THE
CLEANER

THE
CLEANER

ELISABETH
HERRMANN

MANILLA

First published in Germany in 2011 by Ullstein Taschenbuch Verlag GmbH, Berlin

First published in Great Britain in 2016 by Manilla Publishing,
80–81 Wimpole St, London, W1G 9RE
www.manillabooks.com

This paperback edition published in 2017

A CIP catalogue record for this book is available from the British Library.

Paperback ISBN: 978-1-7865-8020-7
Export trade paperback ISBN: 978-1-7865-8024-5
Ebook ISBN: 978-1-7865-8005-4

3 5 7 9 10 8 6 4 2

This e-book was produced by IDSUK (Data Connection) Ltd

Manilla Publishing is an imprint of Bonnier Zaffre,
a Bonnier Publishing company
www.bonnierpublishing.co.uk

Yuri Gagarin Children's Home
Sassnitz, Rügen Island, East Germany, 1985

Martha Jonas stood in front of her open wardrobe and pressed the Bakelite headphones even more firmly to her ears. The hissing intensified. The station disappeared beneath the other electromagnetic waves. Pulsating voices and fragments of music from neighbouring stations overlaid the frequency. She held her breath and turned the dial a fraction to the right, then to the left. In vain. She had lost it.

The portable radio was hidden behind a stack of neatly ironed, folded and numbered bedding. She frantically reached for the antenna cable. Time was running out.

For a brief moment Barry White's deep, sonorous voice sounded out through the ether. Martha pulled the wire towards the window. The Marine Forecast regained command of the frequency and monotonously announced the wind speeds in the German Bight in an endless loop. A couple of seconds later the East German youth station DT 64 pushed its way in and a hit song took over. That was it. The end. She was so furious she could have snatched the radio from the wardrobe and hurled it against the wall.

A beam of light pierced the window and raced eerily over the almost bare walls. Martha hesitated. Then she took off the headphones and stowed them in the wardrobe along with the cable. She locked it carefully, breaking an unwritten rule. She went to the window and cast a frustrated glance at the starlit night sky.

This close to the sea, the stars and moon shone brighter than elsewhere. It could almost have been romantic. But romance was the last thing on Martha Jonas's mind. Not on Sunday evening between ten and midnight. Clouds were ideal. She didn't know why exactly. They seemed to reflect the radio waves better. It was August and all she wanted was rain and clouds. She would try again in an hour.

The blinding light from the headlights burst into the room again. The car was almost 200 metres away on the bumpy road to Mukran. She was just about to pull the curtains closed when it turned off and headed towards the front gate of the children's home, stopping directly in front of it. The headlights went out.

It was so unusual that Martha instinctively slipped behind the curtain, peering out through only a tiny gap. Someone must have been expecting the visitor, because Martha heard the front door easing open downstairs, and saw a tall, dark figure move quickly towards the wrought iron gate. The figure was in a hurry, as if wanting to avoid being exposed by the moonlight any longer than necessary.

It was the assistant director of the home, Hilde Trenkner. In her late fifties, she now enjoyed more power and influence than her boss. Trenkner was well connected with the local government committee – and to other, nameless men. Perhaps men very much like the one outside, who at that moment was starting his dark Wartburg sedan before driving slowly through the open gate. Trenkner shut it behind him as quietly and carefully as she had opened it. The car stopped between the playground and the steps. The man got out. He was wearing a khaki duster coat over his suit. He opened the passenger door. He removed a large bundle wrapped in a blanket and followed Trenkner into the building.

Slowly, making as little noise as possible, Martha crept across her room and opened the door a tiny crack. In front of her was a dark, high-ceilinged hallway. Pale moonlight filtered through the gable-end window, distorting the shadow of the window's crossbars into a grotesquely elongated crucifix. To the right and to the left were two dormitories. Long wooden benches stood by the doors. There was no indication that this was anything other than a completely normal night. Lights out around seven, the last warning at eight and silence by nine. Anyone intent on causing a disturbance after that had to have a damn good reason – or risk an ice-cold shower in the basement. For a while, nothing disturbed the silence. Then, quiet footsteps. Trenkner was coming up the stairs.

The assistant director of the children's home usually announced her presence with a staccato stride and the rattling of the countless keys she always carried with her. This time though, she looked around cautiously before ordering the stranger over to her with a nod of her head. Martha couldn't make out his face in the darkness. He must have been almost a head shorter than Trenkner, but made a powerful impression, even as the blanket started slipping and he struggled to keep the bundle in his grasp. The blanket fell down and for a moment Martha saw the pale face of a sleeping child.

So that's what it was. A new resident. She carefully closed the door and went to her bed. She sat on the edge and wondered whether or not she should show herself. It must be an emergency admission. That happened every now and then, when the police had to intervene in a family. There were families that, according to the relevant Socialist rulebook at least, were simply an impossibility. Officially, neglect didn't exist, and the living evidence it did disappeared into special homes such as this one. Here, every possible measure – including, when there was no alternative, physical force – was taken to make something decent out of them, against all odds. It was just unusual that it wasn't a police car parked outside.

A Wartburg. So, someone important. Martha stared at the floor and waited for the unexpected visitor to leave. By midnight it would be too late. She would have to wait all week long, until next Sunday.

A door was closed gently, soft steps padding away. Martha waited. After a couple of minutes, she started to wonder why the car wasn't driving off. What was taking Trenkner so long? Maybe she'd gone into the office with the man to take care of the paperwork. Sign admission reports. But that could also be done the next day. When the new child was formally admitted and introduced to the others.

Your locker, your bed, your clothes, your shoes. Here are your school supplies, there is your smock. There's no room for disorder in the children's collective. Just like in life. Childhood is a time for learning. You too will understand what that means. Sooner or later.

Trenkner had a powerful voice. Her unusual size intimidated most people. But she also had other methods. The cellar was among the least of them. Unlike her boss, Martha shied away from corporal punishment. She had studied at the university, because she had liked Pestalozzi, Korczak, Blonsky, Sukhomlynsky and, of course, Makarenko. And yes, of course, children too. Good children. Children who had lost their way. Confused children. Children she could offer a second chance at being a functional member of society. Twenty years later, she was a woman in her mid-forties who had shed many illusions but actually only shed tears over very few of those lost. It was a bitter realisation that it was possible to like a child. Perhaps even two, three, maybe even a dozen. But never 223 of them. The only way to maintain control of that many was with firm structure and unwavering discipline.

'Mummy?'

The voice was subdued and full of fear. The blanket of silence over the home made it sound so close.

'Mummy!'

Martha jumped out of bed and opened the door. The girl was wearing only a single shoe. She was tow-headed, with loose curls falling into her face. She was wearing a short summer dress, and over that a thin cardigan hugged her narrow shoulders. She stared wide-eyed at Martha. The girl looked different from the other children who normally came here. Perhaps it was the way she carried herself – not subservient, but as if she had been scared half to death. Maybe it was the way she was dressed – she seemed much better groomed than the usual antisocial elements who landed here. In fact, she reminded Martha of the tinsel Christmas angel. It lay in a box in the cellar now, since Easter and Pentecost had been done away with and a socialist 'festival of peace' was celebrated instead of Christmas.

'I want my mummy.' Tears ran down her cheeks. The child's lower lip started to tremble.

'Hush!'

Martha walked towards the girl. The child flinched and pulled the cardigan even tighter around her chest.

'Go back to bed.'

She shook her head defiantly. Martha sighed and sank to her knees so she could talk to the girl eye to eye. She didn't do it very often; it was terrible for her blood pressure. But the little girl looked like she could break down at any moment. She was swaying as if she could hardly stay on her feet, fighting off heavy fatigue. The child was around five years old. Six at the most.

'What's your name?'

'Christel.'

'Christel . . . ?'

'Christel Sonnenberg. Where's my mummy?'

'Come along.' Martha stood up slowly and tried to take hold of the girl's wrist. But the little thing pulled free. As she did so, she dropped a stuffed animal.

'Give it back!'

The girl jumped on Martha like a weasel. But Martha was faster and held the stuffed animal out of reach. It was hard to recognise anything in the twilight darkness, but she could have recognised this thing blind, just by touch.

'Hush. You'll get it back. It's a teddy bear! Where did you get it?'

'From my mummy.'

Martha looked around uncertainly. Children with behavioural problems from anti-social families didn't often have toys from the West. They usually didn't have any at all. That was two violations against the norm already, and Martha started to work up a sweat.

'You can't keep it. But maybe you'll get a black bear.'

'I don't want a black bear! Give me my own bear!'

'Quiet,' Martha hissed. 'If someone sees it, then it's gone either way. Black bears are just as nice. You know what, even better. That's because they're from the GDR. Where's your bed?'

All new admissions were shown their bed straightaway. It was their fixed point in the children's home.

'I don't have a bed.'

'But of course you have one.'

'But someone's already lying in it.'

Dorm IV was currently occupied by eighteen girls. Nine on the left, nine on the right. New admissions and departures were discussed at the daily briefing in the director's office. So the girl could be right. They were a bed short. Martha carefully opened the door to the dormitory and peered inside.

In contrast to the ground floor, the windows weren't barred. On the gable end there hung a portrait of the Chairman of the Council of State, Erich Honecker. Next to it, but not as prominent, a picture of Yuri Alekseyevich Gagarin, the Soviet cosmonaut who died so young, the first man in space.

'Where were you supposed to be?' Martha whispered.

'Over there.'

The child pointed to the last bed on the left side. Martha straightened her shoulders and entered the room as she always did on her rounds. She convinced herself that the children were asleep and not just pretending, tugged a duvet into place, placed a pair of carelessly removed slippers carefully under a bed and then went to the corner where number 052 lay – Judith Kepler.

But there was no one there. The covers were thrown off, even the slippers were still there, and there was a black bear on the floor. A dark-brown, raggedy bear, twice as big as the teddy bear Martha was still holding in her hands. And twice as ugly.

It had to be a mistake. Martha looked around helplessly, but Judith Kepler was nowhere to be seen. Maybe she was in the washroom? She made sure that the communal showers and toilets were empty. When she returned to the little girl waiting in the doorway, she noticed that several of the girls in the dorm were sitting up in bed and rubbing their eyes.

'Lie down!'

They dropped back down like they'd been shot. An unpleasant heat spread through Martha, which she always felt when a situation got out of control. Half of the dorm was already awake. A child had disappeared. Another was standing in the hallway. What the hell was going on here? And where was Trenkner? She bent down to the little girl.

'I'll sort this out,' she whispered. 'It'll all be fine.'

The girl shook her head wildly. 'I want to go home to my mummy.'

'But where is she?'

'With Lenin.'

'Where?'

'In a palace with gold and windows made of jewels.'

'Lenin doesn't have a palace. Not one like that.'

'But I saw it!'

Martha had already heard too many lies not to know that there was always a kernel of truth with children at that age. The mother had probably told the child this fairy tale then abandoned her somewhere, or simply left her at home, help-less and alone. There was a steady stream of cases like this. She had already taken in a number of children of those fleeing the GDR to the West. They never stayed long. Martha didn't know where they were sent, but it was said that in contrast to the mentally deficient and anti-social children, they were very easy to place.

'Where are you from?'

'Berlin.'

Where else? And again and again, the sea was an escape route to what represented freedom for these people. The coast was no more than ten minutes away by foot. The girl had probably been picked up roaming about while her mother was trying to flee. Relieved to have finally found a plausible explanation for the nocturnal disturbance, Martha remembered the radio. She might have luck shortly before midnight.

'Give me my teddy back.'

'No.'

'I want my teddy back!'

Martha was about to take a deep breath before making it absolutely clear to the child that the time for special requests had past. Then she saw the girl's eyes widen with fright, and heard a quiet, not unfriendly voice behind her.

'Good evening, Judith.'

The light in the hallway flickered on. Scared to death, she turned around. The girl hid behind her and clung to her skirt.

He was about 45 and of middling stature. He had the round, bright face of a North German, but his skin was unusually pale and pasty for this time of year and covered with freckles. The girl withdrew even more fearfully when he stretched out his hand towards her.

'Who are you?'

A gaunt, tall figure appeared behind him. Trenkner.

'Everything is under control.'

The assistant director held out a pair of pyjamas to the girl. They looked neither new nor ironed, but rather wrinkled.

'Put them on.'

Behind her back, Martha could feel the child shaking her head.

'Put them on!'

'No!'

Trenkner lifted her head with a jerk. She had reached the open door of the dorm in three strides. She went inside, looked around and came out again, carefully closing the door behind her. Martha took a deep breath.

'Mrs Trenkner, this child here . . .'

'Judith. Yes.' A furtive smile flashed across the woman's lean, long face. 'You shouldn't be strolling around in the hallway at night. You know what happens with children who do that? The jigaboo comes and gets them.'

The girl pressed herself even tighter to Martha.

'Excuse me, but this isn't Judith, Mrs Trenkner.'

The assistant director of the home and the stranger exchanged glances.

'Follow us into the office. And you,' Trenkner looked at the child strictly, 'go to your bed. And if I catch you in the hall one more time, you'll go to the cellar. Forever.'

Again she held out the pyjamas to the girl. After three seconds went by and the girl still hadn't touched them, she let them fall. Then she turned around and walked away. Martha followed Trenkner down the stairs, through the vestibule to the Office of the Director. Trenkner took a seat at the large, old desk as if she had always sat there. The small desk lamp cast a diffuse, yellow light. There was a thin file on the desk in front of her. She slid it closer and opened it.

'Please have a seat.'

It wasn't clear whom she meant because there was only one extra chair in the room. The stranger nodded to Martha. She suddenly became aware that she was wearing a pink leisure suit and hadn't removed her make-up or combed her hair before going to bed. She held the teddy bear as tightly as the little girl had before.

'Judith Kepler, born 22 September 1979,' Trenkner began in her emotionless, cool voice. 'Application by the school, and by the supermarket that employed the child's mother, for the child to be taken into care. The youth welfare agency found a neglected apartment, the child's clothing was slovenly and dirty. The mother, an apprentice, later employed in the supermarket's returnable bottle post, is described as mentally weak and alcoholic. She expressed negative, malicious and destructive opinions about the powers that be in the school and society. Residential care in a home was initially ordered for a period of two years.'

Trenkner sat up. Her gaze fell on Martha, who had already been forced to listen to the same report a few weeks ago. A briefing in this very room. The director had sat in the seat that Trenkner now occupied. The educators in front of the desk, lined up in a row. They had deliberated which building would be the best fit for Judith. In the end, it came down to a question of space. Martha would have liked to pass on this child. The report from the chair of the youth welfare agency sounded like more than just behavioural problems. In practice, that meant a harsh approach that would unsettle the rest of the group. She couldn't shake the feeling that Trenkner had it in for her. That's because it was Trenkner and not the director who ultimately decided that Judith Kepler received the number III/052 – building three, child 52, educator responsible: Martha Jonas.

'That girl up there . . .' Martha began, but the man interrupted her.

'That girl up there has repeatedly run away. She was under your supervision. How can you explain that we picked Judith up in Mukran in the middle of the night?'

'Judith?'

Judith was a brown-haired, stocky child with a button nose. She had language difficulties, often stuttered, and seemed apathetic and mentally as well as physically retarded. But in the six weeks she had spent here she had made amazing progress. Eating habits and table manners had improved drastically. Thanks to the most stringent monitoring, bodily hygiene was in a normal range by now. Trenkner had cured her of her non-normative manners with her special 'drink cure': soap suds. Those weren't exactly the progressive teaching methods Martha had once dreamed of, but they brought discipline and order to the children's lives. Judith had become an integral part of the collective after a very brief acclimatisation period. She had only left the grounds with the group and under supervision. She had never run away. Judith was a child that subordinated herself, not one that rebelled, like the girl up in the dorm.

The man casually took a seat on the edge of the desk. Martha was surprised that Trenkner allowed it. He seemed calm and relaxed. Only the slightest swinging of the tip of his foot betrayed him.

'Where were you tonight at around 10 p.m.?'

'In my room. I had made my rounds before that and checked that everyone was lying in their beds, asleep.'

'When were you due to perform the next inspection?'

She remained silent.

'Are you hard of hearing? The next round?'

'Eleven p.m.,' she said quietly. Once again, she felt the heat slowly rising in her body.

'Did you do your patrol at 11 in keeping with protocol?'

It was a rhetorical question. The man knew the answer. She slowly shook her head.

'And where were you instead?'

Trenkner leaned back and crossed her arms over her bosom. There wasn't the slightest indication of empathy in the elderly face with the pinched lips.

'In . . . my room.'

The man shifted his gaze to the assistant director. Martha felt her throat tighten. *They know.*

'You're in your room every Sunday between ten and midnight. What do you do there?'

'I read.'

'And?'

'I do my laundry. My delicates, I mean.'

'And?'

Martha looked at the tips of her slippers. 'I listen to the radio.'

'Which station?'

'DT 64. Voice of the GDR. And in summer the holiday frequency.'

'Look at this.'

He reached into his jacket pocket and extended his ID, which was secured with a leather strap. It was filled with authorisation stamps. She was dizzy for a moment, felt as if she would fall into the abyss.

He pocketed the papers again. 'OK, once more. Which stations?'

'DT 64,' Martha whispered.

She could sense what the man thought of the somewhat pudgy, no longer young woman in front of him listening to the state broadcaster's youth station. It sounded so implausible that she immediately followed it with the next lie, just as transparent.

'And the Voice of the GDR.' That was one that no one listened to voluntarily.

'Please. You could have simply used the house receiver for that.'

There was one of those little wooden boxes on the windowsill with five station buttons and marks on the scale, so that no one accidentally hit the wrong station. The man looked at Trenkner, who was enthroned behind the desk like a stone monument of mercilessness. Honecker hung on the wall in the partial darkness and watched her. Always and everywhere. Martha felt blood roaring in her ears and beads of sweat appearing on her forehead. Trenkner quietly cleared her throat.

'I don't completely understand the structure of your mentality. For some time now I've had the feeling that your awareness of your political and pedagogical responsibilities has suffered.'

They know everything.

'Above all, on Sunday evenings you neglect your responsibilities.'

But I was so careful. No one noticed anything. I did my rounds and only shifted one a little earlier and one a little later.

'Ms Jonas,' the man said. 'I'm asking you for the final time: which station did you listen to today?'

'Radio . . . Radio Luxembourg, London,' Martha stuttered.

The man raised his eyebrows.

'And the shipping forecast.'

She kneaded the teddy bear with her damp hands. It had soft fur and a taut, hard belly. Completely different from the standard issue East German bears, which became ratty and somehow lost their shape. Now that everything was over, she suddenly sensed what something like this must mean for a child. Hadn't she had a doll herself once? Nothing as nice as this toy, there simply wasn't money for that just after the war, and then they had had other worries. A doll with blonde hair and big blue saucer eyes. It looked a little like Christel, no, Judith . . .

'The shipping forecast,' the man repeated. 'Ms Jonas.'

'I didn't mean to!'

Martha looked up desperately. Tears were forming in her eyes. 'I just slipped into it! You don't have any bad intentions, and suddenly . . . It's not my fault . . .'

What would come next? Sent to a work camp? Would they interrogate her? Beat a confession out of her? If only she had never given in to it. She cursed the day she first . . .

'I'm going to tell you what you will do. I assume you secretly procured a high-powered receiver to listen to the British hit parade, as an educator at a state home.'

Martha wasn't completely sure that it wasn't all a dream.

'Right?'

'Yes.'

'I listen to it too sometimes.'

Eyes blinded by tears, she stared at the man, who then pulled a pack of Casinos out of his jacket pocket with a satisfied smile and lit himself a cigarette. While doing so, he looked at his watch, as if remembering a meeting at that very second.

'Cyndi Lauper is at the top of the charts this week. But I like the old stuff better. And you?'

Martha didn't know if it was a bad joke.

'The . . .' she had to clear her throat because it was so dry, 'The Bee Gees.'

'*Zee Beachies*,' the man repeated. He pronounced the name like someone who didn't say it frequently. 'It's easy to forget you need to be a role model. I understand.'

Martha slowly nodded. She didn't really understand all of this. What did the two of them actually want? Trenkner pushed an ashtray towards the man without taking her eyes off the accused.

'But there were children entrusted to your care in order to nip the symptoms of a socialist aberration in the bud. Or are radio stations from the West allowed here in this home, perhaps? Are these completely new methods?'

'Of course not,' retorted Trenkner.

'And then this.'

He shook his head with endless regret. Uncertain, Martha buried her hands even deeper into the soft fur. She observed how he knocked off the ash from his cigarette and cast a glance in the file that was still lying open on the desk in front of Trenkner. He pensively picked up the admission form.

'Judith Kepler. That is indeed our little runaway, correct?'

He held up the piece of paper for her. There was a photo of Christel pasted to the form. The man must have seen her bewilderment because a light smile covered his thin, pale lips.

'No confusion? Look at it closely!'

Martha obeyed. The photo was perforated on the two long edges. She recognised a partial stamp in the lower left corner. It must have been removed from an ID.

'Judith Kepler,' she read aloud. 'Bachstrasse 17, Sassnitz . . .'

The man returned the paper. A tower of ash fell from the tip of the cigarette onto the desktop. Trenkner bent forward and blew it decisively over the edge.

What's going on here?

The man took a long drag and gazed meditatively at the smoke he then exhaled.

'What are we going to do with you?'

What are they going to do with me?

Trenkner interjected again. 'In the interest of everyone involved, I think it would be best to put the matter behind us.'

Then she smiled. It was the kind of smile that made the hair on the back of Martha's neck stand on end. She had already seen it so often on this face.

'What in the world do you have there?'

Martha looked in her lap. Slowly, almost hesitantly her hands revealed the stuffed animal.

'A teddy bear.'

The man stretched out his hand. She handed it over without a word.

'Western radio, western toys . . . this place seems to be out of control.'

For a moment Trenkner lost her temper. The smile disappeared, sheer rage came over her, and she was barely able to get a grip on it.

'This will naturally have consequences.'

'It's not mine!' Martha almost choked up with emotion. 'It belongs to . . .'

The two of them stared at her. The man leaned forward to hear her better. Suddenly Martha saw a dark spot on the lapel of his coat. Her gaze skipped down to his shoes, which were dusty and dirty.

'Well?' he asked quietly.

He threw back his coat, and the spot disappeared into the fold. Martha could have sworn that it was blood. She instinctively looked at Trenkner, but she narrowed her eyes to slits. Had she also noticed the spot? Had she noticed that Martha had just discovered it? The assistant locked her in her penetrating gaze. Suddenly she knew that this was the moment she had to decide. And she did what she had always done when she stood between aspirations and loyalties. Between Pestalozzi and Semilivich. Between relationships and responsibilities.

'Judith,' she completed the sentence.

The man lifted the bear and inspected it with interest. 'Our runaway? But that's an unusual specimen.'

Martha nodded. He exchanged a quick glance with Trenkner. Was she mistaken or was he much more nervous putting out the cigarette than he had been lighting it? He stood up.

'You're right, it's late and I'm still expected elsewhere. Ms Jonas, we're not monsters. On the contrary. All we can do is make your life pleasant or unpleasant. Which would you prefer?'

'Pleasant,' Martha answered hesitantly.

'Then let's agree that you'll pay closer attention to Judith in the future. The child needs close attention. She appears to be confused.'

'Confused,' Martha repeated and nodded.

'She shouldn't leave the grounds for the time being. She should be separated from the others until the excitement of her excursion has settled down.' He looked at Trenkner. She pursed her lips and returned his gaze without batting an eye. Then he turned back to Martha. 'The state has put this child in your hands with a great deal of trust. Please don't disappoint it.'

Martha nodded. She still felt the warmth in her lap where she had held the stuffed animal close, and she suddenly began to shake.

'Then the state won't disappoint you either. It will give you a chance to make it up. I believe you'd like a new radio. And a couple of records. Do you have a record player?'

Martha shook her head.

'Then we'll give you one. And something from those Beachies along with it. Take a day off next week and pick it all up from us in Schwerin. At Demmlerplatz.'

'Thank you very much,' she said quietly. 'Whom do I need to contact?'

'Ask for Hubert Stanz.'

He nodded and left. Martha heard his steps in the hallway. First they were slow, then, as if he believed he was outside of earshot, they became fast, almost hasty. She stood up uncertainly. Trenkner took the admission form, placed it in the file, and closed it.

'Bring your old radio in for safekeeping. Anything else?'

Martha didn't know if she was free to go. She shook her head. Trenkner opened a drawer, and placed the file inside. Then she took her massive set of keys and, finding the right one instantly, turned the lock.

'You heard what Mr Stanz said.'

'Yes.'

'Then I hope that you also understood.'

Martha paused at the bottom of the stairs. The Wartburg out front started up and pulled quietly away. Her heart beat heavily, pounding like a blacksmith's hammer. She felt for the light switch with shaking hands and pressed it. The snap was as loud as a gunshot.

You got away, once again.

Schwerin. Demmlerplatz. The headquarters of Department XV of the Ministry for State Security and the Stasi's infamous prison. Hubert Stanz. She slowly went up the stairs, carefully rationing what little air was in her lungs. She stopped in front of the door to Dorm IV. Then she slowly pushed the handle.

Quiet breathing and wheezing – nothing more could be heard. Carefully, without causing any unnecessary noise, she felt her way through the rows. Her eyes needed some time to adjust to the darkness. Just a thin slit of light illuminated the dorm towards the back, so that she could only recognise the outlines of the beds and the two large, dark rectangles on the wall. She stopped in front of number 052. The girl was lying on her back and staring at the ceiling.

Two hundred and twenty-three children. They came and went. Some of them returned to their parents, but most only changed buildings, age groups, or school. They went to other homes, moved out at some point, and the trail was lost – disappearing like the colour from the ancient class photos. Fading in memory, pale and more transparent, dissolving and flowing into the river of forgetfulness that carried everything along with it – names, numbers, faces, and finally the hope of something better, which one had once hoped to establish, back then, when they were all young and confident that they were on the right side of history in the right country.

'Judith?'

The child cried with eyes wide open. She wasn't blinking and didn't wipe away the tears. They just ran out of the corners of her eyes, over her cheeks and into her hair. She looked at Martha.

'Where's my teddy?'

'It's gone.'

Martha sat down on the corner of the bed. She took the bedraggled black bear that had fallen to the ground and placed it next to the pillow.

'I want to go to my mummy.'

'Judith, your mummy . . .'

'My name is Christel!'

Martha's hand jerked up and pressed over the girl's lips. Luckily the others were asleep by now.

You're crazy. Get out of here. You're risking everything.

But Martha didn't go. Maybe it was because of the odd smile on Trenkner's face and the dark spot on the duster coat, and the frigid fear and the feeling of helplessness that had enveloped her down in the director's office, like a black hood that had almost suffocated her. Or because number 052 had suddenly become something else. Martha couldn't say what it was. It was clear to her that she was under observation from now on and that these were the last minutes that the girl's real name would exist. She carefully removed her hand, bent over and whispered into the child's ear.

'From now on this is our secret. Only you and I know. Now you have to be very well behaved. You understand? And if you do everything that we tell you, then one day your mummy will come and pick you up.'

The girl finally turned her head and looked at her.

'Do you swear?' she asked. 'To God?'

Martha would swear to whatever. If only the child would just forget what had happened before. It was the only thing that could still save Martha's neck.

'I swear. If you behave.'

'Then I'll behave.'

The girl closed her eyes. Martha placed the Tiemi in her arms. Then she stood up, and petted the girl's head. She slowly went outside, turned off the light in the hallway and crept to her room. Only when she had closed the door behind her did a vague and hesitant feeling of security spread inside her.

The radio was still in the wardrobe behind the stack of bedding, exactly as she had left it. She paused. It was just before midnight. And she had permission, from Stanz himself, to listen to the British charts. She pressed the button, slipped on the headphones and waited until the radio warmed up and the station covered the humming sound. She looked at her alarm's fluorescent display. It was time. Time for the Number One hit.

The humming became louder, and suddenly Cyndi Lauper disappeared.

'... German Bight: East, becoming cyclonic, 3. Slight. Outlook: Southeast 7 to 5, strengthening west. Belte and Sund: Northeast 3 ... *time after time* ...'

She took off the headphones. Visibility seven to five. She took a deep breath. The dead drop was empty and could be filled. With a message. This time it would have nothing to do with the Russian forces. She quietly gathered her coat and her sturdy shoes from the wardrobe.

1

It was not a good place to die.

Judith Kepler pulled the handbrake and turned off the motor. She watched the grey tenement building through the windscreen of the van and felt her stomach contract. Her palms, clinging to the steering wheel, were moist. And to top it off, she had an absolute beginner with her this morning.

Along the busy street there were rows of discount chain clothes stores, brothels and shady used car salesmen. A district where everything could be had on the cheap: women, cars, even apartments. Several of the building's windows were boarded up. In others, blankets and towels took the place of curtains.

Her front-seat passenger looked longingly at a run-down Ford Fiesta that could be driven off the lot for the monthly payment of only ninety-nine euros. Provided you had a steady job. Kai had neither ninety-nine euros, nor a job. He was a broad-shouldered, tall boy with a stylish Beatles haircut with the fringe combed into his face. It lent something unintentionally poetic to his powerful features, something he probably had no clue about. She flipped down her sun visor and looked into the mirror. What did twenty-one-year-olds think about women over thirty? They didn't even come into consideration, probably. She brushed back a strand of hair and at the same moment thought how vain she must seem to him. She did it every time she went onto a job site: hands washed, hair combed. First impressions mattered. That was true for apartments, jobs, men, and everything else that had to be taken care of properly.

Kai tore his gaze from the Ford Fiesta, raising his eyebrows all the way up to his fringe and asked sullenly, 'We going up there now or what?'

You'll be talking differently by the end of the first shift, Judith thought to herself and tried to keep a straight face.

She got out. Behind her back, she heard him do the same. He followed her like a puppy. He would probably turn on his heels as soon as he registered what he had got himself into, so she might just as well treat him with consideration in advance.

By the main entrance to the building the penetrating smell of urine reached their noses – an unmistakable sign that the night crawlers had taken over this part of the metropolis and marked their territory here. The door was 1950s hideous with an aluminium frame and security glass with multiple fractures. It was opened from the inside. An employee from the funeral home stepped out and locked the doors. He nodded briefly to Judith.

'Man, oh man.' He reached into his jacket pocket and extended a small metal tin. The gesture was a silent summary of what awaited her upstairs.

'Thanks.'

Judith rubbed the menthol cream under her nose. Then she passed the tin to Kai, who sniffed at it and gave it back. He hadn't graduated from school; the employment agency had told him this internship was his last chance. He had showed up at eight-thirty instead of seven, mumbling some vague excuse about a broken alarm. The fact that he was still along for the ride was only because the doctor they were due to meet there had had an emergency and Judith had been forced to wait. And because Judith might be the only one at Dombrowski Facility Management who knew how alarms worked. She had four. Distributed throughout the apartment at strategic points, all hard to reach, and programmed to ring one minute apart. The last one was in the bath.

'Take it.' Judith offered him the tin again.

But Kai either didn't get it or considered menthol cream kid's stuff. His choice. Judith returned the tin to the mortuary assistant. He gave her a brief nod and lit himself a cigarette while casting a glance at the summer sky, which was just freeing itself from the hazy morning.

'Six weeks under the eaves, in this weather. We're just happy we managed to get her into the box in one piece.'

They knew each other. Not well enough to know the other's name. But in the way that at some point you get to know everyone who works in this strange profession: the administration of death. Everyone has their place. The doctor, who issues the death certificate. The undertaker, who picks up and arranges the corpse. The cleaner, who makes the house inhabitable again. They had a utilitarian mode of communication, eschewing all the fake half-tones of lamentation and concentrating on the essentials: the job.

Kai turned even paler than he already was. The nice caseworker at the agency apparently hadn't prepared him for this. Facility cleaning. Scouring. Anyone can do it. Go there and take a look. And then this, right on the first day. Scuffling steps approached. The doctor, recognisable by his assiduous haste and a bulky leather bag, came down the stairs. He was followed by two rapid-reaction police officers.

'We're finished up there.' Like so many members of his guild, he referred to himself in the plural. 'Natural cause of death, passed away peacefully. My God.'

Two semi-trailers rumbled by. The physician stepped onto the wide footpath and inhaled a lungful of the ammonia and diesel mix. Then he shook his head and rushed to his car. The two officers followed him. The mortician was smoking.

'Then let's go.' Judith made the motion with her head that people use to command dogs into the house when it's raining. Kai trudged behind her.

They climbed the stairs. There were buggies in the hallway, shoes and clutter. Every storey got them further away from the street noise and closer to forgetting. Judith smelled the sweet hint of death in spite of the menthol. Six weeks, the man had said. And the only thing the neighbours had finally noticed was the stench.

Kai panted.

'What smells so bad?' he asked, but he had already guessed the answer.

Judith didn't intend to go easy on him. Whoever came along with her had to be ready to push their limits further than they wanted to. The public health department had called Dombrowski Facility Management. And Dombrowski had sent Judith. And Judith wasn't one to wrap rookies in cotton wool.

'This way.'

A narrow hallway with a threadbare runner, old wallpaper, winter coats in the wardrobe despite it being the height of

summer. The first impression was that of poverty and mean-
ness. This had dominated the life of Gerlinde Wachsmuth.

And the solitude, Judith thought as she entered the bedroom.
There was a simple wooden cross hanging over the narrow bed.
The second assistant mortician was just closing the zinc casket and was doing so with special care. Even the staircase was
cramped; they would have to transport the corpse upright at
some spots. His colleague returned from his cigarette break. The
two stood next to the casket, folding their hands and murmuring a quiet prayer.

Judith asked herself if they also did that when there were no
witnesses nearby. She was just about to give Kai a sign that, in
keeping with the situation, he should also conduct himself reverently when she noticed the expression on his face. He stared
past her, looking at the bed. His lower lip began to tremble. He
swallowed frantically, his Adam's apple bouncing up and down
his strong throat like a rubber ball. He clapped his hand in front
of his mouth and lurched out of the room.

'His first time?'

The two had finished their prayer. Judith nodded. She
looked at her watch and hoped Kai would vomit quickly.
They had already lost a lot of time. But the sounds that ema-
nated from the bathroom sounded more like an extended
coughing fit. He was more likely avoiding work rather than
having a true emergency. She would have liked to send the
boy straight home. The wheat separated from the chaff at the
bathroom door.

'I'm going to start,' she called. 'It'll all be subtracted from your
lunch break.'

An argument that often worked wonders with people like Kai. Maybe someone should have advised him not to eat anything before this assignment.

First she examined the bed and the state of the mattress. It was positioned with the headboard against the middle of the wall. Pillows and covers were on the floor to the left, the casket was to the right. The only thing left of Gerlinde Wachsmuth was the impression of her body on the sheet. She must have been a small person, who lay down to sleep and didn't get back up. A silent death. A peaceful, expected departure. A quiet exit. Judith felt the peace and the absence of fear. Sometimes death was the only friend who wouldn't forget you.

And then Gerlinde Wachsmuth's corpse had had six weeks to dissolve during high summer in a poorly insulated apartment on the fifth floor. The silhouette of her body was a soft yellow, where her arms, legs and head had lain. But the shade darkened towards the middle of the body, almost reaching a dark violet, nearly black coloration. White dots were moving in the middle of the dark hollow.

Judith didn't have to look under the bed to know that fluid had collected underneath, contaminating the air. Although the assistant mortician had opened the window and the menthol cream burned on her upper lip, this smell burned its way into her pores like a sandblaster.

The two men lifted the casket and carried it out of the apartment as carefully as possible. Judith waited until she heard the toilet flush.

'Everything OK?' she called down the hallway.

The door opened. Kai emerged, staring at her with the 'I want to go home' look everyone had the first time they saw behind the pleasant façade of how everything meets its end.

'I need safety goggles, a full-body suit. Disinfectants and cleaners. Cling film. A spray can, formaldehyde steamer, thermal and cold-process foggers. The locked poison box – larvicide, acaricide, phosphine and hydrocyanic acid. And of course the boxes with the scouring powder, hard soap, brushes and scrubbers. Understand?'

Kai shook his head.

'It's all in the back of the van.'

Instead of answering, he stumbled back into the bathroom and slammed the door behind him. Judith counted down from ten and waited. The gagging receded. Of course she could have gone down herself. But she didn't want to.

'Are we almost ready now?' She looked at her watch. 'I'll give you exactly one minute. Then I'm calling Dombrowski and telling him he should pull you.'

You could hear the toilet flushing, shortly followed by the sound of a tap splashing. When Kai opened the door for the second time she turned around, expecting his departure.

'Got something for my nose?' he asked.

'Respirator mask.'

'Two, if possible.'

Judith grinned and pulled two out of her trouser pocket.

'There we are. Never go without.'

Judith bent down in front of the bed. Like Kai, she wore paper overalls, and rubber gloves reaching her elbows. She motioned to the spot that had spread out on the carpet.

'Chlorine and oxygen. But you still never get rid of the stench. The carpet has to go. If you're lucky there's a wood floor underneath that can be sanded.'

She stood up. Kai was still staring at the white dots in the middle of the mattress. They had stopped moving after Judith had sprayed them with larvicide. She removed her respiratory mask.

'Maggots. Seen with a little love, they're just another of God's creatures. At least they were. Cling film?'

'Wait . . . just a sec.'

Kai trudged into the hall and came back with the heavy roll. Luckily enough, Gerlinde Wachsmuth had passed away on a single bed. The mattress wasn't heavy. But the noise caused by some of the maggots falling onto the plastic they had spread out was causing Kai problems. It was like a handful of raisins.

'Is it always so disgusting?'

'No,' she lied. 'Usually you just have to strip the beds and clean up thoroughly.'

This was relatively harmless. Cleaners were regularly confronted with much worse. He was probably still here so he could tell his friends about this freak show, and how he was allowed to dart across the screen once as an extra. Wow, maggots. Corpses. Undertakers. Call me a hero. Judith removed the carpet knife from the toolbox and cut the rest of the plastic to length.

'Man, what kind of job is this? Why do you do it?'

She thought for a second. Given the lack of young people entering the profession, telling the truth probably wasn't advisable.

'Because I can. And lots of others can't.'

She cut off the last piece of plastic, retracted the blade and went towards the wide-open window. The midday sun had spread over the city like a bell jar. You could see the autobahn from here. She admired the symmetrical semicircles of the on and off ramps, over which the avalanches of metal rolled. The best view was from the TV tower. Sometimes Judith treated herself to a trip to the observation platform. Then she stared down at the city from above and was overcome by its restless beauty. She thought about how she wanted to drive out to the Lusatia region with a telescope tonight, searching for the ultimate dark spot, the place with the lowest levels of light pollution. She wanted to finally see a really starry sky again. August. The weeks of the Perseids, the meteor showers, granting the eternally hopeful human race a multitude of promises in the form of shooting stars.

She unzipped her overalls and removed a small pack of tobacco where she always kept a few cigarettes she had rolled beforehand. She offered Kai one of the crooked sticks.

'How did you know you could?' he asked. 'Did you do a suitability test at the job centre?'

He gave her a light. She leaned forward and saw his hands, which he held up, protecting the flame. They were young hands, with narrow fingers and big knuckles. Ten years more, and they would be the hands of a man. She inhaled the smoke and blew it past him, towards the window. He would understand in ten years, at the earliest.

'There are jobs you don't apply for. They come to you.'

'Just like that?'

'Maybe you don't get it yet. This here is a chance.'

Kai rested his forearm on the windowsill and looked like he wanted to give himself a little more time to think about it. They stood shoulder to shoulder, and the only sounds came from the traffic noise down below and the quiet rustling of their overalls. They smoked, and Judith blinked at the bright daylight and counted down the years separating them. She arrived at eleven. He was too young for everything that could cross your mind on a day like this, when the sweltering heat brought the blood in your veins to a boil and you suddenly thought about shooting stars in a dead person's apartment. She stubbed out her cigarette on the outer windowsill, donned her mask, which didn't make any noticeable difference, and went back into the room. Five minutes of fresh air had been enough to forget the stench of hell. It hit her like a sucker punch.

'And the deceased?' He wouldn't let it go. 'How do you deal with the dead?'

'We don't have a close personal relationship, if that's what you mean.'

Of course he didn't mean that. She sounded as callous as one of the doctors from those American television series that ran around the clock on cable. But it simply came down to the fact that for her, humans remained human, even after dying. They were given one last show of respect.

They walked up to the bed from either side. Kai bent over and lifted the mattress on one side, she from the other.

'I've never seen a corpse.'

'Won't be too long.'

'Maybe you should have become a cop, if you like dead people so much.'

The mattress fell to the ground. 'The door's over there,' she said.

Kai's eyes widened, staring at her in disbelief.

'I'm serious. You can go.' She reached for the roll with the tape, which she had put on the nightstand. 'I don't want to work with people like you.'

'What do you mean by that?'

'Just what I say.'

Kai cast an indecisive glance toward the hallway, the path to freedom, and an easy afternoon at the beach bar.

'And what will you tell the boss?'

She ripped off half a metre of tape, cutting it with her teeth because she didn't want to ask Kai for the carpet knife.

'That you're a fucking idiot.'

'What do you mean?'

Judith wasn't the slightest bit inclined to explain that to him as well. She folded the plastic sheet over the mattress, but the tape got tangled. Kai squatted down next to her and had the sheet under control with two quick steps.

'Sorry,' he said. 'Won't happen again.'

She furiously ripped off another piece of tape, extending it towards him. He cut it in the middle. They worked together in silence the next couple of minutes.

Judith started to sweat. Even if it was from a single bed, sealing the mattress was not an easy task in this weather. The overalls were like a sauna, and the mask didn't exactly help you breathe.

'I actually meant – you're a woman . . .'

'What does that have to do with anything?'

'What do you tell guys when they ask you what you do?'

'Depends if I want to get rid of them or not.'

She could tell from the look in his eyes that he was smiling. He was probably hoping it wasn't so bad after all.

She turned the mattress so Kai could make a clean rotation with the tape. The tape ripped, the sheet slipped out of her hands, and the mattress went straight over the nightstand, knocking off everything that had been on top. Glass shattered. Judith stifled a curse. There was a commandment that couldn't be broken: leave an apartment clean but undamaged. Kai bent over.

'Just a picture frame. And the light bulb from the lamp.'

'Put it back up.'

She took the frame off his hands. The glass had cracked. A photograph of a man aged around thirty was trapped behind it. The faded colours betrayed that the picture must be at least two decades old. She carefully removed the shards of glass from the wood and returned the frame to the night stand.

'What are you doing?'

Judith spun round. She hadn't heard the man coming, but his tone of voice and the first visual impression were a match. He was thin, almost gaunt, and the unhealthily red face revealed that he was either suffering from the stairs or was an alcoholic. A glance at his jaundiced eyes suggested that the latter was more likely. She discerned a vague, almost caricature-like similarity with the man in the picture.

'Hello. We've been assigned to de-putrefy the apartment.'

'What?'

'De-putrefy. The opposite of putrefy.'

'Not by me. Get lost.'

'According to the federal infectious disease laws, this apartment has to be properly cleaned and disinfected. I don't know if you're qualified to do it.'

'I'm not paying. Just so you know right now. What were you doing with my mother's nightstand? Don't think I didn't see you messing around with it.'

His gaze flitted around the room, coming to rest on the wrapped mattress.

'And leave that here. Don't touch a thing, you understand? Otherwise I'll call the police.'

'Was that your mother who was lying here for six weeks?' Judith removed her rubber gloves. 'My condolences.'

'Get out of here. Immediately.'

Kai took a step towards the man. Judith reached for his arm, but immediately let him go.

'No. You go,' she said. Her hand was still thinking about that contact, but her head blocked out the thought of the touch. 'I can't permit you to be here until we have finished.'

The man hadn't counted on resistance. Only now did he notice the changed chemistry of the room. He inhaled sharply through his nose. With remarkable transformational power his face revealed exactly what he felt: surprise, recognition, disgust.

'What's going on?'

'Your mother's body was picked up two hours ago. The funeral home will get in contact with you. You don't look as if you've made a long journey. So stop playing the doting son and let us do our work.'

'She's dead,' the man repeated. 'The people next door said that.'

He turned around and left. They heard sobbing from the living room.

Judith instructed Kai to bring the mattress to the car. While he was gone, she began to disinfect the room. The use of further poisons wasn't necessary – the decay hadn't spread that far yet. Every time she fought her way through the narrow hallway into the bathroom she saw the man sitting on the couch, bent wide over as if he was searching for something on the threadbare carpet. On the fourth or fifth time she stopped and watched him. He wasn't looking for anything. He was just moving with the erratic motions of an addict.

'We're almost done here,' she said.

The man looked up.

'I have no one else left.'

Judith shrugged her shoulders. She didn't want to be sucked into a conversation.

'I know what you're thinking,' the man said. 'I should have taken better care of her. And you're right. Yes. You're right.'

He started to rock back and forth. She went back into the bathroom and filled a bucket with water. Of course she was right. But it wasn't her business to judge what had gone wrong in the life of Gerlinde Wachsmuth and her son. His photograph had stood next to her bed. He had been in her life but she wasn't in his. It was that simple and brutal. The old rage boiled up in her, but she had learned to keep it under control. You had to differentiate between what was right, what was necessary, and what was pointless. It was absolutely pointless to tell men like him the truth. It would roll off him like drops of rain on a dirty pane of glass.

She turned off the tap and then went back to the bedroom without wasting another glance on the hypocrite in the living room. A little later Kai joined her and they worked until the early afternoon without looking up once.

Judith slipped out of the overalls and stuffed them in the blue bin bag. Her work was done. She was satisfied. She instructed Kai to carry the sacks of rubbish down and followed him into the hallway.

'Mr Wachsmuth?'

The door to the living room was closed. She opened it and uttered a quiet sound of surprise. Kai, already almost outside, turned around and came back to her.

'It can't be true,' was all he said.

The doors of the living room cupboard had been ripped open. The drawers had been pulled out, their contents spread out across the floor. Several picture frames were scattered carelessly on the tiled coffee table. Their backs revealed that someone had searched for something with great haste and little care. Light-coloured spots on the wallpaper glowed where they had hung. Judith lifted one of them. It was a poor facsimile of Spitzweg's *The Poor Poet*.

'The pig is gone.' Kai, having inspected the entire apartment once again, returned. 'What now?'

Judith held the print in front of a spot that would have been the right size.

'We have to clean up.'

She put the picture to one side, knelt down, and started to refill the drawers. Shot glasses, shoehorns, half-burnt candles, lace doilies, a box of photos. All had been tossed to the ground, spread across the floor all the way to the couch. Kai sighed, picked a cushion off the ground and fluffed it repeatedly.

'If I ever see that guy again . . . First he leaves the old woman to rot and then he steals from her.'

'Gerlinde,' Judith said. 'The old woman's name is Gerlinde Wachsmuth.'

She was holding a photo of a man, a woman and a child. Taken sometime in the sixties, when people still assumed a pose in front of the camera, but were no longer spruced in their Sunday best. The man was broad-shouldered and rather stout. Although he gazed sternly into the camera, he had draped his arm around the woman's shoulder. There was an almost girlish smile on her round face. The boy's lower lip protruded. He looked up to his father and grinned at him.

Judith flicked through the remaining photos in the box. The man appeared several more times. The child developed into an ugly teenager with sideburns and long hair and began to assume a similarity to the wreck that she had encountered in this apartment a couple of hours before. Then the man disappeared. The woman appeared a few more times, posing in front of the Eiffel Tower or on a beach boardwalk. The rest were portraits cut out from passport photo machine prints.

A pictorial history of the pursuit of a little happiness. Father, mother, child. A family. Not perfect. Rather pathetic even, when the son goes as far as to steal from his dead mother. But Judith had a weakness for families. She pocketed the photo. The box would land on the rubbish heap anyway, just like everything else from the old woman's belongings that couldn't be turned into cash.

'Are you swiping something?' Kai had re-hung *The Poor Poet* and was straightening it.

'Not really. I collect family photographs.'

'Don't you have any of your own?'

'No.'

Kai must slowly be getting the message that her sense of humour was limited. But he had learned enough today to know when it was better to keep his trap shut.

The heat tasted like burnt rubber. When Judith opened the driver's door it felt like she was climbing into an oven. Despite taking the autobahn, she needed almost an hour to get to Neukölln. The rush hour traffic was stop-start in both directions. The further south she went, the more frequently she was passed on the shoulder by low-riders with tinted windows and boots full of subwoofers. She wiped sweat from her forehead and rolled up her long sleeves.

Kai had fallen asleep on the passenger side. His head lolled against the side window, the exhaustion so extreme that not even the potholes roused him from his coma. She risked a second glance. Did everyone get so tired at that age? She tried to remember how she had felt when she was that young. But she only ran into a blazing flame of self-hatred, vague yearning and depressing despondency. She saw the scars on the crook of her arm and rolled her sleeves back down.

Kai only jolted upright when she reached Dombrowski's headquarters and turned off the motor. She motioned to a pockmarked steel container rusting away next to the entrance.

'That's where the rubbish goes. Your job.'

She removed the key and tossed it to him. He was still too groggy to react and let it fall to the ground.

'Should I come on Monday?'

'Do you want to?'

'I have to think about it.'

He searched for the key. She had already got out by the time he had found it and resurfaced.

'Hey!' he called after her.

Judith didn't turn around. She raised her hand in a fleeting parting gesture and walked across the dusty asphalt to the old tyre storage that her boss had converted into an approximation of a real company headquarters. There were lockers, showers, changing rooms and a break room in a building with a flat roof. To the left, a narrow hall led to the offices. Judith went to the bulletin board next to the entrance and with a single glance registered that no one was still on assignment except for Matthias, Josef and Frank, along with a small cleaning crew. It looked like a quiet weekend. She would take a shower, drink about four litres of water and then make her way to her apartment, where she only had to collect her telescope and sleeping bag. She went over to her locker and removed her duffel bag, which contained the essentials for becoming a human again after a day like this.

After the shower she dried herself off and paused briefly in front of the mirror in the bathroom. She lowered the towel she had just used to rub down her hair. What did someone like Kai see in her? A woman who had, at some point, missed the exit marked 'pretty' and come to a rest with a stuttering motor next to 'mousey'. Only with great effort did she make progress on this bumpy road called life. She had already choked the motor completely a couple of times; the last time it looked like she had totalled it. She had to watch out. Every day, again and again. Not become complacent. Always keep in mind that the next exit could be marked 'terminus.' The fact that real work wasn't about an eight-hour shift, but how you coped with sixteen hours. She had already survived two years and was stuck in one lane at work. She forced herself not to avert her gaze as long as she could. Then she turned away and slipped into her jeans and an old but clean T-shirt. She returned to her locker with the bag in hand.

'Dearest Judith.'

She needed a moment to register what those two words meant. Dombrowski had crept up in his plimsolls. His plump face beamed with fake joy over seeing her again, the grey locks spinning their way over his high forehead like wet spider webs. He looked a freshly bathed Buddha, even if he wasn't just emerging from the showers, like her, but from an office with no air conditioning.

No, she thought. Simply no. He raised his arms as if he wanted to apologise.

'We have a cold starter.'

2

Quirin Kaiserley left the autobahn in Adlershof in his fourteen-year-old Golf GTI and steered towards the glowing city of glass and dreams. He had already lost his bearings by the first traffic light. Cursing, he turned and tried his luck in the other direction. He thought about the cathedral in Cologne being built over the course of 600 years, with people being able to get accustomed to the sight. But Berlin put entire new quarters up so quickly that you sometimes thought it was a mirage. He glanced nervously at his watch. Almost six. His edginess and impatience increased.

Buildings in which particle accelerators and satellite systems had been developed appeared in front of him. Quirin vaguely recalled a visit over twenty years ago. Back then, no one had thought of a so-called science and technology cluster. Adlershof had seemed unapproachable, closed. State broadcaster of the GDR. Ammunition depot for the Felix Dzerzhinsky Guards Regiment. Previously the Reich broadcaster and an aerodynamics testing facility. Grey barracks, bumpy roads. Conspiratorial meetings between the CIA and the BND, Germany's Federal Intelligence Service. Exploratory talks. Meetings on neutral territory. Exchanges of information. Troop withdrawal. Logistics. The world had changed since then. But the people remained the same.

Quirin followed the signs to Adlershof Media City. He turned off the motor, but didn't get out. He took a deep breath. This wasn't stage fright. He had already spent too much time seated in the fake leather couches, bathed by spotlights, and had mastered the role of intelligence expert so well that it was almost routine. This was the tense expectation that he could barely contain. The time had come.

Quirin adjusted his rear-view mirror so that he could see his face. His eyes looked tired, a wreath of wrinkles around them. The blue from his eyes had faded. Twenty-five years on the hunt had left traces. He had spent nearly half of his life looking for a phantom. It had cost him his job, his family, his friends. He saw himself pulling up to the iron gate in the Munich suburb of Pullach. In his hands lay a work reference issued by the Federal Asset Management Munich for ten years of salaried work in the branch office for special assets. Parting by mutual consent. Hardly worth the paper it was printed on. A web of lies to the end. You could always rely on the BND for that.

Quirin reached for the briefcase on the passenger seat, left the car without locking it – he would be on the winning side of a theft with this scrap heap – scurried over the car park, and slowly climbed the front stairs to the studio complex. The doorman knew him and held out a visitor's badge that had already been filled out for him. The seating area in the foyer was empty.

'Did anyone ask for me?'

The man was a fossil from the era of state broadcasting, a survivor of seismic shifts because his grey cotton uniform made him nearly invisible. He adjusted the reading glasses on the bridge of his nose and studied the visitor registry with unnerving meticulousness.

'No.'

'Or leave anything for me?'

Absurd. No one would leave material of such explosive nature in the hands of a frustrated studio doorman, of all people. The man rose with some effort and walked to an empty wooden shelf, which he viewed contemplatively, as if seeing it for the first time.

'No.'

Quirin nodded and walked towards a group of chairs, but only set his briefcase on the ground next to it. He walked back and forth and kept an eye on the entrance. She would come. She had to come. Just an hour left until they started recording. Until the moment of truth. Until their triumph. A young unit manager, recognisable by her headset, clipboard and black-framed glasses, hurried through the foyer.

'Good evening! You must be Mr Kaiserley.' She wore her hair combed back neatly into a ponytail and was dressed in the uniform nerdy chic of the hip upper-middle class. 'I'm very glad to meet you. I'm Kirsten.'

Kirsten-without-a-surname beamed at him with that hopeful maybe-we'll-get-drinks-afterwards gaze, solely because his face was not unfamiliar in the media.

'I'm still waiting for someone.'

Kirsten tapped her schedule with her pencil. 'I'll take you to your dressing room and let the doorman know.'

'Is Juliane already there?'

Her smile lost a degree of warmth. She adjusted her glasses and glanced at her schedule.

'Ms Westerhoff is in make-up.'

Kerstin led the way. Quirin grabbed his suitcase and in passing cast a glance through the wide opened studio doors. *Three to One*, a political talk show, was produced in Adlershof and broadcast every Friday at the end of the main evening programme, after the crime serial and before the midnight news. The time slot was well chosen, the ratings excellent. Domestic political topics of an explosive nature were his specialty. *The camera likes you*, Juliane had explained one evening at the obligatory after-show party. Heat, wine and too much adrenaline that coursed through his veins like champagne after the show. *And I like you too.*

How long had they known each other? A quarter-century? He had kept an eye on her career, and she had followed his. That is, as long as he had a career. His crash had been from the greatest heights. She was one of the few people who hadn't turned their back on him afterwards. Had he thanked her for that back then?

Tonight, he thought. Today they would both celebrate. Page one. Top ratings. Juliane's glowing eyes. A couple of days of springtime in his soul.

When Quirin had called her up a couple of weeks before and told her about his source – with all due caution – she had been fired up with excitement. She wanted to light the fuse at the end of the show, but like any good journalist, had asked for evidence.

'We'll present it.'

'Who's we?'

'Sorry. Protection of sources.'

I know what happened back then. I'm in possession of something that will be of interest to you and 3,000 others. Codeword 'Rosenholz'. *Interested?*

Rosenholz. Quirin's pulse had accelerated when he read the email. The sender's name was *Aquavit*, and at their first and only meeting had turned out to be a woman. Mid-thirties, no-nonsense, with a hard, northern accent.

She didn't give her name. The wide, pale face with the narrow eyes below an overgrown fringe seemed detached. She wore a white T-shirt with a Coca-Cola logo across the front. She had been waiting for him in the back room of a bar on Oranienburgstrasse , a small tin in front of her. Florena cream. When he opened the lid and saw the rolled microfilm he knew she hadn't been lying.

'Do you have the full file?' he had asked her, holding his breath.

'Yes. Filtered from hundreds of thousands of index cards. Produced in 1984 during the filming of the Stasi archive. This is the original. Not the pitiful leftovers that the KGB and CIA gave you after the fall of the wall. These are the real names of all of the GDR's foreign agents.'

'What do you want for it? I don't have any money.'

'But you have contacts. I want the highest price a German media company is willing to pay. Because this here,' patting her bag, which the tin had disappeared back into, 'will finally make heads roll.'

She waited for his answer. She was well informed. About him, about Rosenholz, about what had happened back then.

'Where did you get it from?' he had asked. 'And why only now?'

'I have my private reasons. I'm not just here because of you. I have to take care of a couple of things before you shout it from the rooftops. Don't you dare try to cheat me or follow me. Whoever was able to hide this material for twenty-five years is better than all of you put together. So: *Deal or no deal?*'

'*Deal.*'

'How do you picture it going down?'

'A bombshell.'

The woman's narrow eyes became even more tapered.

'*Three to One*. The talk show with Juliane Westerhoff. Everyone will be there. *Spiegel, Focus, Stern*.'

'Cash? I want 100,000 euros.'

'I have to negotiate.'

'Then do it.'

Quirin nodded reluctantly. He was disturbed by the greed, the way she tilted her head.

'Good,' she said. 'Write me when and where. No tricks. I know how to handle them. Any attempt to track me and the deal's off.'

'Under one condition.'

'Which would be?' she asked quickly.

'I want to be the first to see the films.'

'A score to settle?'

'Yes.'

'Sassnitz?'

If he had needed further evidence – this single word sufficed. She was an insider. She was far too young. She couldn't have been there back then.

'What do you know about Sassnitz?'

'Enough,' she replied. It was the first time he heard a hint of candour in her voice. 'Believe me. Enough to know that you would give everything to get a glimpse of the only existing material.' She took her bag and got up. 'Settling scores is a hard business. They are never completely settled. Least of all through morality or justice.'

He had watched her go. She was right, he thought. Kirsten glanced at her watch.

'I'll pick you up in twenty minutes. You have your own dressing room. We've provided for everything. Even the special requests.'

She smiled tellingly and rushed off. Quirin entered a sparsely furnished room. His gaze fell on a machine in the middle of the room with a platform for microfiche and a lens. He flipped the switch and checked if the lamp and automatic film feed were working. His hands were shaking. A quarter-hour left. Where the hell was she? He placed the briefcase on a chair and opened the bottle of mineral water that stood next to the device, along with two glasses, poured himself a glass and gulped it down. Scores to settle.

The stale air, mixed with the smell of plastic adhesive and disinfectants, almost took his breath away. He opened the window, looking out on the car park, and saw someone closing the door to his car and hastily walking away. Tough luck. He didn't even have a car radio. And whoever thought that a former BND agent would leave anything of value inside a car was an absolute beginner.

He took the electric razor, which he always had along on such occasions, out of his briefcase. Beneath it lay a file labelled *Rosenholz*. Without the new material it was as worthless as a bundle of old Reichsmarks. He went to the small sink next to the door and while he ran the device over his cheeks he sensed that his nerves were already stretched to breaking point. Someone knocked quietly. He left the razor in the sink and jerked the door open.

'Quirin! Are you alone?'

Juliane Westerhoff slipped inside. The heavy make-up gave her face the mask-like beauty of a diva from the silver screen.

She had already adopted a certain public persona, vaguely reminiscent of Marlene Dietrich at the beginning of her career. Chilly gaze, high cheekbones, finely drawn eyebrows, her dark-brown hair combed away from her face in soft waves – that's how she was known on screen. No one would recognise her on the street. The mask was a shield she wore like a second skin.

She smiled at him. He hoped that she wouldn't notice how wretched he felt.

'Your big night. How does it feel?'

Her green, unnaturally large eyes examined him as if she wanted to test his suitability for television. There were icy grey strands running through his thick dark hair. At six foot one with the wiry figure of a passionate long-distance runner, he was a man who was given gifts by age instead of being robbed by it. For now.

He motioned to the open briefcase. 'My publisher wants his advance back if I don't deliver soon.'

'Then you have it?'

'Listen . . .' He had to let her in the loop. 'I think there's a problem.'

'A problem? What problem? The station's legal department is on standby. The journalists are sitting in the front row. I even saw several of your former colleagues in the audience.'

She moved a step closer and looked deep into his eyes. 'We've prepared some establishing shots. Archive material about the old cards in the Stasi Records Agency, exteriors from Pullach and the BND construction site in Berlin. The colleagues from the late news have their weapons ready, are waiting to hear every single sentence from your lips and pass it on to the news agencies. A representative from the domestic security agency VS is among the guests who will make sure that the material can be transferred and analysed immediately after the show. So I'm asking you . . .'

She moved yet another step closer and he registered a whiff of Opium, the perfume that Dietrich was said to have worn. Her voice became hushed, nothing friendly remained.

'. . . *what's the problem*?'

'She should have been here long ago.'

'You're kidding.' But she could see that he wasn't joking. 'She's not here?'

She looked around as if someone could have hidden themselves somewhere in the room, which was as Spartan as a jail cell.

'But you said you were going to bring her with you!'

'Yeah, I know!' He turned away, slamming his briefcase shut with a loud bang. She twitched, but then immediately got herself back under control. One simply does not endanger one's schedule or one's make-up so close to the taping. Stony-faced, she looked to the side and mechanically ran her right palm over her midnight blue blazer.

'Oh fuck,' she murmured. She removed her walkie-talkie from her blazer pocket and spoke into it. 'Check if a "Florena" is waiting in the foyer. Immediately.'

They had agreed to use this name after Quirin had told Juliane how the source transported the films.

'No?' Her big eyes looked at Quirin. She put the device away. 'She's not there. What does that mean? She should be here! With you!'

'We had an agreement . . .'

'Agreement? Am I hearing "agreement"? I thought you were Siamese twins! Do you have any idea what this means for the show? For me? The entire statute of limitations debate would have been top of the agenda. And now?'

Stasi Background Checks: For or Against? The trailer had been running on television the entire week. *This is the topic on Friday evening with Juliane Westerhoff. My guests: representatives from the parties in parliament, the state government in Brandenburg, the head of the Stasi Records Agency, and the former BND Agent Quirin Kaiserley.*

Someone knocked. Kirsten peeked inside. A short technician dressed in faded black appeared behind her.

'Ms Westerhoff? The parliamentary speaker from the left-wing Linke party is here. And Mr Kaiserley should be wired by now.'

'In a moment!'

Kirsten pulled her head back and disappeared. Juliane took a deep breath.

'Where are the films?'

'I don't know.'

'Dammit! I've been running the trailer for a week now! I believed you!'

'And I saw it. With my own eyes!'

'So *what*? You still don't get what all of this is worth without evidence? Have you learned nothing?' Quirin watched Juliane shake her head, close to despair. 'They're wild accusations, pipe dreams of a crazy former agent!'

He didn't understand at first. She slowly calmed herself and chose her words more carefully.

'This story has already hung you out to dry once before,' she said quietly. 'You'll look ridiculous.'

Ridiculous.

When had it begun? The day he handed over his badge? Or much earlier, when no one believed that he had returned from Sassnitz? Perhaps it had also been a gradual process. A long, meandering downward path from BND superstar to being a target in a shooting gallery.

'OK. I'll go.'

'You're staying. It's too late now. Concentrate on your role as an expert on intelligence agencies during the cold war. Then I might still be able to save the show.'

'That's not what this is about.'

She instantly raised her index finger. 'Oh yes it is. That's exactly what this is about.'

Without taking her eyes off him, she went to the door. 'It's about your cold ashes after you burn at the stake.'

The spotlights on the rig flashed. The images from the six cameras were already being shown on the monitors in the production booth. A production assistant entered the studio from the lobby. The soft murmur of the audience, kept happy with wine and salty pretzels, was muffled but perceptible.

A technician handed Quirin the transponder of the wireless microphone.

'Sound check, please.'

'One, two, three, four,' Quirin said.

The man listened to what the distant voices in his headset were saying, and then nodded. The production assistant asked Quirin to take the last seat on the right.

'And one at position one,' he heard the floor manager from the loudspeakers.

The boxy silhouette of a mobile camera emerged from the semi-darkness. Two young men pushed the pedestal towards the stage. The little red light next to the lens glowed. Up in the control room Quirin's face filled monitor one.

'Please don't look directly into the camera,' the production assistant said. She seemed jittery, stressed and slightly out of her depth at barely twenty years of age. In contrast to Kirsten, she looked like she worked a side job as a roadie for a rock band. Quirin nodded. The spotlights were blinding. He squinted and spotted Juliane, who was engrossed in a quiet conversation with her managing editor behind the stairs to the audience seats.

'Two and three, please.'

Two cameramen with Steadicams circled him.

'Would you like your mineral water sparkling or still?'

'Sparkling,' Quirin answered. 'Did someone ask for me? Or was something dropped off?'

'No. But I can check again in a second.'

The production assistant leaned down to him.

'Stupid question, but did you feed the meter?'

Quirin pondered, but then he shook his head. He hadn't seen a machine anywhere.

'They've started towing recently. I'll take care of it for you, if that's OK.'

Quirin forced a smile. It took some effort to act as if everything was the same as normal. 'That's more than OK.'

She knelt down. 'I really inhaled your last book. Completely captivating. I kept asking myself: do those old Russian arms depots still exist?'

She was referring to his second to last publication. He had exposed the fact that any treasure hunter could dig up the hastily buried remains of the departed Soviet Army practically without trying. To the best of his knowledge, nothing had happened beyond the initial hysterical outcry. The girl in front of him gave him the impression she would have liked to head off to look immediately.

'Not really,' he lied. Maybe it was better if some things weren't made public after all.

'Too bad. Oh well. I'll go get your water.' She stood up and scurried off.

Quirin took a breath. He felt as if this short conversation had taken the last of his energy. He would have liked to get up and go. Somewhere where he could be alone and scream out the disappointment that was churning in his guts.

'The four. Where's the four?' The floor manager sounded irritated. 'Thank you. And the next.'

Following the command, the arm of a crane swept past, just a couple of feet from his head. Camera five.

'And the six. Teleprompter. Frontal.' The last camera was pointed directly at the semicircle. 'Thanks, everyone. That's it. In position in twenty minutes.'

Quirin stood up and left the stage. His source had vanished. He was sitting high and dry.

The seventh camera on the lighting rig moved. Its lens was barely larger than a finger and with its black metal casing it was almost indistinguishable from the mounting brackets. It followed Quirin's movements through the room until he disappeared behind the stairs with a short nod in Juliane's direction.

The CCTV camera was produced by Great Choon Brothers, a top manufacturer from Shenzhen, and sent high-resolution images to a transponder via a secure frequency. This was not located in the AMC control room, but beyond the studio in the cracked stump of a transmitter mast formerly belonging to the Reich Broadcasting Company. From there, the encrypted signal travelled ten miles across the city in a mere 0.87 seconds. It arrived at a computer that sent it two metres further, to a television screen on the wall of the Executive Suite of the Hotel de Rome in Bebelplatz.

Angelina Espinoza removed the headphones.

'Zoom in.'

She had a voice used to giving commands, the voice of a high-ranking woman, but she could combine her authority with a kind of steely charm that weakened the knees of every man within a hundred metres.

Tobias Täschner, known as TT to colleagues, nodded. He was nervous and glad that he was seated. Espinoza was in her late forties, so a good ten years older than him, a CIA agent, and her real identity was surely completely different. Their last encounter had also started professionally, before ending rather privately. At the moment there was nothing to indicate that she could remember that night at all. She put the headphones back on and nodded to him briefly – 'let's roll.' He zoomed so close to Kaiserley that his face filled the screen. He had set up his equipment on the coffee table, which was so huge that a roller-skater could have pirouetted on it. Everything in this hotel was huge: the bed, which he had only seen in passing through a half-opened door, the flatscreen on the wall delivering brilliant images, the massive chair, the columns in the foyer, the backs of the ten-foot-long crescent-shaped benches a doorman had led him to with a friendly smile, and even he was at least a head taller than TT at around six foot six. When he entered the building in the stone heart of Berlin and had looked around his first thought was 'Mussolini meets Versace.'

Angelina Espinoza, in contrast, was a dainty five two. Yet when she entered a room, she was as assertive as she was graceful, as if a hotel suite of this size was her custom-made stage, and the rest of the world was too small. She had shoulder-length brown hair that fell across her face in curly waves however often she pulled it back. She wore a trouser suit in subdued beige, paired with a white blouse, all in all a proper business outfit, but TT was still nervous in her presence.

He had met her in Virginia when he, along with the then foreign minister and his entourage, had made a kind of excursion to the CIA with several colleagues from the 'Federal Office for Telecommunication Statistics, Analysis Department.' In Langley, they had celebrated the opening to civilian use of GPS, which until then had been used purely militarily. The headquarters had impressed him with the sheer number of buildings on the campus, the auditorium and the expansive memorial garden. The only reminder of the plantation it had once been was the old mansion, Scattergood. Their American colleagues had held a small reception there. Kellermann, his boss, had acted like the Sun King and not even noticed how TT had suddenly found himself trapped in the dark eyes of Warrant Officer Angelina Espinoza behind the back of his superior. Before he could count to three, she had conquered him, led him away and transferred him to her apartment half an hour from Langley, where he enjoyed the rest of the evening and the entire night in near ecstasy: Angelina knew who he was and who he worked for. No tall tales, no silence, no 'I'm an IT technician at the Berlin Continental Savings and blah blah blah bank,' but rather the truth, about which it didn't pay to talk because their experiences were too similar.

The only thing they didn't do was say their real names. That was taboo. Even – especially – in situations like this. He was Täschner; she was Espinoza. They worked for their respective agencies and were known publicly by these names. Additional aliases and legends were nothing unusual. TT had internalised his work name to such an extent that he could hardly remember his birth name. Or hardly wanted to. The latter was more likely.

Their affair was barely worthy of the name, and so they had left a reunion to the rules of chance. TT welcomed the fact that chance had taken him in hand with this assignment in Berlin, of all places.

She had checked in under the name Sandra Kerring, and he had introduced himself as Oliver Mayr at reception. So he hadn't known who was awaiting him at the door. His job consisted of recording the live images from the CCTV in Adlershof here at the Hotel de Rome, setting up a dedicated line with Kellermann, and preventing it from being interrupted at any point during the operation if at all possible. And of course anticipate the every need of the specialist from the Agency, who had been specially requested for this mission and was being paid by the BND through a consulting agreement. The instant that Angelina opened the door, he was ready to do his duty with the utmost enthusiasm, even put his body on the line if necessary.

Not her. She was thinking of nothing but her assignment. She reached for a glass of mineral water, drank and TT stared at the light imprint of lipstick her mouth left on the rim of the glass. That would probably be the furthest her physical commitment would go. She seemed focused, the consummate professional.

'Go back to him and the young woman.'

He moved the joystick and stopped the recording at the beginning of the conversation. The CCTV had an excellent directional microphone – he didn't even need to hack into the radio signal from Quirin's mic.

'Would you like your mineral water still or sparkling?'

'Sparkling.'

Angelina nodded. 'Continue.'

'Stupid question, but did you feed the meter?'

She squinted and observed Quirin's reaction. Then she had the passage replayed repeatedly in slow motion. Finally, she signalled to TT with a flick of her hand to let the recording continue.

'Do those old Russian arms depots still exist?'

'No.'

Angelina smiled and looked at TT. 'He's lying. No one took care of finally cleaning up those dumps. Who's the girl? She's doing a good job.'

'No idea.'

The girl was new to the covert operations team and belonged to Kellermann's exclusive group of favourites. Depending on the boss's mood, TT was another. But despite all the collegial solidarity and, as closely as they were sitting next to each other, he couldn't forget that Angelina was working for the competition. And this evening, quite possibly not even exclusively for them.

It was nothing unusual by now. CIA agents supposedly even trained brokers on Wall Street in tactics and disguise, provided through so-called *research and advisory firms*. They taught their clients the art of deception as well as the detection of lies. Agents had been regulars at Goldman Sachs and SAC Capital Advisors – and had pocketed fat consultancy fees. What was perfectly unremarkable in America, hiring state specialists for private aims, would be unthinkable for virtuous German civil servants. TT didn't even want to know the sums that would land in Angelina's private bank account after this job. The suite was surely on expenses.

He zoomed even closer on the face of the renegade. So this is what Kaiserley looked like when he was lying. The traitor. Fouling his own nest. Angelina was occupied with the former agent's facial expressions, frame by frame, for a solid fifteen minutes. TT followed her orders without interrupting her once. Finally she leaned back on the sprawling cushions and closed her eyes.

'He winks. He doesn't blink.'

TT pushed the rack to one side so he could put his feet on the edge of the coffee table and get comfortable himself.

'And what's the difference?'

'Blinking is something you can't control. Winking, you can. Besides . . .'

She shifted back into an upright position, much to TT's regret.

'His pupils contract. Just for a fraction of a second. And then he has one quirk that's very rare. He . . .'

She wrinkled her nose.

'What?'

Angelina laid her head on her left shoulder. Her hair slid in front of her face like a glistening veil. She bent forward and TT had to pull himself together to prevent his eyes wandering to her plunging neckline.

'That,' she said, 'is the difference between the pay scale of a federal civil servant and ten thousand dollars. We've got twenty minutes.'

She kissed him. Adrenaline shot into TT's bloodstream. It was like in Langley. Hot, quick, and nearly honest. He asked himself if he had mentioned in her personal dossier back then how quickly she got down to business. Then the time for thinking had passed.

Quirin Kaiserley cast a sideways glance at the neighbour to his right, a deputy leader in the Brandenburg State Parliament. Still fifteen minutes until the end of recording. Right now, he was lecturing on why, in his opinion, the regional government should continue to rule, despite the fact that at least a quarter of them, including the party leader and chairman, had cooperated with the Stasi in the GDR. Juliane wouldn't let him get his excuses out.

'In the other states in Germany, Stasi "informal collaborators" are barred from the state legislature. In Thuringia they were even declared "unworthy" of parliament. The western part of the Federal Republic isn't familiar with the problem. But it exists. Because the former West Germany wasn't a Stasi-free zone.'

A video recording was played over loudspeaker and monitors. Juliane's voice came from offstage.

'What's certain is that the Ministry for State Security also recruited a large number of citizens in the Federal Republic of Germany. Their names can be found in the so-called "Rosenholz" file.'

Quirin flinched in a way that was hardly perceptible. He searched for Juliane's gaze. She was looking at her moderator's cards and sorted them while the segment was running on the screens.

The piece explained that *Rosenholz* was the name of an intelligence operation in 1993. German Federal Intelligence Officers flew to Washington and were permitted by the CIA to view selected files from the Stasi archives. After long, arduous negotiations the files were returned to the German Federal Government and the Stasi Records Agency – of course only after their American friends had finished their analysis. There were gaping holes in the lists of names, either because CIA agents had also worked for the Stasi, or because the Americans wanted to protect certain sources.

Rosenholz was a bone that had been gnawed clean.

The film didn't say how the files got to Virginia. It didn't mention that they had been hidden for weeks in an allotment garden just off the B1 federal motorway before it takes you out of Germany. That had been in Mahlsdorf, just inside the city limits. Quirin had had a tip and immediately informed his colleagues at HQ in Pullach.

It was said a Stasi general and a KGB officer had hidden the material in the cellar of a *dacha*. But the BND didn't retrieve it. Why this unique, historic chance had been missed – this was another of the nagging questions that Quirin had never had an answer to. Who was being protected? Who was protecting themselves? And who sat high enough up to keep the hiding spot secret from his own people?

Juliane's beautiful face reappeared on screen. She looked past Quirin right into the camera before turning to him.

'Over 3,000 West German citizens might have been Stasi spies. Has the *Rosenholz* file really uncovered all of them? Quirin Kaiserley, you're a former agent of the German Federal Intelligence Service, the BND, and are more than sceptical in this regard.'

Quirin saw himself in the monitors. He was too surprised to answer immediately.

'You say that *Rosenholz* isn't the whole story. Is that right?'

He cleared his throat. 'Yes.'

'How so?'

'Part of the files were missing after they were finally given back by the CIA following tough negotiations.'

'Which parts?'

'Among others, the entire alphabetic register from La to Li.'

'So the files were manipulated? By the CIA, the KGB or the Stasi?'

She wanted to corner him. Wanted a public execution. And he was putting his head on the chopping block for her.

'I can only say that far from all of the Stasi's foreign agents have been uncovered. They're still around. They're holding high and influential positions in this country. Not just this country. They're susceptible to blackmail. They've never spoken to their families about it. They fear for their reputations in politics and business. So they have a great deal of interest in putting an end to the debate.'

There was a slight commotion in the crowd.

But I won't let that happen, Quirin continued the sentence mentally. They had already tried it in Sassnitz. An entire family was erased. They had trusted me and I failed them. And all the efforts to find the mole were unsuccessful. Maybe I'm not the only one who can't forget.

Somewhere out there a complete microfilm file existed. The original. It should have been here on this table, in front of the eyes of millions of viewers. And he would have finally known who had betrayed all of them. Could have finally closed that chapter of his life.

Instead, once again he stood there with empty hands. The audience was whispering in their seats.

'Mr Kaiserley?'

Quirin jumped.

'Is there evidence for these claims?'

The murmurs fell silent. Juliane shot him daggers. He breathed deeply.

'Yes,' he answered. Everyone should hear. Above all, those who had felt secure for twenty-five hellish long years. 'Yes. There's proof. I've seen the files.'

'And where are they now?'

Everyone stared at him. Quirin stared at himself through the monitor.

'Mr Kaiserley, when did you see them? In what circumstances? Do you have evidence?'

'No,' he answered. 'Not yet. But I'll find it.'

Angelina lay naked on the huge bed's velvet blanket. TT had connected the equipment in the bedroom so that they could follow the taping from a horizontal position. The CIA agent had stared at the screen the whole time and instructed TT to show her the last thirty seconds once more.

'Split screen.'

The image on the monitor separated. On the left were the pictures from the AMC camera, the right showed what the CCTV caught. Angelina put her headphones back on, TT followed her cue.

'Give me Kellermann.'

TT made the camera pan over the rows of audience members and paused at a man in the second-to-last row. He zoomed a little closer. Kellermann was leaning back, arms crossed, a town crier condemned to listen. He was in his early sixties, powerful, good-looking in a casual way with a large nose and uneven facial features. His short hair and brawny physique gave him the air of a wrestler in a tailored suit. But he was one of the highest-ranking department leaders in the BND – and he loved it when his opponents underestimated him. The closing remarks were being presented and you could see the audience to his left and right preparing to leave.

'Kellermann?'

She pronounced his name in an American way, which almost sounded like *Killerman*. If TT's boss was pleased, then he only let it show through the slightest smile.

'He's telling the truth.'

Kellermann gave the signal: he clicked the cartridge of his pen and put it in his left jacket pocket.

'Give me the other positions.'

The CCTV swung around to the production assistant, who reached to her ear at that precise moment, listened attentively, left her position at the foot of the stairs and hurried towards the exit. Then the camera panned to the four other spots, all in the first row. The men who had been seated there had already got up and had slipped away into the mass of people streaming towards the exits.

The left half of the monitor went black. The taping was over. TT used the joystick to direct the CCTV at Kaiserley. He was trying to get rid of his microphone cable without tearing his shirt off.

'You would have arrested him on the spot, right?'

TT let out a sigh. 'No idea.'

Angelina laughed quietly. 'Don't try to fool me. I spotted one guy from VS and two from BKA. Not to mention the mutts from the press. It wouldn't be the first time the guy pissed in your . . . muesli?'

'Cornflakes,' TT corrected her attempt at German slang. He was upset that Kaiserley got away and was allowed to continue to spread his lies unpunished. The man trampled on everything that the service had once meant to him. He had been a role model for TT. His role model. And now . . .

Angelina ran her fingers softly through his hair. 'Don't let it get to you. There are dogs like that everywhere. And you always blame us . . .' She softly bit his earlobe. 'If the full files existed, wouldn't you have found them long ago?'

TT looked at her with astonishment. Relations between the two intelligence agencies were close, for long stretches almost brotherly. Although there was no doubt who was the little brother. In the nineties the working relationship was so close that there were even joint operations between German and American agents that Pullach only found out about after the fact. But that was a long time ago. Before TT's time. Sometimes Kellerman talked about it in his office after he was off the clock. Those were stories like the ones cowboys in the Wild West told around the campfire, or veterans at D-day anniversaries. Kaiserley occasionally appeared in them. Kellermann's eyes glowed then, until he remembered what had become of his great hero: a journeyman labourer who continuously spread lies and half-truths about the BND.

'If you don't have them . . .' TT said, consciously leaving the end of the sentence hanging in the air.

'The real Stasi identities?' Angelina stood up and went into the bathroom, which could easily have swallowed TT's entire one-bedroom Munich apartment. She continued talking while wrapping herself in a soft, voluminous terrycloth bathrobe and filling the bath.

'We really have other concerns. I don't think those original files still exist. Whatever is still in circulation are counterfeits. Things like that always surface. Alleged copies of the Stasi file cards were already floating around on the market in the eighties. They were offered to several newspapers. But at the time no one had the courage to snap them up. So why the big fuss now?'

She returned to the bedroom. 'What's so important about these ancient lists of names?'

TT shrugged his shoulders. 'It's above my pay grade. You shouldn't ask me.'

She loosened the belt on her bathrobe and came closer.

'Who then? *Killerman?*'

She lowered herself onto his lap and TT instantly felt his willingness to deepen transatlantic relations. He was able to reach past Angelina and turn off the monitor. She purred like a cat.

'Don't try to fool me. You're looking for a real bastard.'

She kissed him. 'Then you lot have to set a trap for him.'

She kissed him again. 'So give him some bait.'

She kissed him once more. TT's phone rang. He needed a minute to find it. It lay under the bed, and he asked himself how it had got there. Then he noticed the chaos around them and he didn't wonder anymore, he just grinned. Unknown caller. Headquarters must have patched him through because his number was secret.

With the uneasy feeling that always overcame him when somebody called him around this time of night, he answered.

'Yes?'

'Everything OK?'

TT recognised his boss's raw voice, filtered to sound chummy.

'Couldn't be better.'

'Listen, I know it's late. But I need you to do me a favour.'

That didn't sound good. When Kellermann was acting pally, stress was on the horizon. TT shot a glance at Angelina, who was just getting a bottle of champagne from the minibar. She sensed something had changed as TT sat up and listened with concentration. Finally he nodded.

'I'll take care of it.'

He hung up and got out of bed. Angelina raised the bottle and looked at him questioningly.

'What about this?'

'I'll be back in an hour. There's something I need to take care of first.'

'Business or pleasure?'

TT pulled on his pants and grinned. 'Business. The hunter is checking the traps.'

3

Dombrowski, Klaus. Late fifties. Judging by his voice, stature and demeanour, he was still the furniture-mover he started off as more than thirty years ago. In the meantime he'd turned businessman, master of more than 350 more-or-less legal employees. His empire comprised fourteen moving trucks and teams, thirty-one street-cleaning and salting vehicles, twenty-three crews of cleaners and the countless day labourers under his rule, whom he still had lined up at five in the morning in front of the employment agency at Nordhafen to personally pick them out as required. He knew every one of them by name. He had an attitude that would have seen him out on his ear at any normal job, even the army, effective immediately. He led his company like a berserker, but he worked like one too. He appeared unexpectedly everywhere to check, curse, insult, rampage, but he had also hauled more than one of his troops out of detention at the last minute before they were deported. The way in which he had got expired papers extended could only be called 'cutting through red tape' if one was very generous (not every house move, not every service for civil servants' cottages on the edge of the city had to be on the books), and there was a recurring rumour that he had even paid bail money and stood as security for employees from time to time.

Dombrowski himself had no comment. Perhaps he might have said something if he was asked. But people didn't talk to Dombrowski; at most they talked about him. His curly, shoulder-length hair was greying and thinning significantly. On special occasions he wore it down, and otherwise tamed it with a rubber band. He cultivated a reputation as a former hippy who in his long march through the institutions had always carried the moving boxes of others to higher and increasingly more elegant offices and now swept the back steps of the powerful. Perhaps he also took care of other kinds of dirt, but that was just a rumour. He paid permanent employees twelve months' pay instead of the thirteen or fourteen common in Germany, squeaked past the minimum wage by just a few cents, but then once a year, at Christmas, added a bonus in the manner of a pre-revolutionary Russian feudal lord – provided you had been able to drag yourself to work with a temperature of 105 and work unpaid overtime for the sheer joy of working and being needed. With him, something wasn't bought because it was new or modern, but only when its predecessor had simply fallen apart. He had got the office furniture for a bargain when the contents of the GDR Ministry of Foreign Trade had been sold off for pennies on the dollar. It was said that the head of the ministry, Schalck-Golodkowski, had personally sat on the chair that now groaned under Dombrowski's massive body. The computer monitor on the shabby desk belonged in a museum. When he turned in Judith's direction, because naturally she had been compelled to follow him and listen before she rejected his doubtless outrageous request, the joints of the chair squeaked pitifully.

'Here. Look at the roster. No one's here.'

'Then call someone.'

'On Friday evening? Anyone still in their right mind wouldn't pick up.'

'Then how stupid do you think I am?'

Dombrowski gave her a smile that would have frightened anyone else. It was as wide as the grin on the wolf that had just eaten your grandmother. She stood still. Pure curiosity: how far would he go? Maybe more than that – she was unable to draw a line in the sand.

'Judith, my dear Judith.'

No. Just say no. She began to visualise the two letters. A precautionary measure. A jagged, clear, N – a barrier. An emphatic O – like a zero. No.

'A cold starter. You know what that means. I can't send just anyone.'

The term actually came from heating oil specialists, and described people whose heaters stopped working in the middle of winter because they had run out of oil. Emergency cases, for which quick delivery could bring in exorbitant fees. No one knew why Dombrowski had adopted this phrase, of all things. Perhaps because you needed specialists who had the brains to turn off their hearts and sense of smell the moment they were confronted with something that was worse than letting your own mother rot for six weeks. There were only a very few specialists who fit the bill. Judith was one of them.

'I don't have anyone else. So don't act that way. Kastner is on holiday. Josef is on the crew at the IHK.'

'And Dieter?'

'Dieter is sick.'

He wanted to hand her the keys to the car. Judith crossed her arms.

'Maybe I have something planned?'

A dark spot in Brandenburg wasn't what people generally understood under the word date. But it was still a plan. And it had something to do with her personal life, a phrase that Dombrowski had erased from his vocabulary.

He gently waved the set of keys, like a piece of meat to a dog.

'You don't have anything planned, Judith. You know what the industry is like. If this works out, then we'll get a city block. If not, it'll go to MacClean.'

They had lost Friedrichstrasse to MacClean last year. After that, Dombrowski had cut the Christmas bonus for the first time ever.

'Please.'

Her *no* evaporated. She took the car keys with an angry sigh.

'What's the issue?'

'Like I said before, murder.'

He motioned to the chair in front of his desk, steel pipes with burst foam cushions, left over in the furniture truck during some move. Judith reluctantly took a seat.

'The corpse will be picked up soon. So no de-putrification, just disinfection and cleaning. However, and this is the problem, forensics took ages. The entire apartment is a wreck. The painters are coming on Monday. Tuesday is the first of the month. On Wednesday the next renters will already be sitting there on their new couch from social services. That's the way it is. And now you're on board.'

That sounded like a dry run. Nothing damp, sticky, black, no gluey mattresses, no bugs, worms or insects that fled in every direction as soon as you turned on the light, no stench. Maybe it had even been a 'clean' murder – poison, strangulation, suffocation. Or a shooting – small calibre, instantaneous death, little blood. Then she would only have to erase the outline of the body and clean thoroughly. On Monday the painters would be puzzled by a couple of faded tomato juice spots on the wall paper.

'The perp?'

This was important. Once, a cleaner had been attacked by a mentally ill man who had stabbed his wife in a state of delusion and had disappeared. On the day the apartment was cleared, the murderer returned to the scene of the crime. The colleague survived. But since then, Dombrowski maintained even closer connections with the police.

'At large. No leads yet.'

'I don't like it.'

'Then take the gun along.'

Dombrowski pulled open the desk drawer, removed a pistol and held it out for Judith. 'It's an apartment building. The janitor will let you in, neighbours are watching, you have a phone. The police know we're sending someone over. Nothing will happen.'

'But something did happen.'

'OK. I can't force you. I can only ask you to.' All the while, he stared unwaveringly at her with the innocent look that he only risked in rare moments of true helplessness. Judith asked herself where her *no* was. Why did it always disappear when she needed it most?

'What about the furnishings?'

'As far as I know the apartment is furnished. That's a job for . . .'

He rummaged through his stacks and pulled out a slip of paper.

'Fricke. That's the janitor's name. He's expecting you in exactly twenty minutes at the front door of Marzahner Promenade 48.'

Bewildered, Judith accepted the note. 'That's right around the corner from my place.'

Dombrowski leaned back in relief and removed a half-sucked cigarillo from the ashtray. Since his second bypass he only occasionally stuck it between his teeth, without lighting it.

'Then you don't have far to go once you're done. The police cleared it this morning. If you do your job properly they can rent it out without a loss.'

He noticed her hesitation.

'Don't show me up. You can do it. There'll be something extra in it for you at the end of the month. When we get the whole city block. And take the smock with long sleeves.'

He looked at her arms. She stood up and went to the door. He bellowed after her: 'I've got a box for you.'

'Professor's estate from the Free University. Josef told me that's your kind of thing.'

It sounded like they had cleaned out a dominatrix's secret chamber. Judith took the box and carried it outside. Books. The leftovers from estate sales rejected by antiquarians, which could only be got rid of at flea markets with grinding effort. When she pushed the box onto the floor of the van she opened the lid and took a quick look inside. There were picture books and tour guides, mostly from the sixties. She pulled one out. Mountains, the sea, serpentine roads, colourful houses. The Amalfi coast. It could be Italy. But Judith wasn't completely sure.

Fricke was a small man. He paced back and forth impatiently in front of the entrance to the apartment tower and peered in all directions instead of opening the boom gate to the car park. Judith repressed a curse and drove twice more around but didn't have a chance with the bulky van. It was thirty-three degrees, Hertha Berlin, the local football team, had a home match – a lazy weekend. Everyone was home, barbequing on the balcony.

Finally she parked the vehicle half on the sidewalk, hazard lights on, twenty metres away and got out. The promenade in Marzahn was an example of poor eighties urban planning: anonymous residential hives, fast-moving streets, battery humans. But in summer, at night on her balcony on the tenth floor, with a bottle of ice-cold white wine beside her and a quiet rustling in her ear when she lowered the pickup arm into the groove and listened to the last of Johnny Cash's *American Recordings*, then the Marzahn Promenade was the perfect place for aliens like herself. You had to love feeling physically out of place, but at home in music. Only then could you love this glittering view of endless building façades.

Judith opened the back doors of the van and looked indecisively at her equipment. The sealed hazardous materials container. The bucket with scouring sand, laundry soap, brushes and scrubbers. The heavy blacksmith's hammer they sometimes used to knock apart beds or rusted window catches. The toolbox with a side compartment for the skeleton keys that could open any apartment door. Gently swinging yellow rubber gloves, hanging from diagonal lines with clothes pins: her work gloves. The stack of blue smocks, 'Dombrowski Facility Management' stitched on the front and back in white lettering. Two lay scrunched up in a cleaning bucket. She had forgotten to tell Kai where the laundry basket was. She tried to remember his face under the fringe, but she had forgotten it already. He wouldn't return on Monday. It didn't even pay to remember his name.

Her gaze wandered up the front of the tower block. Horizontal purple stripes made counting easier and helped with orientation. The building opposite had yellow stripes, others were blue, red or green. She felt the throbbing nervousness in her ribcage. A crime scene. In contrast to Gerlinde Wachsmuth's quiet solitude. She slowly turned back to the cargo bay of the van and took a deep breath. City air, with that slightly metallic taste on the tongue: worn tyres, sun on asphalt and rotting compost.

'Peppi!' someone screamed. 'Stop it!'

An elderly lady two doors down was desperately trying to drag her mutt out of some shrubs by its collar. The dog, a knee-high, dark mongrel, growled and drooled over a pile of rags someone had thrown into the bushes. As small as the dog was, the woman was simply overwhelmed.

'Aren't you going to do anything?'

The woman looked outraged, as if Judith was responsible for all the rubbish in the world.

'Everyone just throws their rubbish around. And the administration doesn't take care of anything!'

She noted the car with the open window.

'Are you from the housing administration?'

'No.'

The dog suddenly bolted, letting a slobbery, indefinable bundle drop directly in front of Judith's feet, as it had been trained to do.

'Wait a minute!' Judith demanded.

The problem was solved as far as the woman was concerned. She simply kept walking. The dog raced behind her, passed her and jumped around the next corner.

'Hello? What's the going on here?'

Fricke looked over to her briefly. It wouldn't make a good impression if she just kicked the thing against the curb now. Furious, Judith retrieved a rubbish bag from the car and lifted the bundle with fingers splayed. She didn't even want to know what it was, so she simply let it fall into the sack and tossed it far back on the ramp.

She pulled on a fresh smock and smoothed her hair. Then she made her way to the janitor, who was rattling his keys and peering back down the street. The path to the glazed entry hall was neatly swept. The man took his job seriously.

Fricke only noticed her when she stopped directly in front of him. The small eyes in his owl-like face spread wide. Perhaps he had been expecting the allied power of ten veiled martial artists. Or perhaps a cohort of Turkish cleaning ladies. She was familiar with this reaction and extended her hand towards him, which he shook hesitantly.

'Judith Kepler,' she said. 'I'm the cleaner.'

Fricke seemed to have had something else planned for the evening. He concealed his bad mood inadequately beneath a silence that lasted eight storeys. Then the elevator doors opened, and without looking back at Judith, he led the way into a bright, well-lit hallway painted pale violet with matte beige PVC flooring. Judith counted six apartments: three to the left and three to the right. At the end of the hall there was a large sealed window. Fricke headed towards the last door on the left side and cut through the seal with a key, as if he did it every day. The nameplate read 'T. Borg'. When Borg opened the door he would have seen the residential tower opposite and Landsberger Allee to the right. He could also have seen her – Judith's – apartment. A tram rolled by. But Borg wouldn't be opening the door. Fricke did that now. He held it open and waited for Judith to walk past him inside.

'You have to dispose of the rubbish yourself.' He motioned towards two blue sacks standing in the hallway. 'They probably thought I would take care of it all. But they were mistaken.'

He stood in the doorway, fumbled with his key ring and then deposited three security keys in Judith's hand.

'This one is for downstairs, that's for upstairs. And this here's for the mailbox. There's still a seal there, which also has to go. Will you take care of it from here?'

'Yes.'

'Your boss has a lot of faith.'

The elevator doors opened. The elderly lady with the dog appeared. She was frightened, and wanted to move past them quickly to the apartment opposite, but the dog had other plans. Quick as a flash, he ran towards her, sniffing and waving his tail.

'Peppi!' the woman called. 'Heel.'

Fricke grabbed the animal by the collar. It squeaked indignantly and began to yowl.

'Dogs belong on a leash!' He snapped.

The woman dared three steps forward and reached for her darling. She cast a curious glance into the apartment where her neighbour had lived until recently, then retreated without a word.

'OK then. The rubbish has to go. All of the woman's possessions. Wasn't much. You dispose of it, OK? Any questions?'

So it was a Ms Borg who had lived here.

'Were the relatives already here?'

'No relatives. No inheritors, it appears, but she didn't have anything that would have been worth saving. It was like she was passing through. Hardly moved in and already dead. So make sure that you're finished quickly. There are parties interested in the apartment.'

Judith kept a straight face. It was really easy when you maintained an invisible wall between you and other people.

'Yes.'

'And don't just put the rubbish behind the house. You've seen how the dogs just roam around here. OK?'

'OK.'

'And by Monday it'll be spotless here.'

Judith didn't say a word. Fricke looked at her with irritation. Judith nodded.

'All right then . . .'

Fricke tapped his forehead and went back to the elevator.

'The keys in the mailbox.'

'Aye, aye, boss.'

'And do a proper job. I don't want the painters vomiting. They're pals of mine.'

'Will do, master.'

Fricke thought for a second. But he couldn't think of anything else, so he pressed the button and the elevator doors opened.

'I don't want the sacks in here either.'

Judith cast a glance down to the car park through the window in the hallway. The cars looked like toys from up here.

'All right.'

The elevator doors closed. She waited until she heard the jolt from the lift on its way down, then she clicked the keys onto her karabiners and removed the rest of the official evidence sticker from the doorframe. She wanted to steel herself against what awaited her. But that hadn't ever worked. It was different every time. Just as every murder was different and distinct from those that came before.

4

It starts in the living room. The armchair across from the three-piece living room suite is soaked with black blood. The woman must have sat there for a while, severely injured and bleeding from a deep wound, before managing to jump up. A last, futile attempt to escape the unavoidable, because she only made it to the balcony door. Maybe she wants out, fleeing, jumping. Flight impulses are irrational. The dried blood on the bright laminate is smeared with bare footprints and heavy shoes. He catches her, pulls her back and flings her across the room to the bay window.

Judith prowls around. He must be furious. Enraged. The situation slips through his fingers, gets out of control. He doesn't get what he wants, even though it had almost been within his grasp. He points the gun at his victim. He aims. He pulls the trigger. Once. Twice. The window has a bullet hole. So does the wall, between the windowsill and the radiator. He misses her. Is he playing with her?

Borg falls to the ground. Rises again. Drags herself through the connecting door into the bedroom. Brushes the frame with her wounded body and tries to close the door. In vain. He kicks the door open. Raises the gun. Shoots. Once. Twice. Shoulder and arm. Ragged splotches of blood on the wallpaper. But Borg is still alive. Why doesn't he finish her off? Is he talking to her?

Yelling at her? She slides down the wall, a wide, rusty trail marks her collapse. She doesn't give up. Crawls further. He stands over her, the gun cocked. Hits her. Kicks her, she rolls up, rolling over the cheap chenille rug to the bed, panicked and instinctively looking for shelter, and he watches her dying, until he raises his gun one last time.

A white chalk outline marked the position of the body between the wardrobe and the single bed. A dried puddle of blood with rosy edges where her head had lain. Judith knelt down. She discovered the scar left by the bullet and the scratches from the tools of the technicians that had dug the slug out of the floor. The crumbs strewn around everywhere were the remnants of cerebral matter. Borg had been shot at point blank range.

Staggering, she stood up and lurched to the window. She ripped it open, leaned out and drew the heavy, warm air into her lungs. Something under her soles crunched, and she hoped that it wasn't bone fragments or parts of the ear canal.

'This is a job. Nothing more.'

Dombrowski's voice rang in her ears, as if he was standing next to her. She remembered the blood. Blood everywhere. Streams of blood, knee-deep and choppy, on the tiles, on the floor.

'This stuff is damn hard to get rid of.'

There had been four of them. One after another had left the room. In the end, she was the only one left. That afternoon Dombrowski had returned and saw the results. A gleaming bathroom with black grout.

'It's porous, girl. No one goes at it with scouring powder. What breaks down protein compounds?

'Hydrogen peroxide in a fifteen per cent solution or a chlorine bleach solution.'

'And why don't you use chlorine?'

'Because it's all gone.'

He growled in dissatisfaction. 'Where are the others?'

She shrugged her shoulders. Dombrowski looked around the training room in which he had spread buckets full of pig's blood that morning, to no little amusement at the theatricality. This is where he put them to the test. This is where it was revealed who had the chops to become a disinfector, pest controller or crime scene cleaner. The room looked like new. Except for the grout.

'Couldn't stand the sight of blood, eh?'

That was before Dombrowski had had his bypasses. He offered her a filterless. She took off her safety goggles. Then they sat next to each other on the edge of the bathtub and smoked a while.

'What about you?' he interrupted the silence. 'Why can you handle it?'

He was the first person who'd asked her. Judith pushed the cleaning bucket in front of her feet a smidge to the right. She tapped her ashes into the water and shrugged her shoulders.

She was clean. After completing the last round of rehab she had started at Synanon rehabilitation agency as one of many untrained employees who had to fight their way back into a world with alarm clocks, work schedules and the binding nature of agreements. But the exit was a dead end. No one wanted her on the real labour market. A glance at her résumé was to recognise a system of failure in a string of short, fitful false starts. She had run out of chances by her early thirties. When she heard a rumour that Dombrowski was looking for people for his special training and wasn't finding them, she'd applied for the test.

Using short sentences he had explained what it was about: transforming the horrible into the bearable.

Dombrowski looked down at his powerful mover's hands.

'Death isn't the brother of sleep. And even less ash and dust. It's decay, rot, putrification. It stinks for a while, and then something new comes along. Nothing was ever truly lost on our planet. If you know that, then it's more than just a job.' He stood up. 'You can start tomorrow if you want.'

Nothing was lost.

Maybe that would have been the right answer to Kai's question. Maybe she should have told him that the difference between getting up and staying in bed was as significant as the difference between everything and nothing. And that every day she fights against nothingness anew, and still hadn't figured out why it paid to fight.

She could see into her apartment from the bedroom. The moon was already visible, bright in the evening sky. She banned herself from thinking about dark spots and examined the building opposite her. A man was standing on one of the many yellow balconies, watering flowers. Two storeys below, someone had started up his smoky grill. Children were playing between parked cars. Stop-and-go traffic on the autobahn. Hertha Berlin FC had won and drivers were honking their horns and swinging their scarves out their windows in euphoria. There was an apartment on the eighth floor of the violet building that needed to be cleaned so that someone could move in two days later. Such is life.

Half-full yet looking somehow deflated and exhausted, the bin bags stood in the middle of the hallway. The hooks on the coat hanger were empty; no shoes, no doormat. Fricke had probably stuffed any personal effects the homicide investigators and CSI hadn't taken with them into the bin bags.

The black traces of fingerprinting 'soot' still clung everywhere, the door frame, walls, light switches and door handles. Laundry soap was the best thing for that. She raised her hand and carefully ran it over a smudged, dark spot. She found the red print of a hand underneath the dirt.

The armchair in the living room couldn't be saved – that was a case for Fricke. Thinning agents were necessary because the blood had caked long before. Chlorine, magnesium oxide and gasoline would be sufficient for the walls and carpets. Pumice, soda and chrome polish for the bath and kitchen, possibly sewing machine oil if the grout darkened and the appearance needed to be evened up. Oil was also good against the sticky remnants of the seal. Maybe a bottle of ethyl alcohol to be on the safe side. She'd need the trolley if she didn't want to keep going up and down. There was a pair of gloves underneath the bed. Fricke must have overlooked them. Judith kneeled down and wanted to pick them up, but then she paused. Pink terrycloth slippers, carefully placed in the middle, exactly a millimetre apart. Shaking her head, she took them and carried them into the hallway with the bags. Then she inspected the cupboards and wardrobes again. They were empty. There was a towel hanging on the door of the bathroom, black spots of rust indicated the people from CSI had used it to dry off. Hastily removed disposable gloves and adhesive paper lay in the bin. The medicine cabinet was sealed. Judith tore the sticker and inspected the contents. Nothing special, except for the four tins of Florena cream, smudged by CSI dusting everything.

She took the bin and threw everything inside, including the two rolls of toilet paper stacked on the tank. She paused once again. There wasn't any roll in the holder. Instead, someone had torn off the paper, piece for piece, and stacked it carefully on top of the tank. Corner on corner. A quirk that had nothing to do with frugality.

Judith looked at her watch. Time to go home. Tomorrow was another day. She grabbed the bin and emptied it into one of the sacks. Then she called the elevator, dragging the sacks behind her and pressed the button for the ground floor. Fricke could go to hell. He was probably already drinking his post-work beer. The thought of something cool made her throat seem even more dry. A sack fell over. A neat little stack of undergarments fell out. Cotton, washable at all temperatures, ribbed, ironed. A hint of lavender wafted up to her nose. The elevator suddenly started moving with a jolt.

She watched the blue plastic sacks in a daze, as if they might suddenly transform themselves into something else – a picture behind a picture, a door behind a door, and then Judith saw it, and the scent of lavender and floor polish filled her nose. The sun shone onto the floor through a tall window. The shadow of its wings drew a gigantic cross. The elevator doors opened in front of Judith like an iron curtain.

'Hello?'

She jumped. Peppi's mistress stood in front of her. The dog strained at the leash.

'Are you going to clear that away already?'

A deliveryman appeared behind the woman, who knew by her tone not to address her. With a furrowed brow, he examined the mailboxes, which were almost impossible to take in due to their sheer number, and with a sigh began to read them name by name.

Judith stared at the bag that had keeled over. Finally, she squatted down and collected everything. Tea towels, pillow-cases, jumpers. A television guide, mockingly opening up to today's programme, half-used cosmetics. All the while, Peppi's mistress pressed the hold button and observed the proceedings with a stern gaze. She hoped the old woman cleaned up after her dog as fastidiously. She was taking it for a walk so often, it prob-ably had the squits.

Judith dragged the sacks into the main hallway. She pulled out her pocket knife and began to remove the seal from Borg's mailbox.

'Excuse me,' said the messenger. He was dressed completely in green, sweating, and appeared to be in a hurry. 'I'm looking for Christina Borg.'

Judith lowered her knife. 'Yes?'

'Are you her?'

Relieved, he turned to her and pulled a large envelope out of his bag. She raised her hands in defence.

'Christina Borg is . . .' She paused. The envelope was light brown. '. . . no longer alive.'

He thrust the letter in front of her nose to indicate urgency. Judith reached for it hesitantly. The writing was in pen and written in the sort of hand that was no longer in style, remi-niscent of a Victorian clerk. She turned it over and inhaled sharply. She stared at the address of the sender in disbelief. Yuri Gagarin Children's Home, Strasse der Jugend 14, Sassnitz, 2355. Printed and real. An original, and she almost expected there to be a GDR stamp on it. But the mark and the stamp were new. The letter had been en route for three days, a very long time for express mail.

'For Christina Borg?'

It was impossible. It couldn't be.

'Yes. She isn't here?'

The messenger clearly considered Judith someone who was informed about Borg. Which was true, to a certain extent.

'No. And she won't be returning.'

'Then it has to go back.'

He reached out his hand but Judith hesitated.

'The address no longer exists. This home was closed as soon as the wall fell.' Which was a good thing too. It no longer existed, even for Judith – until this letter had landed in her hands. And suddenly it became clear to her what had irritated her so much in the apartment and in the elevator. The slippers. The toilet paper. The linen, neatly stacked.

'But I can forward it.'

The messenger scratched his head. 'Registered.'

'With receipt?' Judith asked. 'Then you have the sender after all.'

'No, just registered.' The man looked at his watch. 'I have to go. What are we going to do?'

'We' sounded good. Judith unfastened the set of keys from her belt and opened Borg's mailbox. It was empty.

'Give it to me. I'll take care of it.'

The messenger glanced at the name on the mailbox. The fact that Judith had the key seemed to make him trust her.

'All right. Sign here, please.'

He pulled a clipboard out of his messenger bag. Judith scrawled an illegible scribble in the list of names.

'Have a nice evening,' she said.

The man nodded with relief. He left the building on squeaking rubber soles. Judith examined the envelope. Sassnitz. Sea gulls. Ships. The wide world and provincial narrowness. A port city way up at the end of the country. The ferries to Malmö, Ystad and Trelleborg. Narrow alleyways, crumbling houses. Banquet of the sea. Fish factory. Interzone trains. Train station. Cellar. Darkness. Cold hell.

It was so long ago.

A couple of noisy teenagers kicked empty beer cans along the road. Wearing heels that were far too high and far too cheap, two girls giggled towards Landsberger Allee. Friday night. Jeans and a sweatshirt clung to Judith's body, which screamed for a shower, wine with lots of ice cubes and her bed. She hoisted the sacks onto the floor of the van next to the boxes of books and sat down in the open door, envelope in hand. The word 'Sassnitz' pulsed behind her temples. The scent of lavender and dust mixed with the city steaming from the heat. She lit a cigarette. The smoke bit into her parched throat, and she inhaled so deeply that she became dizzy for a moment.

She ripped open the envelope and held a file from the home in her hands. A thin, light green leaflet made of woody paper. Printed on the front, the name Judith Kepler. She still didn't understand. Her hands began to shake. The documents were carbon copies of an original that was produced with a mechanical typewriter. A photo was pasted to the first page. A little girl around the age of five with long, blonde, angelic curls and unnaturally big blue eyes. The photo must have been taken from identification papers because the remains of a stamp was still visible in the lower right corner. Judith stared at it until her eyes burned. Then she read the first lines of the admission form.

> ... apartment in a state of neglect ... child's clothing dishevelled and dirty ... mother feeble-minded alcoholic ... to be committed to YGKH ... for two years ...

The words dissolved – they liquefied. Judith blinked. Her cheeks burned as if she had just been given two sharp slaps. Just like back then, when she had dipped her spoon once too often into the jam jar. When her shoelaces had come undone. When she had been caught not going straight back to the home after school, but had walked to the train station instead. To the train station, not the port. How could that be explained? Yearning for the sea and the horizon, sure, but the station? The station, again and again. Over the years Judith forgot what had drawn her there. But it always ended the same way. Trenkner's gloating, poorly concealed joyful anticipation when she drove Judith ahead of her down the stairs to the cellar, pushing her into the dark, dank room, and beating her until the child was a whimpering ball. You're slovenly and dirty. Antisocial and squalid. She had heard these words so often that one day she started to believe them.

Was there hatred? Yes. Were there questions? Thousands. Answers? None. There was only a grave in Sassnitz, but no one who could or wanted to remembered the person who had died. Marianne Kepler. Died shortly after her daughter had come to the home. A small granite stone, almost enveloped by moss.

The last time Judith had stood in front of it was more than ten years ago, searching desperately for a feeling inside that was more than emptiness, pain and absolute indifference. She had felt like a monster when she didn't find it. Back then she had filed a request to access the records. She wanted to know more about herself than just her date of birth, the day she was admitted to the home and the name of her mother next to the 'X'. But nothing was found except a few file cards with the transit stations of her life. 1989, people had explained and shrugged their shoulders. The wall coming down. The shredders had been running day and night in children's homes, not just in the Stasi headquarters. We're sorry, Ms Kepler, but we were unable to find more than the basic data on your admission and release at the former city council. She had gone down to Bachstrasse, but the houses there were crumbling and the people no longer recognised her. She'd asked around and never received more than friendly indifference. Marianne Kepler. A forgotten name. And her, Judith. A forgotten child.

Judith raised her head. The coarse cries of the teenagers echoed over the building walls. They sounded like the mating calls of an unknown, carnivorous species. Her apartment lay on the other side of Landsberger Allee. She needed wine. She needed music. But above all, she needed to find out about what Christina Borg had to do with the slumbering monster inside of her.

Judith turned back her carpets and emptied the rubbish sacks onto the bare floor. Then she climbed over the evenly distributed piles, a fogged-up glass of wine in hand, and sat down on the couch. The file from the children's home lay next to her. She was tempted to read it again and again. But first she had to find out who Christina Borg was. She took a long sip and examined the things in front of her.

Fricke had been right. It wasn't much. One mound was made up of clothing. Not expensive, not flashy. H&M, Zara, Mango. Cheap, international products that could have been bought anywhere in the world. Trendy, middling income, inconspicuous lifestyle. No relatives, Fricke had said. So this was everything Borg had owned. Perhaps there was more in the evidence room at the police station, but the police normally only take things like computers or phones. After a thorough search, they would leave all the private things behind that weren't considered evidence.

The other pile was made up of daily basics and domestic waste. Empty bags from the bakery, a couple of yoghurt containers, scraped clean. Dish towels. Toiletries. A bottle of body lotion with the lid carelessly screwed on had expired. Maybe that's where the scent of lavender came from. Dishes – two coffee mugs, one of them used, a cereal bowl, plates, cutlery. Books. A city atlas of Berlin, a picture book about Rügen. Dan Brown, *The Da Vinci koden*. Anna Bovaller, *Svärmaren*. Pia Hagmar, *Som i en dröm*. Judith leafed through the novels. They were all in Swedish.

Judith stuffed everything back into the bags. The TV guide fell to her feet when she picked up the book. A two-week guide, opened to the last day on the programme, Friday, today. She scanned over the colourful pictures and show times. The bottom of the page caught her eye. *Three to One*, the talk show with Juliane Westerhoff.

The guests: blah, blah, blah. One name was circled along with his picture. Quirin Kaiserley, former spy. Judith retrieved the bottle of wine from the fridge, topped up her glass and fell back onto the couch. It was the only show Borg had marked.

Borg probably liked to watch talk shows, or perhaps was a fan of Westerhoff. She was on every week, just like clockwork, and beaming tirelessly and with a steely determination would declare to the republic what kind of machinations she had uncovered. Over time, the shows and topics blurred into one another, and you got the vague feeling of having heard it all before. So why would someone mark a Westerhoff show weeks in advance?

She examined Kaiserley's picture once more. He didn't look unsympathetic. More like an intellectual Harley-Davidson biker than a spy. She was about to toss the paper in the bag and look at what little Borg had apparently brought along to Germany from Sweden, when it occurred to her that Swedes don't watch German talk shows. Judith grabbed the remote control.

'*You claim* Rosenholz *is only an incomplete picture?*'

Juliane Westerhoff, made up like a waxwork model, was taking a good-looking man in his early fifties to task. It was Kaiserley. He was saying something about microfilms and informants. The debate about the statute of limitations. Judith sat up. An unpleasant man made a comment. The moderator dug deeper and Kaiserley looked as if he was explaining to four-year-olds why bad boys had stomped on their sandcastles.

'Do you have evidence?'

'No,' he answered. 'Not yet. But I will find it.'

The camera panned over to the audience. Judith turned up the volume. The Stasi issue frequently bubbled up out of the dregs of the summer silly season. Quirin Kaiserley. Former BND agent. Intelligence expert. Years ago, there'd been a scandal when someone had quit the spooks and started washing their dirty laundry in public. Was that him? She topped up her wine again and watched with interest as Kaiserley was put through the wringer, good and proper. He appeared to be a good loser, because when Westerhoff said farewell with a few parroted phrases and the credits were scrolling across the screen, she saw him shaking hands in parting with the other guests.

She turned the television off and reached for the children's home file again. She examined the photo of the child that she once was. Antisocial. Feeble-minded. The old scars throbbed.

She took the wine bottle, nearly empty, opened the glass door to her tiny balcony and stepped outside. At this height there was a light breeze that ran through her hair. It was still very warm. A tropical night, as the weather broadcasters did not tire of saying, as if the country was transformed into a botanical garden in which cockatiels bustled about instead of blackbirds. She raised the bottle and drank a sip. Christina Borg, a Swedish woman, came to Germany, and got hold of Judith's file, abracadabra, and was killed. And no less than five hundred metres from this balcony.

The realisation hit Judith with such force that she was within a hair's breadth of dropping the bottle ten storeys. It was so clear. So unequivocal. As apparent as the labels sewn in the underwear and the number that you carried around with you the rest of your life, as if it were tattooed onto you. Borg, she thought, and squinted in order to make out the apartment in the sea of buildings on the other side. My God. Why did you come here?

She found the story on the other side of Landsberger Allee. The windows were brightly lit, and a black shadow darted through the rooms.

5

TT still had the master key in his car. It hadn't been long since he'd wired the apartment, and he was sure that no one had found the cameras and the microphones, and that the police weren't on his tracks.

He carefully placed a kitchen chair on the coffee table. The construction was shaky but it was his only chance if he wanted to get at this camera. After all, he couldn't drag a ladder into the apartment. He had already taken down all the other units and dropped them in the side pocket of his cargo pants. Just not this last one. It was located in the smoke detector, an infrared that worked at night and against backlight. He had no idea where the images were sent. When he looked around, he didn't even want to know. He only wanted to get out of there as quickly as possible.

Avoid complications, that's what Kellermann had said. Maybe sockets would be swapped out during renovation, and then even the stupidest electrician would catch on that this apartment has more in common with a TV studio than a normal flat. 'Had', past tense, he corrected himself. His hands were still shaking and his palms sweaty. He tried not to stare at the armchair with the big, black stains. There could hardly be more complications in this apartment.

He climbed up and unscrewed the casing of the smoke detector. Untouched, the camera was located exactly where he had installed it, but he wasn't able to move the clip to loosen it. Sweat pooled on his forehead. He suddenly felt hot, and a wave of nausea rose up from his belly. He had to get hold of this thing, otherwise he'd throw up on his feet. When they said there was never a dull moment in this job, he doubted that was what they meant.

A draft of air brushed over him. Even before he could turn around, he knew that someone was in the room. Out of the corner of his eye he saw a shadow, and then he heard a clear, cold voice.

'What are you doing here?'

He jumped and almost lost his balance. His eyes spread in astonishment because there was a woman in the doorway. She wore white overalls and a gas mask dangled in front of her chest. She held a gas cylinder clamped underneath her left arm and in her right hand she held the hose and the nozzle that she pointed at him like a trigger.

'I'm from property management. And who are you?'

'What are you doing here?'

The construction beneath him shook. TT was aware of the unfavourable position he found himself in. He wanted to climb down from the chair but the woman came closer, quick as lightning, and now stood less than two steps away, the nozzle pointed directly at him.

'Answer!'

'I can prove my identity. You can call the number here.'

He feverishly tried to think of who he could reach in the middle of the night to confirm a cover story. There was surely a procedural number for this operation and people that sat next to telephones, around the clock, to confirm all the fairy tales their colleagues told all around the world. But that was only true for people on operative assignments. He belonged to the department for technical procurement, and this job fell into the category of damage control – even though it looked like the exact opposite at the moment.

She looked at the lid. 'What's that?'

'A smoke detector.'

'Do you think I'm stupid?' She waved around in his direction with the nozzle. 'I have a litre of magnesium phosphide, a phosphorus-hydrogen compound. I wouldn't want to breathe it. A man of average build would die after a few seconds. We use it for rats.'

She took a step closer. TT realised she didn't necessarily mean the four-legged kind of rats. He tried to hold his breath. He had never heard of magnesium phosphide.

'That may be the casing for a smoke detector. But what's inside?'

TT couldn't produce a single word. His entire body began to shake. He had no idea what had happened in this apartment. The only thing he knew: it wasn't over. And regardless of who had sent her, she used weapons that had been considered inhumane at least since World War I.

'Well?' She pointed the nozzle at him like a pistol. Her finger touched the vent. For a split second gas hissed out of the opening. She took a step back.

'Oops. Sorry. That little bit won't hurt. At least I think.'

TT felt his throat was constricting. He couldn't breathe, the floor beneath him rocked and swayed towards him, then retreated, and he only had one last thought: *I want out of here*. In London, they had poisoned an FSB agent with radioactive food. Maybe the stuff came from Iraq or Turkey. The woman looked like she knew what she was doing with that gas cylinder.

'What's that?'

'A camera,' he answered. Rule number one: lie as little as possible.

'And what's it for?'

Rule number two: if you do lie, then stay as close to the geographical, personal, and causal circumstances as possible. 'For surveillance.'

'You a joker, eh?'

She tapped the vent again. TT jumped. She waved her free hand, and if his senses weren't playing tricks on him, then there was suddenly a hint of bitter almond in the air. His stomach lurched. Too many cheese crackers in the Hotel de Rome. He tried to concentrate on a cover story that sounded halfway plausible.

'This apartment was a meeting place for organised crime. That's why. Can I come down?'

'No!'

She wasn't completely normal. And she was cold as ice. She moved like a soldier on manoeuvres; in her protective clothing, she looked like an alien in a car wash.

'Organised crime?'

Apparently she knew as little as he did. So she wasn't working for another service. That made the issue considerably easier.

'Cigarette smuggling,' he answered because it sounded so harmless and the members of the various triads decimated each other with numbing regularity. 'Lots of Vietnamese live here.'

She put on the gas mask. Not good. Then she directed the nozzle directly at his face. Not good at all. Her voice sounded muffled underneath the visor, but no less menacing.

'Maybe you read the nameplate before you broke in. It sounds as Vietnamese as your tall tale about facility management. Who are you?'

Now he had even forgotten the cover name he'd used to gain entry. Günther Leibrecht? Gerd Schultze? He had smuggled himself into so many buildings with so many different identities that now, at the critical moment, he had simply lost track. The first time he had been in the apartment he had used an ID from a private security agency that patrolled this neighbourhood.

'Hands up! What's your name?'

They shot up, quick as an arrow. At the last second he remembered.

'Karsten Drillich.'

'Was that you?'

She used the nozzle to point at the bloodstains on the armchair.

'No!' He tried to appear as cooperative and harmless as was possible in this situation.

'But you recorded it with that thing there.'

'I only take them out. You have to ask my boss. Wait.'

He went to reach into his trouser pocket to remove the forged ID, but the gas hissed out of the nozzle again. His eyes began to water. He wheezed and gasped for air.

'Over to the wall. Move!'

He clambered down and stumbled backwards with his hands raised.

'Listen, this is all a misunderstanding. I have nothing to do with any of this.'

She patted him down and found the cameras he'd already removed and the coiled wires. She let them fall back into his pocket with a snort of disgust. The car keys and IDs were the next to fall into her hands. But the icing on the cake was the folded card made from the finest handmade paper that held the key card for the hotel suite. She flipped the paper up and studied the personal data with great interest.

'This, right. Explain to me, Mr . . . Karsten, Michael, Tobias or Oliver?'

He stared at her, aghast. He had mixed up the names. He was Oliver Mayr in the Hotel de Rome. He had fiddled with the telephone line belonging to one of the drivers from the parliamentary fleet as Karsten Drillich. He had entered this building as Michael Schiller. But right now he simply felt like Tobias Täschner – lousy. The last ID was his access authorisation for 'Federal Asset Management Munich.' The BND internal ID.

'I'm calling the police now.'

As a technician, TT had never been trained in close combat. He weighed his chances of knocking her out with a precise blow, before the gas could checkmate him, and arrived at sixty/forty. He spun around, lifted his leg and hit her with a mix of centrifugal force and muscle tone. She was flung back, the ID cards and set of keys were sent flying through the air, the mask slipped, the nozzle hissed and she tumbled backwards over the coffee table. The cylinder fell on the glass, which shattered with an ear-splitting crash. The hose developed a crazy life of its own, white gas shooting out of the nozzle and spreading in the air. TT held his breath, grabbed the car keys and dove towards the front door. He raced into the hallway, reached the door next to the elevator and kept going at top speed down the stairwell.

He flung himself into his car, started the ignition and accelerated to take the next corner at fifty miles per hour. Only when he reached the autobahn on-ramp and was certain no one was following him did his brain start to settle back into a logical thought process.

Phone. Luckily he had placed it in the breast pocket of his shirt. He pulled it out and dialled a number. *Come on*, he prayed. *Pick up.* Finally he heard Kellermann's voice. TT took a deep breath. Wonderful, dirty air, contaminated by exhaust fumes.

'Boss,' he said, 'we have a problem.'

Judith straightened herself with a groan. She carefully touched her face and let out a cry of pain. She freed herself from the wooden frame of the table in which she had landed, and stumbled into the bathroom.

A sliver of glass had brushed her cheek. The wound wasn't deep, but was bleeding profusely. Because there was no toilet paper left, she just washed it, carefully. Her lower lip didn't look good either and had begun to swell. The gas cylinder had hit her chin with a glancing blow, the equivalent of a medium uppercut and had knocked her out for the few valuable moments that the bastard needed to escape.

Judith returned to the living room. Oxygen was still streaming from the nozzle. She sealed it and opened the window so the gas could escape. As harmless as it was, there was the danger of explosion at high concentrations. Then she collected the IDs that lay strewn around the room. *Karsten Michael Oliver Asshole.* The rage almost burned a hole in her stomach. It was unforgivable that she had let herself be taken down by a man that she had put on the back foot like that. That was self-defence 101.

A drop of blood fell to the floor, right onto the trail that Borg had left trying to crawl away from certain death. Judith rubbed it out with her foot.

She lifted the cylinder and tugged the strap over her shoulder. The black eye of the camera appeared to follow her movements. She climbed onto what remained of the coffee table and stared directly into the lens. Somewhere in this country sat a nameless black shadow, staring back. He had watched Borg being murdered. And at this very moment he was looking down on her from far, far away and very high above, protected by cables and electronic transmission systems, by encrypted signals and high-security connections. He sat anonymous and cowardly in front of a monitor and dared to look into her eyes.

'Give Karsten Michael Oliver warm greetings from me. He should dress warmly. And you should too. Because I'm going to get you.'

She shot a hissing round of cold gas, two hundred degrees below zero, at the camera. A thick layer of frost instantly covered the lens. She held the nozzle tight until the bottle was empty, until the hissing became quieter and finally died. Only then did she let her arm sink and examined the thick layer of ice that had formed around the smoke detector.

If this was a video game, she would already be at level two. And the man whose face had been circled with a pen and with the stupidest name since the invention of Sesame Street would explain everything else to her: Quirin Kaiserley.

In a car heading down the A9 from Berlin towards Nuremburg, Kellermann watched the image on his smartphone disappear.

He could still hear the sound of glass and metal snapping. He tapped the red stop signal. A window opened on the screen.

Are you sure you want to interrupt the recording?

Yes.

He copied the content of the folder onto a mobile two-terabyte hard drive located behind him on the back seat of the car. Only then did he send the forwarded signal to the agency and remove the earbuds from his ears. They were passing the massive Merseburg shopping centre. The furniture stores and gas stations that had suddenly appeared on the right dwindled in the rear-view mirror just as quickly. The car glided over the six-lane motorway like a phantom, swam inconspicuously in the eternal moving stream from which it should have departed hours later on the Munich-Schwabing exit towards Garmisch-Partenkirchen – if everything had gone as planned.

The enormous motorway interchange at Leipzig-West appeared. 'I have to go back. Bring me to Leipzig Central Station.'

Peter Winkler, who had just flipped the indicator to change lanes, cast a brief glance at Kellermann and his phone and stopped overtaking.

He was an inconspicuous man in his late-fifties, and had been seated in the first row of Juliane Westerhoff's audience. Head of Division 11F, German intelligence, departmental head Special Operations. Coordination and cooperation with partner agencies. He should by rights control communication within the national intelligence agencies, but in Kellermann's eye, he was more of a bureaucrat than a coordinator. He prevented more than he made possible. Kellermann had no respect for bureaucrats. Never had.

Because not only the BND, but also the VS repeatedly showed an interest in Kaiserley, Kellermann had brought Winkler along on this business trip for two simple reasons: to keep a sharp eye on their colleagues and to drive the car. And there was a third reason: Kellermann needed every single vote if he was going to make the shortlist for the next BND president. He had been Winkler's boss for twenty years. And he wasn't planning on quitting any time soon.

'Now? Why?'

Kellermann closed his eyes. 'An operation has been exposed.'

'Not good. A field agent?'

'No, a technician removing cameras.'

'By whom?'

Kellermann thought about the images on his smartphone. The motion detector activated the camera whenever someone had entered the apartment. He still had the images of this gruesome, unending murder before his eyes. Now they had been joined by new ones: a woman who had followed the trail of blood like a hunter tracked a wounded animal. When this woman, of all people, had surprised TT, he had asked himself who had trained her and who she was working for. He still didn't know, although he did know that often the most absurd explanations were also the most accurate.

'A cleaning lady.'

'No, are you serious?'

Winkler looked over at him, but Kellermann only wrinkled his fleshy lips and made his phone disappear into his suit pocket.

'And who'd she catch?'

'Täschner.'

Winkler made a noise that sounded vaguely like a laugh. 'Täschner. Of all people. Honestly, I don't understand how you still let him loose on humanity. A cleaning lady!' He slowed down as a blue sign reading 'Weissenfels' whipped past them.

Kellermann said nothing. He could understand Winkler's comment, but he had his reasons for keeping Täschner. For protecting him. For pampering him with assignments like this. For explaining to Angelina Espinoza on the phone that she would be paid almost double for the assignment if she continued to be 'friendly' to Täschner.

'*Not as kind as you are to me*,' he had added.

Once in a while they met, and he hoped that her laugh and her wonderful groaning when he lay on top of her were authentic. Faith and hope. Together with love, the triumvirate of the weak. Kellermann examined his wedding ring.

'You know why he's so important for us. At some point Kaiserley will make contact with him. Turn to us.'

'Yes,' Winkler growled. 'But not because of a pile of old microfilm.'

'Have you heard from him again?'

Winkler shook his head. 'No. You?'

'Me neither. He didn't look good tonight.'

'No. Not good.'

'I think the turn is coming up.'

Winkler left the off-ramp and merged onto the B48 towards Leipzig city centre. Kellerman leaned back on his upholstered seat and wondered why hotels and fodder silos here were built next to each other, just off the autobahn.

6

Quirin Kaiserley was vain. He wouldn't have achieved the notoriety he had otherwise. With astonishment Judith registered the large number of interviews he had given for the publication of his books. Somehow she had completely missed out on this man's existence. She hardly ever read a newspaper since she had so many crates of books from her cleaning colleagues to get through and her image of intelligence services came from the James Bond movies. The fact these movies had actually been used by the KGB as instructional material was just one of the little fluffy factoids that Kaiserley used to decorate his actual message.

What you reveal about your friends today on Facebook would have taken lots of torture to extract before.

Judith didn't have any friends, much less any on Facebook. For the last two hours she had been occupied with nothing but searching the internet for articles by and about Kaiserley.

In fact, she learned almost more from the journalists' questions than from his answers. That his marriage had fallen apart because the pledge of secrecy infected personal relationships like a virus and destroyed them, sooner or later. That he no longer had contact with his son, who apparently couldn't handle his father's public image. That distrust, subconscious or otherwise, weighed on his friendships and soured new beginnings with every person he met. Quirin Kaiserley kept his cards close to his chest, but nonetheless there were clues in what he said. And whoever could decipher them was able to discover more about him that he would have liked.

She had already scribbled two pages on a block notebook. There was a city map spread out next to the rubbish sacks, a compass and her GPS, with which she could find any dark spot in the world.

The construction of the new BND headquarters on Chausseestrasse should suggest a new kind of accessibility. In reality it is a maximum security unit in a residential neighbourhood. Every time I drive past on my way to the office ...

Kaiserley's office address: Hausvogteiplatz in Mitte. But she needed his private address. For that, she needed to find as many points of reference as possible to fix him in her crosshairs.

Judith searched the map for the former Stadion der Weltjugend on an area as large as fifteen football fields where the new secret agency headquarters intended to take a soft approach with the public. Bright, modern, friendly, with a cafeteria and souvenir shop. Its own boarding school – for whom, exactly? – its own university, its own power supply, probably its own bunker, although this city within the city was supposedly being built without a basement. But that is why the entire ground floor of the main building disappeared into a fifteen-foot deep pit – to fend off gatecrashers from evil powers, in case they hadn't already failed at the metal fence.

The work that intelligence agencies do has changed funda-
mentally in the last ten years. Observation and surveillance
has been displaced by a gigantic flood of data. Hackers
are replacing personal experience and assessment.
– How should we understand that?
People make mistakes. But through them, there is the
chance of disrupting plots. It's wrong to bet the house on
highly specialised data surveillance when terrorists have
long returned to messages in a bottle and smoke signals.
Besides, the nets of overall dragnet investigation always
turn up the wrong people.
– There are laws against it. Remember the large-scale
eavesdropping operation?
Everything there's a law against is nonetheless still done.
Otherwise we wouldn't need laws, right?

Judith grinned. No wonder that Kaiserley's former colleagues
didn't think highly of him. She scrolled down to the end of the
interview because that was where the personal questions usually
came in.

I like the area around Mauerpark, although I always have
to park my car somewhere else the night before May Day
so it doesn't end up a burned-out wreck after the inevi-
table riots …

Mauerpark. Judith wrote it on her list. She had collected more
than twenty pieces of information that made reference to his
routes or his neighbourhood. Kaiserley went to the market on
Kollwitzplatz on Saturdays, liked the bars around the water

tower, like to take the tram and loved to watch the sunset. Not bad. She might have made it as an old-school spy.

She went to her laptop and entered the positions into Google maps. The result was Kaiserley's personal corner of Berlin. If she added the fact that his apartment was west-facing and included his mention of 'climbing stairs' as a sport, then he lived in the fourth or fifth storey of an old house without an elevator. It was likely near to a tram stop, and a wine shop that supplied him with his beloved Fendant du Valais.

Bingo. Marienburger strasse, Prenzlauer Berg.

She went into the hall and grabbed the van keys. It was four thirty in the morning. The time when people slept most deeply.

Quirin Kaiserley awoke because the quiet scratching noises weren't part of the repertoire of sounds his ears had become used to and in that warm night he had only fallen into a kind of light doze. Behind the blinds there was a hint of pale morning light, allowing him to recognise contours and outlines. He heard the scratching again. It sounded like a cat was going at his door.

Quirin knew how rare it was for cats to want to get into other people's apartments before sunrise. He got up and walked barefoot into the hallway, wearing only his pyjama trousers. No doubt about it, someone was trying to pick his security lock. And to Quirin's great astonishment, it seemed to be working.

People who had weapons tended to use them, which was why he didn't have any at home. Although he had learned how to handle guns in the army, and he occasionally trained with the latest models, he was wary of the false sense of security they provided. He trusted the moment of surprise and his apartment door more.

It opened to the left, so he positioned himself so that it would hide him, and then waited. This was no professional, at any rate. He heard the quiet clinking of a set of keys falling to the ground, and a suppressed curse. An amateur. Maybe a teenager who wanted to get some cash, and quickly. But why fight your way up five storeys instead of letting the couple on the first floor with the Bose loudspeakers have the honour, the ones who liked to blast the entire street with their questionable taste in music? He would find out first-hand from the intruder shortly.

Clink. Scratch. Click. Contact.

The cylinder rotated, the door opened without a sound. A figure, mid-sized and slender, slipped through the crack. Quirin threw himself against the door. A fraction of a second later the burglar was pinned in the doorway and let out a yelp.

Quirin had already flipped the light switch when he realised he had trapped a woman. He had caught her from the left shoulder down. She groaned and tried to push the door off in vain.

'Well, who do we have here?' he asked with astonishment, and at the same time noticed how stupidly grandfatherly it must sound.

'Let me go!'

She only came up to his shoulder and must have been very athletic because keeping her in check demanded a significant amount of energy. He grabbed her by her right arm and pulled her roughly into the hallway. She yanked herself away with an angry cry of pain and rubbed her shoulder.

'Have you completely lost your mind?' she hissed.

The accusation was so spontaneous and so heartfelt that Quirin almost laughed. She wasn't pretty in the ordinary sense, no longer very young, but her eyes sparkled with fury, and she looked like a woman who knew no fear. Apparently she had recently been in a fight, because there was a deep scratch running diagonally across her cheek and her lips looked unnaturally swollen. Despite this, she didn't look like a thief. More like a . . . his gaze fell across her hands. They were rough and reddened, as if they often came in contact with chemicals. Although she made a fairly battered impression, he didn't overlook how very fit she actually was.

'Who are you?' he asked, closed the door, and positioned himself in her escape path with his arms crossed. If she wanted to run off now she'd have to knock him out. Quirin didn't doubt she could. For a moment he even wished she would try. It had been a long time since he'd last been in hand-to-hand combat, and she looked like she could start with him at any time.

'That's not relevant.'

Instead of looking for a way out, she looked around attentively and took a couple of steps back into the hall, her gaze slipping away from him to the rest of the apartment. She moved past him towards the living room. Quirin followed her.

'You're mistaken. You're misjudging the circumstances under which you gained access to my apartment.'

'Really?' she turned around lightning-fast and disappeared into the bedroom. The ceiling light flashed on, and she returned.

'Are you alone?'

'Yes,' Quirin answered, only restraining himself with difficulty. His surprise over the unexpected visitor was slowly being displaced by annoyance. 'Just the two of us. Are you sure that's what you want? It's going into the lion's den.'

She returned. She looked down at his pyjama trousers and repressed an amused expression, which annoyed Quirin. He wasn't in that bad shape.

'Yeah. Really frightening. Quirin Kaiserley?'

'What do you want?'

'You're the only person who talks about the shitty BND. Do you know this Karsten/Michael/Oliver person – the asshole?'

'What on earth are you talking about?'

She pulled out the IDs and held them up for him, but pocketed them again before he could grab them.

'His real name is probably completely different. What does it mean when a guy takes down cameras in an apartment and forgets his own name as he does it?'

'I'm assuming you caught him in the act.' He was catching up fast.

She nodded hesitantly.

'Then your apartment was probably under surveillance.'

'Why?'

Quirin ran his hand through his hair. They shouldn't be having this conversation in the hallway.

'Come with me.'

He led the way into the living room and offered a Scandinavian-looking armchair made of leather and curved cherry wood.

'Take a seat. I'll make us coffee. And next time, let me know in advance that you're coming.'

She nodded and looked around. Quirin went into the kitchen and turned on the coffee machine. He scooted into the bedroom and slipped into a linen sweater while the machine was warming up. Still barefoot, he padded across the wooden floorboards back to the kitchen, made two cups of coffee and returned to his odd visitor.

The woman had sat down and looked tired. It seemed like more than physical exhaustion. She was slim, tough and limber. She had clearly calmed down, and when she looked up at him he noticed her eyes. Clear, blue – dark blue and shadowy. Her curly hair was pulled up in a careless bun. Some sort of dirty blonde. A couple of wild strands fell into her face and onto her shoulders. She had a smooth kind of physicality, and even in the grey morning light, her narrow face seemed classically severe, like an angel painted by Gustav Klimt. His first impression had been misleading. She wasn't pretty. She was beautiful. In a very unique, cagey way.

'Sugar? Milk?'

'No thanks.'

She didn't hold the cup by the handle, but rather cradled it in both her hands, as if she wanted to warm herself. Yet the morning air was still unpleasantly humid. The heat accumulated under the roof, which wasn't properly insulated, like so many other buildings in this part of the city.

'So your apartment was under surveillance.'

'Not mine. The one I'm currently working in.'

He asked himself what kind of job she had. She wasn't a journalist – she was too blunt and uncalculated for that. He guessed something between a soldier and a bike messenger. Urban guerrilla. Street fighter. Amateur boxer.

'OK. And you thought to yourself, I'll just break into Kaiserley's place and ask him, because he's so knowledgeable about all the evil things in this world. Why didn't you just call?'

She looked up from her cup. 'I didn't have your number.'

'And where'd you get my address?'

A smile flitted over her face, lighting up her battle-weary features for a moment.

'From you.'

She must have noticed his surprise because she put down her cup and raised her hands.

'It was easy actually. You reveal too much about yourself. Including where you live.'

'Really?'

'You live alone, are quite isolated, but still have good contacts with your former colleagues, otherwise you wouldn't be so well informed. You like to eat well, because you go to the market. You have few friends – maybe none at all. And you miss your family. Once in a while you fall off the wagon, probably because you think about how old you are now and whether it was worth it all.'

She picked up her cup again and took a sip. It gave Quirin the chance to process what had just been said. She was exactly right. Every word.

'You're the only one in the building with no name on your doorbell. And something in the past caused your fall from grace. What was it?'

'Something in the past.'

She waited a moment longer. Then she understood.

'What do you want?' he asked.

'Why is someone put under surveillance?'

'Because they have or know something that someone wants.'

'Who does the surveillance?'

'Public authorities, like the police, internal security, military counterintelligence service, the BND. Or private security contractors, security firms. Your neighbour, your landlord, your ex-lover.'

'And why would someone have four different names?'

'That indicates you're dealing with a pro.'

She let out a sigh of irritation. 'I guessed that.'

'Let me see the IDs for a second.'

She pulled them out of her trouser pocket and handed them over hesitantly. His eyes widened for a second when he saw the photo named as 'Karsten Drillich'. He recognised him immediately, even though he hadn't seen him for more than ten years. TT. Bachelor of Engineering, average graduate at the Bundeswehr University in Munich-Neubiberg, with a dual degree including practical training at the BND. Good marks, technically OK, completely unsuitable for leadership roles and only taken on permanently thanks to his, Quirin's, support for him after two extended probationary periods. The boy had never forgiven him for burning his bridges. They hadn't seen each other since.

He checked the other cards. He paused at the BND ID, shook his head and handed them back to Judith.

'You haven't even introduced yourself.'

'My name is Judith Kepler. I'm a cleaner.'

He didn't say anything, waiting. But she didn't deliver a punchline, so it wasn't a joke. A cleaning lady. He wouldn't have guessed that, never in a million years. A quiet hilarity rose inside him, but he didn't allow himself to show it. It wasn't every day that you got assaulted by a cleaning lady. Any comment about that would have been extremely politically incorrect. She impatiently tapped the IDs on the arm of the chair and then threw them on the coffee table.

'You clearly know the guy. So is it someone from the BND?'

Quirin nodded. 'The BND is the foreign intelligence service. If he was doing surveillance on an apartment in Berlin, then your client came from abroad, or had contacts there that were of interest.'

'She came from Sweden.'

Sweden.

Al-Qaida. Right-wing extremists. The main hub for Russian agents. Technology transfers, the arms trade. A quarter of all officers in Russian intelligence agencies have Swedish as their first foreign language. You'd want to keep out of Sweden if you didn't know what you're doing; if they want to send you there, you get a doctor's note or have your grandma die, but you don't go. If that doesn't work and you still have to go, don't forget your Geiger counter before you eat. Avoid Belgian pralines. Tidy up. Prepare. Be ready for anything.

That was Sweden.

Judith Kepler should throw the IDs in the closest bin and never cross paths with Täschner again. Whatever she was involved in was a couple of levels beyond what could be handled by a . . . building cleaner.

'I'm so sorry I can't be of help. You've been caught up in a surveillance operation by chance. It's not pleasant, but it happens. Just forget about it.'

'Is that it? I thought you were against a state full of snitches.'

'Against scaremongering and general suspicion. But you've just crossed paths with a BND information technician in an apartment in Germany. That means you've obliviously walked into a foreign information service operation. I wonder how you got the IDs. Honestly . . .' He leaned forward and looked her over closely. 'I wonder how you got out of it alive.'

Her nostrils flared. Infinitesimally, but for a moment it gave her face the expression of a warrior whose honour had been insulted.

'You're kidding me.'

'Not in the slightest,' he retorted quietly.

She wiped her hair away from her forehead in a restless gesture. Yet in the next moment she appeared composed.

'So it was them.'

She stood up and walked towards the hallway.

'Who was what?' Quirin called after her.

'They killed her.'

She was already almost at the door by the time he could stop her. She whirled around in fury.

'Wait a second.' He tried to make his voice soothing. He had exaggerated to protect her from herself. But she appeared to take the matter more seriously than it warranted.

'Who killed whom?'

'The BND. A woman.'

An intuition arose in him, so improbable that he couldn't consider it. She went to open the door. But Quirin had already grabbed her by the shoulders and pressed her against the wall.

'And who, do you think, the BND killed?'

'A woman from Sweden.'

'How old?'

'Around my age.'

'When?'

'Two weeks ago, approximately. Her name was Christina Borg.'

Quirin let go of Judith. *Borg*. Christina Borg. That was impossible. That couldn't be.

The cleaning lady stood still, rooted to the spot. He held his hands in front of his face because he couldn't handle her stare, directed at him like an x-ray.

'No,' he said. 'No . . . I . . .'

He remembered the rough accent, and that she had known about Sassnitz. The murderers from back then were still alive. And they had killed again.

The cleaning lady was still staring at him.

'Why do you want to know all of this?' he asked. 'Why don't you just do your job and go back home?'

'Because Borg was an institutionalised child. Just like me.'

'Did you know each other?'

'No.'

'Then how do you know that?'

Her gaze finally slipped away. She looked for something in her bag, and produced a small packet of tobacco. She removed a roll-up and lit it without asking for permission.

'It doesn't matter. How are you involved with the dead woman?'

'We met once. She had something that she wanted to give me.'

'What?'

'Nothing. Nothing of interest. To you, I mean.' But an absurd thought crossed his mind. 'Did you find anything while cleaning up the apartment? Perhaps tins of Florena?'

'Yes. Four of them.'

Quirin thought he hadn't heard correctly.

'Where are they?'

'In the bin.'

'What? What was inside? Did you look inside?'

Judith felt her way a couple inches closer toward the door. She probably thought he was completely crazy.

'Forensics already took care of that.'

'And?'

'Cream. In all four. Otherwise nothing. Does that have something to do with me?' She exhaled the smoke as slowly as she took the next drag. 'With my past?'

It was absurd. The entire situation was off the rails. Christina Borg was dead. The microfilm had perhaps been destroyed long before, or would never reappear. And there was a smoking cleaning lady standing in his apartment at five in the morning wondering if this catastrophe had anything to do with her screwed-up life.

'No. You can go home reassured. You're too young. You don't understand all the ins and outs.'

'Ah, the big picture.' The ash from her cigarette fell to the floor.

Quirin rubbed his face with his hands. 'Listen, Ms Kepler, I don't want to be impolite. This is all a shock to me. Can you understand that? I only knew Christina Borg briefly. Nevertheless, I'd still like to be alone now.'

She went to the door and placed her hand on the handle. Then she turned around.

'You're a really bad actor. Not just on television.'

She left without a word of farewell, and quietly closed the door behind herself.

Täschner's IDs still lay in front of him on the coffee table. He picked up the orange-coloured one and studied the photo. Tobias. Something deep inside him shifted, but he refused to allow himself a fatherly feeling about his young former colleague.

Täschner was and remained a complete idiot. Was Kellermann still his boss? Then TT would have to confess to him how this unbelievable glitch had happened. Kellermann would talk with the cleaning lady. Offer her a little money to forget about it. Perhaps a job at the nice new headquarters building, with a confidentiality clause in her contract.

But would a woman like Judith Kepler go for that? He pensively placed the IDs back on the table.

He went to the window, which was wide open, and looked down on the deserted street. The street lights were flickering for the last time and going dark. A tram rumbled over Prenzlauer Allee. Lights were burning in several rooms. At the end of the street a shadow disappeared around the corner. Quietly, inconspicuously, a chameleon that adapted to the colours of the waking city, already forgotten in passing.

It was bright as day when Judith returned to her apartment. This time she took the crate of books up with her and put it in the living room, then collected Borg's possessions and dumped the sacks in the hall. She showered and put on fresh clothes. When she stood in front of her record collection she couldn't decide: the ancient Dean Martin record that Josef had once given her, beaming, with the words, 'saved it for you'? Or the new one from Antony and the Johnsons, which she had bought just a year before? Judith no longer listened to CDs since she discovered vinyl. Although everyone thought she was crazy, she believed there was a difference. Besides, she loved the moment when a record slipped out of its cover and onto her fingertips; she carefully blew over it and then played it. Vinyl needed time and devotion; CDs and files were more about immediate accessibility.

She decided on 'The Crying Light' because she needed a voice like Hegarty's after that seething cauldron full of violence, lies, apathy and condescension. Music like the good kind of silence after a conversation with friends. At least that's the way she imagined it. She put the record on, retrieved a new bottle of wine from the fridge and stumbled over her carelessly abandoned work clothes. She stuffed the things in the washing machine, and when she turned over her dirty jeans, the old family photo of Gerlinde Wachsmuth's fell into her hands again. She carefully removed it and smoothed it out. It looked like a failed dream that had left a bitter taste. You thought he'd come. *He'll come someday. And then it'll be like it used to, when we simply loved each other. He was your son, after all. The only child you had.*

Together with the file from the home, she placed the photo with the others in her desk drawer. Judith remembered every single one. The names of the people on the photos and the haste with which their apartments had been taken apart and sold off. It was a compulsive quirk. Crazy. But it was Judith's way of stopping death in its tracks. It shouldn't be our last friend.

She gave herself two hours, lay down on the bed and fell asleep seconds later, while Hegarty sang about the crying light.

7

Judith had finished her assignment by Sunday afternoon. The apartment smelled of bleach and castile soap. The painters only had to putty over the bullet holes and paint the walls. Before she left, she checked every lamp, every socket, every corner and every crack in the furniture, but she couldn't find any microphones or further cameras. She probably didn't have the necessary know-how, and for the sake of the next renters she could only hope that Karsten Michael Oliver Asshole had at least been thorough before she had appeared.

During the inspection, she told Fricke about the camera. He had retrieved a ladder while cursing quietly, removed the device and put it in his trouser pocket. His irritation over additional work was so authentic that Judith thought it was unlikely he had known about the surveillance. She had asked him whether he wanted to notify the police, but he retorted that the camera had probably come from them.

'Who actually called them?' Judith had asked. 'I mean the cops.'
'No idea.'

Fricke was in a hurry to leave. He was as enthusiastic about working on Sundays as the rest of the world. 'Keys in the mailbox. Invoice to the renting agency.'

Judith nodded. Fricke pushed off, rattling his ladder. Judith picked up a forgotten cleaning sponge and put it in a bucket and rolled her trolley into the hallway, clattering quietly.

As if on cue, the apartment door opposite opened and Peppi shot out. He ran at her, sniffed and barked, trying to get past her into the other apartment. Judith pushed him out with her knee, and would have liked nothing more than to grab him by the collar but his mistress was already following him. She paused at the sight of the trolley.

'Done already?'

Her voice was sharp as a potato knife.

'There wasn't much to do.'

Judith pushed the dog aside and locked the door carefully. Then she pushed the trolley slowly behind the woman and dog, who had already reached the elevator. In passing she read the names on the doorbell. Schneider. Peppi panted nervously back and forth.

'Did you actually witness anything that happened?' Judith asked.

Mrs Schneider fixated on the metal doors, as if any second now an answer would appear. Judith adjusted the trolley.

'You were neighbours, after all. People hear things, right?'

'They came at night. I always sleep with earplugs, because of the autobahn. And the antisocial people down there.'

The elevator came and Judith let the two of them go ahead. The she pushed the trolley after them and sucked in her tummy to the doors would shut.

'And otherwise?' she asked. 'What was Ms Borg like?'

The neighbour shrugged her shoulders. 'No idea. She hadn't lived here very long. Stayed, I mean.'

'She came from Sweden.'

'Yes.'

The elevator stopped at the third floor. An elderly gentleman immediately assessed the situation and let them continue. Peppi yapped.

'Did she ever say what she was doing here?'

'No. Where did you take all the rubbish?'

'To the city dump.'

That appeared to comfort the woman. When they had reached the ground floor she put her precious Peppi on the lead, pushed past Judith without a word and let herself be pulled to the street.

Back at company headquarters, Judith studied the schedule and realised angrily that Dombrowski hadn't given her a single day off in lieu for her blown weekend. Her next shift began at six in the morning in a hospital in Wilmersdorf. That meant hitting the shower, eating a pizza somewhere and then a couple more hours of sleep.

'Was everything OK?'

Once again, Dombrowski had snuck up so quietly that she hadn't heard him. For a second she considered whether or not she should inform him of all the things that weren't OK.

'Yep. Everything was OK,' she finally answered.

Dombrowski studied her with squinty eyes. Then he went back into his office, but left the door open, a sign that she should follow him. Sometimes Dombrowski demanded feedback after these kinds of assignments. Judith had neither the time nor desire for it, but she trotted in with a reluctant sigh.

'Here.'

The Spartan decor of his office was thrown into absurd relief by a huge bouquet of yellow roses. Blooms as big as apples, and at least thirty of them. They outshone everything with their waxy beauty and would have been more fitting in the middle of a massive reception hall than this tight, threadbare room. Dombrowski paused in front of the arrangement, almost a metre across, and studied it with a look that he usually only gave to vermin. Judith had never even seen him in the vicinity of flowers. With quiet amusement she realised that they unsettled him.

'For you?' she asked. 'Wow.'

'Neither for me nor from me. They were brought by a man who asked about you and wanted your number.'

'And?'

'Of course I didn't give it to him.'

Dombrowski motioned to a small envelope that was stuck in the flowers. Judith picked it out and opened it. It opened suspiciously easily. Dombrowski had probably taken a peek before her.

'We regret that you were inconvenienced. Please call us back,' she read aloud. Underneath there was a mobile number. She immediately though of Karsten Michael Oliver Asshole, but as hard as she tried, she couldn't imagine that the man even knew how to spell the word flowers.

'What did he look like?'

'No idea. Mid-sized, older, a mix of bulldozer and health inspector.'

Dombrowski scratched the back of his head and looked at the roses as if they exuded a mysterious threat.

'So tell me: did someone bump into the van?'

'No.'

'Then I want to know what the deal is. If it's an admirer, I couldn't care less. But this isn't a delicate bouquet. This must have been a major argument.'

'Take them to your wife. Doesn't matter which one of them.'

'Am I crazy? I'm not even capable of getting in so much trouble that she'd accept them. Who's the guy?'

He motioned to the note in Judith's hand. She shrugged her shoulders.

'I don't know. You have to believe me. I really don't know.'

Bocca di Bacco was located on Friedrichstrasse and was busiest during the week around lunchtime. However, on Sunday nights at around seven, it was still relatively empty. Only later on would it fill up with those who believed they had to bolster themselves with almond gnocchi, cinnamon scampi and pheasant breast before, during, or after their other evening activities.

The man sat at the window. Early, maybe mid-sixties, powerful. Half-bald, remaining hair kept short. Fine threads, expensive watch. Looked like a former bare-knuckle boxer, but acted like he had bought the joint long ago. He was used to taking up a lot of space. The table was covered with his smartphone, iPad, key ring and newspaper so that the person he was clearly waiting for would have to make themselves fairly small.

If he knew that he was being watched then he didn't let it show. He had already arrived a half-hour before the appointed time, had selected a bottle of red wine, and then conducted several telephone conversations. Now and again he stared out into the street in boredom. When the half-hour had passed, he looked at his watch with increasing frequency. He ate a slice of white bread he had dipped into a saucer of olive oil, and shifted his body language almost imperceptibly. From relaxed, to attentive, and finally, annoyed. When he was sure he had been stood up, he seemed nervous. After an hour he motioned to the waiter and hurried off towards the next Underground station. He was about five foot eleven, walked upright and purposefully. His coarse features twisted in annoyance when he had to wait for a gap in traffic – apparently he took it personally – to speed cross the road with loping strides.

Seven forty-two. The next train would arrive in four minutes. Without rushing, Judith pocketed her binoculars and carefully stepped back from the fake silk skirt of a mannequin. The large plate-glass windows, which stretched almost to the ground, were directly across the road and belonged to a cheap clothing chain that MacClean had pinched. A former colleague was shining the floors one storey above. She climbed a couple of steps on the escalator and waved at him. He registered her farewell with a short nod of the head. Then she left the building through the employee entrance.

She paused for a second halfway down the stairs to the Französische Strasse Underground station and waited until the vibrating floor announced the next train was approaching. It rolled into the station. The loud screeching of the brakes and the enormous draft of air drew the attention of the few waiting passengers and Judith saw the man board a carriage close to the front without turning around. She waited until the recorded announcement had played and she was truly the last person on the platform. Then she jumped on board just as the train started to move.

The man sat alone on a bench next to the window, facing the direction of travel. When Judith plopped down next to him he looked up in irritation, because except for two students and one Asian woman struggling with an incorrectly folded city map, there was no one in the carriage. He saw her threadbare jeans, the old trainers, and the faded T-shirt.

'I was delayed,' she said.

He raised his eyebrows and that was the sole moment of surprise he granted her.

'Ms Kepler?'

She nodded. He extended his hand to her. Judith ignored the gesture.

'Jürgen Weckerle. I'm pleased to meet you. You look better in the flesh.'

If that was supposed to be a compliment then he was out of practice. At least now she knew that he was the person she had said a few last nice words to before icing the cameras.

The train left the tunnel and arrived at Stadtmitte station. The carriages rumbled over the switches. Judith shifted a bit to the edge of the seat because she wanted to avoid any contact with this man who didn't look like he had been born Jürgen Weckerle.

'What kind of device was that in Borg's apartment?'

Weckerle looked around but the few fellow passengers were seated too far away to catch anything from their conversation.

'I could ask you the same question. You removed government property.'

'The cameras? I assume the janitor will sell them at the flea market.'

His powerful lips curled. It was supposed to be a smile but his face didn't completely cooperate, stalling it in the early stages.

'Then we hope he'll still get something for it.'

'Who's we?'

The train continued on.

'We're a security firm with a diverse portfolio of tasks and challenges.'

'You recorded a murder.'

Weckerle looked out the window, behind which the walls of the tunnel flew by, black as soot.

'You watched and didn't do a thing. You know who the killer was and what he was looking for. Hello?'

Weckerle turned to her with a regretful sigh.

'We don't know.' He had light brown eyes, under which lay dark, nearly violet shadows. In the neon light of the car he looked anything but healthy. 'He was disguised. Just like you.' His half-smile became shaded by something dangerous.

'Nice try,' Judith said. 'But you can forget that approach right now. As long as there's officially neither a murder nor a murderer then I'm probably safe.'

'I'm glad you see it that way. For what it's worth, it's a widespread fallacy that the police announce every death from the rooftops. Sometimes forensic investigations only reveal weeks later if it's a homicide. There was a case in which the police went before the press months after the fact to announce, 'whoops', that fall down the stairs or the supposed suicide was a crime after all. No. Believe me, the public is only subjected to what they can handle. Most of the time.'

'Don't make the cops out to be dumber than they are.'

'You're an unusual woman.'

Judith was familiar with this kind of patter. She hadn't asked for an assessment of her character.

'And no one else has ever managed to scare off one of our technicians. What was actually in the cylinder? He called in sick.'

'Oxygen. He should actually be doing splendidly.'

They were silent while the train pulled into the Kochstrasse station with an ear-splitting screech.

'Let's talk frankly,' Weckerle continued, after the disruption of people getting on and off had ebbed. 'You have something we're looking for. Give it to us.'

'The ID cards belonging to Karsten Michael Oliver, etc.? Quirin Kaiserley has them.'

Judith watched his every move, but he had himself under control. She only saw a hint of well-acted confusion.

'Who's that?'

'Now you're making a fool of yourself. I don't have to explain that to you.'

'That writer?'

'If you like, yes.'

'And why did you give the material to him to keep track of, of all people?'

Because I was an idiot and forgot them, Judith thought. *But I can retrieve the IDs any time I want.*

'Mr Kaiserley should be able to do something with them. His area of specialty is, if I'm not mistaken, international security firms.'

Weckerle crossed his arms. She had actually expected him to have a big car with a driver, and had planned to catch him climbing in. The fact that he was riding the train didn't fit.

'I have to warn you,' he said. 'Kaiserley isn't trustworthy. Whatever he tells you, I'd check and double-check it.'

'That's what I'm doing right now.'

Weckerle's expression changed. He appeared to be examining her, patting her down, perhaps even considering not just sending her back home. She stood up to his gaze.

'Did you find anything else?' he asked.

'Nothing.'

'Ms Kepler, why aren't you being honest with me?'

'Ask yourself the same question and you have the answer.'

'You and the dead woman, did you know each other?'

Judith stared at the station map that hung in every carriage.

'I can almost imagine that you did know each other. And that Kaiserley is the missing link. What did you want from him? The same thing as Borg?'

Her head snapped around and she eyed him warily.

He smiled mildly. 'Bring me what you have, please. Bring it to me and no one else.'

'And if not?'

He stood up. Next station Hallesches Tor. She followed him to the door. He held on to the grab pole and waited for the train to come to a stop.

'We live in a free country. You have the choice. No one is forcing you to do anything.'

'And if not?' she repeated.

The air pressure hissed as the doors opened. Weckerle let his arm fall and made to extend his hand in farewell but Judith ignored it. He turned away with a shrug and stepped onto the platform.

'Step back. Doors are closing.'

Weckerle raised his head and sensed something, as if he had been brushed by a draft of air.

'Then Sassnitz will also be your curse.'

'Sassnitz?'

The doors closed. Judith threw herself against them, rattled the handle and finally smacked the scratched windowpane with her palm, but the train sped off. As Weckerle walked up the stairs, she moved away from him, ever faster, until the walls of the tunnels swallowed every view of the outside and she was drawn into the dark web beneath the streets of Berlin.

8

Kai lay on his bed, undecided if he should dive back into the primeval mud of his dreams or at least make the attempt to wake. His body was light, almost floating, somehow dissolved. It transformed into a pastel yellow sea of vibration, white dots that fed off of him.

He jolted upright and stared at his bed with eyes wide, moved his legs, feet, lifted his arms, smelled his T-shirt, jumped up and ran into the bathroom. He had stayed at home for the whole weekend – hadn't painted the town red with the others for fear that they would notice the smell that seemed to stick to him like tar.

It was the craziest job he had ever heard of. While he soaped himself again and again he thought about what he would tell his caseworker at the employment agency and whether he should sue them. Damages for pain and suffering. Sick leave. Trauma. What he had seen, smelled and felt far exceeded anything the soft psyche of a twenty-one-year-old could handle. What made a woman like Judith do that kind of thing?

Because I can. And lots of others can't.

And he had stuck it out. He had expected a word of appreciation for coming back and continuing. Instead she hadn't even said goodbye. As if it was completely obvious that he would have had enough after just one day. Who did she think she was? He dried off and went into the kitchen, the towel wrapped around his waist. In the bin he looked for the instructions on the piece of paper that had been put in his hand on Friday by a hulk of a man wearing a blue smock with the name 'Josef' embroidered on it. Sankt Gertrauden Hospital. Work starts at 5:30, meeting point Dombrowski's gateway. Leave at six. Knock off at three. They were crazy. And all that for six euros' hourly minimum wage? Whoever went along with that was a complete idiot.

But Judith wasn't a complete idiot. She considered him to be a loser who couldn't even manage a draw in his daily battle with the alarm clock. Kai had something against the idea that she could be right.

An hour later, just before twelve, he was standing at the back entrance of the hospital, where everyone who couldn't survive without cigarettes could be found. He didn't have to wait for long. A flock of cackling blue smocks, all women of various nationalities, came through the rotating door and looked for a spot in the shade. The last of them, separate and silent, was Judith. She checked her phone, but then put it away without calling anyone. He was looking forward to her expression when he appeared before her. If she wanted to give him the boot, then she should say it to his face. Kai had experienced enough firings to be able to divide them into two different categories: the soft sell; compassionate, but simultaneously begging for understanding. And the taciturn approach: the papers already in the outbox, 'pick them up yourself and you'll save two days waiting on the mail and can still get back to the agency today'. Judith didn't belong to the bowl of cherries camp. He girded himself with defiance and the carefully checked fury that he felt every time people labelled him a loser.

He was just about to approach her when he noticed how she was looking around carefully. Cigarette in hand, she casually strolled across the driveway towards the street and then quickly scurried to her Dombrowski van. Kai sprinted after her and reached her just as she was opening the door.

'Calling it a day already?'

If he had surprised her then she didn't let it show. She turned away and opened the driver's side door.

'Or are you deserting?'

She climbed in. He positioned himself in the doorway so that she couldn't close it. Finally she forced herself to acknowledge him. He looked her in the eyes and knew something had happened. His apology poured out before he could hold it back.

'I'm too late. I took a shower for four hours.'

'Only four hours?'

She smiled weakly. He had expected a variety of reactions but not this. It was a disappointment but also a relief. He noticed for the first time that she had dark blue eyes. With big black rings underneath. Either she hadn't slept or she had a full-blown hangover.

'Are you done staring at me?' She had switched into attack mode in a matter of seconds. 'Get in. I don't have all day.'

The ride to the station took less than fifteen minutes. She didn't say a word. Just when Kai asked her if she wanted to pick someone up or jump into the next train herself, she took a right past the massive building and merged into Invalidenstrasse.

'Where are we going?' he interrupted the silence. 'Do you have a new assignment? Something that no one else can do again?'

She changed lanes with a hazardous manoeuvre and at a complicated intersection crossed lines to go to the other side, despite the honking of the other drivers.

'WLB,' she said. 'Work life balance. I've got a date. The person I'm going to see once started just like you. So don't worry about your career. Just do what I tell you. Stay in the car. If someone starts asking dumb questions, just drive around the block.'

They had arrived at a set of gates. Judith pressed the intercom button.

Kai studied the grey building with the faded concrete façade. *Berlin Municipal Health Management Institute* was printed on a sign on the wall. The barrier swung up. Judith drove into a car park with several reserved spots. She parked in one that was actually reserved for a Prof. Weihrich, nodded and stepped out.

Kai slid over to the driver's side. Judith went to a side building and disappeared into an open gateway. Kai watched her go. *Work life balance. What had she meant? This didn't really look like a date. Did a woman like Judith even date?*

He had difficulty estimating her age. For Kai, the interaction between people of different genders took place largely below the waist. Women over thirty weren't a part of his worldview. For him their attractiveness was on the level of zimmer frames and balcony plants. But for some reason Judith was stuck in his head. Purely on an intellectual level. She had a way of simply provoking him. She didn't expect anything, neither punctuality nor order. And she hadn't thrown him out.

He got out and strolled to the gateway. Behind that there was yet another courtyard where several green delivery vans with white labels were parked. *Forensic Medicine.* A second sign read *Autopsy Department.* Kai needed a moment to connect the two concepts and picture what that involved. He was standing in the courtyard of a mortuary.

Kai spun around on his heel and walked back to the car. Judith was a freak. It wasn't just her job – even her dates were morbid.

'Does he belong to you?'

Judith peered over Olaf Liepelt's shoulder, which wasn't easy as she only came up to his chest. Everything about him had been stretched too far – arms, legs, nose, back – not to mention that he also couldn't stand still and constantly rocked back and forth. He wore the uniform for the lower-security area, a white smock. His ginger hair was cut so closely that it looked like a seal skin. As he also wore a moustache and had wrinkled his forehead into deep furrows, the overall impression he gave was distinctly seal-like. He removed a pack of gum from his smock pocket and offered Judith a piece. She declined, noting that Kai had retreated to the van with some speed.

'A newbie, absolute beginner. He's always either throwing up or snooping around. I'm not sure what to make of him.'

'Kick him out. You're usually not this way.'

'Exactly. That's why I'm hardly ever given anyone anymore. So what?'

Liepelt felt sorry for the threatened intern. After all, he had once been one himself.

She turned away from the window and went to a hanging file rack on the desk. Liepelt had taken her into the room behind the reception, a small office under the direction of Professor Weihrich, who would be returning from his lecture at the Charité Hospital in less than fifteen minutes, and would be less than pleased to catch his autopsy assistant and a stranger with their hands on his files. Not to mention the occupied parking spot. Liepelt stood next to her and after a brief search, removed a spring binder that he examined carefully, squinting.

'Christina Borg. There we go. Delivered two weeks ago, autopsy the same evening–'

'Give it here.'

Judith nearly tore the file out of his hands. She opened it and leafed through the crime scene photos. A woman in T-shirt and knickers, lying unnaturally twisted on the floor. Her face, pale as wax, with a reddish-brown circular wound on her forehead. Her mouth was slightly open, her features relaxed, eyes closed. Peace after the murder.

'Give me that!'

Judith turned away from Liepelt and looked at the autopsy photos. Her chest. Shoulders. Bullet holes. Close-ups. Lab results. Autopsy report. Liepelt came around the desk reaching for the folder. She dodged him.

'What are you so interested about?'

'Everything.'

'Why?'

She looked up briefly. 'I was the cleaner.'

'Oh, shit,' said Liepelt. 'You shouldn't always take these kinds of things personally.'

She shook her head in frustration and skimmed the autopsy report.

'Judith, we don't have time!'

'Was there anything special about her?'

'She was shot.'

'Very funny. Particular indicators? Anything out of the ordinary?'

'Indications of abuse as a child, I believe. Two fractures, not treated and poorly healed. But that's pure speculation.'

No. Not speculation. 'I want to see her,' she said suddenly.

'Who?'

'Borg.'

'Are you crazy?'

But Judith was already at the door. The photos were the snapshot of a crime. But she wanted to see the person, the woman who Borg had been who had suffered the same fate as her as a child. No one who hadn't been in a home could understand that. In life, and even more so in a mortuary.

'You still have her. Show her to me.'

Liepelt lifted his long arms in a desperate attempt to talk her out of her plan. Judith tucked the file under her waistband.

'You know I can't do it. Weihrich will kill me!'

'Weihrich won't know a thing. And even if he does find out,' she grinned, 'you can always come back to work with me.'

'That's precisely the kind of shit I can do without. I'm so stupid to have let you in here in the first place. Give me the file!'

'Later. This way?'

She opened the door, peered into the hall, and disappeared.

'Shit,' Liepelt murmured. 'Shit.'

Quirin Kaiserley stood in front of the homicide building on Keithstrasse in Schöneberg. His chances of finding out something in the Borg case verged on negligible. He knew that. He had researched all weekend and hadn't found notice of the death anywhere. So first he had to find out if this Judith Kepler had been telling the truth. If she was, and after two sleepless nights and going through all alternatives, he assumed that she was, then there had at least to be a record of the crime with the police. A file number. An address. Circumstances of the crime. The call log, the address of a neighbour, the fire fighters, the forensic team. CSIs, witness statements. Even if everything had been classified immediately, there had to be someone who had initially worked the case. Borg had been murdered in an apartment in Berlin. Even if the various authorities had fought over the case, there had to be witnesses. If not to the crime, then to what happened after that.

The woman at the reception was in her mid-fifties and was talking loudly with someone on the telephone who was supposed to repair a washing machine and apparently wasn't succeeding. She didn't put aside the phone as she turned to Quirin.

'How may I help you?'

'It's to do with the Christina Borg murder case. I'd like to speak with the officer in charge.'

'Wait a second.' She sighed, and with barely concealed reluctance spoke into the telephone. 'Not the pump. It can't be the pump. I'll call you right back.'

She hung up.

'What was the name?'

'Borg. Christina Borg.'

'I got that. And who are you?'

'My name is Quirin Kaiserley.'

'Excuse me?'

He patiently spelled out his name.

'And you want to file a report?'

'No. I want to speak to someone working on the case.'

'So a statement.'

'I want . . .'

Quirin stopped. The woman studied him as sceptically as she had spoken to the repairman.

'We don't give out information. You'll have to go to public relations. Either you make a statement or you want to file a complaint. Then you'd go to the department . . .'

'A statement,' Quirin interrupted.

'So relevant information about a murder case? Which case?'

'Borg. Christina Borg.'

'Then take a seat for a moment.'

The woman motioned to a wooden bench in the hallway. Quirin took a seat under a poster with the composite sketch of a bank robber and watched her pick up the phone and dial a number. He couldn't hear what she said. But he saw her posture change suddenly. She nodded slightly, hung up and stared at him as if he was sitting directly beneath his own wanted poster.

Liepelt followed Judith with his rocking stride, the tails of his smock billowing behind him. He caught up with her at the end of the hallway in front of the admission area.

'Keep your distance. This is where the new admissions land.'

Judith allowed herself to be manoeuvred through the halls by staying a half-stride behind him and lowering her head as soon as anyone approached them. They were just two people in work smocks on their way to quickly take care of a small catastrophe, as happened so frequently. It smelled of disinfectants and Liepelt's cologne, which he must pour on by the pint.

'You owe me one.' They arrived at a heavy door made of polished dull stainless steel. Liepelt looked around. 'Here.'

He tapped the opener with his elbow and walked ahead into a heavily refrigerated, tiled room.

'This here is the top security area.'

He motioned to a light blue curtain that hung on the wall next to the sink. Judith slipped through it. Liepelt waited until she was ready, then he took a deep breath, looked at his watch and opened the second door.

'You really want this?'

Instead of answering, Judith pushed past him. The first thing she registered was the icy air. According to the large thermometer on the cabinets opposite, the temperature was minus six Celsius. This was where the corpses were stored, stacked in four rows, each of them placed on a sliding shelf and packed in white plastic sacks. Liepelt closed the door behind them. Two living beings among forty-some dead ones.

'Hand it over!' he growled.

She handed him the autopsy file. Liepelt threw it on a long trolley to his left and compared the registry number with the labels on the cabinets. He bent over, searching the lower region of the cabinet and then went back to the left, carefully comparing the numbers. After a couple of steps he stood still. He returned the file to Judith because he needed to pull the trolley in front of the cabinet. Judith used the opportunity to put it back under her smock. Liepelt pulled out a stainless steel mortuary tray. A dead woman lay on it. Medium-sized, packaged, registered, deposited, unmourned.

Judith's skin tingled. It was either the cold or her nerves were playing tricks on her. She wanted to finally see the woman who had tangled with the BND and who had been sent her file from the children's home. She gave Liepelt a sign and he opened the zipper of the body bag.

Long, brown hair spilled out. Judith's first glance fell on the bullet hole in her forehead. It looked like an exotic tattoo and gave the dead woman the appearance of a strangely severe deity. Borg was no beauty. Thick, dark eyebrows, wide cheekbones, a narrow, serious mouth. Judith asked herself if this woman had laughed often and how she would have looked then. Laughing changes people. It shows their soul for a fraction of a second. Open and generous, giggling and childish, or gloating and mean. Laughter was tell-tale. That was why Judith didn't laugh very often.

She had never seen the woman before. And she would have remembered someone like Borg, because even in death, her face revealed something unrelenting, a strength she must have once had. You didn't forget a woman like that. Dangerous for those who weren't on her side. For Judith it stung a little that they were strangers and would stay that way.

'Do you want more?'

Cold. Like marble under ice. Judith ran her fingertips over Borg's face.

'Where did she come from?'

'No idea. No one called. As soon as the cops clear this here we'll let Schneider know.'

Gerhard Schneider Mortuaries. They were the kingpins of the undertaking world. They must have had a deal with all the hospitals and prosecutors in the city, because Schneider and his fleet were always the first ones on the scene.

'Crematorium, I'm guessing. Makes it cheaper. No relatives. At least none who called here. Listen, you're not going to pass out now, are you? What's going on with you?'

'Nothing,' Judith whispered and took a deep breath.

Nothing. Liepelt closed the zipper. He pushed Borg's hair back inside so that it wouldn't catch. And so that someone would touch her face this one last time, now disappearing behind the white plastic. No relatives. And her last journey was to the crematorium because it was cheaper.

Liepelt slipped Borg back into the cabinet. Judith waited until he had arranged the tray. Then she followed him silently outside. Only then did she suddenly feel a pang in her heart. She hadn't even realised she had one.

'Mr Kaiserley?'

A slender young man in his early thirties, either freshly showered or with his hair so gelled that it glistened, approached him in squeaky trainers. Quirin stood up and shook the hand extended toward him.

'I'm Franz Ferdinand Maike. And with my name believe me I have to put up with a lot of jokes.'

Quirin smiled a somewhat tortured smile.

'I'm a homicide detective. Please follow me. You want to make a statement?'

Quirin let Franz Ferdinand Maike believe that. Maike was slightly shorter than he was. A nimble, agile man he walked past the elevator without bothering to ask and made Quirin sprint up three storeys. By the time Maike had reached the top, Quirin was half a flight behind him, and Maike still looked like he was freshly showered. He held open the door to a small, very neatly kept office and asked his visitor to take a seat.

'Mr Kaiserley. What exactly brings you here?'

'Are you investigating the Borg homicide?'

'Hmmmm . . . yes.'

Maike folded his hands and placed them on his green civil servant desk pad.

'Why aren't you going public with the case? I knew Christina Borg. I'd have liked to have known that she was dead.'

Quirin still felt a cold fury. He had stumbled right into the trap on Westerhoff's show. Borg had been murdered, and no one in the city seemed to have taken official notice of it.

'My apologies. You knew her?' Maike bent forward. 'From where? And since when?'

'Christina Borg contacted me through my publisher. I write non-fiction books.'

'Oh, yes?'

Maike kept a straight face. Either he had really never heard Kaiserley's name or had just placed him in the category of an hysterical author.

'We met here in Berlin,' Quirin continued. 'She was interested in the same topics as me and offered to help me with my research.'

'Which topics would they be?'

'Domestic security, the debate surrounding the statute of limitations, the BND. And Section A of the Ministry for Security, Division XII.'

Maike nodded. 'And was she able to help?'

'Unfortunately not. She didn't come to our last meeting. That's why I'd like to know what happened.'

'We'd also like to know.'

Maike leaned back and glanced out the window. The office looked out onto the courtyard. Nothing except the grey façade opposite was visible.

'You surely understand that we're not allowed to give any information about current investigations. But,' Maike opened a drawer and pulled out a form, 'please leave us your personal information and where we can reach you. We'll get in touch at the appropriate time if we still have any questions for you.'

He slid the paper over the table. Quirin took it and carefully and slowly ripped it into tiny pieces.

'You surely understand that I don't believe a word you said. What's the name of the department head at Berlin's Department for the Interior? Or is it already in the hands of the Federal Ministry of Justice?'

Maike stuck out his jaw, giving his young face, not yet marked by disappointments, the expression of an abandoned pitbull.

'And before you reach for the telephone to inform your superior, remember that he's also no longer involved. I already told you, domestic security is one of my hobbies.'

'I'm sorry I can't help.'

'Then I'll explain what I can do for you. First of all, I'll mobilise the opinion guerrillas in this country. The press will pound down your door. A young woman murdered, unsolved to date, and the public doesn't know a thing. Who ordered this completely unprofessional approach?'

'You're not expecting me to . . .'

'I want to know where the case was sent.'

Maike reached for the telephone. Quirin leaned over and put his hand over the receiver.

'Is it still a simple homicide or much more? Is someone in the hot seat?'

'Get a grip on yourself!' Maike's self-confidence was starting to evaporate. 'You're crazy if you think you'll learn anything from us.'

'And you're naïve, Maike. Mr Homicide Detective Maike. What does the nose ring feel like, the one they lead you around with?'

Maike's hand sped toward the telephone again.

'Tell me who is really investigating the case, and I'll let you do what you call work.'

Maike extended his lower lip. A couple more years and he'd look like a nutcracker.

'I shouldn't have to listen to nonsense like this.'

'But you are.' Quirin felt his opponent's defences starting to crumble. 'Why don't you call your boss, the one who's just as castrated as you are? Have some other eunuch in this building toss me out.'

'A copy of the files were sent to Schwerin. Ask there. If you can.'

'Schwerin?'

'To the Ministry of the Interior.'

The Borg homicide was now at a level that required more fire-power. Old connections, very old. Quirin asked himself who he still knew that he could ask for help.

'But you didn't hear it from me. We only led the crime scene analysis here.'

'With what results?'

'Nice try. But as you're already here, can you tell me if you know this person?'

Maike removed a picture from a pile of documents. Quirin glanced at it. It showed Judith Kepler crossing the room with rubber gloves and a cleaning bucket. The name Dombrowski was inscribed on her smock. The company was known across the city and was surely already being looked into by the investigators.

'No. Who's that?'

'So you don't know where she is currently? You're not in contact with her?'

'No.'

'Mr Kaiserley, contact me immediately if that changes. And if you're cultivating conspiracy theories – remember, we're the good guys.'

Maike returned the photo.

Quirin stood up. 'Perhaps you'll remind me of that once in a while.'

Dombrowski. At least now he knew where he could find Judith Kepler. She had something, and she knew something. And she couldn't be left alone with either.

Judith followed Liepelt back into the tile-covered vestibule. Outside it was almost unbearably hot after those few minutes in the icy cold. She took off her cape, folded it up and placed it on the shelf. Then they raced back through the hallways to Weihrich's office. It was 12:27. Liepelt returned the file to the cabinet. Weihrich wouldn't notice that almost half of it was missing.

'We lucked out. But don't ever ask me for something like that again. Unless . . .'

Judith stepped to the window and looked into the courtyard. A black BMW was just coming through the driveway and heading towards the reserved spots.

'What?'

'. . . we can go get a drink sometime. If I'm not mistaken I've asked you more than once.'

Judith squinted and watched as Professor Weihrich, unhappy to be parking his car in one of his colleague's spots, gave Dombrowski's van a withering look. Where had Kai gone, she wondered?

'Your boss is on his way.'

'Shit. Come on, get out of here.'

Liepelt ripped open the door and ran into the hallway.

'Come on!'

At the entrance Liepelt pushed Judith through the turnstile just as Weihrich entered it from the other side. He accompanied her to the courtyard.

'We lucked out,' he said. The relief that he had Judith out of the building was visible on his face. 'Well, how about it?'

Liepelt was in his early thirties. He was a nice guy. He provoked an instinct to protect. And for that reason he was absolutely unsuitable for Judith. He needed a woman who could keep him ship shape. With her, even window boxes were doomed.

'Friday night? Just a beer?'

'I don't drink beer.'

'Then something else?'

'Sorry, got to go.'

She was too fond of him to waste his time. In the driveway she turned around once more. Dejected, Liepelt still stood in the courtyard. She had been a hair's breadth away from taking pity on him. But autopsy assistants were about as sexy as crime scene cleaners. And they didn't like each other's jobs.

When Judith opened the driver's seat door Kai almost fell out. He rubbed his eyes in surprise.

'Everything OK?' he murmured and slipped back onto his seat.

'Great.'

Judith felt the file against her skin. It scratched. Kai was annoying her. She had to get rid of him and get a look at the autopsy report as soon as possible. Abuse. Fractures. And in the end, she died like a dog. She waited for the boom gate to rise and accelerated onto the street with such a sharp turn that the chassis rocked. She thought about Dombrowski's gun and regretted having turned down his offer.

'Watch out!' Kai screamed.

She just barely managed to pull the steering wheel around. The truck's horn blasted. A collision, then her side mirror departed with an ugly grinding noise. She careened back into the right lane. The buckets and tools clattered in the back and the hammer rumbled across the floor. In her rear-view mirror she saw that the truck driver hadn't noticed or didn't want to notice the damage.

'Holy shit!' Kai was wide awake.

At the next red light Judith rolled down the side window and examined the damage. The mirror had been an ancient, no-frills model. Dombrowski would send someone to the junkyard that evening and get a replacement. Kai shifted back and forth uncomfortably in his seat. He would have preferred to get out.

She patted the panel with her hand, as if it was the flank of a horse, grinned at him and hit the gas.

'Don't be like that. Nothing happened.'

She handed him her pack of tobacco. He removed two pre-rolled cigarettes, lit them and handed her one.

'Listen,' she said. 'Do you actually want to work, or keep on living off my taxes?'

'I don't have any desire to have such an uncool discussion.'

'OK.'

She concentrated on the traffic and chose the Tiergarten tunnel for her way back. Two or three kilometres straight ahead. Breathe and think. Borg's face appeared in front of her. *Who are you?* Judith thought. *You lived in Sweden and came to Berlin. With my file from the home. I was never in Sweden. But we must have crossed paths at some point. You knew that. I didn't.*

The realisation came so quickly that she almost yanked the steering wheel. The envelope. The sender. Post from the depths of Hell. Sassnitz was between Berlin and Sweden. That is where the threads came together. The sender must live somewhere there. She had to go there.

When Judith stopped at the back entrance of the hospital several of the patients were standing around a standing ashtray. Her phone vibrated. She didn't have to look to know it was Dombrowski.

'What needs to be done?' Kai asked. He had been silent for the rest of the ride and had calmed down.

Judith turned off the engine.

'Mop. Empty the bins. In crews, so relatively easy.'

Dombrowski would hit the roof when he found out. Sometimes he came by with a stopwatch and studiously recorded the length of time needed to clean a floor, shaking his head and grumbling to himself. Days later there were orders to improve seconds per metre. To date such orders were ignored in a kind of silent agreement.

'And the shift is over at three?'

Judith glanced at the clock on the dashboard. Two minutes to one.

'Yes.'

'But that's still considered a working day, right? I have to get a full week in for the employment agency.'

'Don't push it.'

He wanted to get out.

'Wait a sec.' Judith reached into her shirt pocket. 'This is my time card. Go inside and find Josef. Tell him I've got to take care of something. Once you're at the headquarters, swipe it.'

Kai stared at the plastic card. 'You're not coming along?'

'Am I speaking Chinese? Do the job and shut your trap.'

He took the card and pocketed it. 'OK, but this isn't a one-way street,' he said.

Judith shrugged her shoulders. She waited until he had disappeared into the building. She pulled out her phone. Dombrowski had tried to reach her a half-dozen times. She held down the red button until the display went dark. It was time to drive back to Hell, pedal to the metal.

9

Klaus Dombrowski had paternal feelings. Of course they weren't compatible with those that he'd had at the births of his three children by three different women. But he characterised this vague mood of responsibility as such because he couldn't think of a better way to describe the way he felt about Judith.

He stood in his office and watched the return of his employees like a Roman commander overseeing the homecoming of the victorious cohorts: trucks manoeuvred in the yard, vans arrived and delivered the cleaning crew from the early shift directly in front of the door of the changing rooms. He looked at the clock on the wall – a little after three. Josef was the first to climb out. He was followed by that useless intern. Dombrowski had seen at first glance that he either needed basic army training or some-one like Judith to make him get his act together. Six additional workers followed, the last closing the door. The van was empty; Judith wasn't there. And there was a vehicle missing.

Dombrowski furrowed his brow. The bouquet of roses was still in his office reminding him that something strange had happened in Judith's life. He went over to the barracks and was just in time to catch the useless intern swiping a time card through the slot. Dombrowski grabbed it out of his hand, and held up the photo on the card, next to the boy's impertinent face.

'I don't see any similarity. Not in the slightest,' he growled. He turned 'Josef?' he yelled. No answer. 'Josef?'

The second call rang out through the tiled room like a trumpet blast. Josef, smock half off, peered out of a door in the hallway.

'Yeah, boss?'

'Come along. Both of you.'

Josef and the useless intern stood before him in his office with heads hanging low. Dombrowski prowled back and forth and almost chewed his cigarillo to bits in his fury.

'Where's she gone?'

Josef looked up. 'No idea, boss. This guy here showed up and said he was supposed to fill in for her.'

The boy was chewing on his lower lip, leaning against the wall in a James Dean pose, hands in his pockets. Dombrowski stood in front of him menacingly until he finally bothered to look him in the eye.

'It's no big deal,' he said. 'It's not like I'm coming back.'

He pushed himself off the wall. Dombrowski grabbed him by the shoulder and pushed him back into his starting position. 'I only did her a favour . . .'

'Where'd she go?'

'She didn't tell me.'

'And where's the vehicle? What happened to the vehicle?'

'How the hell would I know?'

Dombrowski's gaze swivelled to Josef.

'She was suddenly gone,' the foreman said. 'I don't ask *who* does the work. Main thing is that it gets done.'

Dombrowski huffed. He knew things happened in his company that he'd rather not know about. He'd always turned a blind eye up until now. The time card trick was the oldest thing since the time-punch machines had been invented. He tossed the plastic card on the table and felt stupid as he said: 'It's fraud. Instant dismissal.'

'I'm not even employed,' the smarty-pants intern pointed out and stared insolently at the massive bouquet of roses. You could see on his face what he thought about men who decorated their offices with wax-yellow flower arrangements over three feet high. Something snapped inside Dombrowski. He would have liked nothing better than to slap the boy. But he restrained his inner boxer and nodded.

'And that's exactly what we'll do now. Josef? The boy will take Judith's place. Until she returns. And if you're not here first thing in the morning at 5:30 tomorrow, I'll knock down your door and pull you out of bed myself.'

'Nope.' The boy started shuffling towards the door. 'Not happening. I did her a favour. You can't lock me up for that.'

He tore open the door, fast as lightning. Dombrowski signalled to Josef who grabbed the runaway, and hauled him back.

'Hey!'

Josef stood in front of the door and crossed his arms. He was at least a head taller than the intern.

'I think we have to explain something to you,' Dombrowski said. 'How things work with us. Some people say, cling together, swing together. Others just call it keeping your word.'

Dombrowski took the card and held it under the boy's nose.

'You promised you'd stand in for her?'

The boy glanced quickly at the door. Josef shifted his weight from one foot to another.

'Yes.'

'Then do it. Until she comes back. You'll sign in with this card in the morning and sign out each evening.'

Josef nodded in agreement. He made it look like a serious threat.

The boy looked at the card. 'How long?'

'Are you deaf? Until she's back. Or until you can remember where she headed off to.'

'Sure.' He put the card in his back pocket and shrugged. 'I don't know where she wanted to go. She went to the mortuary and then she split.'

Liepelt. Dombrowski spat out a crumble of tobacco.

'Out.'

Josef and the boy disappeared like bolts of lightning. Dombrowski went to the desk and fell into the chair. Olaf Liepelt. Also one of Judith's protégés. She had pulled him out of the alley and organised a job for him at the mortuary a year later.

Dombrowski pulled open the drawer. The gun was still there. He'd give Judith twenty-four hours. If she didn't show up after that, he'd have some choice words with Liepelt.

The telephone rang. It was the same guy on the line who had been annoying him all morning.

'No! She's not here. She'll get back to you!' he yelled and hung up.

He kicked the drawer shut with a bang. Paternal feelings. Fucking hell. She had run off. She'd never done that. Maybe there was a man involved. Not the one who was constantly calling and had already left his number a million times. Someone who sent yellow roses and acted mysterious. Someone who didn't call, just sent his message via a bouquet. Dombrowski went to the window, ripped it open and sent a shrill two-finger whistle across the yard.

'Josef!'

Already on his way back into the locker rooms, the foreman jumped and turned around.

Whoever sends a wreath like that to a woman was either gay or wanted something. Judith wasn't the ideal candidate for either option. But there was nothing he could do while he couldn't get his hands on her. Dombrowski looked at his notebook. There were three telephone numbers written down. The first belonged to the rose gentleman. The second to this annoying guy, Kaiser-whatever, who kept hassling him with questions. The third was a cop who claimed to be called Franz Ferdinand Maike. He pulled up his rolodex and turned it to L. Liepelt. There we go. He carefully wrote down his number as the fourth on the list. He took his cold cigarillo and sucked on it thoughtfully. From zero to four in forty-eight hours.

'Boss?'

Dombrowski motioned to the bouquet.

'Get rid of it.'

Josef nodded. When the office looked like an office again and not a drag queen's dressing room, Dombrowski leaned back in his chair. He took the notebook and looked at the numbers again. He'd call them, one after another. And if any of them was responsible for Judith's being in trouble, Dombrowski would break every one of his bones.

Josef carried the bouquet across the yard ignoring the jeering comments of his colleagues and threw it in one of the containers due to go back to the recycling plant in the next couple of days.

There were two rusty spring mattresses stacked next to the container and several small pieces of furniture, remnants from apartments that the clean-out crews had deposited in the yard. He used the opportunity to toss everything into the container. All the flowers were squashed, except for one bloom that was severed and rolled a bit further into the corner. If Josef had looked more closely, then he might have recognised a two millimetre long piece of silver wire that protruded out of the broken stem. It had been connected with a ferrite rod only a couple of seconds before, which delivered energy between 0.6 and 6 volts via a button battery. That power was sufficient for a radius between fifty and one hundred metres.

The assembly kit had a value of around eighty cents and had been a bit of DIY equipment. Most of the intelligence services built their own bugs, partly because of cost – specialised listening devices could easily cost a hundred times more – but also, because homemade bugs were much harder to identify and therefore corresponded to the maxim of plausible deniability.

Josef knew nothing about this principle, but then Watergate and the Iran-Contra Affair probably also wouldn't have interested him. In his eyes, plausible deniability simply meant: you're lying. And if you were caught lying, you had to pay. Not getting caught was the trick.

He ran quickly to the changing room. Time to knock off.

TT sat at a desk in the ground floor of the Department for Technical Reconnaissance – SIGINT – and looked out at the three cameras that were watching over the entrance to Heilmannstrasse 30 in Munich Pullach. A faded concrete wall shielded the compound from the outside world. The secret city.

Streets, tennis courts, loosely grouped units of buildings, sepa-rated by park-like green areas.

The SIGINT building was opposite the Leadership and Infor-mation Centre, or 'General Situation' for short. His days in Pul-lach were numbered. When the headquarters moved to Berlin, he would go along too, but he would miss all the green and the exclusivity of this workplace. He had seen a model of the new intelligence headquarters. They could sugar-coat it as much as they wanted but it still remained a concrete bunker in the mid-dle of a metropolis. Nothing comparable with the West German stolidity and the small-town charm of Pullach.

In Berlin he wouldn't have a direct line of sight to the park-ing spaces of the department directors. There he wouldn't know that Kellermann had arrived at the General Situation two hours before and still hadn't let him know. Not a good sign. TT was on tenterhooks.

He tried to concentrate on his task: evaluating Angelina Espi-noza, confirming her identity, her character, her preferences – it was precisely at this point that he was having serious problems. He would have left it out if it had been possible.

Ms Espinoza explained openly that she was paid for the analy-sis of the target person, and fulfilled her task with great expertise and competence.

He stared at the computer monitor. He had taken a half-hour to write that sentence. And only because he wanted to avoid get-ting to the point. Of course he could explain the quickie. Things like that happened and were even desirable, from case to case. The more that was known about a person working for another service, the better. Who knew what these compromising details could be worth someday?

After the conclusion of the observation of Quirin Kaiserley, there was a continuation of non-work activities. However, this was initiated by Ms Espinoza . . .

He deleted the sentence.

Despite her forty-eight years, Ms Espinoza is in excellent physical condition. This can be attributed to her athletic activities. I was able to confirm that no noteworthy external changes had taken place since our last work contact.

Did Kellermann read the reports? What was he doing? He should been long done with his session with the department president. Surely the Berlin mishap was discussed. TT looked back over to the General Situation building but except for two dark Mercedes Benz limousines, carelessly parked in front of the entrance rather than in the subterranean garage, nothing indicated that anyone was there at the moment.

The president was hardly ever seen anyway. Whether he was staying in his work mansion in Berlin – the rumour that it was located in Wannsee had surfaced repeatedly – or in his office in Pullach, his whereabouts were known only by his secretary at best. Perhaps also by people like Kellermann, who had connections at the top because they had pushed everything else out of the way. From time to time there was speculation about Kellermann's retirement, but he had stayed put, despite some hiccups in his career. He was like a boxer: knocked down occasionally but never knocked out. By now he had established himself so firmly that his name was being whispered as a successor to the current president.

Kellermann belonged to a different generation. One of the most senior department heads, it was rumoured he had once looked Khrushchev in the eye via satellite. A cold warrior. A power seeker.

Someone who rolled up his sleeves and occasionally put his foot down. And that was exactly what branded him a dinosaur in the eyes of younger agents.

For TT the future of the intelligence services was in the hands of those who had grown up with computers rather than an abacus. What he had to do with this report had little to do with the intelligence service as he understood it. Reports. Confirmation of identities. That was yesterday. Tomorrow belonged to those who could line up zeros and ones. He was overqualified for this shit.

OK. There was no way around it. TT bent over the keyboard. Angelina Espinoza had probably already written her report. Everyone did that. Allegedly shady characters were even invented for the purposes of assignments to test if they would correctly report everything. TT would have liked to know what Angelina wrote about him.

Sexual activity occurred. However, this remained within the context of the usual and did not take an excessive nature.

The last sentence excited him because it was greatly under-stated. The telephone rang. TT recognised the Berlin area code. Angelina? He didn't know how long she wanted to stay in Germany. Maybe she missed him. Maybe she was also busy writing something like . . . *was a form of stress reduction attributable to work and the situation . . .* or *Tobias Täschner is an extraordinarily experienced lover for his young age . . .* TT grinned. The security conference in Munich was starting in two weeks. Maybe . . .

'Tobias?'

TT didn't reply.

'Or Karsten Michael Oliver Whatever? I can't ever decide whom I should address. So many names. You're carving out a career.'

'TT,' answered TT. 'Simply TT. Can I do anything for you?'

'Yes.'

'I mean can I patch you through or something like that?'

'I'll be in Munich in two hours. I want to see you.'

'No.'

TT hung up. Kaiserley. How did he get his number? And the aliases? The telephone rang again.

'Don't have time.'

'I reserved a table at Rabenwirt for six p.m. We have to talk.'

'I'm sorry. Find someone else if you're lonely.'

Kaiserley didn't say anything. TT cut the connection. The telephone rang again but he didn't pick up. A colleague from next door, on his way to the coffee machine, stopped in front of his open door and glanced inside.

'Everything OK?'

TT nodded, and the colleague continued on. The telephone rang again. Repeatedly, persistently and noisily. He would have liked to rip the device from the wall and fling it onto the car park. He stared at the keyboard. The colleague returned.

'Why aren't you answering your telephone? Kellermann wants to talk to you. In his office.'

Kellermann's office was on the top floor of the same building. Nothing special. A metal cabinet for the files, a picture of the Federal President on the wall, a large desk with steel corners and his own shredder. Next to the telephone the customary framed photograph. TT didn't know who was in the picture but he guessed it was the wife mid-golf swing.

Kellermann motioned to the pair of Le Corbusier style, black leather sofas. TT took a seat and examined the crystal bowl on the coffee table. Probably from the stock of gifts that the foreign heads of allied services brought along with pleasant regularity. Presumably there was a rumour circulating internationally that Germany was running short on crystal bowls.

Kellermann's secretary, a middle-aged woman with the charm and erotic charisma of a parking warden, served coffee and biscuits. Kellermann took the thermos can and TT held out his cup. His hands were shaking and the cup clattered on the saucer. The secretary left and they were all alone.

'Dumb mistake,' the boss said and took a seat. He pushed the plate with the biscuits in TT's direction. 'But no reason to get nervous right away. We know a lot. But how cleaning ladies divvy up their time is one of the great mysteries of the universe.'

TT took a biscuit.

'It was a fluke. Things like that can't happen but they do anyway. The human factor. Was this the woman who ambushed you?'

Kellermann went to his desk and took a photo, handing it over to TT. Presumably taken by Unit 6, the camera that TT had left in his hasty departure. TT nodded.

'That's her. But she didn't have some kind of smock on, she wore a special suit instead. And she had a gas cylinder along with . . .'

He paused.

'Oxygen,' Kellermann completed the sentence. Without losing sight of TT, he sat back down. 'She was there to clean up the crime scene. A death scene cleaner. However, what she was doing in the apartment at this time of night is beyond our knowledge. But we'd like to know.'

Kellermann took the photo out of TT's hand and placed it on the table.

'We need to know what she has planned.'

TT nodded and drank a sip of coffee. Only after the pause in the conversation had stretched out a little too long did he realise that he was expected to give an answer.

'Yes,' he said.

Kellermann put his fingertips together and studied the photo as if it was a snapshot from an American spy plane.

'Her name is Judith Kepler. She works at a building cleaning company by the name of Dombrowski Facility Management in Berlin Neukölln. Everything you see was put together by dearest Clary.'

Kellermann never used the proper name of his secretaries. And 'dearest Clary', 'little Mary', 'Annie' all accepted this habit with stoic serenity, aware that a boss who didn't demand much more than physical presence was a rarity in the Munich metropolitan area.

TT nodded.

'We have to find the woman. But we don't know where she is. You've got to help us.'

Now the chummy stuff was back. Perhaps his situation must not be that bad after all.

'Phone?'

'Turned off.'

'Credit cards? Cash machines?'

'That's your job.'

TT thought. 'A Trojan?'

They weren't allowed to hack into computers but they did anyway. Every once in a while there were initiatives to make such operations subject to authorisation, but this was always vetoed by the Minister of the Interior. As long as there weren't any relevant regulations and every single online investigation had been registered with the Federal Parliament's Control Committee, then they were in a grey area.

Kellermann crossed his arms and nodded. TT set down his cup.

'So when you order something like that . . .'

'That's not an order. It isn't even a question. This conversation officially never happened. Just like your nocturnal operation in Berlin and the loss of Unit 6. You talk to me and no one else. You inform me immediately when you've found out what Judith Kepler is up to. You'll get new cover stories, and the case will be closed. Do you understand?'

TT nodded quickly. Kellermann's abrupt move from the informal to the formal irritated him every time. His boss handed him the photo.

'One question.'

'Yes?' Kellermann snapped.

'What happened in that apartment? Was that us?'

Kellermann looked at him for a long time. Only when TT no longer expected to get an answer did he say: 'I have no idea. And can I tell you something? I don't even want to know.'

10

Judith reached Sassnitz late that afternoon. Dark clouds were building over the isle of Rügen. It was oppressively humid. Not even the breeze through the van windows cooled her. When she got stuck in a traffic jam close to the port at Mukran the air in the vehicle reached boiling point. A ferry must have just arrived from Klaipeda because cars from Latvia crawled up the hill and helplessly lost camper vans compounded the chaos. Only after she turned off the B96 did it get better. She abandoned the advertised tourist routes in the city centre to the others and turned right after entering the city limits, entering a shabby residential area with four-storey buildings that had only been half-heartedly renovated or not at all.

Sassnitz. Before 1990, it still used the old spelling, with a 'ß.' A port city. A trans-shipment point. A restricted area. No turn-of-the-century charm, no Wilhelmina spa architecture. A heavily guarded transit for tourists, commodities, and the Soviet Army. Later, somehow forgotten and pushed aside by ostentatious beauties like Binz, Göhren, and Sellin. The port was moved six miles south, and with that the city lost its last remnants of industrial raison d'être. What was left was the view of the ferries as they floated past, far out to sea.

Judith drove more slowly and studied the derelict buildings. The best maintained were the garage blocks. Maybe your own car was the only thing worth taking care of around here. She remembered the Saturday afternoons when the men circled their boxy Trabi cars, leaning back on their heels, giving each other the once-over and exchanging tips, messing around with the engines and the exhaust, and constantly wiping down the mudguards with a rag.

The sun slipped through a narrow gap in the clouds. It hung low in the sky and Judith saw the Baltic glittering in the distance. The sunset glow gilded the old port area; the beach promenade, and the part of the cliff coast that drew the tourists a couple of hundred metres further on with its promise of views from Caspar David Friedrich paintings. Maybe that was Sassnitz's fate: missing everything by a hair's breadth. The eternal way station.

The bus stop to the right, a graffiti-covered ruin. Judith almost missed it by a whisker. Behind that was the *Strasse der Jugend*, paved with cobblestones and bumpy. Snaking along sharp turns, she drove through the woods and down to the water. The old fish factory, a huge, abandoned area now only good for getting rid of bulk waste. And then – Judith's hands cramped around the steering wheel, and she instinctively slowed to walking speed – a group of tall buildings made of brown bricks to the left and right. She let the car roll to a stop on the edge of the road.

A near ghostly calm lay over the entire compound. It seemed abandoned, despite new windows and an intercom with *Haus Waldfrieden* inscribed on it. Judith ignored the bell. The gate opened easily – the first and perhaps most important difference from the days when the notice read *Yuri Gagarin Children's*

Home. She didn't head towards the main entrance, but rather went to the left, where the ground fell away towards the edge of the woods.

The playground equipment seemed new; even the benches and sand boxes looked orderly. She slowly continued toward the edge of the property. The fence was tall, but the barbed wire was gone. Only the concrete posts were the same, but they were less threatening and were more of a help for climbing than a deterrent for anyone who was seriously intent on running away. A gust of wind whistled through the tips of the trees, the harbinger of a storm. Judith suddenly had the feeling of being watched. She looked around but the building behind her still seemed silent, forbidding and deserted.

She breathed in the scent of woods and sea, but something essential was missing. Just as she turned to go back up to the house she saw a figure standing way back, where the larches almost grew up to the sky. A girl, ten or twelve years old, with long blonde hair. The girl looked over to her, and for a short, completely irrational moment, Judith's heart began to pound. It couldn't be. She was crazy. A hallucination. A chance similarity. For a moment, she had really believed she was seeing herself just because the girl had light curls. The little girl disappeared. Judith began to move, slowly at first, then running towards the trees, seeing the way the light shone down into the undergrowth once again.

'Hello? You there!' Someone from the building was coming quickly towards her

Judith stood still. The child had disappeared. Maybe she had never been there.

'What are you doing here?'

The woman was in her early twenties and wore a suit and high heels unsuitable for this terrain. Her heart-shaped face was without make-up; she wore her brown hair straight and chin-length.

'Are you looking for someone?'

Two nights with hardly any sleep and then returning to this nightmare, which, with its well-trimmed lawn and the freshly painted fence, seemed as if it had never existed. Judith rubbed her eyes with her hands, blinked, and concentrated on the young woman who had stopped in front of her, a little out of breath.

'Who are you?'

The question was sharp, the first attempt towards kicking Judith off the property.

'My name is Judith Kepler. I was here as a child.'

'OK.' The woman adopted a friendlier facial expression but wasn't particularly successful. 'You have to call ahead. You need an appointment if you want a tour.'

'I don't want a tour.' Judith studied her interlocutor. The first words indicated that this was someone who prevented more than she made possible. 'I want to know who leaked my file.'

'That must be a mistake. We don't release any files.'

'I had it in my own hands.'

Judith didn't know why the answer made her so aggressive. Maybe it was the smile. Without any empathy; without the slightest understanding. That's the way Trenkner had smiled when she reached for the bottle with the soapy water. She suddenly remembered that she was still wearing the blue smock. People talked differently to you when you were wearing a smock.

'When I came of age, I was told that my file had been shred-ded. But now it has suddenly reappeared. But not sent to me. It was in the hands of complete strangers. *Haus Waldfrieden* must be the assignee of *Yuri Gagarin*. So either I find out how that happened, right here and now, or I'll press charges.'

'Something must have gone terribly wrong. How terrible for you!'

The woman widened her eyes in apparent sympathy. It seemed a little exaggerated and about as real as her chilly smile.

'Of course that can't be allowed to happen. But unfortunately I can't do anything for you. Please contact the regional archive in Rügen. There's the inventory from the "District Committee" in the National Education and Youth Assistance division. The assistants in the reading room will surely be able to help, even with questions about file access times and . . .'

'What do you think I've been doing for the past few years?'

'This isn't the right place. Not right at all.' The woman extended her hand. Judith took a step back.

'Where's Trenkner?'

'Who?'

'The assistant director of the home back then. Or Martha Jonas, one of the teachers? Trinklein, the physical education teacher. Blum, Wagner, Stoltze. Where did they all go? The peo-ple, the files?'

'We're an independent agency. We took over the property twelve years ago. The buildings were empty. None of the former employees are still here. I'll have to ask you to go.'

'I was 3452.' The rage transformed Judith's voice into a hoarse whisper. 'Building three, dorm IV, number 052. I spent nearly ten years here. There must be something left.'

'No. There's nothing. And if you don't leave, I'll call the police.'

She took out her phone and weighed it in her hand, waiting. She looked like she was accustomed to unpleasant visitors and knew how to fend them off. This was a dead end. The woman really didn't know anything. But she might have gone to the trouble of finding out what kind of home she was in charge of.

'OK,' Judith said. 'I'll leave. But I'm coming back.'

'With an appointment. I'll follow you.'

Judith walked up the lawn to a small forecourt. There used to be flag ceremonies and public punishment for the children who hadn't developed into the proletarian ideal. Another gust of wind swept over the yard and whipped up dust and a couple of withered leaves. Two basketball hoops hung from the brick wall. It was still unnaturally quiet.

'Where are all the children?' Judith asked.

'At supper,' the woman answered.

It was five-thirty.

She had to get her feelings better under control.

Judith walked along the edge of the woods. The wind picked up and shook the tops of the trees. Breathless, she reached the old factory compound. The first drops slipped from black clouds. They slapped on the slabs of broken road like huge, dead insects. *Sassnitz Fisch* was written on a sign with red lettering, the rest of the paint having peeled off long ago. The spelling revealed that there had been work here for at least a couple of years after reunification.

Spread across several acres, and slowly being reclaimed by nature, were abandoned factory buildings. Production, cold storage, storage halls, smoke-house. Not a single pane of glass was still whole. Bulk waste was stacked inside almost up to the ceiling, the overgrown roads and paths were lined by the leftovers cast off by the city. Thunder collected over the sea, and rumbled towards the land as a warning. The drops fell heavier. Then the heavens suddenly opened their floodgates. Judith ran to the storage hall IV and reached the awning over the ramp. The pelting rain battered the treetops.

She leaned against the wall, where the plaster was peeling, and pulled out her package of tobacco. Had she smoked her first cigarette here? She had been fourteen. Old enough to work after school. *Subbotnik*, Soviet-style voluntary work. There had been no question about its voluntary nature. There was herring in tomato sauce until the cows came home. She had enjoyed the work. There were always twenty-four cans in a box. She didn't know why it always had to be exactly twenty-four. Maybe it was a special kind of Advent calendar. She hadn't touched a tin of fish since then. She rolled a cigarette. When she licked the papers and looked back up, the girl was standing in front of her.

The child wore a white summer dress and was sopping wet. On her feet she wore cheap, bright pink plastic clogs, the kind tourists bought on holiday and threw away when they got home. The girl stood in front of the loading ramp, letting herself get soaked, and said: 'Hello.'

So it hadn't been a hallucination after all. She climbed up the loading ramp like a weasel and stood next to Judith. She was up to her shoulder. A thin, tall girl with freckles and unnaturally fair skin. A mythical creature who seemed at one with the cloud-bursts and the overgrown ruins.

'My name is Judith.'

'My name is Chantal.'

Chantal. Who inflicted these names on children?

'You were at the home?' the child asked. 'I'm there too.'

Judith lit her cigarette. Children in homes were used to worse things than the sight of an adult smoking.

'How long?' Judith asked.

'Only for a couple weeks. Until the people at social services say I can go back home. My father hit my mother. And me, too. Look.'

She pushed aside the strap of her summer dress. Judith recognised the healed scars and welts on the skinny shoulder.

'Shit,' Judith said.

The girl put the strap back. She didn't appear to have a big problem with the scars. At least not with the visible ones.

'And what's it like?'

'OK. If my mother could be there it'd be really good.'

'Is there still a cellar?'

The child looked at Judith in surprise. 'You mean the bicycle cellar?'

'The coal cellar,' Judith answered. Every era had its own cellar. It didn't always have to be deep underneath the surface.

'They don't heat with coal. I think there's a machine in there, and an oil tank. Mrs Langgut kicked you out. Why?'

'Because I didn't ask if I could come. And you don't do that.'

'Why did you want to come?'

'Because I wanted to talk to someone from back then. From when I was at the home.'

'Why?'

'Because . . . it used to be something like my home.' Inside Judith bristled at the idea of using that word even vaguely in that context. 'I was there for ten years.'

'Ten years?' Chantal's eyes widened. For her it was a lifetime. An eternity. 'Why?'

'Because my mother couldn't take care of me and died.'

'And your father?'

Judith smoked and watched a wet crow hopping over an old blanket, searching for something.

'I don't have one,' she finally answered.

Chantal already had another 'why' on the tip of her tongue, but kept it to herself this time. She ran her clogs over the ribbed surface of the loading ramp.

'Another woman came who had once lived there,' she said. 'It was only last week. She was in the building at night and was caught and she screamed and they took her away.'

'Who?' Judith asked.

'An ambulance. With lights.'

'I mean, who was the woman?'

Chantal raised her narrow shoulders. 'No idea. She was old. And really terrible. She took dirt and threw it at the house and then rubbed it over herself. Creepy.' Chantal shuddered.

'Do you know where they took her?'

'To the Stasi home.'

'Where?'

'You know, where the criminals come from.'

'You mean prison.'

'No. The Stasi home. There's lots of old people there.'

Judith flicked the cigarette butt down into the dripping weeds. Chantal could only mean a nursing home or a retirement home. There weren't any Stasi homes. There wasn't any Stasi anymore.

'How do you know that the woman was from back then?'

'The first thing she did was go to the fence. Just like you.'

The rain dissipated. A muffled, stale smell emerged from the inside of the storage hall.

'Where's this home?'

'Down by the old harbour. Behind the tracks. We used to play there. But now we're not allowed over there. Everything is fenced off, and dogs patrol at night.'

'Well then, it's better to steer clear of that. That's dangerous.'

Judith jumped off the ramp. Chantal followed her.

'And you're not allowed to play here either. Didn't you see the sign over there? Caution!'

She pulled Chantal aside, who was just about to step on one of the steel floor panels covered by weeds.

'They are loose down there. If you fall in you'll never get out.'

'OK.'

Chantal didn't look like she would take the advice seriously.

'How old are you?'

'Ten.'

Judith smiled. You were invincible at ten.

They separated up at the road. Chantal ran quickly down the wet cobblestones, so quiet on plastic soles that Mrs Langgut certainly wouldn't hear her when she secretly slipped back into the *Waldfrieden*. Judith waited a couple of minutes before turning over the van's motor and letting it slowly roll down the hill towards the old harbour.

A Stasi home. Amazing what kids managed to make out of whispered words and rumours. The road lead directly into the woods, took a curve to the left and went steeply downhill. Along the road there were the remnants of the restricted area. Concrete shafts, iron plates, wire mesh. This far and no further. Forgotten barbed wire hung limply from the tops of the poles.

She remembered how the harbour was one of the best-guarded areas of the city. The sea shone through the woods, grey as a wool blanket pulled over the sky. Heavy drops were still falling on the windscreen but they came from the treetops, not the sky.

The path became even bumpier and led directly to the old piers. Judith drove past an abandoned little guard-house with barred doors. A sign on a concrete pole was labelled 'Harbour Border.' She rumbled over the potholes and old, rusty rails. It had to be somewhere here. The track wasn't paved with asphalt, just made up of large concrete plates, and led down behind Sassnitz along the water and to the right toward Mukran, but then was lost in that direction in barren wasteland after just a few metres.

Judith turned off the engine, got out and went over to a small path as close to the water as the old foundations allowed. She looked to the north: the view went past several sheds to the former ferry terminal. Misty screens of fog hung over the woods and the roofs of the buildings. The city was steaming. The rectangular silhouette of the spa hotel sat enthroned over the shore.

She looked to the south: wasteland. In the distance there were a couple of cranes, a passenger ship was approaching from the sea and kept course for the new piers and terminals. Chantal had been mistaken.

Judith turned around, went back, and was just about to get back into the van when she stopped, stock still. On the other side of the path, in the woods, surrounded by a thick green hedge and a rusty fence, lay a pretty white house. Perhaps it had been a hotel once. Maybe an official agency – the old harbour master's office? Or a sanatorium.

Judith slammed the open car door. Or maybe an old folks' home.

Massive lilac and cherry laurel bushes almost completely covered the fence. As far as Judith could determine, the property couldn't be accessed from the shore. As she approached she heard dogs barking.

There was a house. There were dogs.

Judith turned around and went back to the van. She wouldn't make the same mistake that she had with Mrs Langgut. She would shower, change clothes, and then come back well prepared.

The air smelled fresh. She suddenly realised what was missing. The stench of diesel and fish.

11

TT sat in front of his laptop and twiddled his thumbs. Judith Kepler was fairly straightforward. She had a bank card from a savings bank, health insurance, and had been talked into joining an animal welfare association six months ago. Rent, telephone, and electricity were paid by direct debit. Two times per month she withdrew cash from her account and apparently used it to pay for all of her daily expenses. A couple of times she used her bank card, usually at a record store at Nollendorfplatz, where, compared with her usual expenditure, she went on a spending spree and never left without having spent at least two hundred euros. She had an internet connection, but her computer wasn't turned on, so the Trojan was a no go. She didn't own a vehicle, and she almost never used her landline. At most, she'd order a pizza or call the company, Dombrowski Facility Management. Her phone had last been logged around noon in front of a hospital in Berlin Schöneberg.

A fairly unspectacular life for a woman who was interested in the intelligence services. But that was normal. The more inconspicuous, the more interesting. He decided to shoot off a passport query. Maybe she had gold in the Caymans or a safe deposit box in Liechtenstein.

No luck. Judith Kepler didn't even have a valid passport, and she would have to renew her ID soon. His stomach began to growl. In expectation of being fired, TT hadn't eaten anything all day. The car park in front of his window was already almost empty. The BND was just another government agency: office hours were sacred.

He reached for his phone and called Kellermann. But he only got Dearest Clary on the line, who relayed a load of nonsense about a meeting. Six o'clock, on a Monday evening? With an empty car park? In any case, there weren't any more meetings in Pullach. Unless the Russians were on their way. Ha-ha. TT asked her to deliver the message to Kellerman. Then he decided to call an end to his less than productive day.

He found the temporary visitor ID in his jeans pocket. The gatekeeper knew him and nodded to him briefly. TT tossed the paper into the turnstile bowl and left by the automatic gate, exit monitored by three cameras, and went out to the street to the bus stop.

The cameras should have caught the taxi, which slowly rolled behind TT and only caught his attention by honking.

TT jumped onto the pavement in surprise. The passenger leaned out of the side window, and a mocking smile on the somewhat aged, but still striking face of Quirin Kaiserley appeared. He held four colourful ID cards fanned out in his right hand like aces in a card game.

TT stood still and stared at the plastic cards. Hadn't Kellermann claimed he had them? Not literally, of course, but in the sense that Kellerman held all the cards and therefore his fate?

'Get in.'

TT looked around. No one close by. This was beginning to be interesting.

Judith Kepler stood in front of the entrance to the *Sassnitz Institute and Care Home for German Seniors*. She wore a spotted summer dress made of sweatshirt fabric with elbow-length sleeves. Her hair was loose and fell to her shoulders. Dombrowski wouldn't have even recognised her from up close. She felt strange in her own skin.

The driveway was not on the sea side of the house and was so well hidden that it was almost as if it didn't want be found. A small path through the woods led from the *Strasse der Jugend*, and after several bends, led eventually to a new, white wooden fence. The house lay in the shadow of the trees. Although the sky was still light on this long summer evening, the lights were on in all of the windows. Here, hidden from prying gaze, emerged a property that was almost as substantial as the factory compound, and included lawns, flowerbeds, and abandoned deckchairs. A gravel path led past a fountain to the entrance. The pump had been turned off; water lilies and cattails were reflected on the surface of the water. Stone carvings of mythical creatures with pointed snouts, nymphs, and fish decorated the balustrade. During the day the water probably projected playful arcs into the air.

The impression of long-ago affluence was abruptly dispelled when Judith stepped through the front door into the massive hallway. Shiny linoleum, new stair runners and an ugly neon lamp destroyed any remnants of turn-of-the-century charm. Corridors with rooms leading off ran to the left and right. In front of one door a hospital bed stood empty.

A woman in a white uniform left a room with a tray in her hands. She noticed Judith and came striding over. A small nametag identified her as Sister Reinhild.

'I'm sorry but visiting hours are over.'

She had the ageless radiance of a Florence Nightingale and an appearance intended to seem friendly. Under the surface an authority hard as nails. Judith was familiar with this kind of woman. She had prepared herself. She thought of the sentence she practised to herself several times on the way there, but it wasn't as easy to say it out loud. Her heart pounded in her chest. She only had one chance and only one name. She stepped onto unstable terrain. The first words she said would be critical. They would either carry her forward or sink her.

'My name is Judith Kepler. I want to see Martha Jonas.'

'Martha Jonas?'

Sister Reinhild must have noticed the slight hesitance in Judith's voice. She furrowed her brow and was just about to say no, when Judith recognised her mistake.

'If you could please make it possible. *Please.*' Of course. Please, please, please. How could she forget? 'I know I've come at an inopportune time. But it is very important.'

And please say that she still exists. That she's alive and that she's here. She was the only other person at the *Yuri Gagarin Children's Home* who also looked up at the moon. And at night, on her rounds, sometimes she tucked me in. Judith knew she should have looked for her much earlier. But who looks for a woman who was part of the system that broke you?

'Come back tomorrow morning at nine.'

Sister Reinhild considered the conversation to be finished. She went to a serving trolley that stood next to the entrance.

There she put down the tray. Judith followed her. A cheese sandwich, untouched; a small, half-empty bowl of fruit compote; a pot of tea.

'That is too late. I have to catch the ferry to Trelleborg tonight. It won't take long. I have a message for her.'

'Our guests have a daily routine.'

'I know. I wouldn't disturb her for long. But I know Ms Jonas is waiting for me.'

Sister Reinhild looked indecisively at a screened-off nook in the hallway. Like everything else in this house, it had been a later addition and looked like it. Schedules on the wall, a desk with a visitor registry, and several filing trays. Under the desk stood a Styrofoam box which was used to transport food or medication.

'What was your name?'

'Judith Kepler.'

Sister Reinhild drew her lips into a thin smile, as if she had just remembered something. But she regained control of herself almost immediately.

'Ms Jonas hasn't received visitors for years now.'

'But, no,' Judith answered. 'Someone must have been here just recently.'

If Borg had really come via Sassnitz, if she had really found the Care Home for German Seniors, if she had visited Martha Jonas, then that meant that . . . Judith held her breath.

'A woman from Sweden,' she uttered. 'Christina Borg.'

'Are you her relative?'

'No,' Judith said. 'Not exactly. We were at the same children's home.'

'In Sassnitz?'

'Yes.'

'So you were at *Gagarin*. Why didn't you say that right away?'

Sister Reinhild went to the nook. On the table in front of her lay the visitor registry. Judith looked around. There was a room chart on the wall. She tried to cast a glance at it unobtrusively. The nurse opened the book.

'Ms Jonas is almost never visited by her former charges. Very unfortunate, I think. These people did so much, sacrificed themselves, and ultimately took the blame for others.'

'Yes, very unfortunate,' Judith heard herself say. 'But it's said this is a house of shelter.'

The nurse didn't look up. She was studying the entries, row for row. 'A pleasant thought. Yes, we're something like that. A house of forgotten heroes.'

She shut the visitor registry.

'There is one entry, in fact. Also without notice. Which surprises me, because Ms Jonas may only be visited with the approval of Dr Matthes. At least those are the orders.'

'Is she ill?'

'No. Dr Matthes is the director of this house and also a psychologist. We have orders to call him over if there are unexpected visitors. There have been occurrences of people sneaking in here and bothering our guests. So-called "victims" who attack the so-called "perpetrators."'

Judith nodded. A house hidden in the woods, isolated patients, a psychologist that ruled over the right of access. And a home for those for whom the new categories of guilty and innocent meant nothing. Spending their quiet sunset years undisturbed in the circle of kindred spirits.

The nurse appeared to have come to trust her. She ushered Judith out of the nook and into the hallway.

'We have several very prominent guests,' she said. 'But we make a point to avoid things like barriers and professional security. We take care of things in a different way. Unfortunately Dr Matthes isn't here this evening. But I'm sure tomorrow he will allow a visit by a nice woman like you. Come back tomorrow.'

'But Ms Jonas wasn't important. She was only a care assistant.'

'It's not our job to judge that.'

'I want to see her. Please.'

'Before that Dr Matthes would like to . . .'

'Does she live here as a free person of her own free will?'

The nurse's eyes narrowed. 'Of course.'

'Then I'd like to see her now.'

The wheels behind the smooth forehead of the nurse were spinning. She looked at her watch and cast a stealthy glance down both of the corridors that branched off from the main hallway. There was no one to be seen.

'Well, then. Go. Room eleven. Down to the left.'

'Thank you.'

Nurse Reinhild watched her go and then hurried back to the reception.

Judith knocked and opened the door quietly. No lights were on in the room. The treetops cast it in a shadowy twilight. It could have been an office, with the standard austere filing cabinet if there hadn't been the bed.

It stood against the wall; a crucifix hung over the headboard. An emaciated, old woman lay in the bed. She bore only a vague resemblance to the woman who Judith had known. The sturdy care assistant from back then with the ruddy complexion had become a skeleton, the skin sagging from a delicate body, a testament to age and illness.

She had her eyes closed. Perhaps she was asleep, perhaps she was only dozing to pass the hours. Judith sat down on the edge of the bed and touched Martha Jonas's hand. She felt hot, as if she had a fever.

'Ms Jonas?'

A twitch passed over the sunken cheeks. She must wear dentures because the slightly opened lips spread back over a toothless jaw and formed a black hole in the place of a mouth. Judith studied the stranger's face. She searched for the hate but found only a confused mixture of fear, rage, and sudden empathy. Martha Jonas had been the only person who had occasionally shown some kindness. Never enough to truly stand up for her wards, but a stolen stroking of a head, a plate with sandwiches, quickly and secretly brought down to the cellar in the middle of the night, a lullaby when someone cried and couldn't numb the pain inside. Judith was touched by the unexpected reunion. She pressed the old woman's hand.

'Ms Jonas?'

The eyelids fluttered. Her mouth moved, as if she wanted to say something. Judith found a glass of water on the nightstand. She lifted it to the old woman's mouth.

'Ms Jonas, are you awake? I need to talk to you.'

Martha Jonas swallowed and opened her eyes. Her dull gaze wandered over Judith's face. At first she looked fearful and uncertain, but then something suddenly kindled. She raised her hand weakly only to let it sink halfway towards Judith's face.

'You?' she whispered.

The pain shot into Judith's heart and she was instantly cata-pulted into the past. It was night, and she stood in a hallway, and a woman bent over her and asked her name.

'Do you recognise me? I'm . . .'

'Christel.' The black hole in Martha Jonas's face transformed into a thin line. She smiled. 'Christel Sonnenberg.'

'What? What are you talking about?'

The old woman's gaze moved over her hair and face. She raised her arms again and finally, her hot hands came to rest on Judith's.

'Were you always this well behaved?'

Sister Reinhild waited for the computer to find the list with the names. It was so long and comprehensive that she had to use the search function. Kepler, Judith. The combination of numbers and letters in the line behind the entry told her what she needed to do. She picked up the telephone, dialled a three-digit number and waited until a familiar voice answered on the other end.

'Judith Kepler is here.'

She listened to what the voice told her, nodded, and hung up.

Sister Reinhild was forty-two years old. She knew little about the fates of those entrusted to her care. Some were old, others ill, most of them were both. In other homes it could lead to unrest when it became known who the nice patient in the next-door room used to work for. This was a privately run house. *The Mutual and Humanitarian Society*, or MHS, had the same problem as all the organisations that supported an unbiased ver-sion of the GDR past: its members weren't getting any younger. Dementia was a dangerous illness. People forgot. First the little things, then the more important ones. And at some point they forgot they had signed a confidentiality agreement.

Sister Reinhild had also signed one. In those turbulent times before the wall came down, when not only a country, but an entire system had suffered irreparable damage, she had done so consciously and with deep conviction. When bananas and the freedom to travel were at the top of wish lists, she and the last decent people like her recognised that countries and systems might change but not loyalty. Here her wards found a place where they were safe from persecution and malice and the like. It was rumoured that the high standard of living was not just thanks to the support from the MHS, but also from some other low-key endowment funds from West Germany. The discretion that surrounded the house was valuable – not only for its inmates, but for what some still called the 'new' government.

And if anyone came to disturb the calm, action was taken.

Sister Reinhild looked at her watch. Dr Matthes would be here in five minutes.

The tables under the linden trees on the banks of the River Isar were almost completely occupied. It was a warm summer evening, and Quirin felt as if he was on home leave after a long deployment abroad. He had been born in Bavaria, in a little village near the Austrian border, and he missed the blue sky with its faint hint of the Mediterranean. And taverns like the *Rabenwirt*. All the beach cafés and sea lodges in the world couldn't replace an honest Bavarian beer garden.

The hostess nodded at him politely. He didn't know if she remembered him or if she recognised his face from the media. They had frequently conducted their briefings here, accompanied by wheat beer. Evie had always reserved the table way back in the back of the dining room, to the left. The bar staff knew the gentlemen from headquarters. They were well disposed. Pullach didn't have many employers whose employees ran decent expense accounts and had paid decent prices to the locals for the land on which they built their family homes. With the move to Berlin, the real estate prices must have hit rock bottom. Quirin could imagine how the relocation had been received here. Not a good topic on the left bank of the Isar.

The hostess put down two wheat beers and asked for their orders from the menu. TT shook his head. Apparently he had taken to heart the maxim that one doesn't eat with the enemy. His revulsion was hard to miss. Quirin studied the still youthful face of the man opposite and recognised the first, small wrinkles around his eyes. TT must be thirty-four by now. And he still had that pouty expression around his lips, which Quirin remembered well.

Quirin ordered a snack platter. He waited until the hostess had gone to attend to other guests, then placed the ID cards on the table.

'Take them. They're only food for the smartphone grave anyway.'

That's what they called the huge shredder on the first floor of the General Situation, which ate entire file folders and spat them out as dust. If someone was dumb enough to keep their ID cards, phones, and keys in their breast pocket and lean over too far while unloading, then everything fell into the grinder and was lost forever. Along with the plastic cards, three meticulously constructed CVs with cover addresses, bank information and valid personal papers would also disappear into the shredder. A great deal of work destroyed in one moment of carelessness. Judith Kepler should congratulate herself. Not many managed to do that.

TT took the colourful cards and pocketed them.

'Where did you get them from? From that crazy woman with the gas cylinder?'

Quirin took a sip of beer and then wiped his mouth.

'I'll get to that. I assume Kellermann ordered the surveillance of the apartment.'

'I don't know. And if I did, I wouldn't tell you.'

Especially not you. The unspoken addendum hung in the air. Quirin nodded.

'You're loyal. Unlike me. At some point I recognised that you can only serve one master.'

'Sure. The inner voice. And it told you that only other people make mistakes.'

'Sassnitz wasn't about mistakes. It was a betrayal. Three people died. To this day, it remains one of the greatest defeats of the BND in the Cold War.'

'Sassnitz never happened. It's one of the great lies that people like you put out into the world because they haven't been able to find a position after the collapse of the old order. You're out-dated. Even your war against the BND is out-dated. You just don't get that times have changed!'

Quirin looked around but the beer garden was so noisy no one would have heard TT's outburst.

'I thought you were great.' TT hadn't missed Quirin's look, and he bent over and spoke more quietly. 'I looked up to you. Quirin Kaiserley, the madman who had documented the Russian retreat for the CIA. Who took pictures of surface-to-surface rockets from a moving Jeep. Those are the stories they still tell about you, to this day. And then, suddenly, someone brainwashes you and you turn around completely.'

'The Wall fell. We had new information. We were betrayed in Sassnitz.'

'Is that what the Stasi says? They screwed you over! There was no mole. We would have found it long ago. You fucked up back then. Just you. You can't handle that.'

'I wasn't alone.'

TT, who had raised his glass, put it back down.

'There were six of us.'

12

Heavy flakes of snow fell and danced in the orbs of the street lanterns. The radio was playing the American Top Forty.

Quirin hummed along with the refrain to *Islands in the Stream*, even though he didn't like the song. The eighties had given the charts nothing but simple pop. He regretted it wasn't Saturday evening when he could have listened to BFBS and John Peel. He drove down Clay Allee, past the American barracks, the movie theatres, and the Post Exchange Store, or PX, reserved for the army. Everything heavily guarded and largely blocked from the gaze of the outside world. The Zehlendorf area of Berlin was as American as Spandau was British and Reinickendorf French and the whole east was Russian. The Western Allies were present, but in a parallel universe, which didn't have much in common with the lives of the people of Berlin.

Quirin had landed at Tegel airport an hour ago on a PanAm jet from Munich. He had rented a VW Jetta and had every reason to hope he'd be on time. In the airplane there had been some deliberation about whether they should land in Hamburg instead due to the snowfall.

After Angentische Allee he turned left and drove up to a metal gate. There were already two dark limousines parked in front of the rolling gate, waiting to be processed. One was armoured and carried the British flag. Christmas carolling with the Commander of the American Sector. Allied holiday sing-alongs under the Christmas tree of the intelligence service station, a must for everyone who belonged to the tiny class of political and business elites in the Western part of the city.

Quirin waited in his Jetta until it was his turn, and a sergeant from the Military Police took his ID and invitation. The massive iron gate rolled to the side to reveal the snow-covered, expansive garden. Every tree, every bush, and every windowsill in the compound was decorated with glowing lights. Quirin didn't know the lady of the house, but she must have grown up in Disneyland. The British car rolled off towards the illuminations.

'Mr Kaiserley?'

The sergeant reappeared next to his car.

'Please follow us.'

The sergeant motioned him through the gate and pointed to a car park. There were two cars parked there with Munich plates. Kellermann and Langhoff were already here. He parked next to them and climbed into a Jeep that had appeared out of the blue. His ID and invitation would stay at the security checkpoint until he left.

The lights were reflected in the black helmets of the military police. They wore sleeve covers initialled MP, smiled pleasantly, and made jokes about the similarities between the Great Wall of China and an American chief's villa – both were visible from space – and while Quirin was still laughing, they had already arrived at the back entrance of the basement apartment. The MPs transferred their ward to a different GI wearing a full dress uniform who directed him inside with his white gloves.

The sounds of piano and singing floated through the house. *Hark! The Herald Angels Sing*. There was the scent of warm food and cinnamon. A staircase led up to the ground floor where the reception rooms were located. Lots of red, lots of gold, lots of glass, lots of lots. Thick carpets, heavy silk curtains, polished, dark wood panelling. Quirin had stumbled up there once, looking for the bathrooms and had a brief opportunity to cast a glance around the massive round table in the entry hall, the fireplace with artificial fire and the huge oil paintings, before two very friendly young gentlemen caught up with him and accompanied him back downstairs.

Down below were the rooms where the action took place.

Now there was a real fire in the hearth. Kellermann stood at the bar and was looking for something strong. He briefly nodded to Quirin and paid him no further notice. Langhoff, Section Chief Region East Procurement, was admiring a painting by Thomas Cole, *Hudson River and Catskill Mountains*. Langhoff was a tall, slender man with an artificially noble attitude, which Quirin liked as much as he liked Langhoff's habit of constantly looking at his polished fingernails while speaking.

There were only two other people in the room. A very young woman, who looked as if she might be Puerto Rican, was talking to a man who had just turned toward the door. He came over to greet Kellerman.

'Lindner,' he introduced himself. He sounded nervous. Looking for allies who would help him through the evening, Quirin thought. 'Richard Lindner.'

Lindner must have been in his mid-twenties, so just a couple of years younger than Quirin. He was a good-looking man, but someone who seemed out of place in these circles. He wore a cheap suit, and his tie hung slightly crooked. He was nervous. No one else was. It was an unofficial meeting under Allied supervision. Everyone in the room knew that except for Lindner.

Quirin introduced himself. The Puerto Rican gave him a Colgate smile.

'Angelina Espinoza. I work at the American Embassy in Bonn-Bad Godesberg.'

Her German was nearly unaccented. Quirin returned the handshake. She wore a navy blue suit with flat pumps that would have seemed boring on every other woman. Although she was so young, her behaviour left no doubt: she knew what she wanted and she knew how to get it. Top university, Department of Foreign Affairs, career. Hungry and ambitious. He also guessed that she had an affluent background, but then again maybe her diamond studs were too small for that.

In the meantime Kellermann had found the bar and served himself a double shot. He swirled the tumbler and approached Quirin, keeping Angelina's backside in view.

'Shitty weather,' he said in greeting and raised his glass. 'I hate Berlin in the wintertime.'

Angelina laughed, Lindner remained silent. Langhoff pulled himself away from the painting and graced them with his attention.

'Kaiserley. Always around when there's a chance to fill your pockets, am I right?' Langhoff patted him affectionately on the shoulder. 'One of our best men. He'll recruit anything that moves before you can count to three.'

'Shitty weather,' Kellermann repeated.

He had an alcohol problem. Everyone knew that. No one talked to him about it.

A waitress with a starched apron approached and offered an approximation of a mini-hamburger. Lightly roasted beef tartar with caviar and crème fraîche. Kellermann shovelled one into his mouth and refused the proffered napkin. Lindner declined. He hadn't come here to eat. His gaze repeatedly returned to the door, behind which an additional MP was keeping guard.

'I love Berlin,' Angelina said. 'It's a place with history.'

'Everywhere is,' Kellermann spoke with his mouth full. 'Even the San Andreas Fault. I prefer Düsseldorf or Munich. Clean streets, intelligent people.'

'Hamburg,' Langhoff said, examining his fingernails. He didn't like Kellermann. Quirin, by contrast, could deal with his boss's uncouth manner. They were both action men, rather than manicured theoreticians of culture. 'Are you familiar with Hamburg?'

The question was directed at Angelina.

'Unfortunately not. And you?' She turned to Lindner.

Lindner jumped slightly. Everyone was looking at him.

'No. Bonn more so.'

'How boring.' Kellermann took the next hamburger from the tray. 'Prague, Moscow. St. Petersburg. All places where I don't want to be hanging over a fence dead. Well, that'll change soon.'

Quirin wondered what Kellermann was referring to. There had been another change of power in Moscow. The Russians hadn't had much luck with their helmsmen. Andropov and Cherenkov had come and gone, and the military had just recently installed the latest marionette, a certain Gorbachev, who probably wouldn't survive long either. The US was using the infighting to badger the Russians a little. They were supporting some madmen in Afghanistan who would have liked to bomb their occupiers out of the country. The Cold War had flared up a little on the external borders of NATO and the Warsaw Pact, but had otherwise entered into a phase of bored stagnation. Nothing was moving for the better, but luckily also not for the worse.

'For him, I mean. He's supposedly at a conference,' Kellermann said, motioning to Lindner with his half-eaten hamburger. 'He flies back to Budapest tonight. If Applebroog cooperates. What's the situation?'

Angelina shrugged her delicate shoulders. 'I don't want to speak for the Commander. But the plane is waiting at Tempelhof.'

Lindner looked like someone who would get sick at the very thought of flying. Quirin wondered whether he was a prospective agent from the East, a double agent or a defector. That he would fly back to Budapest that night ruled out defector. He seemed too inexperienced to be a double agent. What remained was a prospective agent: a man to install in the power centres of the opponent and let him climb the ranks. Lindner probably didn't even know what he was getting himself into.

'Gentlemen?' The sergeant with the white gloves returned. The MP at the door stood at attention. 'The Commandant, United States Commander Berlin and Commander, US Army Berlin, General Charles Henry Applebroog.'

The sergeant hadn't completely finished when Applebroog came through the door, a glass of punch in hand. He was a friendly seeming, average-sized man who looked just as good in a uniform as in a tuxedo. A diplomatically gifted soldier – a combination that Quirin wished occurred more frequently in positions of power. As the most influential Commander in Berlin he usually decided things that affected the Three-Powers status in West Berlin, but did so with a refreshing restraint and in a way that let the people of Berlin believe they were still governed by their elected mayor. He had probably been standing one floor above them and chatting with the Brits about the speed limit on the city autobahn.

'Let's do without the formalities. My name is Charles.'

He shook Lindner's hand. Quirin suppressed a grin at the thought of the terrified Lindner addressing Applebroog by his first name. Not even Kellermann had the gall to do that – even after his fourth drink.

Applebroog turned to each of them individually, greeted them each with a handshake and finally asked the group to have a seat in the armchairs.

'Lindner,' he said. 'Where are you from?'

'Gnevezin. Near Anklam. In Mecklenburg.'

Neither the Commander nor the assembled elite of intelligence agencies appeared to have ever heard of Gnevezin. Applebroog still nodded pleasantly. He turned to Kellermann.

'This young man would like to work with us?'

The young man gulped. His Adam's apple bobbed in his throat. Quirin asked himself why he had been sent into the lion's den unprepared. It was clear this was what Lindner thought this surveillance-proof cellar of the villa was.

Kellermann nodded generously at the guest. 'He's the messenger of an offer that can't be refused, as the Italians would say.'

He looked around, begging for applause. Everyone was silent. Quirin asked himself how long someone with so many problems could retain a leadership position in the service. The broken marriage, the alcohol, and the town house in the Fasanengarten district of Munich that was far too expensive, even for a department head. Kellermann needed a coup, something to kick-start his career and his life back into motion. He was only ten years older than Quirin but he looked like he was on his third life.

Lindner looked at the floor. No one would get anything out of him at the moment. Langhoff had been nervously kneading his hands, waiting for the opportune moment. It appeared to have arrived.

'Mr Lindner approached one of our men at the edges of the Fototec in Budapest. He would like to leave the GDR and offers us . . .'

Langhoff hesitated. Pausing for effect. He was one of the many people waiting for Kellermann to make a blunder. Quirin had never participated in these games. He was a man for field work. He didn't get his adrenaline kicks at a desk.

Langhoff looked around. '. . . the complete list of real names of the GDR foreign intelligence service. All of the agents working for the East in the West. Germans, but also Americans, British, French. We could uncover them all at once.'

Quirin held his breath. He asked himself if he was the only person in the room who had no idea what was going on. Then he noticed that Angelina Espinoza was also fighting to maintain her composure. American Embassy Bonn-Bad Godesberg. Tell that to the birds. Ambassadorial staff didn't belong at intelligence service meetings. They sang Christmas carols at orphanages but they weren't present when a peephole appeared in the Iron Curtain.

Applebroog smiled. He knew about this. Otherwise he wouldn't have provided a plane and overridden the ban on night flights. Kellermann and Langhoff also knew. Of course. So it seemed that Quirin and Angelina were the only ones stumbling around in the dark. She probably belonged to her country's foreign service. Typical: the ones who took the rap were always the last to find out why.

'What does it look like?' Quirin asked. He was frustrated by the others' advantage. But such an idea was already logistically impossible. As far as they knew – and their knowledge about these Pandora boxes was more than flimsy – the files of the Stasi agents were located in file cabinets kilometres long.

Lindner was silent. The fire crackled. The ice cubes in Kellermann's drink clacked. Applebroog looked pensively into his punch.

'Mr Kaiserley is right.' Applebroog studied Lindner. He sank even further into the leather padding of the Chesterfield. 'Of course we need information. Proof.'

Proof. The Ministry of State Security was a fortress. There was no proof. Quirin wasn't surprised that Lindner would now apparently rather sink into the San Andreas Fault than this sofa. Applebroog lost a bit of his paternal charm. He gave a sign to the sergeant with the white gloves, who then closed the door in front of the MP post.

'Please don't misunderstand us, Mr Lindner. No one is forcing you to do anything. I want to reassure you: you can get up and go at any time. We'll take you directly back to Budapest, and no one will find out where you were tonight. You have my word.'

Complete nonsense. Lindner would see neither his Mitropa hotel in the Eastern bloc nor the GDR. Instead, he could look forward to a long time under a sort of caring siege.

'The word of the United States of America,' Applebroog added. Even worse.

'She wanted to go to Paris,' Lindner said so quietly that Quirin hardly understood him. 'She has always dreamed of that.'

'Is this about a woman? Your wife? Then we'll fulfil her dream.' Applebroog smiled. 'So we're talking about two passports.'

'Three. We have a child. I'll only negotiate if they're the right ones. I already said that in Budapest. Three passports and smuggling us over.'

Applebroog exchanged a brief glance with Kellermann. Kellermann motioned to the sergeant with the white gloves with his glass.

'Is that a problem?' The Commander's polite question was directed at Langhoff.

Langhoff shrugged his shoulders. 'In twenty-four hours, including cover story. Ironclad.'

'And a visa for the US, of course,' Applebroog added. 'You're in Times Square within three days. And then Paris, for all I care.'

Quirin didn't miss how elegantly the Commander involved his country in the operation. And without any risk on his part. He asked himself how high the price had been and who he had negotiated it with. Quirin guessed Langhoff. Kellermann was digging his own grave if he kept up the boozing.

'In three days, Mr Lindner. Three days. Time to practise your English. *Et français, naturellement.*'

This was absolutely out of the question. An operation like this needed time. Preparation. It had to be planned into the finest details. Applebroog was laying the bait before there was even a trap.

'We won't leave you hanging,' Langhoff said. 'We'll be with you, every step of the way, and watch over you. You're at exactly the right place. But we need security. Information. Tell us what you know about this index. We can't buy a pig in a poke.'

Lindner looked imploringly at Applebroog. The Commander nodded at him. He was back to Charles. A benevolent advisor, a wise friend. It was like a training film from the seventies. Open doors, but pressure in the right direction. Lindner took a deep breath.

'3,000 in total, with NATO top secret information, real names and aliases, evaluation reports, administrative details, filmed by the Real Name Registry at Section XII in Berlin.'

'Filmed?' Quirin asked.

Kellermann raised his hand testily. He didn't like interjections. 'Why only 3,000? We're aware of sixty or seventy operations.'

'A file doesn't necessarily mean that the person concerned is an agent,' Lindner explained. 'We've basically separated the wheat from the chaff.'

This was enormous. The best-case scenario. Quirin shook his head lightly. How would a man like Lindner get at such information? Impossible. Someone in the innermost sanctum of the Stasi, the holy of holies, would have to take every single index card in their hand, check it, and copy it. That might work at the local residents' registration office at some small town in the middle of West Germany, but not at the Ministry of State Security of the GDR.

'Where?' Applebroog asked. 'Where do they keep it?'

'In Berlin. Normannen Strasse, building seven, second mezzanine.'

Quirin bit his lip so he wouldn't interrupt again. The Stasi filming its agent index cards. That was something new. The security measures must be insurmountable. And then someone like Lindner comes along, a pushover, a handsome boy, but definitely not a spy, and announced he could serve them the essence of evil on a silver platter.

The sergeant with the white gloves joined the circle uninvited and took a seat next to Applebroog. He straightened the sharp creases in his trousers.

'Films or jackets?' he asked

'Films.'

'Roll film? Sheet film?'

'In this case roll film.'

'Make?'

'Orwo-DK 5, unperforated, sixteen millimetre.'

'Camera?'

'Carl Zeiss Jena Dokumator microfilm camera.'

It was so quiet that they could hear the water in the logs evaporating in the fireplace. A quiet hissing that was vaguely reminiscent of the whistle of a kettle. The sergeant looked at Applebroog, and nodded subtly. It was the strangest quiz that Quirin had ever witnessed.

The Commander motioned to the sergeant. The man got up, went over to the fireplace and came back with a box of Cohibas.

Applebroog opened it and offered them around the circle of gentlemen. Kellermann took one, the rest declined with thanks.

'Who are you?' Quirin asked.

Lindner looked at him with such surprise, as if only now did he notice that he wasn't alone with the Americans.

'I'm a precision engineer. I develop cameras of various kinds. In the West, I worked for a company in Leverkusen and delivered information to East Berlin.' He cast an unsure glance at Kellermann. 'In close cooperation with your service, of course. Beyond that, I was involved in the development of table-top devices.'

'How did you get to the films?'

Lindner's Adam's apple bounced again. Maybe he built good cameras. Maybe for Agfa, maybe for Carl Zeiss Jena. Maybe even for the Stasi. But he couldn't know what was done with them in a Stasi photography lab in East Berlin under the highest levels of security and out of the public eye. Quirin would have liked nothing more than to get up and leave. This man was a nobody. He might have detailed knowledge and access to all the technical information, but you could also get that if you showed up with a pair of Levi's and approached a student at the State Archive Administration in Potsdam and asked her to make copies of a couple of term papers.

'I can't tell you,' Lindner whispered.

Applebroog puffed on his Cohiba and enveloped them in smoke. He had clearly envisioned the path of the conversation differently. Kellermann and Langhoff stared at the table. It was made of rosewood and decorated with carvings. Cuban cigars in the basement of the American Commander.

Angelina, seated next to Lindner, leaned forward.

'We just want to be sure that everyone gets what they want. You get the passports, we get the film.'

'What happens if something goes wrong?'

'That won't happen.'

'And if it does?'

'Then we'll pay your bounty.' Applebroog had enough of Lindner's nerves. 'The German Federal Republic, of course. But if you're not interested – there's the door.'

The sergeant went into motion.

'No,' Lindner said quickly. 'I want to. We want to.'

'Then please tell us now how you want to access the best-kept secret in the Ministry of State Security.'

Lindner gulped. He looked everyone in the eyes, one after another. Even Quirin was curious again.

'It's very simple,' the man said. 'My wife. She's the one doing the photographing.'

13

'Knock it off. I don't want to hear those old stories anymore.'

TT took a sip of his wheat beer and put the glass down so hard that it spilled over the rim. 'That's all water under the bridge.'

'It would have been a betrayal the likes of which the entire Eastern bloc had never seen. Maybe the wall would have fallen sooner. Maybe it would still be standing today. History would have been rewritten.'

'Dream on. It never happened.'

'I was supposed to smuggle them. Three people. A man. A woman. A child. They had put their lives on the line. And I was young, I was hungry. I thought that it would be an adventure. I didn't know what betrayal meant. Not for those who do the betraying, not for those who are betrayed. Do you know, TT? Do you know who you're working for and why?'

'Fuck you.'

TT stood up, but Quirin's hand shot out. His grip was so firm that TT's face twisted in pain.

'Sit down,' said Quirin. 'And listen to me.'

TT looked around. Several guests were exchanging looks. The waitress was making her way towards them, snack platter in hand. Quirin had the public on his side. They had to behave in

Rabenwirt. The young man took his seat again, the hostess set the plate down and left. Quirin unwrapped the cutlery from the napkin and tried to sound as normal as possible.

'Things like this happen,' he continued. 'We planned, prepared everything, had the passports and had gone through the exact procedure a dozen times. The CIA kept a low profile; it was our job to get the three out. Everything went according to plan – until Sassnitz. Then they disappeared. Without a trace.'

'Because they took you for a ride. Because they got scared.'

'They're dead, TT.'

'How do you know? Maybe they're living contentedly in a cottage somewhere in Oderbruch?'

'They had a car accident that same night in Romania. As much I'd like to believe it, TT, no one can be at the train station in Sassnitz and crash into a ravine in the Carpathian mountains at the same time.'

TT didn't say anything. Quirin offered his plate, but TT declined.

'I needed years to get a grip on it. Then reunification happened. CIA and BND shared offices in Berlin. I requested a transfer. The retreat of the Russians and so on.'

TT nodded. Tales from the times of transition. His face said it all.

'Our American friends still had their network of agents in the foundering GDR. I received a tip that there were still files on a certain Richard Lindner in Schwerin. In Berlin everything had already landed in the shredders. I went to Schwerin to the old Stasi branch office on Demmlerplatz. But I came too late. The shredders there were already smoking. Nothing about Lindner, nothing about that kamikaze mission from the mid-eighties.

All that was left was a cross-reference. A single, tiny note from a completely different department. From another service.'

TT furrowed his brow. Cross-references were dicey. Usually they couldn't be used because they didn't have any validity as evidence.

'Cover addresses and drops belonging to the CIA,' Quirin said. 'Staff and Management Section Department II D.'

Quirin paused for a moment. The establishment of the internal security services in the new German states. Kresnick, who had been sent to Mecklenburg from Wiesbaden in those crazy years, was a bean-counter in his head and a cowboy at heart. He was the one who had given Quirin the tip.

'The night that the handover of the microfilms should have happened, there was an incident in Sassnitz. I don't know exactly what happened, I only know that someone informed the CIA. It was a security Level III message. *HumInt Red* with the directive that it should be passed on to the allied services. Human Intelligence, red. That meant: an operation cover was blown. We should have taken action immediately. That night Lindner was a citizen of the Federal German Republic. All three were under Allied protection! Maybe we still could have saved them! At least one of them was *HumInt Red* – that means a CIA agent had hidden someone, found someone, or knew the hiding place of someone we absolutely had to get out. Immediate establishment of contact!'

Quirin was almost shouting now. TT looked around but the noise level was still high enough that no one had noticed his outburst.

'Why didn't you do anything?'

'We didn't know about it. The message was intercepted.'

TT looked at Quirin for a long time. Then he finished his beer. He wiped his mouth and searched his pockets for enough change to pay. He didn't understand.

'And I'm looking for that person, TT,' Quirin said quietly. 'The one who intercepted that message. For twenty-five years. He has three people to answer for. He also betrayed us. And when the call for help came, he destroyed that too. But the woman who could have helped me was murdered in Berlin. In front of your eyes, TT. Those were your cameras that filmed it.'

Quirin turned away and stared at the Isar.

'Applebroog, Kellermann, Espinoza, Lindner, Langhoff, me. One of us is the mole.'

He heard TT put a few coins on the table and get up. Quirin raised his hand in farewell, but didn't look at him. It was pointless.

'Should I have this packed up for you?'

TT motioned to the snack platter that still lay on the table, untouched.

'No,' Quirin said.

'Then come now. I can't hack into the surveillance material for you. But just this once I'll look in my smart little blue book for you. Once – and then never again.'

TT turned around and left. Quirin leapt up and rushed after him.

Judith bent a little closer to Martha Jonas's mouth. It was almost dark in the room. The woman's voice had grown gradually quieter over the last few minutes. Now her breath seemed exhausted. The words had become so unclear that Judith hardly understood them. Martha Jonas had told an outrageous story. One in which two children were switched.

One girl disappeared; the other had taken her place. And if this story was true, then the only true thing about Judith's file was the photo.

Judith listened and registered the information but she didn't analyse it. Not yet. She soaked up every word, but she didn't think about them. She could think later. As soon as she had left the house. But not now. Every second counted now.

'All these years I thought they would come to get you.' Martha took a deep breath, but her strength was ebbing.

'Who?' Judith stiffened. 'My parents?'

'No, Christel. You don't have parents anymore. Your mother . . .'

'Where is she? What happened to her?'

'Christel, forgetting was for your own protection.'

'Forgetting what?'

Panic crept up inside Judith. Martha Jonas would fall asleep any second; she was exhausted, ill and fatigued. All of this dredging up the past was taking its toll.

'What should I forget? Martha! Tell me! How did I get into the home? Who was my mother? What happened, for heaven's sake?'

'Heaven isn't in Lenin's palace.'

'What?'

'I did everything I could do.'

Judith rubbed Martha Jonas's hand. 'I know, I know.'

'I hid your file behind a framed photograph of Yuri Gagarin. In the attic. I thought maybe you would come back one day. Never . . . I never heard from you, even after reunification . . . And then the others came . . . and they wanted to find you. Then I went back to the home one more time – and of course they caught me.'

She winked at Judith. 'I acted as if I had gone crazy. But everything's OK upstairs. Everything's OK.' She tried to tap her forehead with her finger but she was too weak. 'I've been sick since then. I need medication . . . I'm so tired. So tired.'

Her head fell slightly to the side.

'Ms Jonas? Ms Jonas! Martha, please don't fall asleep!'

Judith felt the teacher's cheeks. Tears were running down her face, but she didn't blink, didn't wipe them away. There was no time for that. She had to get the old woman to talk.

'Martha! Martha . . .'

The despair had her again. The cellar, the beatings, and a promise that this woman had given her, even if it had been a lie. A scream welled up from inside her, that almost suffocated her.

'I was always well behaved, Martha. Always. But my mother never came back. Is she . . . what happened to her?'

'You have to go,' the old woman whispered. 'No one followed up. No one helped. So I erased your past until your new name and your new life had taken hold. I had to erase you, to protect you. Completely erase you. Delete you.'

Judith raised her head. She heard steps in the hallway, and they weren't the quiet footfalls of the nurse. Martha Jonas's eyes grew wide. Pure fear suddenly twisted her features.

'Too late,' she said. 'Too late. They're coming to get you now.'

TT sat in front of his laptop and established a connection to BND headquarters. There was nothing new on Judith Kepler.

The story had touched him. Kaiserley had had three people disappear off his radar screen. That alone would propel everyone into such a deep career hole that they would never again see the light of day. Then, after all this time, a mysterious person surfaced and offered something that was suddenly important for a lot of people. The ancient microfilms – and this time complete. The woman was murdered; the film vanished. And a cleaning lady, of all people, had stumbled into the picture, and she knew more than she should.

Rosenholz.

TT looked at Kaiserley, who stood on the balcony and down at the construction site that got TT out of bed every morning at six. What the hell had got into him, taking this man along? Maybe it was that he had suddenly looked so tired. TT only remembered him as a warrior. A warrior who marched into his defeats with head held high. They hadn't seen each other in years. Suddenly TT had a notion of how relentlessly time, age, and failure could chip away at a person.

He stood up and went outside.

'Sassnitz,' TT said. '*Yuri Gagarin Children's Home*. There was a Judith Kepler there. She was ten years old and then she went astray. Arrested as a minor, a thief, junkie, the whole she-bang. I'm guessing she lies every time she opens her mouth. She'll have seen you on Westerhoff and wants to make herself important.'

'Where is she?'

'She lives in Marzahn, Marzahner Promenade 31. She went to work on time and clocked out just as punctually. She's probably painting the town red and partying.'

'Phone number?

'Here.'

TT passed Kaiserley the slip of paper. While he was dialling the number, TT plucked a withered leaf from his tattered balcony greenery. He just didn't get around to watering enough. Kaiserley came back into the room. He paced back and forth impatiently, and finally pocketed his phone in frustration. Then he spotted the scanned photo of Judith on TT's screen.

'It was taken by one of your units.'

TT stopped in the doorway.

'So what?'

'The police in Berlin also have the same one.'

TT pushed off from the doorframe and came closer.

'So where are your recordings? You were watching the apartment around the clock. You recorded the murder. Why do the police have a photo of Judith Kepler but not one of the suspect?'

TT sighed. They were starting back at square one. Give him an inch, and he'll take a mile, and pull you along behind him.

'Maybe because your cleaning lady and the murderer are one and the same person?'

The laptop went into energy-saving mode. The screensaver showed a man, a woman, and a child. TT went to the desk and quickly closed it down. Kaiserley didn't seem as if he'd noticed anything. He probably wasn't interested. There was no space for memories in Kaiserley's life. Unless they involved Sassnitz.

'Judith Kepler is no murderer.'

'OK. So why is she suddenly so interesting?'

'She has something. She knows something. I want to know where she is. And I want to be one step ahead.'

'Honestly. I don't have a clue what you're talking about.'

'I'm talking about the woman who could be the next victim. And this time, TT, you're in the middle of it.'

'Me? Why?'

'Because you're sending her to her doom.'

'I'm just doing my job. OK? Just my job.'

'I told myself the same thing back then.'

Kaiserley grabbed his jacket from the back of the chair and left without looking around or saying thank you. TT exhaled when he heard the door close. But he wasn't satisfied. Not in the least.

Dr Matthes didn't lose any time. He hurried past Sister Reinhild into Martha Jonas's room. The old woman appeared to be alone. But the window was wide open. Matthes looked out into the dark garden, then he shut the window and turned around to Martha Jonas, who seemed to be asleep.

'Where is she?'

He had a pleasant voice. Everything about him was pleasant. Sister Reinhild felt extremely comfortable in his presence, although he wasn't a handsome man in the ordinary sense. In his late sixties, mid-sized, compact, with a nearly bald head and fine, intelligent features. Freckles covered his face and the brows over his bright eyes were almost white. When he removed his glasses during a consultation and looked at his patients, they felt as if he were looking into their souls. Sometimes Reinhild had the feeling he also looked into hers. Then she felt warm with the thought that he could know what she felt for him.

'Ms Jonas, look at me.'

He stepped to the bed and touched Jonas's arm. She slept, deeply and firmly. If she was pretending, then she was doing it well.

'She can't be far,' Sister Reinhild said. 'Should I inform the guards?'

'Yes. Send the dogs out, and order a patrol.'

Patrol was the word for alarm level two, when someone had escaped who couldn't find their way back from the woods alone. Or if an unauthorised person had got into the house and taken pictures, like that reporter from Hamburg recently tried. The doctor felt the patient's pulse. Then he carefully covered her, almost lovingly.

'She'll come back,' he said. It wasn't clear whether he was saying that to Ms Jonas, or to Sister Reinhild.

They left the room together. The doctor's sleeve touched her forearm on the way out.

'I'm sorry,' she said.

The doctor smiled. 'Don't mention it. It isn't your fault. These people are skilled at concealing their true objectives. I'll have Ms Jonas moved to the first floor. The windows are a risk. But I just don't like bars.' He paused. 'No one likes bars.'

Sister Reinhild watched him leave, walking down the hall to the exit. She rubbed her forearm with her hand.

Judith stood under the window with her back to the wall. She was on the sea side of the house. Beyond a small stretch of lawn the slope went gently down to the woods. She pushed off the wall and ran. She heard the dogs even before she reached the fence by the old harbour. They yelped and barked, their triumphal howling betraying the fact they'd picked up the trail.

Judith raced along the fence. She almost slipped on the rubber soles of her trainers, but she just managed to catch herself.

What by day looked like a carelessly secured property with a pleasant green hedge, was now revealed to be an excellently secured terrain. She could hear the dogs coming closer, jumping down the slope, and spreading out. She wanted to climb up the chain-linked fence but it wasn't stable enough to hold her, and barbed wire circled around the tops of the concrete posts.

Judith clenched her teeth, took a running start and jumped. She got a firm grip of the post and grabbed the spikes. Pain raced through her hands like fire, but she didn't let go. She pulled herself up. She threw her right leg over the loop of barbed wire and felt her dress rip and even more barbs tearing into her skin. A greedy growl rang out from the dog immediately below. She pulled back and kicked the animal, her foot landing directly on its muzzle. The dog yelped. Two more shadows flew past from the thicket like arrows. There were calls from above. Hoarse cries. Panic. Pain. Adrenaline. Each one was the stimulant needed to push Judith over the top of the fence, just as the dogs jumped up at her and the first dark figure broke through the thicket.

'Stop where you are!'

Judith jumped. She landed well, stumbled, and ran.

'You there! Stop!'

She stormed off to the left through the broken concrete slabs of the old harbour road. She vaulted the gate with a single leap, pushing off with her hands, and felt pain coursing through her neck. She landed on the other side, and kept running like she'd never run before.

The cries behind began to fade.

The storage halls came into view. She gradually fell into a trot. Her lungs burned and her heart pumped the blood through her body in pulsing beats. She examined her bleeding hands and wondered if she would be able to hold a steering wheel.

At the first opportunity she turned left and reached the grounds of the old fish factory. She slid into the former processing hall, in which only the brown tiles on the walls indicated that fish had once been sorted on a conveyor belt here. Behind a filthy couch set with broken cushions she holed up and waited. When a half-hour had passed and the only living beings that appeared were a couple of rats, she stood up and left.

A white, fat moon sat up in the light summer sky. She fought her way over the overgrown path to the large patch of wasteland that led out to the *Strasse des Friedens*. Half-collapsed wooden sheds, the garages for the transport fleet, stood at the edge of the road. She had hidden the van in one of them.

The first thing she did on reaching the van was disinfect and bandage her hands. Then she climbed into the back and opened the wood panelling, behind which the boys smuggled their cigarettes from Poland. The autopsy report was still there. She screwed the panelling back on and pushed the tool box back in front of it. Then she sat back down on the floor, smoked a cigarette, and allowed herself to think.

She wasn't Judith Kepler. She was Christel Sonnenberg. Christel. Christina. She closed her eyes and tried to remember how that name had made her feel when she'd first heard it from Martha Jonas's mouth. Sonnenberg. Shock. Hot joy. Black oblivion. She whispered the name. She spoke it aloud. She repeated it, as if it was an incantation, a voodoo curse that would suddenly pull back the curtain that had separated her from her past. But words no longer helped. And thinking even less.

Judith jumped up, slammed the back doors and jumped behind the wheel. She started the motor. She backed out of the garage, braked sharply, turned, hit the pedal, and drove the vehicle over the grounds like a bucking horse. She scraped the curb with an ugly grinding sound and hit the road hard. She ground the gears up through the transmission and left the residential towers in her wake, heard the angry honking when she ignored someone's right-of-way, came to the end of the city, and finally reached the green park with its tall, old trees and the brick church.

She parked the car directly in front of the entrance. The gate was still unlocked as it was open in summer until sunset. She pulled the sledgehammer out of the vehicle, not caring that the blood had already soaked through the bandages on her hands and that her dress hung in tatters. An elderly couple came towards her. The man quickly steered his wife to the side and let Judith pass.

Colourful flowers decorated the graves, the wind was rustling in the weeping willow. Judith kept walking. She paid no attention to the visitors who put down their watering cans and straightened as she walked past. She only had eyes for the wall at the end of the cemetery, the narrow strip of lawn before it, and the small, rectangular slabs of black granite. She turned left, stood in front of the third to last, lifted her hammer, and swung. The impact was as loud as a gunshot. She wound up again, as if she wanted to split the earth. The hammer crashed against the stone. Again and again. The tile broke. Little slivers broke off. Judith panted from the effort, the wall carrying the echo of her pounding over the graves. The letter M burst. Then the K. Someone screamed for her to stop. But she didn't want to. She wanted to keep on going until there was nothing left of the stone. She wanted to pulverise it, destroy it, erase it. The heavy iron shattered the letters, one after another, ground the number to dust – irrelevant. Date of birth, date of death – irrelevant. Name – irrelevant. Everything irrelevant. The stone was a stone and it was a lie. And lies had to be destroyed.

14

Quirin Kaiserley reached the Franz Josef Strauss Airport north of Munich in the nick of time, just before check-in closed. He would arrive in Berlin around ten thirty.

By now the police, BND, and internal security all knew about Judith Kepler. Dombrowski, that bastard of a boss, was stonewalling. Regardless of where Kaiserley went, it was like the tortoise and the hare: someone jumped out of the bushes and was already there.

Quirin bought a newspaper, which he wouldn't read, and made his way to the gate. The trip to Munich hadn't accomplished much. Even more: it had shown that he and the boy didn't have much to tell each other. Quirin huffed. 'Boy' was right. TT was an adult and still ran around with a baseball cap and tennis shoes. At his age, Quirin had already had a family. Had assumed responsibility. Was convinced he was doing the right thing. He had taken TT on board after average grades in school and a lot of convincing. Would he ever hear a word of thanks for that? Maybe the reasons for their falling-out lay deeper than he had previously assumed.

Quirin arrived at the gate. The ground hostess already had the microphone in hand to call out his name. Her smile was stressed.

'Mr Kaiserley?'

Quirin handed her the boarding pass. He just wanted to turn off his phone when he saw that TT had tried to reach him. He took the stub back, went through the gate, and dialled.

'You have to turn off your phone. Immediately.'

She closed the gate with a thick rope. Quirin walked down the gangway.

'Yes?'

Music in the background. Quirin thought he could recognise a line from ZZ Top's *Legs*.

'It's me. You called?'

'There's news: And I'm giving you time until tomorrow morning at eight. Not a second more.'

The gangway made a turn. Quirin saw a stewardess standing in the doorway impatiently waiting for him.

'What happened?'

The flight attendant stepped in his way. 'Please turn off your phone.'

'Your cleaning lady was arrested. Vandalism, damage to property, and . . . an additional offence in keeping with paragraph 168 of the penal code.'

'Your phone!'

'Which paragraph?'

'Aren't you listening? You won't be allowed to board!'

TT produced a sound that only vaguely resembled a laugh when distorted by the microphone. Quirin made a hand motion that was intended to show the hysterical stewardess that he had understood her and would follow her instructions. In a second.

'Violation of a grave.'

'What? I don't understand.'

'Me neither. But apparently it's nothing new with this woman. She was arrested, but then slipped out of the police station.'

'Where?'

'You won't believe it.'

On the plane, now, the stewardess followed him through the rows of seats. The passengers gave him curious, impatient, frustrated looks.

'Judith Kepler is in Sassnitz. Funny, right? That is the only reason why I'm talking to you at all. The second reason is that there's actually a search out on her. Kellermann will also know that in exactly ten hours. I can't help you any more than that.'

'Thanks.'

'Forget about it. And something else.'

'Yeah?'

'Don't ever call me again.'

TT hung up. Quirin turned around to the stewardess, turned off his phone and held it under her nose.

'It's off. You see. It's off.'

She turned around on her heel and acted as if she was checking fastened seatbelts.

A little more than an hour later Quirin withdrew a thousand euros from the cash machine at Tegel, the highest amount that he could get out on his bank card. He drove directly into the autobahn lane towards Hamburg-Prenzlau. He had to be careful. He paid cash at a petrol station close to Greifswald, drank a coffee, and looked at an atlas, examining the stretch that lay ahead. Straslund. Rügendamm. Bergen. Sassnitz.

He reached the city a little before two in the morning. He still had six hours to find Judith Kepler, a woman who not only disturbed those resting and asleep, but also those resting in peace. Quirin didn't know which made her more dangerous.

Kellermann opened the door to his town house and listened. He was met with darkness and silence. Eva was long in bed. He loved his job. He also loved Eva, but if someone had put a gun to his chest and had forced him to choose one of the two, he would probably choose his profession.

There had been a time when that would have been different. He didn't know which he regretted more: that the time had passed, or that he managed so remarkably well with the present.

He laid his briefcase on the table in the hall and went quietly into the living room. On the coffee table lay a plate with a liver-wurst sandwich, covered in cling film. At least this kind of care had remained. Something about this gesture touched him. He was familiar with gala dinners and confidential lunches at three-star restaurants. He had licked chocolate from Angelina's belly and shovelled caviar at Uliza Twerkaja 17 in Moscow, before three women – either on the house or courtesy of his host – had anticipated and fulfilled his every desire. He knew the lunch menu at the Chancellery building by heart, but liverwurst sand-wiches he had only at home.

Kellermann took the plate, carried it into the kitchen, and placed it in the refrigerator. He retrieved some ice from the freezer, put a couple of cubes in a glass and went back to the living room. He took a bottle of vodka from the house bar and returned to the sofa. Then he took his smartphone out of his jacket pocket, it was equipped with several special tools that couldn't be purchased in an app store. *Not for at least twenty years*, Kellermann thought. For instance, it was equipped

with a backdoor to TT's laptop, which in contrast to a Trojan, didn't need to be smuggled in. That detail had been there
upon delivery.

The laptop was nothing more than a transit station for the
data that Kellermann could call up at any time. He was interested in the results of TT's research assignment: Judith Kepler,
the cleaning lady. She knew Kaiserley, and it was only a matter of
time until TT would find that out. Kellerman was not only eager
to find out what TT would tell him, but also what he would keep
for himself. That was what he was really interested in.

Kellermann looked up briefly. The door to the hallway was
open. He didn't want Eva to surprise him again. That had already
happened once when he was watching the recording of Borg's
murder, again and again. He had tried to recognise the voice and
something about that dark, masked figure that could give him a
lead. They were terrible images.

He hadn't noticed Eva coming over to him and looking over
his shoulder. He had once sworn to her that he wouldn't let evil
into the house. Now he carried it with him, day after day, and it
had become his shadow. Now he listened. Only the quiet ticking
of the wall clock disturbed the silence. But it was there. He had
sat in the shadows and waited for the past twenty-five years. The
fools had woken it. And he was the biggest of them because he
had believed that it wouldn't reawaken.

He took a deep drink of vodka.

TT had hacked Judith Kepler over the internal police communication network. He had shot a volley of searches across
the internet, and her name had popped up. Arrested in Sassnitz
due to property damage at a cemetery. Kellermann read the
police report, first bored, then with increasing interest. Kepler

had smashed a gravestone. She had subsequently been arrested without resistance and been taken away. At the station she had been asked to take a seat and wait. But Kepler apparently hadn't waited. She simply stood up and left.

A well-behaved girl. Kellermann closed the report. TT would be on her heels.

He opened the window containing Judith's photo one last time. He studied the blurry, grainy picture. He had believed the ghosts of the past would never return. But Borg had awakened them. And Kepler – Kepler just made them furious.

A grave in Sassnitz. They were getting closer. He would follow her every step. She would lead him. If anything was left over from back then, she was the only one who could find it.

He jolted upright because a shadow darted through the hallway. Eva slipped into the bathroom, light falling through the narrow gap beneath the door. Kellermann emptied his glass. He hadn't been able to kick his drinking habit, but Eva had made him reduce it. Eva. He felt required to feel more gratitude. She had given him so much more over the years than he had given her. But to this very day he didn't know why and he didn't dare ask.

He poured another two fingers of vodka over the half-melted ice cubes, raised the glass, and clinked it quietly. He liked the sound. It sounded like the old days, when people still smoked cigars and dictated the agenda of a briefing into a machine for the secretary in the basement of the Chancellor bungalow, agendas which would then magically appear on the desk of Ulbricht and Honecker in East Berlin by Monday morning.

It was so long ago. It had been a different world, divided between NATO and the Warsaw Pact, and a war that couldn't be won. He had always felt passionate about his work. Yet even that had slipped away during these last few years, just like the clear goals and predictable enemies. Defending freedom was a much less glamorous and more boring a task than winning it.

Sometimes he was overtaken by nostalgia for the old days, on nights like these, when he was sitting alone in a house that was actually inhabited by two people. He drank and savoured the chill that transformed into a fire on his tongue. He thought of the woman in the blue smock, who had awakened his hunting instinct, long believed lost. And he thought of the path that lay before her. Judith Kepler would travel far back into it. Back into a war in which all means were justified: love and death. She would find both, because back then there had been no winner, and there never would be.

A light went on in the hall. A figure in a white nightgown appeared in the door, illuminated from behind, so that he recognised the silhouette of her figure beneath the thin fabric.

'Are you coming to bed?' she asked.

'Yes,' he answered.

People die around the clock, about thirty thousand per year in Berlin. There were around two hundred and fifty funeral homes living off of this fact, more or less successfully. For many of them, being open around the clock was a decisive competitive advantage; death doesn't stick to business hours.

Schneider Mortuary advertised online and with full-page ads in the Yellow Pages. The hotline was staffed with students whom Schneider senior had personally selected according to the degree of empathy in their voices and their ability to schedule. This way, the undertaker was only dragged out of bed after ten p.m. in absolute emergencies. Usually patient listening resolved the question of when the firm needed to visit. It was a quiet job. And because, in addition to the hourly pay, a small commission was paid for every successful assignment, Berthold Geissler was quite keen to answer the telephone when it rang in the office shortly before dawn – the rush hour for death.

He answered with the usual greeting and was careful to sound helpful and constructive from the very first second. On the other end was a woman who didn't give her name. She got straight to the point.

'It's about Christina Borg. Cremation with subsequent repatriation to Sweden. What is the address?'

'I, um, don't know,' he answered truthfully. 'Is the deceased a relative of yours?'

'I have a request from the Berlin Senate administration for city development. Cemeteries, green spaces and crematoriums. I work for the Scan Ferries company in Rostock. We have trained personnel and could, if the remains are to be accompanied, provide a cabin. If not, we have a special container in the cargo hold. I'm commissioned to negotiate a tender.'

'Now?'

The woman on the other end laughed quietly. It almost sounded sympathetic.

'We sail around the clock so we also work around the clock. I could wrap up the tender immediately. Then the time would go by faster. What do you do all night long?'

He looked at the clock. Almost four. He was actually waiting for someone to die.

'When there's not much to do I read.'

'What?'

Geissler looked at the book he had put to the side. 'Fractional infinitesimal calculus.'

'Mathematics?'

'Physics. Grad school.'

The woman laughed again. She sounded nice.

'Where do your ferries go?'

'Petersburg, Klaipeda, Travemünde, Bornholm – all over the Baltic, a mixed bag.'

'I'd love to ride along some time.'

'No problem. Send me an email and I'll reserve an outside cabin. I could do something with an employee discount. We're more or less co-workers tonight.'

He heard a loudspeaker announcement in the background.

'That's our ship to Rønne. Have you ever been there?'

'No. I've only been to the Mediterranean.'

'That's a shame.' She sounded as if she was actually sorry. Maybe the women at the ferry company were trained in empathy, too. 'We should fix that. Soon. We have wonderful weather up here. The sea is calm, the sky blue, it's simply a different kind of travel. Rather like it used to be. You're exposed. To the elements, to the decisions of the captain, to the passage of time.'

Berthold Geissler was starting to enjoy the conversation. Not many people called Schneider Mortuary in the middle of the night to talk about the weather and the sea. A strange woman with a warm, enticing voice. He imagined standing at the harbour and waiting for a ship. Or for her.

'Sounds good,' he said. 'What does it cost?'

'Less than you think. Let me know if you're ever up here.'

'I'll do that. What was the name again?'

'Borg. Christina Borg.'

'And you?'

She hesitated. If she gave him her name then he might write to her.

'You know what? I'll write to you. I promise. If you help me with my request. I don't know when forensics will clear the body but you've probably already received the assignment and a contact number.'

Geissler opened up his computer database and typed the name in.

'The urn goes to Tyska Kerkan i Sverige on Köpenhamnsvägen 23, Malmö.'

'Wait a second. I have to write that down.'

He repeated the information.

'Thank you,' the woman said. 'You've been a great help.'

She hung up.

'Hello?' He stared at the phone. 'Hello?

Berthold googled Scan Ferries. He tried all the spellings he could think of but the company didn't exist. He reviewed the conversation in his mind, but it still came out the same: he'd provided information and she hadn't. He considered letting his boss know, but because he couldn't explain the woman's interest in an urn with ashes, he abandoned the idea. He reached for his book, but before he could become engrossed in the Riemann tensor analysis again, he thought how he really would have liked to get to know her.

Quirin Kaiserley braked abruptly and reversed a couple of metres until the trees revealed a view of the church and the small car park. He rubbed his eyes in case fatigue was playing tricks on him, but there was a vehicle up there and if he wasn't have hallucinations, then the inscription *Dombrowski* was clearly visible.

Quirin looked around. The streets were empty; several dimly lit street lamps glowed, covering the park in a ghostly light. He had spent almost two hours driving round the city and had cursed himself. Judith Kepler would hardly be sitting at a bus stop and waiting for him. But just when he had decided to give up, he had seen the van.

A faint sunrise was already lighting up the eastern sky. He parked the car and walked over the lawn towards the vehicle. Of course it was locked, but it was neither sealed nor clamped, so it hadn't yet been reported as stolen, which meant that the police also hadn't connected it with Judith.

Quiet admiration mixed with his anger. Anger because Dombrowski had lied to him. And admiration because Judith had been able to come this far and even further. TT had said there had been a violation of a grave. Whatever that meant, the van was close by a church and a cemetery.

The church door was closed; the iron gate in the brick wall was not. Quirin entered the grounds and circled round the church. He didn't find any indications of vandalism. He was cross with himself for leaving his torch in the car, but he didn't want to go back. The cemetery was old, with no clear paths marking the uneven slope, and by day it must have offered a breathtaking view of the Baltic. Quirin remembered that many cities on the coast buried their dead on hillsides. Perhaps out of fear that the sea would rise and claim the bodies.

When he had almost reached the other side of the cemetery he discovered an area that had been sealed off. Barrier tape protected the spot and as Quirin came closer, he stepped on the fragments of a smashed gravestone. Someone had pounded it with power and stamina. Quirin picked up a small piece of granite and examined the cracks. They were dry and new. Just then, he heard steps behind him.

'What are you doing there?'

Light blinded him. Quirin raised his hand to protect his eyes.

'Who are you?' A dark figure directed a torch beam directly at his face. 'Does no one have any respect anymore? A cemetery isn't a basement party room! We have regulations! Opening times are from sunrise until sunset! Get lost!'

Quirin dropped the stone.

'I'm investigating this incident.'

'Hmmm.'

The beam of light slipped to the ground. Quirin lowered his hand. Before him stood a small, elderly man with wild, mussed white hair. He wore pyjamas underneath his poplin coat.

'In the middle of the night. Really?'

'Did she do this?'

'That crazy woman? I've never seen anything like it. Who are you?'

'My name is Quirin Kaiserley. I come from Berlin. The woman is still out there. We have to find her before something else happens.'

'Does she frequently do this kind of thing?'

'I don't think she's done this before.'

'Hmmm. She got out of an asylum, right?'

Quirin let him believe that was the case. The man moved the torch over the pile of stone. Individual letters could be recognised here and there, but no more than that.

'Whose grave is it?'

'A Marianne Kepler. It would have lapsed in a couple of years. Then the plot is released. No one took care of it. The fees were paid by the city.'

'You're the cemetery keeper?'

The old man nodded. Quirin turned away from the grave and took a seat on a bench opposite. The keeper followed him, although he stopped repeatedly, pushing dry leaves aside with his foot. Quirin leaned back and stared up at the clear, starry night sky for a second.

'Why would someone smash a gravestone?' the man asked. The cone of his flashlight caught a nicely planted grave with a shiny frame of black marble. 'It's sick. I'm just glad it wasn't a Jewish grave. What do you think would have happened then? State security and such. We already have enough trouble with the young people here.'

'Yes,' Quirin agreed. 'When did it happen?'

'Around nine, just before the gates were closed. She came in with eyes as big as saucers, waving a sledgehammer or something like it. Poor Old Lüttich was terrified. She has circulation problems, even had to go to the hospital.'

'Was she threatened?'

'No. it was the shock. That mad woman just smashed the stone. It'll probably be in the paper tomorrow.'

'Just the stone?' Quirin asked. He had a crazy thought. But in the Judith Kepler case, nothing was too far-fetched. 'Or did she also dig up the ground? Was she looking for something, perhaps?'

The keeper took a seat next to him.

'No. She just rampaged. After fifteen minutes the police finally arrived and arrested her. There wasn't much left by then. It's a mystery to me.'

'The woman was Judith Kepler. Do you know her?'

The man turned off the flashlight. The darkness was so deep that Quirin closed his eyes and couldn't tell. He heard the person beside him breathing. A quiet, wheezing sound.

The silence that followed lasted a long time.

'Judith,' he finally said. 'Little Judith.'

Judith left the telephone booth. The terminal had emptied. Strewn about were torn boxes containing beer cans and half-empty bottles of wine. She grabbed two cans that were still intact and on the way to the ramps she popped one open and drained it while walking.

Trucks, cars and campervans formed long lines in front of the entrance to the harbourside. Peak season. Judith strolled down the rows, as if she was searching for her own vehicle. The gates would open in a few minutes. Lithuania to the left and Sweden to the right. Two huge ships lay in the harbour. The cargo traffic was already in motion, bumper to bumper, disappearing into the massive hold. The cries of the stevedores mixed with the humming motors. Blinding light illuminated every corner. Impossible to slip past the controls.

Christina Borg's ashes had been sent to a German church in Malmö. Judith crept to the right and crouched in the shadow of a small Dutch flower truck, keeping an eye on the guard in the watch tower. She had cleaned herself as best she could under a shower on the beach, but without a comb and with a torn dress she still looked like a vagrant. Her palms glowed. She didn't have any documents, no keys, no phone, no money. Her journey would likely come to an end here.

She sat down on the kerb and opened the second can. The beer was lukewarm, but at least it quenched her thirst.

The police had taken her to the station and confiscated her phone and wallet with the papers. She had taken a seat on the stool in front of the counter while the officers conferred in whispers about whether she fell under the jurisdiction of the hospital, the asylum, or the district attorney in Schwerin. After ten minutes, Judith got up quietly and left the station. No one had noticed her. They were probably still discussing the administrative details, even now.

Slightly groggy from the alcohol, she stared at a truck's massive wheels. She considered crawling underneath and holding on tight until she was on board. Out of the question. She was in no condition for that.

She tried not to think about what Martha Jonas had told her. She tried not to think at all. Not about the fact that she had lost the van and the documents. Dombrowski would have her head.

Fuck Dombrowski. She emptied the second can, tossed it in the gutter, and stamped on it until it was flat. She had to get on that ship. No money. No papers. No ticket. And the cops would almost certainly like to take her in for questioning. A signal chimed from far away, then a bell rang out loudly. As if upon command, everyone started their engines. The flower truck slowly crawled forward, accompanied by the hissing of hydraulics, but stopped again after a few feet.

The passenger side door opened. A man leaned out.

'Want a ride?'

Judith stood up. She stumbled. She shouldn't have drunk that beer so quickly.

'Malmö?' she asked.

The man let his eyes wander over her figure. He was the sort of person that people changed sides of the street to avoid. Greasy clothes, shifty gaze. But then she didn't look much better. Excellent prerequisites for a chance encounter.

'Yes, Malmö.'

The brakes hissed again. Judith jumped back. The truck slowly rolled further forward; the door remained open. She looked around. In the camper behind her sat a married couple. The woman held a thermos can in one hand and a cup in the other. Instead of pouring, she stared at Judith and made a comment to her husband. The corners of her mouth twisted in disdain.

The driver shrugged his shoulders, and bent over to the right again to shut the door. Judith started to run.

'Wait!'

She just managed to climb up onto the passenger side seat. He made a quick hand motion.

'Get down.'

Judith ducked down. The door slammed shut. The truck rocked through the gate and drove past the control booth, over the ramp into the ship. Judith carefully groped underneath the seat and found the fire extinguisher. She unhooked the latch. The driver manoeuvred the truck in the hold. The metal floors rattled. The air was filled with exhaust and the cries of the crew. Finally the vehicle came to a rest.

'OK. Come up.'

Judith crawled on the seat. The camper with the married couple drove past her to the right and parked in the same row. Other cars followed. It would take a while before everyone was on the ship. The driver grinned at her. He had yellow teeth and a face like a punch bag. He motioned behind himself. Judith turned around and saw a bed with a bunched-up, dirty blanket.

'Time to have some fun,' he said.

He reached under the covers and pulled out a half-full bottle of vodka.

15

Marianne Kepler had died in August, 1985. Soon afterwards, three people from Sassnitz had disappeared without a trace and had simultaneously had a fatal accident in Romania. It was in this cemetery in Sassnitz that these individual threads started to come together.

'Who was Marianne Kepler?' Quirin motioned to the remains of the gravestone.

The old man sighed and ran his feet over the ground. His frustration had evaporated.

'I hardly knew her,' he said. 'She was one of the women who, well . . .'

He searched for the words. 'She worked at Rügen Hotel. The big block down by the harbour. The Swedes built it in the seventies. For transit tourists.'

'Westerners.'

'Yes.'

That was an important clue. Whoever had professional contact with Westerners back then had to sign a declaration of commitment. Marianne Kepler must have been known to the Stasi in Schwerin. There must be a file on her. Quirin hoped that her file hadn't gone the same way as that of Lindner and his family.

'As what? Was she a cook? Or a chamber maid?'

'She was, well, a prostitute. She drifted around the harbour and then got knocked up by a john, and kept the baby. She started to drink. I saw her a couple of times down on Bach-strasse, in one of the fishing houses they've fixed up now. They took the child away from her in the end. She was sent to a home, and a little later the mother died. Alcohol poisoning. Sleeping pills. No one knows.'

'The child went to the home before the death?'

'Yep. A couple of weeks or months, I don't know any more than that.'

'What happened to her?'

'Judith? That was a strange thing. I never saw her again. Even though people constantly ran into those brats from Gagarin. But you don't think anything of it. Maybe she was adopted. Or she was taken somewhere else. At any rate, she wasn't in Gagarin for long.'

'Gagarin?'

'Yuri Gagarin. Cosmonaut. The first human in space. The home was named after him.'

Quirin remembered the face of a smiling young man with a white helmet.

Because Borg was a home kid. Just like me.

'And you never saw the Judith you knew again?'

'Never again.'

But the Judith Quirin knew had lived for ten years in Sassnitz. And as a grown woman she had suddenly decided to smash her mother's gravestone, had got mixed up with the BND, and was now on a wanted list. She also had something in her possession that had something to do with Christina Borg.

What had happened to make Judith Kepler, cleaning lady and death scene cleaner, go on the rampage after so long? But she hadn't done it in Berlin. She had made her way to Sassnitz, following the same route that three people had taken decades before. Transit Berlin-Malmö.

'Did the children at the home know where their parents were?'

'I can't tell you that. But I heard that the staff rubbed their noses in it. Used their unfortunate origins for social education.'

'So it can be assumed that Judith Kepler knew about her mother's profession ... that she knew how Marianne Kepler earned her money?'

'That was probably thown at her. We had our reconciliation sessions here after '89. Quite a bit was discussed. The entire leadership of the home was fired, and there was a lot that came to light. Unfortunately not everything.'

'What didn't?'

The cemetery keeper scraped the soles of his shoes again.

'Quite a few chimneys smoked around then.'

'I understand.'

Quirin's neighbour sighed. The first bird awakened. The sunrise became lighter. They heard a ship's horn from far away.

'Malmö,' the small man said. '4:45—you can set your clock to it. I'd better get going. Make sure you find that girl. She's a danger to the public.'

'Ms Kepler might not respect the dead, but this wasn't the act of a mad person.'

'But you said that she was crazy.'

'That's what lots of people think,' Quirin said. 'But she's as normal as you and me.'

'And what was the deal with the stone?'

Quirin stood up. He could have given the man an answer. But at least he shouldn't be robbed of his sleep. 'That's exactly what I'll ask her. Thank you very much. And good night.'

'Good night,' the small man said.

Judith only acted as if she was drinking. She had already tried to climb out of the truck twice. Two times the man had forced her back onto the seat. Judith passed the bottle back to him. She had won enough time. The park deck was full; the passengers already up on the decks. The motors vibrated, the ferry pushed off. It wouldn't turn around now, even if they found a stowaway.

In the meantime the driver believed his dreams were about to come true. He raised the bottle again. They were alone down here, and Judith knew exactly how he planned to spend the rest of the ride over. She pushed the fire extinguisher into the foot well.

The driver patted on the meagre bed.

'Come on.'

'No.'

She bent over and reached for the extinguisher. But she had underestimated the injuries on her hands. She couldn't hold it firmly enough, and the man hit it out of her hand. In the next moment he pulled her head back. She smelt his breath and flailed wildly, but the man was stronger than she had assumed. She screamed, he laid his hands around her throat and pressed. She kicked at the window with her feet and hit the fire extinguisher, which broke with an ugly grinding noise. He loosened his grip, but didn't release her.

'Fucking bitch!'

The blow to her face almost robbed her of her consciousness. She gagged, took a breath, and screamed. The next blow hit her on the chin. The wound on her cheek broke open. She rolled to the passenger side, reached for the door handle, but the man grabbed her hair and pulled her back. The driver's door opened. Even before the Dutchman realised what had happened, he was grabbed and thrown out of the cab. Judith heard the thuds of fists landing, then the furious scream of the man, and after a final blow, which sounded like an uppercut, silence.

She climbed over her seat to the left and stared down the narrow path the vehicles formed in the belly of the ship. A man stood over the Dutchman, holding him by the lapels, and just let him fall to the oily ground, unconscious. He looked familiar. She wanted to say something but she was either too drunk or still too dazed from the blows. She vomited onto the floor of the truck. The man waited until she was finished and had wiped her mouth with the back of her hand, then he came over and helped her out of the cab.

'Judith Kepler. Nice to see you.'

Judith woke up because she was freezing. The blanket had slipped, and a cool breeze ran across her back. She blinked. She lay on a narrow bed in a tiny cabin. Directly above her was a window. If she stretched out her hand she could touch Kaiserley, who was lying on the other bed. He had his arms crossed behind his head and his eyes closed, but Judith sensed that he wasn't asleep. She would have liked to ask him how he had found her. But that would have meant starting to think. She wanted to postpone that moment as long as possible, and so she just pulled the blanket over her shoulders. He opened his eyes and turned to her.

'How are you doing?'

She felt her cheek. Someone had put a bandage over the cut. Even her hands were properly dressed.

'Where's my dress?'

'You mean the tatters I cut from your body?' He smiled. That and the forced intimacy made her uneasy. She had found him attractive back in his apartment, when she had shown up at his place to find out why the BND employed complete idiots like Karsten Michael Oliver Asshole. Back then. That wasn't even forty-eight hours ago. She motioned to the dressings.

'Them too?'

He nodded.

'Thank you.'

Kaiserley sat up and grabbed a plastic bag that lay underneath a tiny desk. It rattled.

'I had to buy three bottles of bourbon to get a T-shirt. The shop on board has a fairly limited selection.'

He tossed her a red package wrapped in plastic.

'XXL. With a little luck it will reach to your knees.'

She tore open the package. The T-shirt was huge, and printed with the name of a whisky brand. He motioned to the narrow door to the right of the bed.

'The bathroom is through there.'

The shower was so tiny that she hit the plastic walls with her elbows. She let the water run over her body so long it grew cold. Only then did she dry off. Kaiserley had rustled up a comb and a single-use toothbrush. The comb broke and even with half of it she wasn't able to untangle her hair. She finally gave up trying.

'Where's my underwear?'

The door opened a crack, and he passed her what she asked for. She slipped into the shirt. White Eagle Bourbon. She looked as bad as she'd ever looked. He must have seen her scars. The most embarrassing thing was the idea that he had lugged her into an elevator half-unconscious and dragged her down a dark corridor. She tried to plait her hair but failed. Finally, she couldn't think of anything that would further delay her going back in.

'Stunning.' He grinned. She looked for her trainers and found them at the foot of the bed.

Kaiserley didn't have any luggage. He must have slept in his trousers, because the linen looked wrinkled, and there was a dark five o'clock shadow visible on his cheeks.

'Did you bring anything else along? Is there anything still with that bastard in the truck?'

Judith shook her head. Something crackled directly above her. From the loudspeaker on the deck came several loud puffs into the microphone, then the announcement in three languages that the ship would reach the harbour of Malmö in thirty minutes. Kaiserley stood up.

'How did you find me?'

Kaiserley pulled the key card from the holder on the wall and opened the door.

'I'll tell you if you tell me what you're looking for in Malmö.'

He waited. Judith moved towards the window, forcing herself between the two beds. At that moment they were sailing under a massive bridge. It led to a distant, rocky shore, above which the haze of a foggy summer morning lay. A city appeared in the distance: suburbs, then modern office buildings, and finally elegant villas and old brick buildings. She heard Kaiserley close the door again.

'What do you have planned in Malmö?'

She laid her head against the window. The glass was cool and eased the pain somewhat.

'A holiday,' she said.

The cafeteria didn't have any breakfast left, just coffee. They found a table up front at the viewing windows that had just been abandoned by an excited family. The room grew empty, most people wanting to watch the entry into the harbour and the docking manoeuvre from the deck. Quiet elevator music bubbled out of the loudspeakers. *Time after time* in a version for Hammond organ. Quirin came back to the table with a plastic tray. Judith had taken a seat at the table, her back to the other passengers. She played with an unused paper napkin.

'Coffee?'

'Thank you.'

She took the cup in both of her hands, as she had done at their first encounter in his apartment. Quirin sat down next to her. They looked at the white railings in silence for a while and the massive cranes they slowly glided past.

'Are you in pain? Do you need to see a doctor?'

She shook her head. He had undressed her and bandaged her. He knew that she didn't have anything with her. Not even her tobacco.

'Would you like a cigarette?'

She nodded. Quirin went to the register in the cafeteria and bought a pack of Marlboro and matches. They went to the middle deck with their coffee. Modern harbour buildings with lofts and glass-faced administration buildings went slowly by. It was just before ten. Judith tried to light up, but couldn't manage it. Quirin took the matches from her and lit her cigarette.

'What did you do to your hands?'

'Cut them.' She inhaled deeply and leant her upper arms on the railing. Kaiserley stood next to her.

'Only barbed wire makes those kinds of wounds. Did you break in somewhere?'

She turned away. 'I'm wading through so much shit I can't even smell it anymore.'

It was chilly on the deck. The wind played with her T-shirt. She looked like a fourteen-year-old: rumpled hair, shirt far too large, thin legs. Then he saw the scars on her arms. He motioned to them.

'Where do you have those from?'

'Are you a doctor? I don't like people playing doctor. I was able to take care of the last person who tried that all by myself.'

'That's not what it looked like to me.'

'What's the deal?' The aggressiveness in her voice was unmistakable. 'What are you doing here? I didn't ask you to follow me. And don't tell me that it was all a huge coincidence.'

'No,' Quirin answered. 'That's just as unlikely as you being here on holiday. Although a couple of days would probably do you some good. Apparently you really went haywire in the Sassnitz cemetery.'

She shook her head in disdain as if to say he didn't have a clue.

'I gave you a piece of advice. You were supposed to keep out of the business with Borg. Instead you set off on your own and left chaos in your wake. Why?'

'My own business.'

'You're mistaken. What do you want to do in Malmö?'

She tossed the cigarette overboard and went to leave. Quirin stepped in her path.

'What did you find in Borg's apartment?'

'Nothing!' The answer came too quickly. 'Leave me alone!'

'You won't get far. Not looking like that.'

He motioned to the red T-shirt and at the same moment knew it was the wrong move. Her face closed.

'Why did you follow me? What about me was so interesting that you followed me all the way to Sweden?'

'You tell me.'

'No, you.'

'We're not going to get any farther this way.'

'Well.'

The studied civility failed to mask the instincts of a wild animal. She would bolt at the first opportunity. Quirin sensed that. He had become the hunter again, and he was just about to bag his prey. Looking at her, he felt neither triumph nor elation, only shame.

'I don't want to do anything to you. I want to understand you. I can take you to a hotel and help you do whatever you have planned. But you have to play with an open hand. At least with me.'

He had spoken calmly, and persuasively – or he hoped he had done. At least she seemed to be thinking about his offer, because she pulled another cigarette from the pack and let him light it again. Several attempts were needed because the wind kept blowing out the matches. She smiled when it had finally succeeded.

'Quirin Kaiserley.' She studied him, her dark blue eyes curious. 'What do you think is in my possession? Please be honest. Then I'll be honest with you.'

Without thinking he said: 'Microfilm.'

She looked at him and blew the smoke in the wind.

'Microfilm,' she repeated. 'Are you serious?'

'Yes.'

She went back to the railing, bent over it and started to laugh.

16

Pastor Volfram Vonnegut swept the first golden leaves of the year from the path. It hadn't rained this summer. The clouds simply didn't make it over the sea. The low-pressure troughs came together in the distance, unloading in the south, over Mecklenburg, Pomerania, East Prussia, but they didn't reach Scandinavia. He couldn't remember the last time they'd had such a long period of drought.

He leant the broom against a tree trunk and sat down on a bench. His gaze ran over the parish hall with pleasure. It hugged the Sankta Anna Kyrkan church as if they had always been inseparable. But it was from the sixties. The church façade, almost twice as old, must have been avant-garde for its time with its unadorned austerity.

He was looking forward to the summer excursion over the weekend. The whole congregation met up at Salsjön near Bråkne Hoby, a pretty forest lake just outside of Malmö. The children wore themselves out with outdoor games instead of sitting in front of a computer. Parents and grandparents met friends and acquaintances, everyone bringing something to eat, and he would man the grill. New members were welcomed and old relationships renewed. It was a functioning and abundant congregational community and Volfram thanked the Lord every day anew that he was able to find his place in this beautiful patch of earth.

The telephone rang. Volfram stood up, making an effort not to put too much weight on his new hip. The operation had gone well a couple of years ago, but his discomfort had been increasing over the last few months and his doctor feared he might need another replacement.

'All right – coming!' he called out, as if the telephone could hear him.

He climbed the stairs to the entrance and reached the small office. On the table sat an old-fashioned telephone. Volfram would have liked to exchange it for one of those mobile devices, to save him having to walk to answer it. Maybe over Christmas. Rutger had one of those electronic stores and had already kindly suggested it, but Volfram could hardly explain in a church service that the offering this week would be for a new telephone.

'*Tyska Kerkan Malmö och Blekinge*,' he said.

The connection crackled. That's the way it was with these old phones.

'Am I speaking with Volfram Vonnegut?'

Although the voice sounded strange, he recognised it immediately.

'Yes,' he answered hesitantly, and wished his wife Gillis had answered the phone and wasn't in the kitchen at the moment, making supper for Madita.

'You remember me?'

'It's . . . been a long time.'

The voice on the other end laughed. The tone was artificially distorted by the membrane. It sounded like a storm was blowing over the Baltic.

'Yes, a very long time. How are you?'

'Good,' he answered. And because he couldn't think of anything better: 'My hip, though. You don't get any younger.'

'Time doesn't spare anyone. I'm glad you're still around. There are fewer of us than ever.'

'I'm . . . I'm no longer active.'

A short pause fell. Volfram would have liked to hang up, but he knew that wouldn't solve anything.

'I'm an old man. Everything has changed. I have too.'

'You're still a pastor. A shepherd who takes care of the worries and problems of his flock. And those can be very diverse.'

'Back then it was a question of philanthropy, not politics. Apparently I wasn't able to make that clear to you.'

He hoped that would suffice.

'I also have difficulties from time to time,' the voice responded. 'Especially in today's world. I don't want to hold you up too long. Your granddaughter is coming home from school any minute now. I believe her name's Madita. What is your wife cooking today?'

An icy hand seized Volfram's heart. He put the receiver down and hurried into the kitchen. Gillis was at the stove frying little meatballs.

'Where's Madita?' he asked.

Gillis shook the pan over the gas flame. A strand of her white hair had slipped out of its bun and fell onto her face. She pulled it behind her ear and looked at the clock on the wall.

'She should have been here long ago.'

He ignored her questioning look, rushing back into the office.

'Where is she? What did you do to her?'

'Little girls lose their way sometimes. Don't worry about it.'

'You heathen bastards!'

He spun around. Gillis had followed him and stood in the open door. He motioned to her furiously but she didn't leave. She nervously dried her hands on her apron.

'Mr Vonnegut, please calm down. And consider carefully again whether or not you want to continue to be active.'

'Leave my family alone! I'll call the police!'

'No!' Gillis came over and ripped the telephone out of his hands. 'Who are you and what do you want? My husband is ill. He's not available.'

Volfram raised his hands but she turned away and listed to the person on the other end.

'Is that all?' she asked.

He sat down and waited. *Lord*, he thought, *let nothing happen to Madita. I know what they're capable of. I was one of them. I have inflicted bitter suffering on others. But she's only a child. Don't let her pay for my mistakes. Lord, take me instead. But protect this young life that was entrusted to us.*

Gillis's voice became a whisper. Fragments of words came to him as from far away. A name, an address . . . not in the computer, but in the old rolodex standing forgotten on the filing cabinet that hadn't been used for years. He saw how he had become weak and how lucky he was over all these years that Gillis carried the weight together with him, that she took action and not him, but it didn't make the matter easier. Perhaps it had been a mistake to sever contact. No contact – no protection. There was no one left who would help them.

She took a deep breath. 'I'll vouch for it. But only on the condition that you leave my family in peace. Forever. Do you understand? Do you hear me?'

She pressed the receiver to her ear; then rattled the connection repeatedly, but it had been cut off. She slowly hung up.

'Gillis . . .' he began.

They heard the hinges of the garden gate squeak and a child's quick, almost running steps.

'Gillis? Volfram? Are you there?'

His wife ran out so quickly that it took some effort to follow. Madita flew into their arms and was kissed from head to toe.

'Where were you? Where were you for so long?'

'I helped a little kitten cross the street.' Madita avoided their gaze.

The icy chill disappeared. Volfram exhaled. For a moment he saw a different child in front of him, a girl with dark hair and a stubborn gaze, who had stood on the threshold of this house not too long ago. Back then he had believed he was helping but in the end he'd been turned into nothing more than a tool in the hands of heathens. The girl had become a woman, and this woman had gone away and had now returned in an urn. Would she still be alive if he had acted differently? He thought about what she had entrusted to him before she had left on the journey that had culminated in her death. He knew that he was only a human, and very vulnerable. A secret was not a secret if you weren't willing to defend it with your life. Volfram only knew three reasons in the world worth dying for. He had two of them directly in front of him. He was ashamed because he suddenly felt disloyal to all of the others that trusted him. Most of all, he was ashamed before God.

Gillis hugged Madita even closer. The child slipped out of the embrace and ran into the kitchen.

'Meatballs! Thank you!'

Gillis wanted to follow her but Volfram held her back.

'What in the world did you do?' he asked.

A pair of jeans, a sweatshirt.

Judith stood in the fitting room and hoped that Kaiserley would be taken in by her indecision. Grey or black? He stood directly in front of the curtain. She could see his shoes when she bent over. Hiking boots, cognac brown. Something expensive.

'It doesn't fit,' she said. 'I need a size smaller.'

He spoke English with the sales assistant without leaving his position. The woman had immediately identified them as tourists and after a brief glance at Judith's outfit, decided not to ask any questions. At least she had an eye for sizes. The jeans were a perfect fit.

Kaiserley passed Judith another sweatshirt through the crack. She took it and put it on the increasingly tall stack. She had hoped there might be an opportunity to slip away while shopping. But the former agent hadn't taken his eyes off of her.

'It can't be that hard,' she heard him say. 'Are the jeans OK at least?'

'Yes.'

She pushed the curtain aside. She wore the trousers and the first sweatshirt she had pulled from the rack. They walked to the checkout, where Kaiserley paid and the sales assistant used a pair of scissors to cut off the price tags. The woman folded the whisky T-shirt with the tips of her fingers, placed it in a plastic bag, and passed both over the counter.

'*Adjö*,' she said.

'*Hejdå*,' he answered.

The department store was close to Stortorget, a popular square dominated by the Renaissance façade of the city hall. It was surrounded by restaurants, cafés, and stores. It was late afternoon. The pedestrian zone was filled with people, both locals and tourists. Kaiserley still hadn't revealed how he had planned the rest of their day, but she wanted to head in the direction of the German church as soon as possible.

He moved towards a coffee shop, walking next to her the entire time. At first he had tried to reach for her arm, seemingly unintentionally while crossing the street. She had immediately pulled away, and since then he had avoided all contact. But his presence was as intrusive as a pair of handcuffs. She knew that he was watching her every step, but she was determined to pretend she didn't notice.

'Do you want something to drink?' he asked.

Judith nodded. They sat down at an empty table in front of the café. Judith placed her bag underneath her chair. She would leave it here.

'You look good.' His gaze scanned her jeans.

'Thank you,' she growled. On the other hand, her options in Malmö were rather limited.

He ordered two latte macchiatos from the stressed student barista and leaned back. The sky was a shining blue with snow-white clouds that moved by quickly. When the sun shone through it became instantly hot.

'Now that we've arrived where you wanted to go,' he started, 'and after your burst of laughter on the ferry, I'd like to know what you have planned.'

'It's private.'

'You're mistaken. After the murder of Christina Borg your private space is no longer private. Your only advantage is that you have brought nothing with you. Because of that, you've evaded the colleagues for a couple of hours.'

'By "colleagues" you probably mean the BND?'

'Not just them. So please answer my questions now, or they will be posed by others. And they won't be as charming as I am.'

Judith squinted her eyes because the sun was blinding. And because charm was almost the last thing that she would associate with Kaiserley.

'Where is the microfilm?' he asked.

'I have no clue what you're talking about.'

'Now you're acting dumber than you are.'

'In all seriousness. I don't know. Does it have something to do with the file they were discussing on that talk show?'

' "Rosenholz", yes.'

The barista placed two glasses in front of them, and managed to spill almost half of the contents. She apologised profusely.

'*Det gör detsamma*,' Kaiserley said. '*Du kan inte hjälpa det. Tack.*'

He reached for the napkin holder and wiped up the spill while the server scurried away.

'You speak Swedish?'

'One of the most important foreign languages for people in my profession.'

'What is your profession exactly?' Judith asked. 'I thought the BND kicked you out.'

Kaiserley lifted her glass and deposited another napkin underneath. 'We parted ways by mutual accord.'

'And why are you so interested in this private matter?'

'This is also my private matter.'

Judith was silent. She awkwardly raised her glass and took a sip of the lukewarm milk, the only thing it had in common with coffee is that had once stood next to a cup of it.

'You've found something and I want to know what it is.'

His voice sounded steely. Judith wondered whether he had led interrogations and what agents were trained in. Killing silently, disappearing without a trace, tactical behaviour, psychological warfare. She didn't know which areas Kaiserley had worked in, but chose to assume the worst, just to be on the safe side.

She put down the glass. 'If I'm supposed to help you further, I want to know what you have planned.'

'You, of all people, say that!'

'Quid pro quo.'

He tore open a packet of sugar and shook it into his glass. 'OK. I have already been to the police, so I could just as well go to the press or tell you. I believe Borg was murdered because she had a roll of microfilm. Highly explosive material. Microfilm we had assumed that the Stasi had found long ago and destroyed.'

'The Stasi.' Judith shook her head and raised her glass of milk. 'And when did this supposedly happen?'

'In August 1985.'

The glass slipped out of her hand. She just barely managed to catch it, and it only spilled slightly. Kaiserley looked at her for a long time.

'And the name "Rosenholz" really means nothing to you?'

'No.'

'The Rosenholz file contains the names of the Stasi's foreign agents. The list is only partial, even today. Borg had the only complete original list still in existence.'

'Where . . . how do you know that?'

'She showed me the film. Thirty thousand names, addresses, real names, NATO top-secret information. With index numbers, file numbers, the administrative information, the postal codes of the agents' home addresses . . .'

'But why are they so important today?' Judith interrupted his litany. He could hardly be stopped once he'd started on his secret service stories. 'It's at least as cold as this coffee here. Hasn't the statute of limitations run out on this stuff by now?'

'There's no statute of limitations on murder.'

'Which murder? Christina Borg was just . . .'

She stopped because he suddenly raised his hand and looked around. All at once he lost all the patronising self-confidence with which he had treated her until now.

'Quiet,' he said.

His gaze scanned the people next to them, the joints of the awning above them, the lantern on the other side of the street. Judith took another sip of the lukewarm milk and looked around. A classic case of paranoia. And then she noticed it. A couple stood in front of a display window. Or were they watching Kaiserley in the reflection? An older gentleman two tables over raised his newspaper in front of his face at the exact moment she looked at him. A couple of steps further away, there was a cash machine in a bank branch located in the ground floor of a brick house. Didn't those machines have cameras? Was there an invisible eye pointed at them right now?

The couple moved on, the man with the newspaper kept reading, and the cash machine was much too far away. Kaiserley had calmed down by now. He bent over and spoke very quietly.

'In the middle of the eighties there was a betrayed attempt to escape the GDR. No one ever found out who was behind it. I had assumed no one had survived, until a couple of days ago.'

'And now?'

'Now?' Kaiserley lowered his voice even further, until she could hardly hear him. He looked at her with that same strange gaze. 'Now I believe there's someone arisen from the grave, sitting in front of me.'

TT stood next to a desk on the first floor of Section II (SIGINT) HQ in Stockdorf, an organisation that went under the name of the Federal Telecommunications Statistics Bureau, where he was scrupulously examining a tactical PSC-5 satellite radio device that had given up the ghost in the middle of an assignment. The antennae looked like an upside-down umbrella.

The portable terminal should theoretically have been set up and torn down within ten minutes. However, although TT had been fiddling around with the high-gain antennae the entire morning, he had been unable to repair it. Maybe he was simply too nervous. That morning he had sent Kellermann an encrypted report via the internal network. A collection of all of the meagre information that he had collected on Judith Kepler. Hopefully Kaiserley wouldn't fuck up. If it got out that TT had passed information along that was actually intended for a department head, then he wouldn't need any ID at all. Or just the one he could use to register with the employment agency.

Kellermann still hadn't responded. TT went to his computer and sent out a new volley of searches into the virtual ether. The programs ran at high speeds. If Kepler as much as coughed, then they'd have her. But the woman had apparently learned something. It was as if she'd vanished from the face of the earth.

TT sneaked out into the hall and looked around. He was alone. Lunch time, and everyone was in the cafeteria or at *Rabenwirt*. He carefully closed the door behind himself and pulled his laptop from his messenger bag. While it booted up and logged into the systems, TT thought about how he could best sell his meeting with Kaiserley if it became known. Anticipatory zeal, perhaps. Or thinking for himself, the thought of which made him grin. They were always encouraged to think for themselves. However, there was never any mention of resulting action. Presumably because it would have to be ordered from above.

Quirin Kaiserley.

He typed the name and noticed how his pulse accelerated. It only took a couple of seconds in which Kaiserley's activities were checked under the usual criteria. Then a list of the individual reports appeared on the screen.

Lufthansa flight LH 236 to Berlin, departure at 9:45 p.m.

A thousand euros withdrawn from a cash machine at Tegel.

Those were the last events recorded. TT clicked further into the past. What he read disturbed him.

Lufthansa flight LH 235 to Munich, departure at 3:45 p.m.

Visit to Homicide Unit 6, Keithstrasse, Berlin.

Several calls to Dombrowski Facility Management.

Pensive, TT closed the programs and turned off the laptop. He stowed it back in the bag. The antennae lay on the table like a huge dead spider.

He should have never met up with Kaiserley. His tracks were as clear as footsteps in fresh snow. And they all led back to him, TT.

His smartphone rang. TT jumped. Caller unknown. He waited. The ringing echoed through the empty room. It stopped after the fifteenth ring. TT waited for a minute, then listened to the mailbox.

'Sweetheart,' he heard Angelina Espinoza's voice say. No name. She sounded in a hurry, as if she were crossing a busy street. 'I'm in the city. Countdown to the big party. Will I see you beforehand? Call me.'

The big party was the security conference. So he must have made an impression on her after all, otherwise she wouldn't be calling him already. He instantly felt better. She knew all the big players but wanted to meet up with him, of all people. He heard footsteps in the hall, laughter, and some random conversation. His colleagues were coming back. He dialled her number and felt his palms moisten.

'When?' was all he asked when she picked up.

17

The high sun over Stortorget had only imperceptibly changed its
position. Judith moved her chair into the shade to sit closer to
Kaiserley. She was annoyed by the fact that they now looked like
a romantic couple innocently people-watching the scene on the
street, but it couldn't be helped.

'Arisen from the grave. How do you get that?'

'I was at the cemetery in Sassnitz and saw what you did.
Someone only does something like that if they have a very large
score to settle. I think that you had a different name until that
fateful night. Do you know what it was?'

Judith nodded reluctantly.

'Your mother's name was Sonnenberg. She was a photo lab
technician. Your father's name was Richard. He was . . .' Kaiserley hesitated a moment before continuing '. . . an agent of the foreign intelligence service. He worked for the Stasi in the Federal
German Republic under the name of Lindner. Your parents
wanted to start a new life, but with that background they didn't
have the slightest chance of leaving the GDR legally. So they
offered us the list of names.'

'High treason.'

'For the Stasi, yes.'

Judith pursed her lips. She didn't like what Kaiserley had told her but she also didn't think he was lying.

'What was she like?'

'I never got to know her.'

'And my father, that . . . *double agent*?'

She spat out the last two words. Kaiserley raised his hand to calm her. He just barely managed to pull it back in time.

'He was a decent man.'

'He put me and her – and himself – in danger! I spent ten years in that home. Ten years!'

'I know.'

'You don't know a fucking thing, Kaiserley. Not a fucking thing.'

Kaiserley bit his lower lip. They couldn't afford to destroy the impression of harmony they had just established.

'At some point I believed what they told me,' she said quietly. 'Your mother came from Bachstrasse. Your father was one of her clients. And every time I defended myself I got punched in the face. I was twelve the first time I ran away. By sixteen I had no fixed address.'

She tugged at her sleeves again.

'Are your scars from that phase?'

She nodded. 'From then and from the years that followed. It's hard to get your act together. It comes down to jail or rehab.'

'And you went to rehab.'

'Three times in jail, a dozen stints in rehab. I didn't count them. Then came a support group. And then Dombrowski. And then . . . then I believed I'd made it. I was able to handle who I was. And then . . .'

She stopped.

'Judith, are you here to find out whether your mother made it to Sweden?'

She blinked and looked away. 'Maybe.'

'That's an illusion.'

'Really? What are my last twenty-five years then?'

'And even if she had made it – a woman who took a strange child and your passport? And who never let you know? That's a monster not a mother.'

Deep inside, Judith felt a burning, stabbing sensation. She'd never thought that far. Up until now she had only been motived by one thing: to find someone who could explain what had really happened. And yes, for a moment she had felt that hot, insane hope that someone from her family had survived.

A monster. Children from the home often had relatives of this sort. Only those who had grown up like that understood that a monster was still better than nothing.

'Christina Borg saved my life,' she said quietly. 'She found out about me and wanted to contact me. She went to Sweden in my place as a child. She didn't do it by herself, right? She was exactly the same age as me. So someone was with her. A woman. Her mother. My mother. But not the person buried in Sassnitz. What happened back then?'

'Irene Sonnenberg boarded the international train from GDR Berlin to Malmö with you in Berlin-Lichtenberg. The idea was that you and she would transfer to the coach we were in with the help of a Swedish conductor, during the hour-long stop at Sassnitz. Irene supposedly carried the key for the film depot along with her. One of the CIA agents had the assignment of checking the depot in Sassnitz and giving us the green light. At that point the plan was that Irene would receive three passports.'

'A shitty plan. Since when could citizens of the GDR simply board a train to Malmö?'

'Of course they couldn't "simply". Lindner and I boarded a through coach in Bahnhof Zoo. It was attached to the Sassnitz express at Berlin Ostbahnhof and remained locked. People from West Berlin and GDR citizens travelled in the same train but their paths separated on Rügen. The through coach was uncoupled and sent toward Trelleborg and the ferry; the remaining coaches went to Bergen. The whole procedure took at least an hour due to the border controls. During this time your mother was supposed to be smuggled out of the East German coach and into the through coach.'

'And?' Judith whispered, her heart pounding. 'What went wrong?'

'You and your mother were pulled from the train and disappeared. Your father became anxious. Time was running short. The operation was over as far as I was concerned. We would have been glad just to arrive at the harbour unharmed and catch the ferry to Malmö. But suddenly Lindner thought he could see you and your mother on the train concourse. He wanted to get out and go to you. I think he thought he still had a chance to deceive the PCO. He thought you still had a chance.'

'The PCO?

'The passport control officers. We were in a restricted area. I tried to hold him back but he was like a man possessed. He wanted to be with you, regardless of what happened. He asked me for the passports. He said if they were able to prove they were citizens of the Federal Republic who had suffered a flat tyre in transit, they might still have a chance. I told him . . .'

Kaiserley stopped.

'What? What did you tell him?'

'No passports without the microfilm.'

Judith looked at him for a long time.

'You absolutely miserable fucking piece of shit.'

Judith would have liked nothing more than to have smashed his face with a fire extinguisher too. Pulled him to the ground and beat him. Kicked him, beat him, broken every single bone in his body.

'You're right,' he said quietly. 'But it was in the best interest of the country.'

'Stop now unless you want me to beat the living daylights out of you.'

'Judith, since then I've . . .'

'Shut the fuck up!' The other guests sat up and looked over. She lowered her voice. 'There is no defence. None. You sent us to our doom.' She wanted to get up, go, run off and scream. 'What happened to my father?' she asked with a hoarse voice.

'You see these scars here?'

He pointed to his right temple. A light, barely visible line ran from his forehead to his hairline.

'That was the emergency hammer. I woke up an hour later and the train was already on the ferry. Lindner was gone and with him the passports.'

'And you never tried to find out what became of us?'

'Of course. The Sonnenberg family had a car accident on their way to their holiday in Romania. Everyone died.'

'Romania. Why Romania?'

'It could just as well have been the Urals. At the time, nearly every Eastern bloc country was available for the GDR to remove names from their registry. You were simply deleted.'

'Deleted,' Judith said.

Kaiserley nodded.

Judith blinked into the light. The rage and hatred diminished, and something incomprehensible and unknown spread inside her. Timid and delicate, she was prepared to immediately disappear into the oblivion and dissolve into nothingness.

'The man . . . my father . . . he knew he might die if he left the train?'

'I believe so.'

'And my mother?'

'I don't know. Your parents hoped they could start a new life. They weren't interested in money. They would have received fifteen thousand marks to get back on their feet. The microfilm was worth at least a million.'

Parents. Her parents. What a contrast to an unknown father and an antisocial mother. The feeling crawled up her throat, stayed there and nearly cut off her air. There had been two people who had cared for her and loved her. That was infinitely more than everything than she had ever hoped to get from this journey. It was so enormous that she couldn't find enough space for it, neither in her head, nor in her heart.

'He didn't even take the fifteen thousand with him, Judith? Or should I call you Christina?'

Judith looked past him and at the cash machine. A young man stood in front of it and had either forgotten his PIN or his account was overdrawn. He looked at the monitor with bewilderment, jabbing at the keyboard.

'Do you have any memory of your time before the home?'

'No.'

'A name? A scene, an image? Anything at all? You're the only witness who was at the station back then.'

Gold. Chinking, glittering glass.

'Lenin,' she said.

'What?'

Judith wiped her hands over her eyes.

'Judith, try to remember. There has to be something remaining, even if you were only five at the time. Experiences, images, or feelings.'

She opened her mouth, wanted to say something, but then noticed she didn't have the words. It wasn't a wall she was defeated by. It was worse. She herself was the wall.

She held his gaze until he turned away in disappointment.

'I'll take you to a safe place now and continue on my own.'

She had to get to the German church. Someone there must know what had become of Borg's mother. Someone in this city must have known her. You don't live a quarter-century in a country without leaving a trace. Maybe a miracle had taken place at Sassnitz train station . . .

'Are you listening to me?'

'Yes.'

Maybe she would find a monster. But maybe she would also only find someone who had waited for her all those years. Who had also been lied to. Who didn't even know that she still existed. Who would remember the child she had once been. Who could smash the stone out of a wall. Who she would recognise.

'Are you listening? Judith?'

She started.

'Borg is dead. Whatever you were thinking just now, Borg might have lived your life.' Kaiserley looked at her, and his eyes darkened, as if her pain could actually affect him. 'But she also died your death.'

TT knew that he'd never go so far as to own his own home. He wasn't the kind of person who would take on a thirty-year debt and torture himself only to end up stuck in a terraced house. He preferred to spend his money on travel, cars and gadgets. His apartment was one of a carefree bachelor with no responsibilities, equipped with just a few status symbols like the huge flat screen television, a shiny chrome espresso machine that he hardly ever used because he always had to re-read the operator's manual, or his Wii console, with which he was currently learning to play tennis.

The furnishings in the apartment were Spartan and modern. He had a cleaning lady who came from an agency recommended by the BND, and a rubbish chute in the hallway, large enough – and this was key – to dispose of pizza boxes without having to fold them first. The bed had been freshly made, and he himself came right out of the shower and opened the door when it rang shortly after six, his bath towel slung casually around his hips.

She didn't say a word, just kissed him.

It was quick, hot and hurried. Afterwards, she rolled off him and laid there, cradling her head in the warm hollow of his belly. TT ran his hand over her dishevelled hair.

'How long have you been here?'

'Since yesterday. In a complete surprise, the Iranian Foreign Minister announced he was coming. *Grande confusione.*

But keep that to yourself. The agencies won't be notified until the week before next, when all the preparations have been put in place.'

She purred as his fingers began to massage her neck.

'I'm staying at the Bayerischer Hof. Next week I'll be getting my old apartment in Bogenhausen again. The Israelis are two floors above me, and I cross paths with the Egyptians and Russians in the morning when I go jogging. It's a small world. I like Munich. Do you have cigarettes?'

'You smoke?'

'Only post-coital.'

He stood up and went into the kitchen where he kept an open pack of Marlboros in a wall cupboard. He lit two, took a saucer as an ashtray, and went back into the bedroom. Angelina smiled at him, took the cigarette, and inhaled deeply. He lay back down next to her and slipped his phone onto the bedside table. He should hold seminars: *Handling mobile telephones – a primer for intelligence service agents who maintain contact with members of allied services.* It would be very helpful for married men as well.

'And yourself? What are you working on at the moment?'

'On a portable spitfire,' he answered and turned back towards her.

'That shit the Brits sold to Afghanistan?'

'Precisely.'

She leaned back and fluffed a pillow under her head. TT's gaze fell upon her small breasts. Her skin had a golden shimmer; her whole body was perfect. In comparison to her, he felt clumsy and hairy as a chimp.

'I keep thinking about Kaiserley,' she said.

TT ground out his cigarette. First of all, he didn't like the taste, and second, he was upset about that name being mentioned in his bedroom.

'Why?'

'I can't get rid of the image of his face when that TV journalist cornered him. I felt sorry for him. He has been chasing after a ghost for years now. Why does he do it to himself? He used to be one of us.'

TT shrugged his shoulders – he didn't know and wasn't interested, either. He passed Angelina the saucer.

'How do you know him?' he asked, although Kaiserley had told him. But he was interested in her version.

She knocked off her ash. 'That's a long story. We first met years before the wall fell. I was very young at the time, just starting out, really. We quickly lost track of each other.'

'You planned the operation in Sassnitz together.'

If he had surprised Angelina, then she didn't let it show. She smoked, letting a mysterious smile cover her lips.

'What actually went wrong back then?' he asked.

'You know we're not allowed to talk about it.'

'Is it true that three people died?'

'The fact is that we never received what we were promised. We were supposed to get the microfilm before the deal could proceed. That's the way things worked back then. Unfortunately, the BND only let us in on the planning stages, but not on the mission itself. It was led by Kaiserley and he failed.'

She rubbed out the cigarette and pushed the saucer under the bed.

'Quirin Kaiserley was entirely responsible for the failure of the operation?'

'No, of course not. He was being watched. Unlike you, we were operating under allied law and could move about the GDR with a fair degree of freedom. They kept an eye on Kaiserley in Sassnitz. He accompanied the decoy and had the passports to smuggle the targets. There was an hour spent in the train station processing the transit passengers, an hour that wasn't documented. Sassnitz and the harbour were restricted military areas, so even we had to bow out.'

'That sounds more or less like the official version.'

She laughed. It sounded so beautiful that TT felt like little glass beads were rolling down his back.

'Of course we also had our people on board the train. A Swedish conductor later reported that the target persons left the train but that Kaiserley merrily continued on to Sweden. You'll have to read the rest in the files.'

'Classified. Even today.'

'Then ask Kellermann.'

She bent over him and kissed him. Her tongue slipped into his mouth and began a tempting game that TT submitted to willingly. He groaned as her hand slipped over his hips and thighs. Then she pulled back before he could let himself fall.

'He knows more than you think.'

Her dark eyes narrowed. TT could see the desire in them but also the enjoyment at keeping him in suspense.

'We only received a brief report that the target persons had disappeared, along with the passports, and that Kaiserley had no idea what had happened. He had apparently been asleep or was knocked out, or had simply drunk too much of that Danzig Gold-wasser. With that, the case was over for us. They weren't our passports. Kaiserley was transferred from operational reconnaissance to headquarters, and all indications were that he would survive the career setback. We only met again years later. In Föhrenweg.'

Föhrenweg was the legendary BND cover address in Berlin after the wall fell. An old villa from the thirties, it had been the secret headquarters of Field Marshal Wilhelm Keitel during the Second World War. Afterwards it was a CIA branch equipped with all the requirements expected from a modern intelligence service, from air conditioning to its own photo laboratory. The BND more or less moved in, subletting, and didn't even bother to install their own coffee machine. As usual, in the basement of world history.

'Kaiserley never stopped looking for whoever it was who betrayed the mission. He went too far with it. He suspected everyone. Everyone – Kellermann, me, even the Commander. He had no proof, and at some point he was a liability. He was an adventurer, a gambler – but not a lucky one. There was something relentless about him. Those kinds of people have no luck. You should steer clear of them.'

TT let himself fall back and stare at the ceiling. If only he had followed that advice earlier.

'A little later the Russians offered to sell us the Rosenholz file. We officially handed over the list of agent names to the unified German republic. But there wasn't a second mole like Guillaume among them. Or at least we didn't think so until now.'

Günter Guillaume, a personal aide to Chancellor Willy Brandt had been unmasked as an East German spy in 1974. Shortly thereafter Willy Brandt resigned. The affair had been a blow for both sides, which weighed heavily on the beginnings of the policy of détente. Markus 'Mischa' Wolf, the Stasi chief at the time, had even characterised Willy Brandt's fall as a huge disaster.

That had been long before TT's time. Everything he knew about it he had learned during his training. He hadn't been particularly interested in it.

'Rosenholz is incomplete. You withheld entire indexes.'

'Not us. The Russians, baby.'

'Even the official version? It hasn't been cleared up completely, even to this day.'

TT closed his eyes and felt her shift her weight and bend over him.

'In case you should ever have contact with him . . .'

'I don't.'

'If you do . . .'

'I don't know any Kaiserley. Never heard of him.'

'If he asks you for help . . .'

Her mouth opened, her tongue played with him, and her hand slid over his belly, down to the centre of his lust, where the blood collected, hot and pounding. He groaned and it took some effort to concentrate on what Angelina whispered into his ear.

'Tell him he should stop. He's rousing the wrong sleepers.'

The hotel was called Linneaholm Slott & Pensionat and was located in a small and not very well-maintained park, bordered by thundering highways. A thermal power station was directly behind it. The hotel only offered three rooms, and long ago it must have been part of a rural estate. Built in the nineteenth century, it seemed like a relic from the past, with its Baltic white walls, the dainty tower, and the curved window, but caught in the middle of a cross-section.

They were the only guests; the car park was empty. While Kaiserley waited at the reception for someone to appear, Judith pretended to admire the shiny parquet and the elaborate mouldings on the ceiling. She asked herself if he would take a double room, and how she should react. She was old enough to know that in some cases temptation was also a question of convenience. He was a good-looking man. She wasn't furious with him anymore. But she also had no feelings for him. A man and a woman in a foreign city, in a room, in a bed. Perhaps it would take more energy to withstand the temptation than to give in.

She was tired. Pain pounded in her palms. She longed for bed and a dreamless sleep. At the same time a flood of feelings threatened to overwhelm her. She would have liked to set off to Köpenhamnsvägen immediately. She dared not let Kaiserley continue researching alone; she had to get rid of him. But she also had to sleep. She had to leave. But she also had to stay. What the hell was wrong with her?

'Thomas!'

A pretty, happy woman in her early forties came in from the garden, her open face laughing. Judith looked around. No one was in the foyer except her and Kaiserley.

'It's been so long!'

'Sofie.'

Kaiserley opened his arms. She ran to him, hugged and kissed him, running her hands through his hair and finally over his stomach. Arm in arm, they turned to Judith.

'Sofie Kirseberg. This little jewel of a place belongs to her. This is Judith Kepler.'

Judith extended he hand and instantly regretted it. A cry of pain escaped her. Sofie immediately let go and pointed to the bandages.

'Are you hurt?' she asked. Her German sounded unfamiliar to Judith's ears. 'Do you need a doctor?'

'No, I'm fine, thanks.'

The two of them appeared to be fond of each other and to have known each other for quite some time, They still stood next to each other, Sofie's brown eyes glowing. She only reached up to Kaiserley's shoulder, had chin-length, dark curls and a broad, plain face. Her skin was radiant. Perhaps from pleasure, but perhaps also because she had just been working in the garden. She wore rubber boots, jeans, and a blue T-shirt with traces of soil on it. She was slender, but in contrast to Judith, had a hint of feminine voluptuousness.

Sofie slipped out of Kaiserley's embrace and bashfully swept a strand of hair from her forehead.

'You should have called. I would have prepared the room for you.'

Her gaze unintentionally turned to Judith with the word 'you.' 'On the second floor, as always?'

Kaiserley nodded. 'As always.'

Something about the familiarity of their interaction disturbed Judith. She was upset that she had just been thinking about sex in the hotel where Kaiserley and Sofie had apparently long shared that experience.

'I'll take a separate room,' she said quickly.

Too quickly. Kaiserley furrowed his brow.

'That's not a good idea.' He turned to Sofie. 'We'll stay together.'

Sofie nodded and slipped behind the carved wooden counter. Kaiserley pulled an ID from his briefcase and handed it to her. Sofie examined it fleetingly and moved to hand it back to him but Judith was faster and grabbed it.

'Nice picture,' she said and inspected the plastic card. 'Thomas Weingärtner.'

The photograph was less than two years old. The ID was laminated and contained a hologram. It was valid for eight years and had been issued by the District Authority in Pankow, Berlin. Where had Kaiserley got such a perfect, up-to-date counterfeit? She passed the piece of plastic over to him. He didn't say a thing. Sofie opened the drawer and removed a key with a heavy brass fob.

'Do you want breakfast?'

She could forget about the 'you plural'. Judith took the key and went towards the staircase.

'No, thank you,' she said.

The wooden staircase creaked so loudly she would have heard if he had followed her.

The room at the end of the hall was pretty and functional in its decor, with a large bathroom and two single beds. There were bay windows on three sides. The view to the south fell on the power plant, to the west the park could be seen, and the heavily trafficked Ystadvägen was to the north.

The windows were old, and as Judith immediately threw herself on the bed on the side nearest the road, the heavy trucks sounded so close she felt she was lying directly in the ditch.

She thought about the Dutch truck driver, about Martha Jonas, and the dogs in Sassnitz. And the scars on her lower arms that sometimes still went tight and itched.

She angrily boxed the pillow into shape. Love. Trust. Security. Warmth. Empty words, all of them. And Kaiserley was a master in playing with those concepts. For a brief moment she had actually had the feeling that he was interested in her. But even with his stories of betrayed betrayers he was only concerned with getting at that microfilm. And his old flame in Malmö.

She wanted to hate him but was too tired for that. She would have liked to experience that feeling once again, that moment when Kaiserley told her about her parents. She didn't know what it was called. And because she didn't have a label for it, she couldn't call it back.

She felt as if an avalanche had swept her along and buried her underneath it. Every single muscle in her body ached. Then she noticed that the weight upon her was nothing other than sleep. She spread out her arms and surrendered.

Judith awoke because she smelled coconut and curry. The sun shone through the window in the west and cast bizarre patterned shadows on the covers. Something rustled. She turned over with some effort and blinked. Kaiserley sat on the small couch and unpacked a plastic bag with food. He placed two plates on the low table and arranged cutlery next to them.

'I hope you like *Thai Kök*. I walked through half the city just to get this Pad Kra Thao.'

He removed the aluminium foil over the disposable plates. Judith sat up. She felt as if she had just woken up from an anaesthetic. She slowly came to and looked around.

Kaiserley had also purchased a carryall in addition to the food. The bag from a discount pharmacy made her hope for shampoo and toothbrushes. There was a bottle of wine on the table and two glasses. He pushed one of the plates in her direction.

'What's that?'

'Stir-fried veggies, chicken, and Thai basil. Lukewarm. But the green mango is worth going the extra mile for. I rented a car on the way back.'

He took one of the white plastic forks and began to eat. Judith pulled her plate closer and sniffed. It smelled good. She took a bite and suddenly realised how hungry she was.

'Outside there's a Toyota with GPS. I know you're planning to go somewhere, but you won't be going alone. We can get going immediately as soon as we've eaten.'

'What time is it?'

'Almost six. Where do you want to go?'

Judith held out her glass and let Kaiserley pour her some wine. He had taken a shower and shaved. She preferred him with a five o'clock shadow. But Sofie probably didn't like that. She pulled herself together. It was good that her single bed would stay single. She made a quick assessment: what would she gain by keeping Kaiserley in the dark? Nothing at the moment.

'The German church. That's where Borg's urn is headed when the investigation is concluded and she's been cremated. If she's to be buried, then the church should have been told.'

Kaiserley lowered his fork, which was almost at his mouth. For a moment he seemed surprised, but he recovered in a fraction of a second. His own glass was full, and he drank half of it in a single gulp. Then he nodded.

'Good research. I'd better not ask how you acquired that information. In case Borg still has a family, I have to meet them. Preferably tonight. The sooner, the better.

'We.'

'I.'

'Why such a rush?'

'Because I don't want you to end up like Borg. We're leaving traces. Regardless of what we do. At some point Borg's murderer will find us. Whoever it is appears to know his way around. There are still plenty of contacts around here from the old days.'

'Is that why you registered under an alias?'

'Yes.'

Judith continued eating. Poor Sofie. She had looked so happy when she'd recognised Kaiserley. But he must have lied to her from the start.

'Only active agents and criminals have fake IDs. Are you both now or what?'

'I still have a couple of friends from the good old days.'

'You have friends?'

'There are a ton of people at the BND who are just as unsatisfied as I am.'

'And they forge IDs?'

Kaiserley shook his head. Judith's obvious naïvety appeared to amuse him.

'They're faithful recreations.'

'Faithful recreations?'

'German documents for fictitious life stories actually do come from the Federal Printing Office. The BND has consultants in the city administrations of all state capitals. They just fill out the paperwork like normal, with the data from the BND.

Name, address, place of birth, passport photo. They get a few extra euros, and then they bag it up with the normal applications from normal people and send it off to the Federal Printing Office. Four weeks later, the agent has his new ID. Truer than true. Along with a cover story, a second, ironclad identity. At times I had up to six of them. Thomas Weingärtner is an insurance salesman who in your case would urgently advise you to get a full-term life insurance policy.'

'And once in a while people who don't happen to work for the BND also get fake documents?'

'Modelled after,' Kaiserley corrected her. He shovelled curry veggies and continued talking with his mouth full. 'The BND produces foreign IDs itself. There's even a separate workshop with true artists. They would never forge anything. That would be illegal.'

'So you're only *modelled after* Thomas Weingärtner? That's bullshit.'

'That's the official terminology.'

'Why do you need a fake – sorry – an ID that's been modelled after someone?'

'For renting a car, for example. To check into a hotel without a notice being immediately sent off to the relevant offices.'

'How practical. Could you order one for me too?'

Kaiserley instantly became serious. He laid down his fork. 'I could. But only if you convince me that you really need one. And if you completely understand what an alias means. Only the very few must know. Cover stories aren't a game. Think about witness protection programmes. Confidential informants. Arms trade and international terrorism. Most of all, think about the fact that agents also have families. When a cover story is blown, the consequences don't only affect one person. It's their entire private life as well.'

Judith pushed aside the thought that there wouldn't be many people affected in her case. She and Kaiserley were similar in several ways, but they dealt with it differently. Judith had become accustomed to her isolation. Kaiserley hadn't. He lived like a lone wolf, although no one wanted to follow his trail, and he suffered as a result. Even if he would never admit it.

'And there are still people at the BND who help you?'

'Don't say that so incredulously. Yes, there are.'

'How do you know that Thomas Weingärtner's cover won't also be blown?'

Kaiserley began to pack the aluminium foil into the plastic bag. 'Residual risk. Done now?'

He looked at her half-empty plate. Judith nodded. So Kaiserley relied on the loyalty of a BND associate, of all people. And she relied on Kaiserley, for better or for worse. She didn't like that. Kaiserley apparently had no problem living with the so-called residual risk.

He threw everything into the plastic bag and tied the straps in a knot.

'Almost six,' he said. 'Time for the service.'

18

The closer they came to the beach the more the houses were hidden behind tall fences and the larger the signs of the security companies became on the gates they watched over. Fridhem, Västervang and Bellevue were the most expensive neighbourhoods in Malmö. The church lay in a hidden one-way street that Quirin wouldn't have found without GPS.

They drove past people taking a stroll, frequently accompanied by large and apparently well-trained dogs. Only at second glance did they notice that almost all of the estates were equipped with surveillance cameras. The pretty Swedish wooden fences had given way to steel enclosures. A city had geared up.

Quirin didn't believe the crime rate had increased that dramatically in Sweden to justify this kind of isolation. He regretted that so many beautiful houses were now out of sight. He remembered a summer day with Sofie, who had taken him down to the old centre of Linhamn. And the delight that a young heart can feel at the sight of something new, something never seen before – whether the sea or the joy in the eyes of someone else.

He looked at Judith. She soaked up every image. The Öresund, which occasionally flashed through the tips of the trees. The tall buttresses of the bridge to Copenhagen. The foreign words on the signs above the shops. The gables of the hidden *fin-de-siècle* houses, only hinting at the splendour hidden behind the walls. She was so hungry to see everything, so curious about everything that was around the next corner. Quirin felt how old his heart had grown.

'Were you ever in Sweden?'

'No.'

'Ever out of the country at all?'

'Brandenburg,' she said and grinned.

He slowed down, driving past the church without finding a parking spot and once again having to merge into the traffic on Limhamnsvägen.

'I was in Italy once,' she added. 'Somewhere on the Mediterranean. I forget the name of the place. It was loud and hot and there was terrible music.'

'What do you do on holiday?'

'Everything that I haven't got around to. I don't have to travel. I think it's ridiculous. Thousands of miles, and then you're stuck in a hotel, the ice cream is bad, and the weather is far too hot.'

She plucked at the sleeves of her shirt again. By now Quirin knew that she unconsciously performed the gesture when things came up that she felt uncomfortable about.

'Then you've never seen the pyramids. Or the Eiffel Tower. or Niagara Falls. The old city of Granada. The grave of Frederick II, or the House of Hohenstaufen, in the Cathedral of Palermo.'

She stared out of the window.

'There are excellent study trips, even for singles. They set you up with the tour guide, get . . .'

'I don't need your advice!' she hissed. 'If I want to see something, then I'll go and look at it. I haven't had any desire to look at the Eiffel Tower up to this point. OK? Can you live with that?'

He nodded. He was an idiot.

The car turned back onto the one-way street. This time Quirin drove slightly more slowly through Köpenhamnsvägen. Sankta Anna appeared. He drove five hundred metres further and then rolled to a stop directly in front of a no parking sign. No cameras. Good. He looked around and adjusted the rear-view mirror, scanning the street behind them.

'Is everything OK?' Judith asked.

'Looks that way. You can never be one hundred per cent sure. We wouldn't be the only ones interested in the congregation after such a long time. It was the first stop for German immigrants. The pastor used to be one of us.'

'Can't you even keep your hands off the church?'

Quirin took one last look round. 'Wait here.'

'Not a chance!'

She unfastened her seatbelt, but Quirin held her hands. For a fraction of a second he felt as if he would like their touch. Hard, slender hands.

'You can't be there when two former agents talk to each other.'

'Bullshit.'

He let her go, stepped out, and activated the central locking system. Judith freed herself from her belt and went to follow him but couldn't open the door.

'Hey!' she yelled, and pounded the window with her fist. 'What the fuck?'

Quirin pocketed the key.

'It's for your own safety.'

'Motherfucker! Unlock the door!'

'I'll be right back.'

He scurried down the street to the rectory.

Judith tugged at the door once more, then gave up. The car was probably customised for agents at a special price. After all, the gentlemen had to travel frequently.

She searched the interior, but couldn't find anything that would have unlocked the doors. Judith was glad that the car was in the shade. She would give him exactly half an hour, then the side window would be a case for comprehensive cover.

She turned the rear-view mirror so she could watch the street. A woman was walking her dog, a huge Doberman. Panic crept up inside Judith at the sight of the animal. She made an effort to breathe calmly. The woman crossed to the other side of the street and disappeared from Judith's field of vision.

You're hysterical, she thought. You're turning into a wimp, bit by bit. Christina Borg hadn't been like that. Borg had been courageous. She had inquired and been persistent and hadn't let herself be bullied. Suddenly Judith was ashamed of herself. They simply deleted you, and you let it happen. Loser.

The side window burst with a bang. Judith whipped her arms up and for the fraction of a second out of the corner of her eye she saw a baseball bat travelling through the breaking glass. The alarm howled. Chunks and kernels of glass rained down on her.

The second blow hit her elbow. She screamed in pain and curled up. She wasn't able to ward off the third blow with her damaged hands. It was as if a firework had exploded directly behind her forehead. She hardly felt the blow, but then the warmth arrived, spreading within her. A powerful, unendingly high wave that took her up and lifted her, far up, unstoppable, toward the terrible, the beautiful.

A million suns flew past her, casting her into a black oblivion. Judith dissolved, more quickly than she ever had before. She left her body behind and sank down on the vibrations of her soul as if a huge eagle lifted her up and carried her away.

Someone was humming a lullaby.

'Lay thee down now and rest . . .'

There was the scent of roses, milk, and love.

'Sleep now, fall asleep.'

She was so tired. A sea of honey held her down, pulling her down to a golden floor. She lay curled up, fetal, trust and bliss covered her like a warm blanket. She tried to open her eyes but she no longer had any.

'Mama?'

It became cooler.

'Mama!'

'Hush. Relax. We'll be there soon.'

Red and gold and velvet and silk. A bird cried, loud and hoarse, as if it wanted to warn of what was about to happen. The moon poured silver over a clattering mill. Clunk. Clunk. Clunk.

Someone stood up. She wanted to defend herself but how could she when she no longer existed? She was nothing more than a breath of air, no more tangible than a confused thought. No being, only awareness.

'It'll be OK.'

She heard fear. The honey became viscous, appeared to freeze. Lenin bent over her. He looked at her with his bronze eyes.

'Mama!'

A man dressed all in white floated from heaven like Jesus. He smiled at her with arms extended. She felt herself flying away with him in the starry night. She wanted to look down at the earth one last time, but she couldn't see, although everything was so vibrant and clear. She was the parallel universe. She was God. She knew exactly what was happening. The man held her and flew with her to a space capsule circling the moon.

'I'm Yuri Gagarin,' he said. 'And this is my teddy bear.'

A big furry bear hopped toward them.

'You can't ever lose it. Do you understand? Never.'

The animal spun around once. It floated in space, slowly, weightless, and a red glowing sun rose in its belly.

Quirin sat in a kitchen, in an atmosphere mocked by its domesticity. There was a pile of meatballs on a platter, glistening, right out of the pan, but no one reached for them. Volfram and Gillis Vonnegut sat across from him, upright, stiff, with stony expressions on their faces, in which only a trained observer could detect mortal fear. With them, Madita, a pretty, sturdy girl with the typically Swedish deep summer tan. She sat on Gillis's lap and cuddled closer to her grandmother.

It was so quiet that only the buzzing of a fly up on the kitchen lamp disturbed the peace. Outside an alarm howled. Quirin briefly thought of Judith, but it would take more than mere fists to break that car. It could only withstand a collision below 30 mph, corresponding to the lowest security standards, and certainly wasn't made for Moscow circumstances but it had a GPS locating system and an anti-kidnapping function. In order to force the car open from the inside you had to know where the release buttons were located.

He turned to Volfram. He had recruited him when he was around the age Quirin was now. In the meantime he had become a grandfather. Kaiserley didn't overlook the silver strands in the pastor's hair and the deep wrinkles in his face.

'Perhaps we should talk in private?'

The pastor didn't answer. Madita clung even tighter to Gillis.

'At least send the child away.'

Madita shook her head. Gillis kissed the parting of her hair.

'Go upstairs. Mama will be back from work soon to pick you up.'

'I don't want to.'

'Madita?' Gillis grabbed the girl under her chin and raised her head. 'Do what I tell you. Then your mother won't find out about the kitten.'

Madita jumped down from Gillis's lap and scurried out. Quirin watched her go.

'What kitten?'

'Today a man approached her on her way home. Russian accent. Apparently she was supposed to help him catch it. We thought . . .' Gillis stopped.

'That it had something to do with the phone call,' Volfram said. 'She called and forced us to accept an assignment.'

He appeared relieved to be able to talk about it with someone.

'She?' Quirin asked. 'Who? One of us?'

He didn't use the expression out of loyalty to the service. It was simply the old division of East and West, good and evil.

'I believe so, but I don't know. Back then she would come and bring money for . . . I thought you knew.'

Quirin bent forward to get a better look at Volfram.

'I didn't know anything. And I was your commanding officer. You should have notified me immediately!'

'But I did! I tried to. But then it was said that you weren't there anymore and someone else would take over for me, but I never heard from you again. Until that woman came.'

'Who did she bring money for?'

'For two refugees. Mother and daughter.'

'How much?'

'A hundred thousand.'

'What for?'

'I don't know that either. I passed it on. I was allowed to keep ten thousand for the congregation. We needed the money. After the wall fell people swarmed here from the Eastern bloc. But they didn't get very far with their aluminium coins.'

Quirin felt a sudden urge to grab this man by the collar and shake him.

'How often was she here?'

'Four, five times. Ten times. I don't know anymore. All within one or two years. But that stopped long ago. Reunification was over twenty years ago.'

'Did she always come with so much money?'

Volfram nodded hesitantly. 'She was wearing a wig, you could see that at first glance. And sunglasses. It was a little like the old James Bond movies. She always had cash in a large envelope.

Sometimes we even drank coffee together. She laughed and said it was an offering.'

'And a tithe for the church.'

Gillis stood up and retrieved plates from a cupboard. Her hands were shaking as she placed one on the table in front of Quirin. She got cutlery and napkins from a drawer.

'You passed the money on to Irene Borg. Does she know her daughter has died?'

'Yes.'

'Where can I find her?'

The old couple exchanged a fleeting glance.

'She's moved away,' Volfram said hurriedly.

'Where?'

'To Kristianstad, I believe.'

Quirin slammed his fist on the table. The plates clattered, and a meatball rolled onto the wax tablecloth with the old-fashioned rose pattern. Volfram started.

'Where is Irene Borg? Or the woman who lived in Sweden unchecked for almost thirty years under that name and using our passport? Ten thousand marks! Three, five, ten times that amount! You didn't get it for nothing! Did you forge the municipal registry? The entries in the church register?'

Gillis sat down. She ran her hands over her skirt, again and again.

'We didn't take a cent for ourselves. Nothing. We only gave it away.'

Tears came to their eyes. Quirin repressed any sympathy he felt. He nearly had them. Just a couple more turns of the thumb-screws and then they'd talk. He hadn't felt this bad in a long time. Like a dirty, awful, godless bastard.

'You'll put Madita in danger if you don't start talking.'

'No!' Gillis almost screamed. 'I had a clear order. I was only allowed to give the address to one particular person.'

'Which address? Does that mean you betrayed her to the caller?'

Gillis looked at the floor. Kaiserley felt the turmoil rising inside himself. Something was going wrong here. Something had happened outside his control and he suddenly felt the fear that he was too late.

'They have Borg's address? And they're waiting there? For whom?'

He looked at Volfram, who reached for his wife's hand. Kaiserley didn't know who was giving whom strength and comfort. 'For Judith Kepler?'

Gillis nodded. 'Yes,' she whispered chokingly. 'No one else can know. Otherwise they'll get our little girl. They hired the Russians for that. They'll do it for only a couple of hundred euros.'

Tears ran down her face. Volfram lifted his hand and placed it on her forearm. He was shaking.

'Where did they wait for your granddaughter?'

'Less than two hundred metres from here. On the corner of Vikingagatan.'

'When?'

'Just before five.'

The arms on the kitchen clock pointed to six thirty. They were here. And they had a head start. They had been watching the house. Probably even knew that he was talking to the old couple. They had set a trap for Judith and were calmly waiting for her to stumble into it. The howling sirens had stopped. The sudden silence rang in his ears like an alarm. They had to have noticed the car. And Judith. The only thing keeping him in his seat was the thought of the kidnapping device.

'Tell me immediately where I can find Irene Borg. If they've harmed even a single hair of her head, then I'll make sure you are held responsible. Maybe not morally. But financially. They bought your silence. The Federal Government will retrieve the money, with interest on top.'

'We don't care,' Volfram said. 'As long as nothing happens to our granddaughter.'

'Take Madita to a safe place. They'll leave you in peace because you've completed your assignment and are out of their sights. If this woman still gets in touch, then immediately contact Sofie in Linneaholm. Understand?'

Gillis nodded.

'She lives on Ryttmästareg four in Rönneholm. Ten minutes from here.'

Quirin stood up and left the room. Gillis's sobs followed him long after he had closed the door and left the house.

19

Judith came out of the cold and oblivion. She opened her eyes and realised that she was lying on the floor in the fetal position. She was watching glow worms with the bright eyes of a newborn. They were dancing in front of her nose. There were so many of them. They looked like yellow grass on a summer meadow, with the wind blowing over it. They rocked, bending up and down, back and forth. Tentacles like sea anemones on the ocean floor.

She blinked, stretched out her hand and reached out. The worms felt soft and woolly. She lay on a carpet, shaggy, and the long floor moved as if it were alive. But the eyes staring at her were dead. And there was a knife protruding from the neck of the woman.

Judith tried to move. But she still wasn't properly conscious. The heroin still flowed through her veins, the trip had cooled, but the little snake was already stirring in her belly and hissing: 'more.'

Spaced out, she thought. *Hallucinations*. She tried to remember her dream. After such a long time, the drug apparently worked like a door-opener for her. But she wasn't able to go back through the crack.

Her tongue was a swollen clump. *Water*, she thought. *I need water.*

She knew that the snake would awaken. It was only a matter of time until the real horror trip would begin. Lenin, Gagarin, and a dead person with a knife in her neck were nothing in comparison.

She tried to roll onto her back and was amazed when she succeeded. She lifted both hands in front of her face. The bandages were soaked in blood, her arms completely blood-smeared. She sat up with a groan. The walls were dancing a tango. Forward, back. Chassé. She looked to the left. The woman was still lying there in a dark red puddle. The armchair was overturned, drawers pulled out of the cupboard, and the contents strewn everywhere.

Judith got to her feet and stumbled into the hall. She held onto the doorframe and tried not to lose her balance. The bath. Left. Right. Here. Tub.

She braced herself again the tile wall and left a red mark behind. When she turned on the faucet ice cold water pounded on her head. She positioned herself, just as she was, under the shower and watched with amazement as the water, light pink and gurgling, found its path to the drain. The snake in her belly roused itself. Judith began to shake, so much that she was barely able to turn off the water. A single thought bored its way through the soft cotton in her brain: cold turkey. It would come. She needed pills.

She got out of the shower and dragged herself to the sink, dripping wet. She hardly recognised her face in the mirror. Her eyes and nose were swollen, her left jaw glowed an unnatural red. She ripped open the mirrored door and searched for medication. Toothpaste. Salves. Tinctures. Shampoo. She cleaned out the shelves with an agitated sweep of her hand, everything falling into the sink. She rifled through her loot with flying haste without finding what she was looking for. Sleeping pills. Everyone had sleeping pills.

Högt blodtrck. Antipsykodika. Akut stressreakition. Bingo. She tossed a half-dozen blue pills into her mouth and drank directly from the tap. She didn't care about the effects. The main thing was that she wouldn't see any more bodies. She hoped that five years without hard drugs had been enough. That her head would cooperate, and her body too. That she could handle it like an accident. And that she would find enough pills. She was about to reach for the bottle with the blue pills when she heard it.

A quiet sound. She lifted her head. Someone had come into the apartment. She looked around helplessly. The window over the toilet was far too small to climb through She took a silent step away from the sink and hid behind the half-open door. The steps came closer, quiet and creeping. Judith tried to concentrate on the tiles. They were beige and the grout wriggled in front of her eyes, forming an amorphous net. The shaking didn't stop. She pressed her jaws together but couldn't do anything to stop her teeth chattering. She slid down along the wall.

Acute stress reaction.

Her knee touched the door, which began to close unbearably, treacherously slowly. The steps outside paused. She fell over. Someone pushed against the wood, but her body blocked the path. She was unable to move. She was pushed aside slightly and saw a shoe, hiking boots. Cognac. Expensive.

'Judith?'

She knew the voice but couldn't think of the name. Someone shook her, tried to pull her up, but she was soaking wet and the bathroom was simply too small.

'Judith!'

He hit her face. From far off her brain signalled pain.

'Wake up!'

She blinked. Kaiserley's grotesquely distorted face came closer. He had the nose of a hippo. If she would tell him that . . . she grinned.

'We have to disappear. Immediately.'

She tried to raise her hand to shoo him off. Annoying, stupid idiot. She had other problems.

'Irene Borg is dead. Come.'

He grabbed her by the armpits and pulled her up. Her trainers slipped, she kicked frantically, but finally she got to her feet, shaking, rocking, bent over like a folding knife. He straightened her and pressed her against the wall.

'It's OK,' he said. He studied her, recognising what must have happened, and suddenly he pulled her close. 'It's OK. I shouldn't have left you alone.'

'You . . .' She fought for air. Her throat contracted. The gag reflex was overpowering but she was still strong enough to think that he hadn't deserved what had happened. 'You locked me in, you asshole.'

'I'm sorry. Judith. My God.'

She pushed away from him. The pills tamed the snake inside her, but they also pulled the rug out from under her feet. She wiped her mouth with the back of her hand, pushed off, and stumbled into the hall. The body was still lying on the carpet.

Something inside her broke. Her heart hammered in her ribcage, and she asked herself why everything she longed for ended in a nightmare. She stumbled toward the woman and went to her knees. She stretched out her hand and comforted her. The woman's skin was still warm.

'Don't,' he said.

He wrapped his arms around her again and pulled her away.

'It's not her. It's not her. Judith, it's not her. I saw a picture of your mother back then. Judith!'

But it could have been her. She pushed him away and bent over the body. Irene Borg had dark hair, streaked with grey. Her lipstick was smudged, her mouth opened as if crying out in surprise. Perhaps she had once been pretty, in an alluring, coarse way that could quickly slip into the vulgar. Judith stretched her hand out once again, but Kaiserley caught her once again and embraced her.

She waited for the tears but they didn't come.

'We have to leave,' he said. 'What did you touch in here?'

'I . . . no idea.'

She tried to wrench her gaze from the corpse, but failed. Kaiserley wiped her wet hair from her forehead and held her tight. She didn't care. It meant nothing to her.

'What did you take?'

'Some pills.'

He turned her face in his direction and forced her to look at him.

'Was that you?'

She pushed his hand away.

'I was in the car. Someone broke the window. And then . . .'

She stopped, looking at her arms. Hastily pushed the fabric up and inspected the skin. Nothing. He placed his index finger on her neck.

'Here. You have an injection site. Heroin?'

She nodded. The snake in her belly wearily lifted its head and laid back down.

'Overdose. It was really intense. My body must still be used to it. It would have killed anyone else. You fall over and lie there with your face in the dirt. After that you're either dead or you get back up.'

'We have to clean up our tracks and disappear.'

He stood up and tried to pull Judith up along with him. He gave up after the third attempt and left her sitting there.

'Bleach,' she said. 'Everyone has bleach. Destroys amino compounds. And soapy water for the finger prints. My hands, in the shower . . . you'll get it with that. But not that over there.'

She pointed to a huge puddle of blood surrounding the body. She'd need Dombrowski's van for that. Kaiserley went into the kitchen and returned with a dripping sponge.

'Once more: what did you touch? Hello?'

She shrugged her shoulders. He wiped the door frames, and a little later she heard water running in the bathroom. Then he came back and bent over Irene Borg.

'We'd better take that along.'

He pulled the knife out of the dead woman's neck and deposited it in a plastic bag. Judith turned her head.

'They'll find something,' she said. 'Hair. Fingerprints. Something will be left over from me. I have a record.'

Kaiserley nodded.

'They'll know that I was here.' She looked up at him. But she didn't get an answer. In the distance, the police sirens were coming closer.

The gulls were crying out. Judith lay on the back seat and saw the façades of houses and blue sky flying by. Kaiserley and Sofie sat up front. The flow of air whistled through the broken side window. Cranes appeared. The air changed, became moister and smelled brackish. They were approaching the harbour. Kaiserley braked sharply; Judith almost fell off the back seat. He hadn't spoken another word to her, just bundled her into the car and picked up Sofie at the hotel. Now he was handing the car key to Sofie.

'Try to get rid of all the traces in the car, and park it somewhere. I'll report it as stolen.'

Sofie took the key and nodded. Kaiserley got out and opened the back door. He held a plastic bag with a knife in his hand. Judith sat up. She felt like a roll of carpet. Dirty, trampled on, and disposed of. He waited until she had climbed out of the car, not an expression on his face.

They were parked directly on the quay. It must have been in the evening, but the sun still hung in the sky as if glued to it. A man leant against the iron railing and casually watched a cutter sail past. He wore a grey suit and didn't fit in the scene. He heard the doors slam shut and turned around. Kaiserley squinted. Judith couldn't tell if he was happy about the man's appearance or if he wished he would go to hell.

'Kaiserley,' the man said. 'It's a pity we're meeting again under these circumstances.'

'Long time no see.'

'But when it comes down to it, old Winkler is still good for something. Right?'

Winkler wasn't so old. Maybe in his mid-fifties, but he looked like he had spent his life in the office and only accidentally escaped. He was a mid-sized, slender man with a high forehead and an easily forgotten face. He had called Kaiserley by his real name. Sofie acted as if it was the most normal thing in the world that her lover was sometimes called Weingärtner, and sometimes Kaiserley. Perhaps she hadn't heard it.

'Who is that?'

Kaiserley didn't pay attention to her. He slowly walked to the railing, opened the bag, and let the knife fall into the water. Winkler looked on without emotion. Sofie didn't let either of them out of her sight. When they began to talk quietly with one another, she pulled Judith away from the car door and towards the boot.

'Old colleagues,' she said. 'They probably have a lot to say. I have something for you.'

Judith turned around. Sofie held a dress in her hands and viewed it with a whiff of melancholy.

'You can't go as you are now. Change clothes on the cutter and throw your old things overboard.'

She handed it to Judith. It was made of dark blue cotton chintz with a row of buttons. It looked elegant. It must have cost her a fortune.

'Thank you.'

'What happened? You look terrible. Did they beat you up?'

Judith shrugged her shoulders. She helplessly bunched up the dress and didn't know what to do with it. The snake in her belly was getting hungry.

'It's OK. I get it. Take good care of him.'

Judith looked over to the two men. They didn't appear to be close friends. Kaiserley had his hands in his jeans pockets and was looking past Winkler to the cutter while Winkler seemed to be relaying something that didn't appear to be very pleasant. The plastic bag had vanished into thin air.

'What do you mean?' Judith asked. Kaiserley seemed to be the type of man who could take care of himself.

'He's still where he was when he left the BND,' said Sofie. 'Mentally, I mean. The wheels have begun to turn again. At some point he won't be able to get off.'

'I think he knows exactly what he's doing.'

'How well do you know him?'

'Not at all.'

Sofie followed Judith's gaze and her eyes softened.

'Don't try to change that,' she said.

Winkler placed his forearms on the railing. It was supposed to look cosmopolitan or at least as if he knew what was going on.

'The inner ring is locked down. By midnight they'll have expanded the search to the second. ID controls on the ferries, increased deployment of security forces at the airport. Discreet but effective. I don't know how you managed to leave the apartment less than two minutes before the police arrived.'

'Did Sofie notify you? I expressly forbade her from . . .'

'She's not the only one who's worried about you. Shut up for once and do what I tell you.'

Winkler pointed to the cutter. 'That's our courier between Kaliningrad and Copenhagen. He'll make an extra round trip for you tonight. You'll be in Sassnitz in six hours. Don't fuck up and make sure you return to Berlin separately by tomorrow morning. Kepler has to go to the police. Voluntarily. I don't know what shit has hit the fan there but she's already far too deep in your shit for you to leave her here. So make sure she gets back safely and that no one knows she was ever here. Understand?'

'So the two of us are supposed to take the fall for you?'

'Be glad that you're still around.'

'Who put the Vonneguts under pressure? Who killed Irene Borg?'

'I don't know. But we're working on it. There are rumours that someone hired the Russian mafia for a special job. Our confidential informant can't say much more at the moment.'

'The Borgs were just freeloaders. Fled the GDR with stolen passports and knowledge that made you guys susceptible to blackmail.'

'No one blackmails us.'

'Why were they murdered then? With the mother I could guess the connections. But the daughter had nothing to do with it!'

'Really? Then why did she go to Germany and throw the Rosenholz originals on the market for the highest bidder?'

'That's a lie.'

'Ask Kresnick in Schwerin. Or Kellermann. The only catch is that none of them will talk to you. You shouldn't have thrown in the towel, Kaiserley. Then most of this would have been much easier. Christina Borg wasn't a noble avenger. She was a cunning bitch. Just like her mother.'

'Is being a bitch a death sentence these days?'

Winkler laughed quietly. He had a dark, deep voice which surprised people as much as his clear, analytical reasoning and efficient manner of working, differentiating him from his direct superior, Kellermann, in nearly every regard. Everyone in the service expected him to leapfrog Kellermann in his next promotion. Some of them even pictured him becoming head of intelligence.

Winkler motioned with his head toward Judith, who came hobbling over. 'Is she still alive then? A junkie? I can see it at first glance.'

'Then you see too little.'

Winkler smiled at Judith and lowered his voice so that she couldn't hear his next words, addressed to Kaiserley.

'Interesting. I didn't know you were like this. You'll explain it to me when the time comes.' Then louder: 'Peter Winkler. Telecommunications and Communications Systems South. I'm pleased to meet you.'

'Kepler. You can pull up the rest in Pullach. Good day, gentlemen.'

She ignored his outstretched hand, stepped onto the jetty, and boarded the cutter. Quirin and Winkler watched her go.

'Charming,' Winkler said. 'I wish you a pleasant journey.'

Judith stood at the small window of the galley and looked at Winkler's shoes. Wingtips. Hand-sewn. Did people earn that much as civil servants? The quay bulkhead ended precisely at eye-level. She could see the car if she stood on her tip-toes. Winkler and Kaiserley said their farewells. The wingtips went to the left, the hiking boots towards the car.

She went to the sink and filled water in a glass that had been standing on a drying rack. A sailor appeared briefly and nodded to her without saying a word. Probably better that way. She drank and wondered if there were sleeping pills on board. Or that stuff for seasickness and motion sickness. The tenfold dose might help her survive the next hour. She went back to the window.

Kaiserley walked up to Sofie and embraced her. Just kiss her, will you, Judith thought. She's been waiting for it the whole time. When he finally did, she watched until she couldn't take the sight anymore.

The ship's medicine chest was in the shower. Judith rummaged through the little cabinet. The usual pain medicine, salves, and tinctures. A little bottle with pills. *Aplicabile la insomnie*. What was that? Italian? Romanian? She tried to remember what Kaiserley had told her about Romania, but she could no longer concentrate. The snake was crawling through her veins like glowing poison. She took four pills at once and pocketed the rest. Then she dragged herself back into the narrow passageway and found a dark, smelly cabin with two folding beds stacked one over the other. She fell onto the lower bed and closed her eyes. She tried to think about the feeling she didn't have a name for but it was gone. Disappeared. Perhaps she shouldn't watch other people kiss.

20

Kaiserley woke her shortly after midnight. He gave Judith some time to collect all five of her senses and waited for her on deck. In the meantime she had taken a shower and then put on Sofie's dress. It smelled slightly of roses and fabric softener. She buttoned it up to her neck, leaving her old clothes for the boatman, then climbed up via the narrow iron ladder.

He stood in the wheelhouse, next to the captain, and looked through a night vision device.

'Good evening,' she said.

The captain nodded briefly to her. '*Buná sera.*'

He was small and perched on his seat like a midget king. The radar sent its fluorescence into the night and bathed what little Judith could recognise in a green tint.

'Coffee?' The captain pointed forward with his index finger. 'Good weather, good journey.'

Several lights blinked in the distance. Kaiserley raised the binoculars and watched the coast. The little captain handed her a cup from which he had apparently just been sipping. Judith couldn't see the contents, and just downed it. Lukewarm Nescafé. Completely OK.

'Where will we be landing?' she asked.

'Wherever you want.'

'Sassnitz, if possible.'

She had to get back to her vehicle as soon as possible. Hopefully it was still parked in front of the cemetery, otherwise she'd have to ask Kaiserley for money. The captain nodded. He moved the joystick, and the motors roared. The ship moved even more quickly through the water.

'How are you doing?' Kaiserley asked.

'Splendid. May I?'

She motioned to the captain's cigarettes. He nodded. She stumbled to the door and smoked outside. The lights came closer. Perhaps another half-hour, and she would finally be rid of Kaiserley.

She had reached the end of the road. She would never find out what had really happened. All of the witnesses were dead. And the microfilm, if it had ever existed, had disappeared into the primordial mud of history. It hadn't been any use, not at all.

Only this new, unknown feeling. A kind of yearning, like wanderlust. Did that exist? A wanderlust for people who have long disappeared? She looked up and was surprised to see the stars so close. The sea was the ultimate dark spot. She found Cassiopeia, but the North Star had disappeared behind a cloud. She tried to remember the legend of the constellation. Cassiopeia had enraged the gods, and had to sacrifice her daughter.

She took a drag and watched Kaiserley behind a window smudged with saltwater. He appeared to be on an even keel. According to the legend, Andromeda was chained to a rock. She was lost. A hero named Perseus saved her. As if sensing she was looking at him, Kaiserley turned his head. Their glances connected. She quickly looked away.

Comparing Perseus with Kaiserley. Absurd. It must have been these last days and this sudden, forced intimacy. She wasn't used to it. She couldn't handle it. She had tried, several times, because she had told herself that a normal relationship was part of a normal life. But that was not a good enough reason to want one. She couldn't handle intimacy. Or what people thought of as intimacy.

A powerful wave rolled under the ship and lifted it. The bow divided the water, which washed over the side of the ship, frothing and spraying. She shivered but her teeth had stopped chattering. Her bodily functions were slowly shifting from red to yellow.

Surely he couldn't believe that she had killed the wrong Irene Sonnenberg? She forced herself to go through the apartment in her mind, and remembered the chaos, drawers ripped out, clothing strewn. It was like a set decoration for a TV show on drug-related crime. Who knew about her addiction? Who had access to her past?

The wind pressed an oily cloud of warm diesel fumes down on them. The smell reminded her of Sassnitz, a city that had lost its past, just like her. The ship slowed, the motor fell into a quiet putter. They were approaching Prorer Wiek bay. Judith watched one building pass by after the next. The moon shone brightly through the fractured clouds, and she began to recognise the dark silhouette of the chalk cliffs. The first lights of the street lamps appeared behind the dark woods. They shimmered like soft pearl necklaces.

The ship headed directly for the old harbour. Judith wondered if the infrastructure still existed for docking such a large ship. The little captain didn't care much about that. He sailed as close as possible to the farthest end of the old harbour basin. The quay bulkhead was still over a metre away. The sailor stood on the redoubt and called up commands. The machines were running at full speed. Suddenly, someone stood next to her.

'You have to jump!'

Kaiserley climbed over the ship's rail, pushed off, and landed nimbly on the shore. He turned around and stretched out his hands to Judith.

'Go!'

She stood at the railing and held on tight.

'It's really easy! Judith!'

The sailor made a universal gesture anyone would understand: get out of here.

The motor screamed, the ship reared up. Judith swung herself over the railing. The ship's side slowly leaned toward the shore.

'Now!' Kaiserley yelled.

She jumped. He caught her but let go of her so suddenly that she stumbled and nearly fell into the water. The ship turned away. The ground swayed under her feet, but she stayed upright.

On the other side of the pier, the breakwater diffused the power of the sea. A mass of water whipped against the stones with a loud bang. It was colder here, rougher here than in Sweden. They walked off towards the shore where a tall building stood. It looked like a huge, black domino with several brightly lit windows. The Rügen Hotel. They reached the entrance at nearly the same time. Panting, Judith stopped to catch her breath. The last guests were still seated in the restaurant. Candles stood on the tables spreading a romantic light. A man held a woman's hand. He said something to her, she smiled at him, and lifted her glass. Judith heard footsteps behind her and didn't know what she should say in parting.

'The bar's still open,' Kaiserley said.

Gabi Jensen was polishing a glass, holding it up to the light, before placing it in a hanging shelf over the bar. The jukebox was playing a schmaltzy love song quietly. She glanced at the clock on the wall, vaguely reminiscent of a ship's wheel. Along with the other nautical knick-knacks, it was supposed to convey a maritime air. Almost twelve thirty. If no other guests came she could close on time.

Svenja, the waitress, came in and skewered a receipt on the nail next to the till.

'Another beer,' she said and left again.

Gabi pulled the glass back down and placed it under the tap. While the foam rose in the tulip glass, she noticed the couple just stepping into the lobby through the rotating glass door. A good-looking man wearing a linen suit with wet legs, and a woman, maybe in her mid-thirties, who seemed to be slightly disoriented. The two of them looked as if they had just survived a capsizing. They didn't stop at the reception, heading straight for the glass door. The man held it open for the woman, who slipped inside and waited for him, so that he could take the lead again. There was something vaguely familiar about him.

'Good evening.'

The beer ran over and she quickly released the tap.

'Mr Weingärtner?'

The woman instinctively made a face, but Gabi had long ago stopped taking much notice of female guests. In the end the men paid and gave tips. She beamed at the late arrivals.

'You've come back again! I almost didn't recognise you.'

Weingärtner took off his jacket and hung it over the back of the chair.

'Fancy you still remembering me! How are you? Gabi, right?'

She smiled, happy he hadn't forgotten her either. His companion climbed onto the bench next to the bar and slid across to the corner, as if she didn't want to be seen.

'I hope we'll still be able to get something from you.'

'For you, always, Mr Weingärtner. Always. We no longer have the Hungarian Bull's Blood wine. But I do have a good Bordeaux.'

He nodded. She opened the drawer where the red wine bottles stood and pulled one out. Then she turned to the woman.

'For you as well?'

Something about her eyes was off. Her whole face looked as if she had been involved in a brawl. Gabi was tempted to offer her an ice pack. She was familiar with those kinds of wounds. But the women that carried them usually looked different. Not so . . . proud.

'Anything 80 proof or more.'

Gabi nodded. 'Our sea buckthorn liqueur is . . .'

'I don't want liqueur. I want whisky.'

Gabi looked at Weingärtner uncertainly. He nodded. Good. If that was what she wanted and he paid for it . . . she poured the wine, and placed a generous glass of Jim Beam in front of her.

'Ice?' she asked.

The woman shook her head and downed the whisky in a single gulp.

'Another one,' she said.

Weingärtner sat down next to her. Svenja came over and picked up the Pilsner.

'How long have you been working here, Gabi?' he asked.

'Thirty years this autumn.'

She held the tumbler up to the opening of the portion controller and pressed it up several times.

'Where are the ladies this evening? Surely they're not off already?'

Gabi placed the glass in front of the woman. She was surprised that Weingärtner would raise the subject of prostitution in her presence.

'Karin and Anita are in their rooms. The others have given up. These days all the girls are from Estonia and Poland. They're young – very young.'

Gabi sighed. She saw her own, plump silhouette in the reflection of the glass door.

'And cheap. I mean reasonably priced. But you surely don't . . . right?'

'No, thanks. Can you still remember Marianne Kepler?'

The woman, who had been staring into her Jim Beam until then, suddenly lifted her head.

'No, I'm not at all familiar with the name.'

'She worked here in the mid-eighties. Looking after the guests.'

'That was before my time.'

She had been told to react to such questions with that sentence. The topic of the GDR past and the role the Rügen Hotel had played during those days didn't exactly fit with its current image.

'Gabi. Thirty years. Service anniversary. Do the maths.'

She turned away and arranged the wine bottles. 'Yes, you're right. Those were the days. In summer they camped on the beach in tents and gave rock concerts. I was even there a couple times. Dirk Zöllner, Feeling B and Autumn in Peking.' She giggled. 'I was really cheeky. Listened to a lot of "other bands" then. And Zöllner. I was head over heels in love with Dirk.'

There wasn't very much left to be arranged. She assessed the order of the bottles and then closed the drawer. 'But he wasn't in love with me. Unfortunately.'

'Marianne Kepler. You have to remember her. She came from Sassnitz and lived on Bachstrasse.'

'Someone from Bachstrasse? What did she look like?'

'Medium size, dark curly hair.'

His wife or girlfriend or chance acquaintance or fellow accident survivor had swallowed the whisky like water and held out the empty glass again without a word.

'That should be enough, from a medical perspective,' Weingärtner said to her.

'But not from a psychological one.'

Her voice was clear. By now the jukebox was playing a soppy love song. Gabi took the glass, placed it in the dishwasher and pulled a new one from the shelf.

'There was someone from Bachstrasse, yes. But she was blonde. Usually. She had a wig but once she slipped and then I saw that she actually had brown hair. You mean her?'

She poured out a triple, and hoped the woman wouldn't fall off the bench.

'Who did she have contact with?'

'It's all so long ago. The girls came because they wanted to buy themselves a pair of Wrangler jeans in the Intershop. Or a little Jacobs coffee. And maybe some of them wanted to meet someone who would marry them and get them out.'

'Marianne Kepler too?'

Gabi reached for the sea buckthorn liqueur and held it up. Weingärtner nodded to her encouragingly, meaning he would foot the bill. She served herself a shot glass. For closing time.

'She wasn't one of them. She didn't do it for the money. At least not just because of what the guys gave her. Occasionally someone did come around, I think he was her case officer.'

'What was his name?'

'You don't really want to know that. They never used their real names. Stanz was what he called himself. Hubert Stanz. I can remember that the name fit him. He looked like someone who notched the edges of the stamps at the post office. Cheers.'

Weingärtner clinked glasses with her. His whatever-you-want-to-call-her raised her eyebrows, as if all of this was some-how amusing. Maybe she was crazy. Or fall-down drunk, although she still seemed sober as a judge.

Gabi drank the liqueur and felt herself relax after her long day. Svenja scurried in.

'Two Sambucas.'

Gabi nodded and searched for the bottle on the shelf.

'Someone from Schwerin?' he asked.

'I assume so. I think she delivered quite a lot of information. She was well liked among the guests. And she made a lot of sales. There was plenty left over for us, because the men were in a good mood. Today I view things differently, of course. But back then we didn't think to ask, if there were a couple of Krone or Mark. We knew what was going on: all of the women at the bar were working for the Stasi.'

'Cheers,' the woman said. 'I think I'm going to throw up.'

'But not here!' Gabi's voice became sharp. 'Would you like to get some fresh air?'

Instead of answering, the woman raised her empty glass. Weingärtner took it from her and put it aside. 'That's enough,' he said quietly, and he didn't just mean the alcohol. He turned back to Gabi. 'What happened to her?'

Gabi put a coffee bean in each of the shot glasses and gave herself some more sea buckthorn liqueur. On the house.

'They said alcohol and pills. That happened from time to time. There wasn't much discussion of suicide in the GDR. She was gone, from one day to the next.'

'And Stanz?'

'Funny that you mention it now.'

Svenja returned, placing the two Sambuca glasses on the tray. She lit the alcohol with a lighter.

'Table two wants the bill.'

'Right away. Another one . . .?'

Gabi looked at the woman next to Weingärtner in surprise. She had the empty whisky glass in her hand, but she was leaning against the wall with her eyes closed and mouth slightly opened, as if asleep. Gabi bent over the bar towards them, as far as her breasts and decency would allow, revealing both.

'Stanz never came again,' she whispered.

The woman slid down the wall and her head landed on Weingärtner's shoulder.

'Can you give me the bill,' he said. 'Thanks.'

Gabi stepped to the till. 'Do you need a room?'

Weingärtner nodded carefully. 'Certainly looks that way.'

When the two had left and Svenja had taken off her apron and said goodbye, Gabi closed the bar.

Marianne Kepler. It was so long ago that the number probably wouldn't work anymore. She had never written it down because the digits themselves would have been revealing. But she had it in her head, even today.

She stepped to the telephone, lifted the receiver, and dialled. And to her great surprise, someone picked up.

21

The sea stretched to the horizon. The morning sun reflecting off the waves was dazzling. Where the sky began a delicate haze hugged the surface of the water. She couldn't tell if that was Sweden already, or just the curvature of the earth.

She sat on the eighteenth storey of the Panorama Restaurant nursing a cup of coffee in her injured hands. Kaiserley had gone down to the reception to use the telephone. He wanted to find out what awaited her in Berlin. Maybe Dombrowski had reported his shitty car as stolen after all, she thought. He shouldn't be such a hard-ass. It wasn't the first time someone had borrowed it for a long weekend.

In front of her lay a plate of scrambled eggs and bread rolls. She slowly lifted her fork to her mouth. She had to eat. She would be back in Berlin by noon. She tried to remember the schedule for the week. Early shift, hospital. She could take her time because with luck she'd arrive just before clocking-off time. The images of the past days resurfaced, and she pushed them aside with all the strength she could muster. But the fork in her hand began to shake, and the scrambled eggs fell onto the plate. *Come on, pull yourself together. Once again, from the beginning.*

Far below her lay the old harbour. The ramps had been rebuilt, no longer leading to the large ferries, but to a museum. Pedestrians strolled along the shore. Judith stretched her neck and peered to the right, but the tips of the trees blocked the view of the old fish factory and what lay hidden a bit further on. It was shortly before ten. Young women wearing white aprons began to clear away the buffet.

She stood up and bummed a cigarette off a love-struck couple. Then she headed off with it onto the balcony. The wind was cold and tugged at her hair. She had showered for a long time and afterwards finally managed to comb her hair properly. Although her head and her hands still ached, the alcohol had numbed her so well that she had been able to get a couple of hours' sleep. Once again, sharing a room with Kaiserley. His bed had been empty when she awoke. He had started the morning with forty minutes of swimming. Great. She felt miserable, but at least she was back among the living. He had returned to the room at precisely the moment she was ready to leave. Showered, refreshed, with wet hair and smelling of water and chlorine. Just a phone call, he'd said. Not from a smartphone, not from the landline in the room. Downstairs, in the telephone booth.

Did payphones even exist anymore? Probably only in Sassnitz, where time appeared to be standing still, somewhere between revolution and resignation.

Someone stepped onto the balcony through the sliding glass door. She didn't turn around because neither Kaiserley nor anyone else was worth the effort. She didn't know why she was furious at him again. It had nothing to do with his annoying athleticism. It was more to do with Malmö and Sofie and those old-boy networks that had never gone away and continued to marginalise people like her.

'Good morning.'

A man stood next to her and took an audibly deep breath. She looked up briefly. He was a head taller than her, light-skinned, and muscular. There were freckles shining on his fore-head. Mid-level administrative officer. Citizen centre branch office manager. She didn't answer.

'I assume Mr Kaiserley still needs a couple of minutes. That's good. We can talk without being disturbed. My name is Dr Matthes.'

She slowly turned around and inspected him, from head to toe. His inconspicuousness was deliberate. At second glance he revealed authority and self-confidence. You had to have both if you dared to set the dogs on someone. Judith could hardly keep her impulse to flee in check. There could only be one reason why he had showed up at the hotel.

'What happened to Martha Jonas?'

'She suffered a minor stroke after your visit. Nothing severe. We'll get it under control.'

'Well. Perhaps you should be slightly less generous with her medication. She seemed in complete command of her faculties to me.'

Dr Matthes gazed at the sea, intently. He folded his hands behind his back and rocked back and forth in a state of complete relaxation. The way people look standing in front of a painting in a gallery, passing judgement.

'You're back in Sassnitz. You surely don't really plan to pay Ms Jonas another surprise visit?'

'And if I do?'

Matthes sighed. For a moment, a seagull hung in the air no more than two metres away from them. It stared at Judith with flinty eyes and then turned away.

'You're not welcome anymore, Ms Kepler.'

'It's a free country.'

'Certainly. But Martha Jonas is under our special protection. This country owes her a deep debt of gratitude.'

'Which? The free country or the other one?'

Matthes smiled. Judith could imagine that women liked trusting him. He looked reliable and helpful. Someone who liked to listen. Unfortunately, with Judith, he had crossed paths with someone who didn't like to talk.

'Both, Ms Kepler, both. Even if Mr Kaiserley would like to tell you otherwise, we've arrived at the here and now. Most of us, anyway. Only a few still live in the past, and every attempt to tell them the truth ends painfully.'

'Martha Jonas doesn't have Alzheimer's, in case you want to tell me that. She's still as sharp as a tack. There's no reason for me to doubt what she told me.'

'And what would that be?'

Judith wanted to push past him, but he blocked her path. The couple was gone. The staff as well. No one would notice if Matthes just took her and . . .

'What did she tell you?' Matthes asked. His voice, warm and soothing just a moment ago, was now cold.

'That her psychiatrist is an asshole.'

Matthes grimaced.

'I can help you if you choose to cooperate.'

Judith's hand groped for the railing. She wanted to be able to hold on if it came down to the alternative to non-cooperation. Matthes was standing so close to her now that she could smell his cologne. Dunhill. It was a scent she would have recognised upwind in a force ten gale. She didn't know why, maybe because it was so heavy and musky and unforgettable.

'What does that mean?' she asked.

'You forget about us. And I'll help you. One hand washes the other.'

Eighteen storeys. She tried not to think about it. His smile was mild and sincere once more.

'Whatever Martha Jonas can tell you, I can tell you. Just ask me. Go ahead. I'll tell you anything you want to know.'

An absurd thought flashed through Judith's mind.

'Lenin,' she said. 'Where can I find him?'

'He isn't here anymore.' Matthes's lips twisted into a regretful smile. 'No one knows where he's gone.'

'Oh, that's a shame. Didn't keep track of him very well, did you?'

How absurd were the conversations she'd been having lately. The whole world was a madhouse. Her hand unclenched, but still rested on the railing. Clearly Matthes was crazier than his patients.

'Good question,' the doctor said. 'But you weren't visiting Ms Jonas because of Lenin. You wanted something else. If you can keep your mouth shut about *Haus Waldfrieden*, permanently, I can give you something in return.'

'You must be scared shitless.'

'Not me, Ms Kepler. I just want to make sure that our beautiful lawn isn't suddenly trampled by a hoard of wild, pseudo-investigative journalists. But then you're in pretty deep yourself.'

Matthes looked around quickly. They were still completely alone. The waiting staff had abandoned the half-cleared buffet and were nowhere to be seen. He went through the sliding glass door, into the restaurant and waited until Judith followed him. Something about the change in his tone and body language made her realise he was slowly losing patience.

'What do you mean by deep?'

'The police are looking for you in connection with a homicide in Berlin. They'll lock down all the cemeteries in Sassnitz once they know you're on the way. And I don't even want to start with what happened in Malmö. You appeared to leave a swathe of destruction in your wake. But . . .'

'What, Malmö? I don't have the foggiest idea what you're talking about.'

He approached the table where the couple had been seated. There was a croissant still in the bread basket. He took it, examined it with interest, and then returned to her with it.

'You're underestimating us again. But you've still made it a long way. Don't endanger everything you've achieved for the sake of a fleeting moment of victory. We're not important. We're only a station on your path. Nothing will happen to you. If you keep your mouth shut.'

Judith sat down on the closest chair. Her legs had begun to shake again. Matthes saw it. He observed all of the visible signs of her withdrawal – the jittery hands, the pale skin, the blinking eyes, and the endless tremors – bit into the croissant and chewed on it thoughtfully, before reaching into his jacket and tossing a tinfoil strip of pills onto the table in front of her.

'Rohypnol. You want to get off the stuff, right? Give yourself one or two days, then you'll be through it. This time at least.'

'What . . .' Judith reached for the pills. 'Is there anything you don't know?'

'If you'll get out of this dead or alive.'

'What do you want from me?'

'Keep Kaiserley off my back. He knows everyone and his dog. I saw him on Westerhoff. I don't want the next show to be something like "Senior Care with the Stasi".'

'There's at least a thousand years of jail time in your joint. What is the level of care you charge for? Do you submit invoices at all? And who are they addressed to?'

'This is exactly the kind of question I meant.'

Matthes returned the half-eaten croissant to the basket and inspected his suit for crumbs.

'Well? You needn't be afraid. You'll leave the hotel in the normal manner. Our methods are different, if we have to apply them at all. On the other hand, it should be clear to you: just because I, let's say, let you go this once, I wouldn't necessarily do it a second time.'

'Then I can go now.'

She wanted to get up but Matthes grabbed her by the arm and forced her to sit back down. She was too weak to defend herself.

'If you cooperate I'll tell you who signed the arrest warrant for your parents.'

'What am I supposed to do with that?'

'He's the only one who is authorised to issue information about how the operation played out from the perspective of the Stasi. You want to know how your parents died, right?'

'Yes,' Judith said silently. *The operation.* 'No. Yes. Does he know that you're telling me who he is?'

'He suggested it himself.'

Alarm bells began to ring in Judith's head. She had been trained to forget. Every memory carefully deleted. And the experiences of the last few days had shown that no one talked to her voluntarily.

'He wants to see me? That's absurd. Now?'

'Soon. And because we all want to get old in happiness and peace, I'd suggest the following: you go to Berlin. You turn yourself in, you'll be questioned, and if you're smart, you won't breathe a word about us. We have first-class connections, well beyond the borders of this country. Our colleagues in Malmö are already waiting for our command, waiting to help you. Forget the BND. Forget Kaiserley. Nothing will happen to you because you're under our protection.'

'Under . . . your protection?'

'Ours. The Mutual and Humanitarian Society. If it makes you feel any better, we're a registered charity.'

Judith's fingers played nervously with the strip of pills. More than anything, she would have liked to take one immediately. But she knew how roofies worked. With two minutes she wouldn't even be able to spell her name.

'Charity?' she repeated. 'Who waved that one through?'

'I don't believe this question is really the most pressing of your concerns. Have we reached an agreement, Ms Kepler?'

'What is going to happen then? If everything goes as smoothly as you suggest.'

'Someone will get in touch with you.'

'When?'

'As soon as we know that you've fulfilled our agreement. Well?'

Judith nodded. 'Regarding your retirement home – I have no problem sparing the world the truth about that. But I want to have access to Ms Jonas at all times.'

'Only through . . .' Matthes smiled, before finishing the sentence, 'my office. After making an appointment. You're a Gagarin, right?'

'Yes,' she said, adding silently: a cosmonaut in space.

Matthes stood up and waited until Judith had also struggled to her feet. The clatter of a service trolley approached. A young woman in a neat dark uniform came around the corner, and parked the wagon in front of the buffet. On the way to the elevator he continued talking, as lightly and casually as if they had met by chance eating breakfast in the hotel restaurant, and were chatting about the weather.

'Not many people know about Lenin. Perhaps it's better that way. Sassnitz is reorienting itself. There's an effort to return to a Wilhelmine spa culture with flags a-waving. But without the ideology this time.'

'What happened to him?'

Perhaps it was one of those statues that had been in every town square until reunification.

'No one knows. The only people who might still know about it are all . . . organised.'

'In your Mutual and Humanitarian Society?'

'No.' Matthes pressed the elevator button. The doors slid apart, and Kaiserley came out. He nodded to Matthes, but was perplexed to see Judith.

'In the model railway club.'

The doors closed on Matthes. Judith turned to Kaiserley.

'Could you please repeat what that gentleman just said?'

'In the model railway club.'

'Thank you.'

'A hobby of yours?'

Kaiserley peered into the breakfast room, saw the half-cleared buffet and shrugged his shoulders in disappointment.

'Not yet,' Judith said.

They stood in front of the roundabout and waited for Kaiserley's taxi. He had parked his car in Mukran, somewhere in one of the huge car parks. His concern about not being able to find it had him nervously playing with his keys. Judith explained to him that she wanted to drive the van back to Berlin.

'That's out of the question,' he had said in the tone of a sergeant speaking to an injured veteran. 'You can't even hold a cup of coffee.'

'I'm driving.'

'You still don't know which way's up and which way's down. I'll take you with me and after your deposition to the police you'll stay in bed for three days.'

Deposition. Interesting how Kaiserley interpreted the search for her.

'I'll see you later.'

Judith marched off, but only made it three steps before Kaiserley caught up with her and blocked her path. Furious, she went to move past him.

'I know full well when I'm capable of driving and when I'm not. So are you going to let me take care of my shit or not?'

'It's done, Judith. It's over. Leave the rest to the pros.'

'Then I'm done, if you mean you're the "pros". Wherever you show up, the best thing to do is take cover.'

'If you had only done that just once!'

'There was no one forcing you to get in that car.'

She crossed the roundabout and walked towards the street. Kaiserley followed her. The traffic was so heavy that, for better or worse, she was forced to wait for the light at the pedestrian crossing.

'We're not quite done yet. Right now, Sofie's trying to find out everything she can about Irene and Christina Sonnenberg in Malmö. Perhaps that will give us something to work with.'

'Us. Sure.' She pounded the signal button with her fists. It was unbelievable how long the lights took to change here.

'I'm in the automobile club. I can have my car picked up. Let's take your van.'

Automobile club. As if she cared. Finally green. He walked behind her.

'You've been through a lot the past few days. I don't want you to be on your own.'

'I'll be fine,' she said, making an effort to keep it together. 'Thanks. Goodbye.'

'It will take you a while to process everything.'

'Are you done now?' She twirled around and glared at him. 'Do you even know how much you annoy me?'

'But I only want to . . .'

'I don't give a shit what you want! Now it's finally about what I want! Leave me alone! Get lost! And thanks for giving me the trip to Malmö. Those were some real magic moments. But I'll be fine on my own now.'

'Judith!'

'Get lost! It's about me, right? Me! Not any fucking special interests! This fucking country killed my parents and almost killed me as well! And don't you start asking me which one I mean. Understand? Get the fuck lost!'

Would he have to be dragged out of the way by the roots of his hair? She wanted finally to be alone. Kaiserley, Matthes, Winkler, Sofie and the mysterious person who wanted to get in touch with her if she cooperated . . . they were all strangers behind masks, playing a game in which human lives were secondary. It was about the interests of the country. If there was something that she'd never forgive Kaiserley for, it was that one sentence.

He looked at her. He sensed exactly what she was thinking. His eyes darkened a shade. That was what had brought them to stand on the side of this street hating each other. He despised the man he had once been. And Judith despised the person he was. She couldn't help him to feel better about himself. She wasn't Kaiserley's redemption. She had to save herself.

A taxi stopped and waited for the pedestrian light to go back to red. It was signalling, apparently headed for Rügen Hotel. Kaiserley waved at the driver.

'At least I can take you to your car.'

'Get lost,' Judith said. 'Get out of my life and never come back.'

He finally understood. He got in. The taxi drove off. Judith turned around and walked off, not caring where the path would lead her.

22

Jörg Optenheide and Gregor Wossilus had been forced into early retirement almost simultaneously. Jörg because the registry office in Sassnitz was being 'downsized.' Gregor because the *Rasender Roland* had been snapped up by the *Bergener Tageblatt* and contrary to promises made, was not continued as part of the Sunday paper. Because the staff only comprised him and his wife, an enthusiastic hobby photographer, this affront had not lead to an outcry from the national union of journalists. Instead, Karin could finally take care of the cottage, while Gregor met up with Jörg in the attic of the train station in Sassnitz during the week, making a hobby into a mission: the complete 1:100 scale reconstruction of the old berth at the harbour.

Gregor, a man with a carefully trimmed white beard and the beginnings of a comfy paunch, who liked to wear short-sleeved shirts and Bermuda shorts in the summer, was inspecting a group of trees Jörg had glued next to the tracks the day before.

'But those aren't beeches!'

Jörg, a slender man, half-bald and with a massive pair of Medicare glasses on his hawk nose, placed his index finger in the official railway timetable for West Germany, 1953, closed it and looked up.

'There weren't any beeches left.'

Gregor snorted furiously. He took a pair of tweezers and tried to shake one of the match-sized trees, but it stood as firmly as only epoxied German oaks can. If there weren't any more beech trees, then you ordered more. You didn't just plant replacements that couldn't be justified after the fact and would be spotted as inauthentic by anyone who knew what they were talking about. There hadn't been any oaks next to the loading tracks in the harbour, even the greatest fool could see that even today.

Jörg looked for a Mitropa menu, of which they had several boxes stashed away, and placed it as a bookmark in the timetable book. He stood up with a groan and pushed through the narrow gap between the individual models. He looked at Gregor over his shoulder.

'No one will notice.'

'I noticed.'

'You old nitpicker. Coffee nip?'

Coffee nip was coffee with Asbach brandy. Gregor looked at the clock – an original from Huai'an, a city whose name no one here could pronounce, but which had been Sassnitz's twin city for three years now, together with Trelleborg, Cuxhaven and Kingisepp in Russia. The representatives from Huai'an had apparently done their research well before their inaugural visit. As a present for the hosts, the small, friendly men had brought along an old train station clock. Manufactured in England in the 1920s, it still worked, or had at least been repaired. It might have been a veiled reference to the broken clock in the station tower, which had been stuck at seven thirty for as long as anyone could remember. Perhaps the reputation of the Model Train Association of Sassnitz had already spread to China, and they had had tried to come up with something extra special for them. No one seriously believed that but it was still a good joke. The celebratory handover ceremony had been covered at length in one of the last issues of *Rasender Roland*. Carefully framed, the picture of the first, and to date only, visit by the mayor to the Friends of the Model Train Association hung over the counter of the little bar in the side room, where Jörg was now headed, moaning and groaning, to make the coffee.

'Almost midday,' Jörg said in his high, nasal accent.

Gregor watched him go and wondered when Jörg would finally go to the doctor. Retirement appeared to be a watershed in people's lives, one he didn't think was properly recognised by society and medicine. Some blossomed – Karin had recently even started taking dancing lessons – others became smaller, withdrawn, invisible. Gregor feared that in another year or two, Jörg would simply disappear.

Shaking his head, Gregor wanted to get back to uprooting trees, when he heard the door below bang and then footsteps on the wooden stairs. He put down the tweezers. Unexpected visitors were rare. Their membership meetings still took place regularly, but there weren't many young recruits. Young people just weren't interested in trains.

The noise made it sound like someone doddery was forcing himself up the stairs, step by torturous step. Gregor had time to get up and go to the landing before he had even made it halfway up.

She, Gregor corrected himself. A woman. And a young one at that. At least at first glance she looked like one of those eternal students: pony tail, flats, dark dress. As she climbed up out of the shadow of the steps into the light, Gregor could see that she was in fact older than he'd first thought, and looked like she had just climbed out of a boxing ring. He had rented *Million Dollar Baby* from the video store once. She looked exactly like that American actress. Not quite as thin and not as grouchy as ... the name escaped him. Besides, this one was blonde. But the way she clung to the rail and kept pausing for breath, she could have come straight out of the movie.

'Hello?' He let the greeting end like a question.

She was still climbing the last steps. Admittedly, the stairs were steep, but even he made it up without collapsing.

'Hi,' she huffed. 'Is this the Sassnitz Model Train Association?'

Gregor cast a brief glance toward the kitchenette. Jörg was still fiddling around and hadn't caught wind of the unannounced visitor. The woman didn't look like she wanted to steal the association funds. But something about her was off. She was sober, but didn't seem completely herself.

'Whom do you want to see?'

She reached the attic floor and looked around.

'Wow.'

The exclamation was so astonished and admiring that Gregor instinctively took a step back in order to not block her view.

'What is that?'

She pointed at the massive set-up: the twenty-metre model of the stretch from Sassnitz to Stralsund. It took up the entire length of the garret.

'That's our exhibition piece. Six circuits, analogue controls, seven commuting tracks, two narrow-gauge tracks.'

'With real water?'

'Of course,' Gregor answered proudly. 'That's the only way ferry transport works, if you take it seriously.'

She stepped up to the spread and walked past every single yard, from Stralsund to Sassnitz.

'Amazing. Is that the old ferry port to Trelleborg?'

She indicated section eight at the left-hand side of the model.

'Just as it was in operation until the early nineties.'

She nodded. 'The old fish factory. It's still standing.'

'Yes. We pay special attention to original details.'

Jörg appeared in the door, two cups in hand. Gregor hoped that he had caught the last few sentences. This woman knew her stuff. She would certainly notice oaks standing where beeches were supposed to be.

'I'm Judith Kepler,' she said and smiled.

'Gregor Wossilus. Deputy Chair. And that's Jörg Optenheide. Our Treasurer.'

She extended her hand. Gregor was astonished how rough and firm it was, and that she had bandaged it. *Mason's hands*, he thought. *A boxer's mug*. But she was interested. That was the only thing that mattered for model train enthusiasts. Jörg placed the cups on the trolley and also greeted the woman.

'A coffee nip for you too?'

'Certainly.'

Jörg handed her his cup and went back to the kitchen to make another.

'May I enquire what brings you here?'

Judith lifted her cup, sniffed at it, and then took a sip, without making a face. So she could take her brandy.

'I'm looking for Lenin.'

'Oh.' Gregor raised his cup and tried it. Good heavens. Was that brandy thinned down with coffee? 'I'm sorry, but Lenin isn't here anymore. If you mean *that* Lenin.'

'How many are there?'

'No idea. Two, three Jörg? Do you have a clue where the Lenins are? And how many of them there are?'

Jörg came over to them.

'We have one of 'em here. In the boxes in the attic. Should I go have a look?'

The woman placed her cup back on the trolley.

'If it's not too much trouble. How many boxes are up there?'

She looked sceptically at the ceiling, as if trying to estimate the size of the storage space in the attic. Jörg scratched himself on his head and mussed the last of his remaining strands of hair.

'Well, dear me. Forty? Fifty?'

'And what is in them?'

'Models. Deconstructed sets and stuff.'

'Would it be too much of an inconvenience for me to ask you to take a look at Lenin? I'd even climb up myself.'

'No need,' Jörg answered. 'We'd be happy to.'

Gregor thought it was time he took part in the conversation. 'Why are you interested in it?' No one voluntarily climbed up to the attic. Cobwebs, mice, dirt.

The woman smiled again. It lit up her face in a wonderful way. For a moment she was almost beautiful.

'A childhood memory. I was five years old. The train station, Lenin and his palace . . . I can't put it together. It could be very important for me, if I could only remember it.'

'There wasn't a palace,' Jörg said. 'Just a Pullman. The only thing we have is the model.'

'In one of the boxes up there?'

Jörg nodded. He picked up the cup and emptied it with a slurp. A soft glimmer coated his eyes.

'You're from Sassnitz?' Gregor asked.

The woman nodded. 'I was a Gagarin.'

Gregor and Jörg exchanged a quick look of the kind that can only mean something for old, old acquaintances.

'A Gagarin,' repeated Gregor.

He bent over and lifted a curtain that ran along the far edge of the ferry display, designed to hide the clutter that there was no room for in the attic. He groped for the ladder, found it, and pulled it out.

'A debt that was never paid.'

Judith followed Gregor up the ladder. Halfway up he removed the bar over the hatch, propped it up and climbed into the attic. Then he bent over and gave her his hand. He pulled her up with such momentum that she landed almost nimbly on the wooden boards.

'Keep your head down,' the model maker muttered.

Hunched, Judith looked around. Only a little light pene-
trated the dusty skylight. She could make out a large number
of removal boxes, carefully labelled and pushed under the roof.
She tried not to appear too curious. That, she sensed, would not
be welcomed by these gentlemen.

She thought of Kaiserley and what he would imagine was
in all those boxes. The missing Rosenholz files? The Stasi files?
What did she care? He had gone, finally. Actually, she should
have been happy. Instead . . .

She followed Wossilus, who was scurrying through the narrow middle passage to the north side of the attic as if he knew
what he was looking for. Lenin's lounge car. She was annoyed
she hadn't thought of it before. While the man dragged one of
the boxes into the bright light under the window, she tried to
remember what she had once been asked to learn in socialist
history class.

*Comrade Vladimir Ilyich Ulyanov Lenin arrived at the port
of Sassnitz in a sealed lounge car belonging to the Royal Prussian
Railroad Administration on 12 April, 1917, in order to board the
'Drottning Victoria' and reach St. Petersburg on 16 April. There he
proclaimed the Russian Revolution.*

'Good Lord.'

Dust flew as Wossilus opened the box. He removed a bundle of scratchy woollen blankets and placed it on the floor.
Carefully, almost reverently, he pulled away the corners.

'Green express coach, six axles. Eight compartments and a
baggage car.'

The model was made of metal. A sturdy, detailed copy of the
original. Judith stared at her nightmare in miniature . . .

'One to forty-eight, standard size zero. You won't find work-manship like that these days.'

She took the coach out of Wossilus's hand and held it up to the faint light. Red velvet on the benches. Brass luggage racks, sparkling like embossed gold. Would a five-year-old girl think it was a palace? Clearly, yes. Anyone who had only spent their life in the sticky, uncomfortable trains of the Deutsche Reichs-bahn would have had saucers for eyes at the sight of this spe-cial edition. She moved the shiny silver wheels. Clickety-clack, clickety-clack.

'At the time, the people of Sassnitz thought they were being visited by some kind of Russian Grand Duke,' Wossilus said. He must have noticed her astonishment because he viewed the model and Judith with the same kind of benevolence. 'Not bad for the old comrade, eh? Looks as good as new, right?'

'Yes,' Judith said and carefully returned the coach. In doing so, a small door fell open. 'Sorry, I hope I haven't damaged it.'

'The baggage part. There's always a weak link.'

With a surprisingly sharp eye given the gloom, he closed the door with a tiny hook that was barely visible to the naked eye.

'The original had a specially made key. There were once four copies of it, but only one of them is still here. And just guess where.'

'With you?' Judith asked.

Like Alberich, hiding the sparkling Rheingold under the earth, Wossilus bundled the coach back into its cardboard box. After it was pushed back into the right place, he patted the dust from his hands.

'Yep,' he said.

'And the coach? The original?'

Wossilus grimaced. Apparently Judith had reminded him of something painful.

'Come back down. The coffee's getting cold.'

She went ahead, Wossilus following her and closing the hatch carefully. Down below, Jörg was already waiting with the next round. Judith took the cup offered and drank it in a single gulp. After all her body had been forced to process over the past forty-eight hours, it could only do her good. But she declined when Jörg offered the next strong coffee.

'I still have to drive.'

'Where to?' the small railway man asked.

'Berlin.'

Both men nodded, as if they wanted to express their sympathy for a long prison sentence.

I was in that coach, Judith thought. *Finally I know what it means.*

'Where's the real Lenin now?'

'No one knows. Gone.'

Wossilus shrugged his shoulders regretfully. 'We would have liked to have kept it. Truly. But when they tore down the old locomotive shed no one knew where to put it. There were plans to make a Lenin museum out of it. But you try explaining that to the people at the ministry of culture.'

Judith grinned. The solidarity surcharge was a burden for East and West equally. In the days when freshly paved roads unleashed fits of envy, a Lenin museum would have been truly difficult to negotiate.

'I understand. But a coach like that doesn't just disappear.'

'Disappears like copper and tracks and cable and scrap does,' Jörg said with a giggle, as if he knew exactly what he was talking about. Wossilus gave him a stern look. Jörg choked, coughed, mumbled something about sugar and milk, and disappeared into the kitchen.

'Are you telling me that you tore the coach apart and sold it as junk?'

'No. Of course not. No one with a heart for the railways would do that.'

Judith believed him. Wossilus sat down on a chair next to the car and studied the smaller display. The sight of a group of trees caused his gaze to darken.

'What is that?'

'The Sassnitz train station as it used to be.'

'The locomotive shed is still there.'

'It's the model of the thirties.'

'Do you have one from the eighties?'

She suddenly realised what a gold mine of memories this represented.

'Eighties? With restricted zones and such?'

'Yes.'

Wossilus shook his head. Judith felt the disappointment in the pit of her stomach. It felt like the elevator in the Rügen Hotel when it stopped.

'But we still have pictures. And a couple of Super-8 films that are on DVD now. Available for purchase.'

'Yes,' Judith said quickly. The DVD sales were probably not that brisk. She wanted to do the man a favour. 'I'd like one.'

Wossilus stood up again and went to the other end of the room. Judith followed him curiously. Behind a door was something like a club room: a little bar, benches from the railway coaches, signal lanterns, route signs.

'You have made it pretty nice here.'

Wossilus grumbled something in agreement and ducked under the counter.

'Under-the-counter goods,' he said, and giggled. He straightened up holding a brochure and a DVD in his hands.

'Sassnitz Station . . .'

'. . . through the ages,' Judith completed the title. She smiled. 'Thanks a lot. What does it cost?'

'You're from Sassnitz?'

'Yes.'

'Nothing.'

Judith nodded, and Wossilus grumbled something unintelligible again. He led her back to the stairs. They said farewell, and Jörg came out from the kitchen and waved goodbye.

As Judith left the train station building, she stopped and studied the area. The locomotive shed had once stood just opposite her. It had disappeared, and with it the railcar in which Lenin had come to Sassnitz. She closed her eyes and tried to remember. How often had she stood here as a child and searched for the missing piece of the puzzle? The erased memory hadn't let her be. Maybe they had been able to destroy the *what*, but not the *where*. And not the *that*. *That* thing that had happened one night twenty-five years before, when she'd stood here once before, holding her mother's hand with one hand and a stuffed animal with the other. Kaiserley had told her that she and her mother had been in the same train and something had gone wrong. They had pulled her off and taken her somewhere else. Not far from here. Actually just a couple of steps past the tracks.

She opened her eyes and saw the shed in front of her, the faded mirage of a memory. There. A tall wooden door. Rusty hinges. Old lights that cast ghostly shadows on the high walls. And in the middle of it all, a palace made of gold and velvet. And then?

The pain shot through her brain like a bolt gun. She bent over and pressed the DVD in front of her stomach. An elderly couple with a travel bag looked over at her concerned, but didn't come any closer. Judith clenched her teeth and took a deep breath. She was slowly able to stand up straight. Good Lord. What was that? As if a part of her brain was sealed with high voltage. Like an electric fence that kept cattle from leaving the meadow.

She stumbled into the small station foyer, took an ice-cold bottle of water from the shelf in a newsstand and sneaked past the cash register without paying. On her way to the cemetery she opened it, drank greedily and poured the rest of it over her head. She slowly began to think clearly again. The van was still there. Relieved, she groped for the small receptacle underneath the bumper and found the replacement key. When she opened the vehicle her nose was met by an overpowering smell of the putrefying, damp rags, and other unidentified ingredients. She rolled down the window, drove off and only after putting Stralsund in her rear-view mirror did she look for a car park so that she could climb into the back and get Borg's autopsy report and the skeleton keys to get back into her apartment. She stuffed it all into an old work bag. When she drove on, she thought for a moment about what it would be like to have another name now, a passport, credit cards. How it would be to keep on driving to Usedom to Świnoujście and then down to Wrocław and Prague until Vienna. And then even further. Always further. So far that she couldn't think of turning back.

Then she remembered what she had told Kaiserley about travelling. Everything was true, but she had lied about one thing: she really would like to see the Eiffel Tower.

23

Franz Ferdinand Maike returned to his office from the coffee machine in the hall with a plastic cup in hand. The telephone rang, and Maike took the call without putting down the cup. At the other end there was a mumbling gentleman who sounded like Holger Ehrmann from the Ministry of the Interior, and who wanted to know he was talking to the right person, to Maike.

'In what regard?'

'A Supplementary Information Request at the National Entry, SIRENE for short.'

Maike put down the cup.

'Why aren't the BKA talking to me directly?'

'Because it was flagged in the Schengen Information System. Don't ask me.'

'Who should I be asking, then? What is this really about?'

Something that had been flagged could be really tricky. It meant that a search initiated from outside the country had been blocked because there were significant legal obstacles in Germany. Maike, who'd been in Homicide for over ten years, hadn't seen one yet. They usually went in the direction of international terrorism, customs and border police.

'As far as I know you're working the Christina Borg case. There's a suspect – her name is Judith Kepler.'

Maike asked himself if there was an agency left that hadn't heard of Judith Kepler. The woman was omnipresent in a way that was slowly becoming eerie. He sat down and shooed the screensaver off his computer.

'Do you have her yet?' Ehrmann changed his tone from friendly to authoritarian, which Maike didn't like at all. 'Do you know her whereabouts?'

'Unfortunately I'm not authorised to give you information about the state of the investigation.'

'Then I'll just answer for you: You don't have her. And you haven't made an effort to. By now there is an international warrant out for her arrest. The Rikspolis informed us over half an hour ago. Why don't you know?'

Maike felt his nerves start to fray. *Yeah, why not?* He looked at the monitor. The box with urgent messages was blinking dark red. *Shit.*

'Being flagged means that even when she's caught there's no extradition, right?' he asked. At least that's what he had learned at the police academy.

'Exactly.'

'And why is Kepler wanted by the Swedish Federal Police?'

Ehrmann sighed because he apparently had to put on his glasses first, then look at his computer or the expedited application.

'Murder.'

Maike didn't say anything. Judith Kepler was one of many people who were being considered in the Christina Borg case. He remembered a grouchy looking janitor, Fricke, and a completely disinterested neighbour whose dog nearly peed on his shoes. Borg had frequented the dive bar Zum Klabautermann, and had brought a friend along once. She had sought contact with Quirin Kaiserley because of a supposed microfilm with top-secret contents. The bar and microfilm were incongruent to say the least, but at least the latter was a connecting point. The summons for Kaiserley's official deposition was already in his outbox.

But Judith Kepler was a cleaning lady. It was unusual that so many different agencies were interested in someone like her and now the material was being requested from Munich to Schwerin. All at once, significant suspicious facts were piling up against her. Sweden even expected extradition, and one of the very top brass had just blocked it. *How nice*, Maike thought, *that I get to hear about it too*.

'Murder,' he repeated. 'But how did the Swedish police connect that with the Borg case?'

'Because Kepler apparently killed the mother after the daughter. Irene Borg was found dead in her apartment in Malmö last night. There's a witness. And he described the dead woman's visitor fairly clearly.'

Maike clicked on the blinking symbol. An internal memo opened and confirmed what Ehrmann had just told him.

'So why no extradition then?'

'Ask the Minister of the Interior.' Ehrmann hung up.

That's exactly what Maike wouldn't do. But he would ask his colleagues in Malmö. And then Kepler would be on the hook.

Klaus Dombrowski knew them all. The nice ones, who politely asked if they could steal a minute of his precious time. The hot-headed ones, who didn't wait, but got right to the point. And the disinterested ones who just acted as if they were fulfilling their duty, but had given up believing in its existence long ago.

Maike must have been new, because he was all of it at once: pleasant, quick and still not completely focused, as if he wasn't very well informed about the state of his own investigation.

'So you say that Judith Kepler hasn't left Berlin in the past two days, and was at her place of work. Why didn't you tell us?'

'No idea,' Dombrowski grumbled. 'Because I'm not a turncoat?'

The wheels were spinning furiously in his head. What the hell was wrong with Judith? He had known her for two years and she'd never once behaved strangely. On the contrary: she was one of his most reliable employees. She appeared to have understood that she had caught the last exit on the highway to nowhere. He had even considered making her the head of the cleaning crew soon. But in the past three days he'd got the distinct feeling that Judith Kepler was a total stranger.

A woman who everyone from Homicide, to former BND agents, and who-the-hell-else were looking for. And of course he was looking for her too. After all, he was her boss.

'I have over three hundred employees. Some of them start at five in the morning, the others are clocking off at the same time. Sometimes I don't get to shake every one of their hands.'

'We're investigating a murder. Perhaps that will encourage you to consider my situation here – and yours, not to mention Kepler's. Where is she?'

Dombrowski huffed and turned to his computer.

'Sankt Gertrauden. Early shift.'

'Till when?'

'Two thirty. 14:30 Central European Summer Time.'

The homicide cop reached for his phone and dialled a number. He was patched through to the hospital and then hung back up.

'Then let's have a look. You could have saved yourself a fair amount of trouble if you'd said that earlier.'

'But I did.'

'To whom?'

'To your colleagues. They're the ones who ran in here.'

The detective didn't like the sound of that at all.

'Colleagues?' he asked. 'Do you have names?'

'Don't remember. I only remember my own arrests.'

Dombrowski remembered the demos and the squats and the days when he had marched arm in arm through the streets with men and women chanting 'Hey ho, the cops have got to go!' Not to mention 'Long live international solidarity!' Several of his fellow combatants had washed up in high office and now acted as if they'd never held a cobblestone in their life. One in particular was now sitting somewhere in America, enjoying a professorship and the third or fourth young wife and taking it easy on his retired minister's pension. That's the other way international solidarity could be seen. Bollocks.

The homicide detective looked at his watch.

'We'll have her in ten minutes.' He glared at Dombrowski, intending to be intimidating. But it would take more than that. Dombrowski leaned back and folded his arms over his substantial belly, yearning for a cigarillo. Inhaled, this time.

'If not, then you'll be prepared to accompany me down to the station.'

'Can I still call my lawyer?'

'As often and as many of them as you want.'

Maike motioned to the telephone, Dombrowski thought about it. Was Kepler worth it? And what did international solidarity mean if it didn't even tie him to his employees? The cops had nothing on him, nothing at all. He thought about whether he still had the small bag of grass hidden underneath his desk drawer or if he had enjoyed it outside with Josef and co. on one of those wonderfully balmy summer evenings. It was the only thing he smoked these days, and only once in a while. Come on. Not even three grams. The judge at the arraignment wouldn't even blink; he'd dismiss it at once.

Quick footsteps approached from the hall, laughter, calls. Babel. Turkish, Lebanese, Vietnamese, Polish. The hospital brigade, back far too early. The bean-counter in him wanted to explode; the bookkeeper advised restraint. Dombrowski looked at the calendar: Wednesday. The mandatory reduction in overtime meant that they were quitting an hour earlier.

Ignoring the detective, he stood up and stormed out into the hall where a chattering cleaning crew was just in the process of breaking up for the day. At the back he discovered a lanky figure.

'Josef!' he bellowed.

The man turned around. Dombrowski realised the cop had followed him.

'Where's Kepler? Did you drop her off at the Underground station?'

Josef widened his eyes in surprise. He came closer. The chatter fell silent. The women in their blue smocks disappeared outside.

'Kepler?' Josef asked. 'At the Underground?'

How stupid could one person be? Dombrowski gave him a sign, but Josef didn't get it. Behind him the boy he had given

Judith's card to appeared. Great. He was even less able to put two and two together.

'The homicide detective would like to talk to you.'

Dombrowski emphasised the title in such a way that chimps would have understood that something was wrong. But not Josef. His face went red, and he turned to his young charge.

'Kai? Where's Kepler?'

'Out in the yard. I think she was getting ready to leave.'

The cop left them standing there and ran after the blue smocks.

'Keep your trap shut!' Dombrowski hissed. 'Give me the card!'

'I don't have it anymore.'

'What?' Dombrowski bellowed. The boy recoiled. 'You don't say a thing. Understand? And you didn't see her.'

'But . . .'

'Let me take care of this, OK?'

Josef and Kai nodded, but exchanged a look that looked an awful lot like 'play along with the madman.' Dombrowski decided he had said enough and followed Maike to the yard to save what he could of the situation.

Judith opened the back door of the van and wrinkled her nose in disgust. Something in here stank badly. Rotting rats? Dirty, damp cleaning rags? She was used to bad smells, but only where they belonged. Inside here it was supposed to smell of disinfectant. She was just about to climb in the back and take a look when she heard footsteps and someone addressing her.

'Ms Kepler?'

Judith spun around. In front of her stood a slender man, halfway good-looking in a traditional way, and holding his ID under her nose.

'Maike, homicide.'

'Anyone can claim that.'

She grabbed the ID, read the name, and returned it with barely concealed contempt.

'Franz Ferdinand. Whoever thought up that one . . .'

'Where were you today?'

'At Sankt Gertrauden Hospital.'

'Business or pleasure?'

He examined the barely healed cut and the bruises on her face.

'I was working. It's called mopping by the yard. We only do the uncluttered surfaces and floors in the hospital.'

'And that there?' He pointed to her jaw.

'A windowsill. Bending over.'

'Witnesses?'

'For what?'

She removed the time card from her overalls pocket and motioned to Josef and Kai, who had just trotted out of the barrack behind Dombrowski.

'We'll confirm that,' Maike said. 'How is it possible for you to work in Berlin and Malmö at the same time?'

'Malmö?' Judith repeated, perplexed.

'You were seen in the vicinity of a crime scene that was subsequently cleaned in a professional way.'

Who would have thought it? Kaiserley had another talent. Josef came closer, examined the back of the vehicle and sniffed.

'What's stinking it up?'

'I don't know.'

Maike cast an interested glance into the van, before taking a couple of steps back and calling someone. In the meanwhile, Dombrowski wandered around it, kicked the tyres, and examined the mudguards. He spotted the missing side mirror and hissed. He appeared to be particularly interested in the front bumper. Judith remembered racing around the old fish factory grounds and the ugly sound the van made as it swiped the curb. She reached for the work bag that lay on the passenger seat. Maike noticed it immediately. He hung up and came back.

'May I?'

Judith handed him the bag. He cast a glance inside and then gave it back.

'Where's your phone?'

'With your colleagues in Sassnitz.'

'This vehicle is confiscated. We have to search it.'

Dombrowski's ears perked up.

'We can't do that. Kepler needs it tomorrow for . . .'

'*Kepler* doesn't need anything,' Maike emphasised. 'Now she'll need to make a statement with an exhaustive list of her activities during the last forty-eight hours.'

'I'd like to take a shower first and change clothes.'

'Of course.'

Judith took the keys and threw them in Dombrowski's direction, who didn't react quickly enough and dropped them.

'Can you drive the vehicle away? I have another appointment.'

'It'd be best left back there.' Maike pointed to a spot next to the bins. 'Then the towing service can reach it more easily.'

Dombrowski huffed.

Judith threw Maike a telling look and scurried into the changing rooms. She could still hear Dombrowski calling for Josef behind her, but he had already disappeared. She waited until she heard the ignition. She had forty, maybe sixty seconds to do what she needed to do.

Judith left Homicide two hours later. It had been so easy. Basically she'd only said what she'd done during the day outside working hours: shopping, drinking wine, sorting through boxes of books, reading.

'What are you reading at the moment?'

'Fractional infinitesimal calculus.'

'What? Mathematics?'

'Physics.'

Maike wrote that down, and it was plain to see that this was only one statement among many that he doubted.

'What do you actually want from me?'

'Did you kill Christina Borg?'

'No, of course not!'

'And Irene Borg?'

'Who's that?'

For a second her nerves had begun to flutter. *Malmö doesn't exist*, she told herself forcefully. *You were never there. They want you to stay silent. You'll be protected. Regardless of by whom.*

Maike appeared to be satisfied with her answer.

'So you went to Sassnitz to smash your mother's gravestone, and then went immediately back to Berlin.'

'Yes.'

'Just so I'm understanding this correctly: why?'

Maike wasn't paid to understand, just to write things down. Judith sighed.

'For me, a person doesn't stop existing just because they're dead.'

'You're not alone in that. We all think that way. But that's also why we honour the memory of the dead, not destroy it.'

'Death isn't a blanket absolution.'

'It is the end of guilt and atonement.'

'Is it really?'

Maike looked at her sharply. 'What did Marianne Kepler do to you?'

'Take a look at my file from the children's home. Then you'll know.'

'I'd like to. It doesn't exist.'

'Then you look for it.'

But please not in my apartment, Judith thought. On her way to Dombrowski's she had stopped off and stowed Borg's autopsy report in a photo book from the sixties about Tuscany. Maike placed the deposition in front of her for her to sign, and then slipped it into a folder. He signalled that they were finished. Judith stood up.

'Is that it?'

'For the moment. You can't leave the city and you have to keep yourself available.'

'Of course.'

'You have a lot of friends.'

She waited for a moment for him to continue, but he didn't. She could have asked who he meant, but it was better to leave him under the impression that she knew just as much about her supposed friends as he did.

Four thirty. She took the next train to Marzahn and decided to wait. She'd kept her part of the bargain. Now it was their turn.

A little later, Maike entered the report onto the computer. From there it took various paths: one, to the internal police information system POLIKS, so everyone cleared for the case could access it there. An additional file landed directly on the desk of Ehrmann in the Federal Ministry of the Interior, where it was passed on to the relevant departments at Interpol and the Federal Criminal Police. However, the flag in the Schengen Information System kept it from being shared within the EU member states, including Sweden. Ehrmann himself passed it on to the desk that had ordered the flagging.

That was the office of the VS, the internal security agency, in Schwerin.

With the help of a Trojan that TT had sent to POLIKS, hidden almost undetectably inside a faked urgent message, an additional copy of the report landed on his laptop at nearly the same time. Together with the blocked search for Judith Kepler in connection with the murder of Irene Borg in Malmö, it reached Kellermann while he was in a meeting a short time later. The agenda was concerned with the organisation of the office's move to Berlin and the question of whether the BND day care facilities should include a playgroup in addition to the after-school centre.

24

Judith stood on the balcony and looked up at the pale turquoise and violet sky as it donned its stars like a grand dame putting on her pearls. It was the hour after sunset, not yet completely dark, but dimming all the time. Sluggish and tired after a hot summer day, the city slipped into the brief calm before night.

The pain had returned. She examined the wounds on her palms and felt as if she'd been crucified. Her body had taken a beating from the stress of the last few days, but through pain and the sleep deprivation, her mind had reached a level of clarity that made her feel almost weightless.

I, Judith Kepler.
I had a mother and a father. And I've made a pact with the devil to find out who killed you.

The lights in the apartment went on. Over there, on the other side of the autobahn, someone was hanging curtains in the eighth floor of a violet-coloured building. Judith squinted to see the small, illuminated rectangle better. A woman. Before she pulled the curtains closed, someone stepped up to her and took her into his arms.

Judith turned away, went into her bedroom, lay down on her bed and fixed the full moon in her gaze. If she closed her eyes, it was the same moon as back then, and its soft light cast a huge cross on the floor, directly over her heart. Yuri Gagarin smiled at her; her, a cosmonaut like him, searching for a lost planet in the darkness, in order to finally plant a flag there.

The next morning she called Josef and told him she was sick. She lowered all the blinds, took the last two roofies, and slept all day. She only awoke when the door buzzer pulled her out of her coma-like sleep. Confused, she groped for her alarm clock. Half-five. In the morning or evening? She rolled over with a groan, but the shrill sound pushed its way into her core, again and again.

She stood up and stumbled into the hallway. The pills were exacting their revenge – she felt drunk but without having enjoyed the pleasure. When she felt along the wall for the intercom, the phone slipped from her hand. It hung from its cord, just above the floor. The buzzer rang again. At the same moment someone knocked on the door. This was multitasking and it was overwhelming her. She let the device dangle and looked through the peephole onto the landing.

Kaiserley.

Her heart stuttered. After everything she had thrown at him in Sassnitz, she hadn't expected ever to see him again. She opened the door and carefully bent down for the handset. The third attempt to hang it up worked.

'Did I wake you?' were his first words. 'I'm sorry, but you have to put something on, I need to talk to you.'

'What?'

She wore a T-shirt and nothing else. His presence confused her, and she blamed the sleeping pills for making her so numb and therefore defenceless.

'How . . .' she searched for the words because thought and language were still hard to put together. Her voice sounded strangled. 'How did you manage to find me?'

'Through my own personal residency index. May I?'

He pushed past her. He was disgustingly awake and smelled outrageously good. It was completely unreasonable. She closed the door and clicked on the hallway lamp, but too late. The muffled sound from the living room revealed that Kaiserley had already stumbled over something.

'Are you moving house?'

'No.'

The ceiling lights became brighter. Kaiserley had caught the corner of the soft cardboard box. It had ripped and several of the books had fallen onto the floor. He bent over with interest and started to pile them up. *And Quiet Flows the Don, Dr Ibrahim, The Rider on the White Horse* . . .' He looked up. 'World literature from a few decades before your time. Do you run an antiquarian bookshop?'

He motioned to the other boxes that stood in front of the bookcases. She bent over and collected several volumes.

'Otherwise they'd end up in the bin.'

'So a kind of homeless shelter for books?'

Judith looked at him to see if he was pulling her leg. Clearly not. She gradually found her voice.

'It happens when places are cleared. Sometimes I feel sorry for a box. Then I take it home.'

Kaiserley went to her bookcase. He tilted his head and read the titles on the spines. Every now and then he pulled one out, examined the volume, and put it back. Books revealed something about the intellectual stance of their owners. The selection was as varied as the owners had been. From Ernst Jünger's *Storm of Steel* to Böll's *The Lost Honour of Katharina Blum*. From the *Trace of the Stone* and *The Adventure of Werner Holt* to Lebert's *Wolfskin* and Lowry's *Under the Volcano*. If Kaiserley wanted to find out something about her from these shelves, and that was the purpose of his visit, then he was welcome.

'And?' she asked. 'What does it say about me?'

'That you're either unbelievably unselective or voraciously inquisitive.'

She went to the bathroom and got in the shower. Water. Ice cold. She brushed her teeth twice and still felt dirty afterwards. In the kitchen, she turned on the coffee machine. She looked through the open doors and saw he was engrossed in a fairly ancient volume of Hesse's *Steppenwolf*. She found the coffee, filled the filter, poured water over it, spilling half of it in the process, and took two cups from the cupboard.

'Milk? Sugar?'

She wondered when she had last said that to a man in this apartment. She couldn't remember.

'Milk.' He held the book in his hands as he walked over to her. 'I used to love this,' he said. 'Until I found out that the guy who'd stolen my girlfriend, he of all people, had also read and loved it. From then on I was slightly disappointed in Hermann Hesse, but it's a mistake to believe that everything is written only for yourself. You always have company. How do you choose your books?'

'I don't choose them. They choose me.'

She turned away so that he would not notice her sudden uncertainty.

'Did you go to the university?'

'Having dropped out of school? No.'

'You should finish school. There are very good long-distance study programmes and night classes.'

'I don't have time. And thanks, yes, I've already heard about them.'

She leaned on the refrigerator and waited until an acceptable amount of coffee had dripped through. Kaiserley went back into the living room. He placed the book on the shelf and then scanned along her record collection.

He called over to her. 'Tell me what music you listen to and I'll tell you who you are.'

'That's really elitist.'

'But usually accurate. The world has become poorer. Why do we let them take our books and music? Instead we get converted files. You can't travel to the Swiss Alps and read Max Frisch aloud to your dearest from an e-book.'

'Why not?'

He let the LP he had just held in his hands slip back into its spot. Santana, *Abraxas*. 1978. She poured the coffee, walked over to him, and handed him a cup.

'No one ever read to me. As far as I'm concerned, they could have been runes on slates.'

'And cassettes? Did anyone ever make you a tape?'

'What for?'

'To express what they thought and felt.'

'On a cassette? How stupid is that.'

Kaiserley shook his head with a smile. 'No. Not voice recordings. I mean music. Songs that express what you feel for a person. That say what you might never speak out loud. I used to spend hours choosing and putting them in order. Every piece was important in itself. I even have a couple left at home. Every few years I listen to them again and think about . . .'

'Yes? What?'

'Not important. The past.'

He drank a sip of coffee and looked around, as if the shelves, the moving boxes, and the abandoned furnishings were a stage set and he was just wondering which play was being produced this evening.

'I haven't ever got a cassette either,' Judith finally said. 'It would probably only have been Death Metal on it anyway.'

'Death what?'

'What do you listen to?'

'Always music that has something to say.'

His eyes locked onto hers. Judith cursed the pills. She felt weak and that upset her. More harshly than intended, she asked: 'And which records? Perhaps something with longing?'

For a sudden, wild moment, inside Judith the fear rose that he might say yes. People talked differently when they had talked about books and music. Kaiserley motioned to the records with his head.

'Face à la Mer. Morcheeba and Les Négresses Vertes.'

'Why?'

'Melancholy. A cemetery by the seaside. It just fits. Fits you.'

A hint of a smile crept over his thin lips. She sat down. Everything was different all at once. He looked at her, and she had the feeling he knew her. Really knew her.

'You don't want to read me a good night story.'

'No.'

'Then . . . what do you want?'

He put down the coffee cup. Judith remembered that she had liked his hands. His arms. His shoulders. His face. His eyes looked so different. There was pain there. Loss. Perhaps . . .

'Who was the man you talked to in Sassnitz? In the Rügen Hotel. In the elevator. The one with the model trains.'

She recoiled. 'What?'

'You received a tip. Don't lie to me.'

She didn't want to show how hurt she was. For a moment she had forgotten who she was dealing with: a man with two faces. A skilled manipulator. A hunter who only had his prey in mind. That's why he could give a cleaning lady the feeling he could gaze into her soul. Something inside her slammed shut. It hurt for a moment, but then it was over.

'Who was that?

'A model train enthusiast.'

'Stop it!'

'I don't know. The kind of person you meet in hotels. Things like that happen. Vicky Baum is also in there somewhere. I'll give it to you.'

She motioned to the bookcase with a spiteful nod. But Kaiserley wasn't to be distracted.

'I know that man. I thought about it for a long time until I realised where I'd seen him.'

'Where? At the breakfast buffet?'

'In Sassnitz. At the train station. Twenty-five years ago.'

Angelina Espinoza sat at a café terrace on Leopoldplatz. The city showed its other side in the evenings: boisterous, happy, almost Mediterranean. She could dive in and let herself be drawn along by the beautiful creatures who flitted around the lights of the bars and restaurants like rare species of moths: colourful, iridescent, dancing, and making courtship displays. She had pushed her sunglasses back into her dark hair and watched life go by as if it were a Fellini film.

Sometimes she longed to stay. But the feeling quickly passed when she saw the youth in the faces of the girls, their unending expectations for life, and when she noticed how few women of her age had fulfilled their promise.

The LED that showed her phone was on standby flickered. It looked like a massive amount of data. A livestream.

Angelina clicked through and on the small screen she saw an apartment in which two people were sitting on the floor, drinking coffee, and talking. The woman didn't look familiar to her, but, although he sat with his back to the camera, she would have recognised the man in a crowd of a million. She inserted the Bluetooth headphones – a dreadful device, but the best technology currently available – and joined the conversation. The man appeared simultaneously furious and concerned. Look at that. Had the old wolf lost his heart once again? She smiled in amusement. But the man's next sentence made her smile freeze.

'His cover name was Stanz, Hubert Stanz. Surveillance expert for the Stasi in Schwerin.'

'How do you know that?' the woman asked.

'From—what does Stanz want from you? Or should I call him Dr Matthes?'

Angelina's hands began to shake. She looked around carefully, but the people at the next table over were preoccupied with themselves.

She interrupted the livestream. Her thoughts raced through her head, stumbling over each other and cutting each other off. Things were accelerating. The situation was getting out of control. She considered what she should do, then finally dialled a number. Someone picked up.

'Oh,' she said in a friendly voice, 'I'm so sorry. And so late in the evening. I dialled the wrong number. I hope I didn't disturb you.'

She hung up and looked at the display and the last numbers dialled until the light faded. Just as slowly, a smile crept back over her face.

Kellermann came out of the shower, the terrycloth towel slung around his powerful hips, and went into the hallway. Eva stood there and looked at him. He wanted to reach for his phone and only then saw that she had it in her hand.

'Did somebody call?' It was his work phone and therefore off-limits to her. The display was still illuminated.

'No.'

She placed it back in the Murano glass bowl and pulled the belt tighter around his waist. 'I just wanted to tell mama good night.'

She did that every evening.

'And why don't you use your own?'

'It's gone.'

'Gone? Since when?'

She avoided his gaze. 'I must have left it at the hairdresser. This afternoon. Or in the taxi. I don't know.' She ran her fingers through her hair in a nervous gesture. 'Is the bathroom free?'

'Yes,' he said and stepped aside to let her past. 'Watch out, it's wet.'

'It always is when you have a shower.'

She gave him a fleeting smile.

'Eva?'

'Yes?' She turned to him one last time.

He pointed to the charger cord that had wound its way from the socket next to the wardrobe to the shelf.

'Your phone is here.'

Disbelieving, she came closer. 'My God, yes! Then I didn't even take it with me! Imagine that . . . old age is getting off to a good start.'

She embraced him so suddenly that he almost lost his balance.

'Please don't leave me.'

'But Eva. Whatever are you thinking?'

She cuddled up to him. 'Just a few more years, then life will start.'

'Retirement can't come soon enough for you, right?' He wrapped his arms around her. 'But what would you have me do? I'd keep pigeons and talk to the radishes.'

'It'd finally be over,' she said quietly.

She released him. He watched her until the bathroom door closed behind her. He didn't want for it to be over. He wanted to keep going. Stopping was stagnation. Stagnation was . . . he repressed the thought and automatically reached for his phone, which was the first thing he always did when he had put it down for several minutes. What he saw made his blood freeze. Eva had accepted a call from a blocked number. She had lied. She wouldn't have had a reason to if it had been a business call.

He hastily swiped over the display until he landed at his private texts. The very private ones. The ones no one should see because they mentioned lust and lasciviousness. Had she read them?

He heard the water in the shower raining down into the tub, and he stood in the hallway in a bath towel with the end of the world in his hand. Something had happened. Something he'd never expected: the false trails he had so carefully laid, suddenly led in a completely different direction. To him.

Judith went into the hallway and opened the door. But Kaiserley didn't leave. He stood in the doorway to the living room, arms crossed, his smile already long since given way to the hard features in his face.

'Dr Sigbert Matthes,' Kaiserley continued. 'Under the alias of Hubert Stanz, expert for Operative Psychology in the Stasi branch in Schwerin. There was a rash of protests when he wanted to open a practice in Potsdam after '89 and no one removed his licence. What is he doing in Sassnitz?'

'I don't know.' Judith tried to sound convincing. So Kaiserley also wanted to take care of Matthes now. 'He told me that if I leave him alone then I get the man who had my parents arrested. And dammit: you'll leave him alone now, understand?'

'Those people are just as dangerous as back then. Their backs are to the wall. They won't let themselves be cornered by anyone.'

'Because I'm a cleaning lady. Is that what you mean?'

Fury made her voice sound hoarse. He pushed himself off the wall and came closer. So close that she instinctively took a step back. He raised his hand. She flinched. It was a reflex no child who had been beaten as frequently as she had could suppress.

'No.' He lowered his hand. 'Because I'm afraid for you.'

She wanted to say something but she forgot it the moment she looked into his eyes. She couldn't wrench herself away from him. *No*, she thought. *No. He was just acting. He was acting again.*

'You don't have a clue what it's really like to be afraid,' she whispered.

He lowered his head. His lips were so close to her mouth that she could feel his breath.

'I know,' he said. 'By God, do I know.'

He kissed her. A good kiss. Very good. And he just didn't stop. Every time Judith started to say something he suffocated her words with irresistible arguments. Passion, overpowering, heat. And something else that suddenly made everything light and simple. Normal. No, not normal. Different. New. Lust, and more than that. A deep desire, a drifting together, as if they were two suns whose orbits had crossed after millions of years. That was how her resistance crumbled.

Her hands felt their way over his body, and were pleased with everything they found. She groaned as he became bolder and pushed her against the wall. He wanted her. She wanted him. It was real, and it was the only thing they could trust. Right there, in the hall, and over and in each other into the bedroom. She felt the heat in her body and the nearly unbearable desire.

Suddenly he stopped.

He let go of her and took a step back. She could hear his breath, panting with arousal, and in the twilight she saw him raise his hands and run them almost helplessly through his hair.

'I'm sorry.'

'What?' she asked. She went over to him and wanted to kiss him again, but he only embraced her and turned his face away.

'Don't. I can't.'

Judith's hand slid down his body to the place that showed his words to be lies, hard and unequivocal. She kissed his neck, her lips found her path to his mouth nearly automatically.

'Judith . . . no. We can't. Not yet.' He carefully disentangled himself from her. She stood there with eyes closed. 'Let's be reasonable. Please.'

Reasonable. Thanks a lot. Judith waited for the length of a breath, two, then she left him there and went back into the living room. Every cell, every nerve was vibrating from his touch. She looked for her tobacco, didn't find it, and would have liked nothing better than to fling her coffee cup against the wall, and Kaiserley too. She felt ridiculous. Just seconds before she had thought of solar flares, and a moment later he had made her feel like a woman who was only lusting for a crazy, hot, quick fuck.

'I don't want that.'

All right, you wimp. Save it for confession on Sunday. But not with me. She found her tobacco and went out onto the balcony. She was so furious that she was only able to roll one on her second try. He followed her.

'It's the difference.'

What bullshit was he coming out with now? 'What difference?'

'Back then you were a child. I couldn't protect you. And now . . . maybe that's what makes this all so difficult.'

Maybe for him, but not for her. Judith knew that men didn't perceive her as a delicate rose in need of protection. She was irritating, annoying. She spoke her mind and made what she wanted clear, sometimes too clear and without consideration. Maybe Kaiserley was someone who couldn't deal with that. Too bad, because he'd actually made a good impression. She lit her cigarette and tried to swallow her frustration. But she choked on it.

'I'm not a child anymore.'

'I don't have paternal feelings. That's not what I meant.'

'Thank God.' Judith exhaled the smoke and watched as it rose in a soft, ethereal haze. 'It certainly didn't look that way.'

He stood next to her and looked down at Landsberger Allee. She felt his body, although he kept it at least a half-arm away. *Too bad. Just too bad.*

'I don't do one-night stands.'

Of course that explained everything. Judith just nodded, but didn't respond, because every word that would have come out of her mouth would have been pure irony. Men were the delicate creatures. One wrong word and they'd blame you for never getting it up again.

'And you?' he asked.

'Do I know what a one-night stand is? Well, you do it. And either it remains that one time, or it continues. I don't approach things like that with firmly held plans.'

'You're twisting my words.'

She blinked at him through the smoke. He was a good guy. She liked him. She liked the way little wrinkles formed around his eyes when he smiled, and his athletic but relaxed figure. His skin was lightly tanned, and the way the sleeves on his linen sweater were pushed up revealed his muscular biceps. So a one-night stand. That's what he was accusing her of wanting. Quirin Kaiserley had discovered ethics.

Calm down, she told herself.

'Peace?' She extended her hand, and he grabbed it.

'Peace. Under one condition. I'm coming along.'

'Never.'

'I won't ever let it happen again. I wont let someone who . . .'

She would never discover what he wanted to say. Her phone rang. She let go of his hand and sprinted into the living room.

'Yes?'

'Am I speaking with Judith Kepler?'

A whispering, hoarse voice sent a chill down Judith's spine.

'Yes,' she said.

'Do you have anything planned for the evening?'

25

The house appeared bent under the overhanging fir boughs. A low, inconspicuous building with a grey façade and a porch that looked home-built. Tall cherry laurel bushes stood along the edges of the property; only the garden gate offered a view inside.

Kaiserley parked his car on the other side of the street.

'What does the residency office say?' she asked.

Kaiserley checked his phone. 'Nothing yet. Our contact there has gone home for the day. But I assume that the name Horst Merzig is real. Just like his career with the Stasi.'

'You assume.'

Kaiserley sighed. His right hand still lay on the steering wheel and Judith thought how just a little while ago that hand . . . she opened the door and got out. There was no room for feelings in her life. They could dissolve into thin air, just like names and people. And the schizophrenia of the Cold War led one to believe that Merzig, whom they were visiting in his detached house, had also been more than just a pencil pusher.

The damp, heavy smell of rotting greenery greeted them. The suburbs. Compost heaps. Lawns with sprinklers, blossoming flowers, tall trees. The birds twittered, and the sky had that post-sunset green that Judith loved so much. The traffic noise from the nearby B1 motorway was muffled. It sounded like a satiated swarm of bees bringing the day's harvest back to the hive.

'No former General Lieutenant of the Main Section II still lives under an alias.'

He stood next to her and cast a quick, examining glance at the surroundings. Small detached houses, built in the sixties and seventies, gaining some patina and slowly erasing the newly built smell of the settlement. Voices and laughter mixed with the fragments of dialogue from the rattling loudspeakers of old tube-type televisions cranked up next to the opened windows. The aroma of bratwurst and charcoal crept into Judith's nose. Someone had fired up the barbeque.

Had she been here before?

She followed Kaiserley across the street. The garden fence was a piece of GDR blacksmith production, the playful philistine counter to socialist modernism. Blue. Sky blue. She extended her hand to press down the handle, but Kaiserley held her back. The initials 'H. M.' were next to the doorbell nameplate. The path to the vestibule was made of exposed aggregate concrete, and under the porch of dirty yellow corrugated fibreboard stood a man. He had the mid-sized, sinewy figure of a garden worker. Slender, almost haggard, with a healthy tan on his finely chiselled face. His eyes, small and shiny as stream pebbles, were almost hidden in a wreath of deeply weathered wrinkles, giving his face an impression of vigilance. *Like a bird*, was the thought that shot through Judith's head.

Had she seen him before?

She was afraid. She wanted to turn around and go. But she knew that there was no longer a way back. Kaiserley looked at her. She didn't know what he was thinking but all of a sudden she was glad that he was there.

In the few seconds she needed to reach the stairs from the garden gate she tried to take in the property again. Rectangular, with the long side to the street, almost hidden, well tended.

'Watch out!'

She'd almost stumbled. The man came towards her, smoothing, feline, and held out a hand for her. Judith grasped it. It was cool and dry.

'Ms Kepler?'

He had a voice like reed grass: elegant, almost whispery, but razor-sharp at the edges. Next to the sickle of his mouth his cheeks dug deep, cliff-like valleys into his skull. It was hard to guess his age. Bad late-sixties, good early-eighties.

'Horst Merzig. I'm very glad to meet you.' The reeds rubbed together. Dry blades, touched by the wind. 'And you are . . .?' He cast a look over her shoulder.

'Quirin Kaiserley. Publicist.'

Merzig's thin lips formed a smile. He extended his hand to Kaiserley.

'I've been following your revelations with great interest. Perhaps there will be the opportunity for an . . . annotation or two. From my perspective.'

Judith and Kaiserley followed Merzig into the house. It was set up so that all of his daily needs could be attended to on one floor: kitchen to the left, bathroom to the right, a Spartan bedroom behind, the living room straight ahead. The doors were ajar, as if Merzig wanted to demonstrate that he had nothing to hide.

The living room was simply furnished. A three piece suite of Scandinavian minimalism, book shelves, grandfather clock, and desk. It was dominated by an aquarium that seemed huge for the setting. Its green light cast the windowsills and the green plants in an almost enchanted light. The fish were as large as trout, shimmering and silvery with deep blue patterns. They moved with a majestic elegance.

'My hobby.' Merzig hadn't missed Judith's gaze. 'Cockatoo dwarfs. Cichlids. Since I retired. So pretty much exactly since the summer of 1990. Would you like to sit down? You look tired.'

Judith nodded and chose the armchair. Nothing in the world would have made her sit on the couch next to Kaiserley.

'The last couple of days have been stressful.'

'I gather.'

Merzig offered Kaiserley a spot next to him on the couch. He pulled a crystal ashtray containing a pipe towards him.

'I hope you don't have anything against smoking. I tend to be inconsiderate within my own four walls. I don't get many visitors.'

He opened a can of tobacco and began to stuff the pipe. Judith didn't let herself be deceived by his demonstration of composure. Merzig was vigilant. And he was an astute observer.

'Then I don't want to keep you for too long,' she said. 'Dr Matthes . . .'

She stumbled and cast Kaiserley a quick glance. What did he think about the fact that she was increasingly dependent on old Stasi cadres? His face didn't reveal anything.

'. . . mentioned you might be able to tell me about the operation in Sassnitz during the mid-eighties.'

'Dr Matthes.' Merzig smiled and patted down the pockets of his washed-out, too large corduroys until he had found a matchbook. 'How's he doing?'

'We're not that close.'

'He's the head of that sanatorium, right? Did you know that used to be an insane asylum? Lots of head cases. Up there, of all places, where the ferries to Sweden were constantly floating by. I would have gone crazy there.'

'A sanatorium?' Kaiserley asked.

He sat down, brushing Judith's knee while doing so. It was like a tiny, electric shock. She shifted in her seat away from him.

'Is that important?' she asked. 'This isn't about Dr Matthes, but about you. Who or what were you?'

'I was head of the counterintelligence service.'

'And signed arrest warrants.'

'Yes, I did.'

Judith took a sharp breath. 'Including one for Irene Sonnenberg and her husband?'

'That's possible.'

'And . . . Christina Sonnenberg?'

Something flashed in Merzig's eyes. Maybe it was just the reflection of the match he was holding to his tobacco.

'No. Children weren't arrested.'

'They were sent to the home,' Judith said. She hoped Merzig wouldn't notice how much his calmness upset her. 'To Gagarin, for example.'

Merzig shook the match until it went out. A cloud of smoke floated through the room. It smelled of wood and earth.

'A model institution. Truly. In contrast to those youth camps. Their educators were much more committed, as far as I can remember.'

'I want to know what happened that night. I kept my promise. Now it's your turn.'

'Judith Kepler?' Merzig asked.

Judith nodded.

'You really want to know how your parents died?'

'Yes,' Judith whispered.

She groped for her bag and felt the cold, hard steel.

26

It was a warm Tuesday in August, and the air streamed through the wide-open window and carried the scent of mowed hay and melting asphalt. Lieutenant General Horst Merzig left his desk and looked over to Commander's Hill, as the cafeteria of the ministry was known. It was just after noon, and the weekly menu listed mashed potatoes, pan-fried fish, and pickles for today. Nothing the company doctor had recommended at the last check-up. More veggies, less fat, is what he'd said. Mid-fifties, that's when the ailments started. Merzig knew he was carrying at least twenty extra pounds around with him. But he had only eaten in the cafeteria since his wife died. The layered cabbage dish was divine. And because the Stasi worked almost around the clock, the cafeteria was open from early in the morning until late at night. He ate more than was sensible – or necessary. Once in a while he'd tried to diet but the women at the counter had seen straight through his half-hearted attempts and enjoyed dumping two more meatballs with onions fried in butter onto his overloaded plate. Eating his plate clean was a habit from childhood days. Merzig reached a point where he only felt comfortable if he was full.

But this morning it wasn't his growling stomach that made him impatient for lunchtime. It was the disheartening news that he'd just received.

The maintenance of internal security at the ministry fell in his jurisdiction. This was primarily directed toward the well-being of full- and part-time employees and their families, instead of any actual danger that could arise within their own ranks. And that's exactly why he and Colonel Kauperth, one of his closest and most senior colleagues, had gone clueless and unprepared into the routine briefing in Building I, completely unaware of what awaited them.

A small circle had come together in a conference room on the fifth floor, and the focus had been on the reports from West Germany that had reached them punctually and reliably at the beginning of the week, leaked to them from their source in Bonn. It was a satisfying feeling, not only to have the same level of information as the West German Chancellor and his closest ministers, but simultaneously being a step ahead of them.

That morning, at 8:15, exactly thirty minutes after he had been served breakfast by his female comrade Major Dresgow in his private quarters, the Minister for State Security was no longer sitting self-satisfied at the head of a shiny table as usual. His shoulders were positioned higher than normal, the round face seemingly petrified. The eyes narrow slits, the mouth pinched, and that's how he waited, unofficially the most power-ful man in the German Democratic Republic and a notorious early riser, until everyone had found their place in their leather seats. Merzig sat opposite Fröde, the head of Department XII, who avoided his gaze. He stared down the surface of the table, as if he had just been karate chopped out of commission.

Markus 'Mischa' Wolf, the Head of Foreign Reconnaissance who had been outed by *Der Spiegel* magazine, was missing. He was supposedly plagued by health issues. The hydra of rumours whispered about private problems, and even Hercules wouldn't have made progress against it in an agency like this. Everyone else was present.

'Merzig,' the minister grunted by way of greeting. The direct address without reference to title was a foible of his. But on days like these it sounded a shade chillier. 'Everything under control?'

'Yes, Minister.'

'I don't believe it. How do you explain the fact that the entire index of our foreign intelligence service is going to fall into the hands of the enemy next week?'

Merzig gulped. He couldn't be hearing right. He looked over to Fröde, who was still sitting there as if his life was hanging from a thread. In that moment everyone would have liked to have private problems so they could avoid being dressed down like this.

'I don't understand.'

The minister pounded the table with his fist. Everyone jumped. The twelve heads of department and their representatives were seated in this room. Everyone in the country snapped to attention in front of these Comrades. But if this little man, a man who took pleasure in collecting dough figures from kindergarten groups, hit the table with his fist, then everyone jumped. Fröde was deathly pale. And an abyss had just opened up under Merzig's chair.

'Please excuse me,' Kaiserley interrupted Merzig's reminisces. 'The information came from Bonn?'

Merzig shrugged his shoulders. 'The briefing on Tuesday mornings was always dedicated to the report from the secret services coordinator at the Chancellor's Office. I don't know how many hands the information passed through on its way. At any rate, it was the essence of what the BND, military counterintelligence, and the internal security guys at VS had collected for that week.'

'Why not Bonn?' Judith asked, annoyed. 'After all, it was once the capital.'

Kaiserley took a breath, preparing an explanation, but Merzig beat him to it.

'You two are pursuing different goals. Mr Kaiserley wants to know who betrayed the operation to the Stasi at the time. You, Ms Kepler, would like to find out more about the fate of your parents. Perhaps you can first agree what it is you actually want to know from me.'

'Who was it?' Kaiserley burst out.

'A secretary. One of the best sources we had. Uncovered by a Romeo with the cover name of Sapphire.'

'Sapphire was uncovered. About a year later. And all of his sources along with him.'

'Another one of those points, dear Mr Kaiserley, on which we could still disagree.'

Judith raised her hand. 'Wait a second. Stop speaking in riddles. Who is Romeo?'

'A Romeo was a lover in the service of the Stasi. He convinced lonely women in West Germany, preferably women who sat in the outer offices of important gentlemen, to betray their secrets.' Kaiserley gave Merzig a quick look, and he nodded. Judith was not unaware of the fact that these two people had met their match. Still hunkered down in their respective trenches, but engaged with complete professional fascination. Why did Kaiserley effortlessly get everything he wanted to know and she had to go around begging for every scrap of information? Merzig appeared to enjoy the exchange of blows, and Kaiserley more than ever.

'Sapphire was one of the top spies. There were more than sixty files on his operative activities. There's nothing that isn't known about him.'

'Then, Mr Kaiserley, you'll also be aware of who his sources were. It's as simple as that.'

'I've seen the files . . .'

'It's as simple as that,' Judith repeated and strengthened Merzig's words. 'You have your turncoat. A typist. May I continue?'

'It wasn't a secretary! This operation was top secret. Not even the secret services coordinator knew exactly what was planned.'

Merzig puffed a cloud of blue haze to the ceiling. 'But then you didn't know the gentlemen very well. Mr Kaiserley, sometimes the simplest solutions are the most ingenious. Did you ever see the movie *Romeo*? With Martina Gedeck and Sylvester Groth? That was Sapphire.'

'I know the film,' Judith said. 'The woman was almost destroyed by the affair.'

Merzig smiled benevolently. 'Don't believe everything that can be told in ninety minutes. To each their own song and dance. Shall we continue?'

Kaiserley nodded; he seemed confused and yet impressed. A secretary. A young girl who was led into sin by a Stasi lover. No Mata Hari, no Third Man. Not even a political 'idealist'. Just someone in love, a naïve woman. Did that fit? He didn't seem convinced.

Merzig drew on his pipe and appeared to enjoy Judith's eagerness, before he continued, taking them on a journey into the headquarters of the grey men who had written the fate of her parents.

'Wildgruber?'

Colonel Wildgruber was one of Fröde's deputies. A young, snappy type, he was different from the old guard who had been through the war, the Nazi dictatorship, the collapse of the country and her arduous rebuilding; who had wanted a newer, better Germany. One in which everyone had a place and there were no class differences. One that had to be protected against the attacks of the class enemy, lurking around every corner, ready to poison the brains of the youth with its imperialistic agitprop and dancing with triumph in front of a mountain of consumables, praying to it as if they were new gods.

Wildgruber was from the post-war generation. He had completed an impressive course of study at the Ministry of State Security's School of Law in Potsdam-Eiche. From the day he graduated his career had followed a steep upward gradient, which he stormed effortlessly, and whose peak he had reached in that moment, in silent satisfaction. All that was left was to clamber atop Fröde's remains. Wildgruber wasn't concerned with Socialism. He was focused on victory. He would have followed the same route to the top in any other ministry in the world.

Wildgruber cleared his throat. All those not directly touched by the terrible events in Department XII lifted their heads and listened with interest. The rest of them gazed into oblivion, paralysed.

'We're aware of reports that select copies of the latest generation of our microfilm archives are supposed to be taken abroad. Due to obvious reasons, I don't want to go into details, but apparently one of the employees of our department was able to get these copies out of the building, over the course of a longer period of time and driven by an unbelievable criminal energy, and, through a middleman, offer them to various Western intelligence services, most significantly the CIA and BND.'

'That's impossible!' Merzig spluttered.

The others whispered and hissed.

'We're not talking about the entirety of our foreign contacts. No. While recording, someone picked out only the files of agents abroad. Based on today's figures, that makes 3,782 Scouts of Peace who will be sent to their doom.'

The murmuring became louder. Merzig heard the blood pounding in his ears. A co-worker at Department XII looked over to Fröde. The extent of this treason was unimaginable. The man needed a glass of water or a doctor. He looked as if he was about to fall off his chair.

'In return, the Federal Republic has agreed to issue three passports for the traitors and smuggle them out of the country with the help of the CIA.'

'Three?' whispered Merzig and gasped for air. The others also looked around in confusion.

'Kauperth?'

Merzig jumped. Why was the Minister addressing his assistant and not him? Kauperth cleared his throat. His Adam's apple bobbed with excitement, but his voice sounded steady.

'I've been familiar with the case since this morning. But in the meantime I was able to reach the relevant colleagues in Schwerin. The traitors' plan is as simple as it is perfidious. And because they'll be in the same train as the class enemy's spies, seizure is . . .'

Merzig could see Kauperth's lips moving but he heard nothing more. His gaze travelled over the faces of the men, who listened to Kauperth's exposition with attention and seriousness. He got caught on Wildgruber, who could barely conceal a touch of triumph. And finally, to his left, Kauperth, his co-worker, who talked and talked and talked, like Merzig had never seen him talk before. With glowing eyes and a level of zeal only held in check with some effort.

'Why don't you arrest them immediately?' the fat one bellowed.

Kauperth stumbled. The Minister's interjection only caught him off guard for a second.

'Because then we'll never find out where the copies are located. And they can't leave the country in any case.'

The Minister furrowed his brow. Merzig sensed what he thought. Water torture and isolation, including a blank cheque for every kind of interrogation – twenty years earlier, it would have been taken for granted. But times had changed. Today they had to proceed more subtly. Today, GDR critics couldn't just be strangled in car parks in Brandenburg anymore. These days the enemy wasn't kidnapped, shot and murdered. There were other methods of dealing with those people. But the old guard and the new fought over which methods were more effective. Merzig stood somewhere in between. He had never been able to warm to brutality.

'We should wait until the mole reveals himself,' Kauperth continued. 'They're in the same train. If we grab them too soon, then we only have the turncoats. But if we get them during the hand-over, then we also have the Western agents in our net. Those are high-ranking people from the CIA and BND who are worth a significant amount.'

The Minister inhaled air through his almost-closed lips. It sounded like a squeaking balloon. He was probably mentally calculating how many West German marks the ransom would bring in. Or how many GDR citizens sitting in West German prisons for spying would be able to walk over the Glienicker Bridge in an agent exchange.

'Merzig?'

Everyone was looking at him.

'Arrest orders. Today.'

Merzig nodded. He almost knew the wording for fleeing the Republic and treason by heart. Was he mistaken or was the Minister looking longer at him? No. He turned to Wildgruber, who had shifted a little further from Fröde.

'You will give Lieutenant General Merzig the names. Understood?'

Wildgruber's bright, alert eyes lit up.

'Gentlemen?'

The fat one stood up. Just as at the emperor's table, everyone else stood up and waited until the Minister had left the briefing room. Merzig remained standing, until the crowd started moving, and then suddenly found Wildgruber standing next to him again.

'I'd like a word with you,' the young Colonel said. His voice, loud enough for a barracks yard just minutes before, had sunk to a whisper.

'Because of the names?'

'Yes. There's something you need to know.'

Merzig pushed out through the door and into the hall. The carpet swallowed their footsteps. Most of them took the stairs; several of those with seniority waited for the elevator. Merzig joined them.

'I don't have to remind you that this is all top secret,' he said. 'The circumstances are clear. I do not and cannot know more.'

Wildgruber stood there. Merzig, who didn't want to be impolite, turned around to him.

'This case is different.' The young man looked past Merzig as if to assure himself that no one was listening to their conversation. 'Do you like Thuringian bratwurst?'

'Yes,' Kaiserley said. 'That's just how I always pictured your working environment.'

Merzig appeared to hide himself behind his pipe smoke. Judith couldn't tell if the memory of that day affected him or not.

'So you signed the arrest warrant for my parents?'

'That was my job. They were accused of having made comprehensive preparations for illegal departure from the German Democratic Republic by eluding the legal requirements. This was compounded by treason and high treason. At the time this was punishable by death.'

Judith began to shake again. This time it had nothing to do with the withdrawal symptoms.

'The death penalty was only abolished in 1987,' Kaiserley said. 'The last person executed was Werner Teske, a Stasi Captain who wanted to defect.'

'What did you do then?' Judith asked. It was so strange and unreal in this bourgeois living room with the beautiful fish. She felt as if she was feeding coins to a machine that spat out information in return.

'We let them believe that no one had noticed anything. We knew that they would only come into direct contact in Sassnitz. That's why we had to prevent the traitors from changing coaches at any cost.'

'Don't call them that.'

Merzig raised his eyebrows. 'What would you call them if the case were reversed? If they had been West German citizens taking the entire agent network of the BND to the GDR?'

'There were no BND agents in the GDR,' Kaiserley countered.

'An interesting, but in no way accurate claim. And one of the points we could certainly talk about at length at the appropriate time.' Merzig reached for a small, silver instrument and poked around in his pipe. 'OK, let's call them your parents, Ms . . . Kepler.'

Judith nodded. It was hard to appear calm.

'The colleagues in Schwerin took command of the operation. So with all I can tell you, I'm restricted to my memory of a file copy that I later received from the branch at Demmlerplatz.'

'Where's the original?' Judith asked.

'No longer in existence.'

'Shredded?'

'Everything was. Mr Kaiserley will be able to confirm this.'

Kaiserley nodded. 'And our mutual friend Dr Matthes as well. However, there are still a great many plastic sacks that we might be able to reconstruct.'

'Have fun,' Merzig replied dryly. 'Every country has the employment policies it deserves.'

Judith wanted to jump up and hit the arrogant garden gnome's pipe right out of his mouth. He clearly enjoyed the opportunity to exert all of his power, one last time. A toppled king who strolled through the treasure trove of his memory with his head held high.

'What happened in Sassnitz?'

Merzig looked over to the aquarium. Two of the cichlids circled each other. Their elegant movements looked like the supernaturally beautiful choreography of a ballet.

'Your mother wanted to go with you to Malmö in the through coach. At that point we wouldn't have been able to reach her. The Swedish conductor had been bought by the BND. However, the Stasi outbid them. So he didn't let you through. He handed you directly over to passport control.'

'Where was my father?'

'In the through coach.'

'How did he get there? Did he have a visa?'

'I thought you knew that. He was a citizen with very special tasks.'

It was so quiet that Judith could hear the fizzing of the tobacco in Merzig's pipe. Perhaps it was because the last few words were echoing around in her head like hammer blows.

'He was . . .' she said silently. She stared at Kaiserley. 'A citizen with special tasks? What does that mean?'

Kaiserley avoided her gaze. But Merzig answered.

'Richard Lindner was, next to Sapphire, one of the best Romeos we had.'

27

Kellermann stood on the patio of his bungalow and lovingly inspected the two rose bushes that he and Eva had planted behind the house after moving in. They had been small, with only four or five shoots. Now the branches climbed high along the patio door and already almost met in the middle. Next year they'll make it, Eva had said, I'm sure of it. Then two will become one.

It had been a hot summer, back then, just like this year. She had brushed the brown hair out of her face and in doing so, had left a broad trace of dirt and earth on her cheeks. Kellermann had lovingly wiped it away, embraced her and admired his house. His castle. His fortress. The lofty wall built around the property. The alarm system. The two dogs playing on the lawn looking so harmless, who could transform into vicious beasts if he just said the word.

He had felt secure. He had done everything to keep the world out. He had even sold his soul. But twenty years later he felt like Faust, cheated, forced to realise that he had got the worst end of the bargain.

He turned away and went through the patio door into the living room. The evenings were becoming fresh, a welcome change to those endless summer weeks glowing with heat. The quiet whispering and gurgling of the sprinkler system intruded. Seven o'clock. He'd treat himself to a whisky and hope that he was already asleep when Eva came home. Regretfully, he noted that a second enemy had crept into his life, along with the past. Habit. The river of life took the hard edges off the banks, smoothed them, polished and shiny, and the emotional world of matrimony transformed into something most closely resembling thankfulness.

The phone rang. It was TT, and for a second he wondered whether he should take such a late call. He was tired of the chase.

'Yes?' he finally said.

'You didn't get my email?'

TT sounded rushed, out of breath.

'Which mail?'

'I sent you a message this afternoon. With an attachment.'

'Wait a sec.'

Kellermann checked his inbox.

'I didn't get any.'

'That can't be. I sent it at 4:42.'

'I'll call you back.'

He hung up and searched his folder. Nothing. An uneasy feeling grew. He opened the recycling bin and found the message. Someone had read it and then deleted it. The attachment was still intact. Kellermann restored both, skimmed the message, and didn't know what disturbed him more: its content or the question of how it had landed in the bin. He called Eva's number, but she didn't pick up. The call went to voicemail, and he hung up.

TT had tracked Kaiserley. He had found out where that crazy man was and opened the Pandora's Box. Kaiserley was with Merzig. And that meant . . . Kellerman's pulse raced, his thoughts stumbled over each other. Things were set into motion that should have been frozen for all time.

Kellermann poured himself a double from his drinks trolley. He knocked back a slug and stared at the phone in his hand, as if he were considering hurling it against the wall.

Where was Eva?

'I'm meeting a girlfriend at Bayerischer Hof. Don't wait up for me. I might be back late.'

He had received the text message at 4:44 p.m. An icy, furious thought arose. She had read his messages to Angelina. His phone was an open book. And if she had flipped around even further back, then she would also know about Sassnitz. And about his attempts to keep the worst of it a secret. And Kaiserley was just about to destroy it all.

Kellermann let the phone fall, and stepped on it. It shot to the side like a cherry pit. He chased it, hammering it with his foot, kicked it against the wall until it broke into pieces and gave up the ghost. He had spilled the whisky. Breathing heavily, he poured himself some more. Then he went to his landline and called TT.

'You have to find Eva.'

'What?'

Kellermann took a deep breath. How do you explain the unexplainable to a boy like that? That you could love someone and simultaneously cheat on them? And that through this, things had come to light that could destroy them all?

'Eva,' he said. 'Eva Kellermann. I have to know where she is.'
He hung up. No secret was safe now.

'A Romeo?' Judith jumped up. She felt as if she was suffocating under the low ceiling. 'What a bunch of unbelievable bullshit you're serving up here. Both of you.'

'He didn't want to do it anymore,' Kaiserley said. 'So he had contacted us at a photography trade fair in Budapest. We brought him to Berlin and there we formed the plan of how we could get him, his wife, his child, and the files out of the country. After that he returned to the GDR and continued to act normally. We scheduled the operation to run parallel to the trade fair in Hanover. Lindner was representing the VEB Carl Zeiss Jena, and I was there too. We met. He changed his identity. I was assigned to accompany him to Sassnitz. I also had his passport: Richard Borg, a Swedish citizen with a West German visa. That's how he got into West Berlin with me, and one day later he departed from Bahnhof Zoo.'

Merzig tapped his pipe empty above the ashtray. 'That's how he became a double agent. The worst case scenario for every intelligence service.'

'When did you know?' Judith asked.

'From that Tuesday in August.'

Berlin Lichtenberg, Ministry for State Security
Corner of Normannen-Gotlindestrasse
Building 22, Commander's Hill, 1985

The cafeteria was a bright, functional room, divided into a self-service area and a reservations-only restaurant. There was room for two hundred diners, but was usually half-empty because only the higher officers were allowed to enter. Merzig had been waiting in his office for Wildgruber. Together they had climbed the hill.

'Leave it. I'm paying.'

Wildgruber pulled out his wallet and settled the 2.74 mark bill. He also put the two plates on one tray, lifted it high, and looked for a spot far from the other guests. Merzig followed him and felt his dislike for the man grow.

'Would you also like something to drink? A Radeberger?'

'No, thank you.'

Wildgruber waved away the waitress who was on her way to them. She turned around and devoted herself to the other guests. Merzig recognised Major General Henze with Colonel Zwedylla two tables over. He nodded to him, but Henze didn't appear to have seen him.

'Well, then, enjoy your meal.'

Wildgruber divided his sausage into several small pieces, then took the fork into his right hand and began to eat.

'We have quite a pigsty to clean up,' he said. 'It's starting up again. It's Stiller all over. Forget it, it's Stiller times ten. Times a hundred.'

Werner Stiller, First Lieutenant at the HVA, the foreign department of the Stasi, had made off for the West with a treasure trove of documents in his luggage at the end of the seventies. Since then, not even a wasp was able to pass the wall without its identity being examined. Stiller had sent almost fifty scouts to their doom.

Merzig placed his cutlery to one side. For some reason he didn't like the taste of the sausage.

'Fröde will bow out. But only afterwards when the operation in Sassnitz is over. We don't want to scare the horses, you understand?'

Merzig's gaze fell on the glass door that led out of the cafeteria and to the elevators. Several sentries were posted there. That surprised him. Was the Chairman of the State Council visiting unannounced?

'That's why we have to know how you will act. Will you sign the arrest warrant?'

'Of course.' There was no question. Merzig wondered why the conversation was taking place here at the table and not behind closed doors.

'Then you have to act just as you always have.'

Wildgruber dunked a piece of sausage in his mashed potato. On the way to his mouth, the mouthful fell from the fork back down into the gravy. Wildgruber's white shirt received several tiny spots.

'Oh, that happens to me all the time. My mother always says I eat like a barbarian.'

Smiling, the Colonel reached for a napkin and started to clean up the mess. Merzig gave his sausage another shot. He chewed, but was hardly able to swallow. He pushed the plate away.

'To be honest, Comrade Wildgruber, I don't know where you are going with this conversation. My department is charged with the exposure of and defence against intelligence service attacks against our country and our employees. Arrest warrants against suspects and those caught in the act are nothing that could influence my actions in the least.'

'Even if it concerned a friend or relative?'

Merzig carefully dabbed at his mouth with a napkin. The question surprised him. No one from his circle had contacts in the West, aside from those necessary for professional reasons and expressly desirable in the service of foreign reconnaissance. They were all party members. And several even worked in the same ministry. His entire background was examined in detail annually, and followed the same routine as doctors' examinations, which checked physical and psychological fitness in the same way. The only thing he didn't have under control was his weight.

'Even that wouldn't have any bearing on things,' he said. 'You don't violate an oath.'

Wildgruber nodded. 'That's exactly the way I see it.'

The next time Wildgruber looked over to the door, the guards had disappeared.

TT didn't have a chance. Eva Kellermann's telephone was turned off. If it wasn't transmitting, it couldn't receive signals. He was surprised by Kellermann's sudden change in tack. Kaiserley, Kepler, and now his own wife – was Kellermann still on top of the situation? And what was the situation exactly?

A melodic beep pulled him out of his thoughts. The spider had spun its web, and somewhere out there in the world something was twitching in a trap. TT opened the window, read, and dialled Kellermann's number with great haste – but there was nothing, no connection. TT jumped up and ran to the balcony. From there he eyed his laptop, as if the machine itself was a Trojan horse used by the enemy to gain access to his most inner sanctum, his apartment.

His phone rang. It was a blocked number, but TT knew who was on the other end. He stayed on the balcony.

'Yes?' Kellermann bellowed.

'There's news,' TT said quietly.

He didn't know how he should break it to his boss. He didn't even know what game was being played. He only sensed that everything was connected and that he wasn't the bearer of good news.

'I was able to locate your wife's phone.'

'And? Where is she?'

'In Berlin. She's leaving Tegel Airport and is on the move . . . wait a sec . . .'

He carefully crept back into the living room and approached his laptop, although he was overcome by the feeling that it could bite him any second. This was absolutely idiotic. He didn't want it anymore. He was a technician. This was about things that were so far in the past that they only survived as legends in the long, dark cellar hallways. These were stories from the days when the lives of agents didn't take place in front of computers in sun-drenched feng-shuied offices, but rather in the catacombs of the old border positions, in the tunnels along the insurmountable wall, places where a bullet to the head was considered a natural cause of death. TT sensed the connections. But he didn't want to know about them.

'Heading towards the east side of the city centre. On the B1 at the moment. And that leads to Biesdorf. And that's where Kaiserley is drinking coffee with Lieutenant General Merzig. Mr Kellermann, what does it all mean?'

Kellermann was silent.

'And that's not everything. Your wife's movement profile shows that she was in southern Sweden the day before yesterday. Malmö.'

He heard a tortured noise that sounded like a groan. TT's concern morphed into dismay. Kellermann was losing control. The old warrior appeared wounded.

'But you certainly know that already,' TT said, not quite believing what he was saying. 'Should I inform somebody?' No response. 'Do you need help?'

'No.' Kellermann's voice sounded like rough sandpaper. 'TT, do me a favour and forget all this, if you can.'

'Aye, aye, sir.'

TT felt a weight fall from his chest. So his strange assignment ended here. He stood there, undecided, with his phone at his ear, and waited for Kellermann to sever the connection.

Kellermann hung up without a word of farewell. TT hurried to his laptop and began to delete everything that had the slightest connection to the events of the past few days. He closed his backdoors and called the Trojans back. He created false trails, and branching tracks and traces, until he believed he had everything under control. Only then did he notice his mistake. It wasn't enough. It was pointless. There was only one solution.

For the first time in two months TT was glad to have a construction site in front of his apartment building. Before going down, he unscrewed his laptop and removed the hard drive. With that in hand, he left the apartment.

Working on the switch in the tram tracks was apparently a complicated task. Two welders were working on the connecting part at once, and the noise was ear-splitting, until one of the two finally looked up and noticed TT standing at the fence, wildly gesticulating and whistling. TT explained what he wanted from them, and passed over a fifty euro note. He was even allowed to stand within a metre of them and watch until the hard drive had become a small glowing clump of metal, which was driven into the hems of the tracks with two hammer blows.

'Do you have a phone?' he asked one of the welders.

The man nodded and pulled a small device from his chest pocket.

Judith stared at Merzig as if she'd like to spray him with an insecticide. The Stasi Lieutenant didn't seem to notice her distaste. Either that, or he simply ignored it, because in the course of his life he had learned to deal with such reactions. He looked thoughtfully at Kaiserley.

'Lindner was working for the HVA. Sometimes in Bonn, sometimes in Hamburg, sometimes in Munich. He had done good work. Excellent, in part. But I blame myself for having overlooked something. The beginning. The moment when a person first second-guesses what he does.'

'Maybe he was just disgusted when he looked in the mirror?' Judith asked. 'Did my mother know about it? That he screwed other women to get information?'

'Of course. She was also working for the Stasi.'

'Both of them?' Judith asked. 'I thought that she . . .'

A phone buzzed. Irritated, Judith looked at Kaiserley. He pulled his device from his pocket, looked at the display, shrugged his shoulders, and put it away. Merzig waited until he could be sure he had their undivided attention.

'I don't know if Irene Sonnenberg was informed about the details. Spouses do talk with one another, even when it's expressly forbidden. But I think that she did know. In the end, you could assume that was the reason why she wanted to leave the GDR.'

Judith looked at her hands. She remembered what Kaiserley had said in Malmö. That you looked for parents and found monsters. Her father, a Romeo. Her mother with the Stasi. The escape bought with betrayal.

'Many marriages broke up because of that,' Merzig said. 'The never-ending lies. The aliases. The questions that couldn't be answered. Am I right, Mr Kaiserley?'

Kaiserley was silent.

'An occupational hazard that probably all agents suffer from. A great deal of character is needed in order to live with such a person. To love them. To trust them. The family is the predetermined breaking point.'

'Your father was a good person.'

Judith raised her head with a jolt. She glared at Kaiserley in rage. 'Oh yeah? How do you know that?'

'I knew him.'

'But you didn't tell me what he really did! And my mother – a photo lab technician! It sounded like holiday snapshots at the lake, not microfilm! Did she do that? Did she?'

'Judith, please don't be naïve. Where did you think the Rosenholz file came from? Found on a park bench? Do you think the BND forged Swedish passports to smuggle a loving family out of the GDR out of pure benevolence and altruism?'

THE CLEANER | 400

'Modelled after,' Judith corrected him with caustic sarcasm. 'That's the name for it, right? And don't you dare call me naïve.'

'Everyone would have benefitted. Your parents, who wanted to start a new life, the CIA, which had been just as infiltrated as the BND, and not least the BND itself, which would have achieved an unbelievable success in one fell swoop. A win-win situation.'

Judith reached for her bag. Her finger touched the pistol she had taken out of Dombrowski's desk drawer when she had asked the detective for ten minutes to change. The cool metal comforted her. A win-win situation. Did Kaiserley actually know what his words were doing? Her fingers slipped past and found the pack of tobacco. She pulled it out and placed the bag next to her. Kaiserley's phone vibrated again. He ignored it.

'But there are only losers left on the battlefield,' she said and tried to keep her voice sounding as calm as possible. 'My parents are dead. I was put in a home. Two others travelled to Sweden in our place. And I was somehow forgotten, right?'

'Stanz saved your life.'

'Stanz? Me?' Judith asked and stopped rolling the cigarette for a second.

'The report about the night in Sassnitz was from Stanz. And the role a very special woman played.'

'Which woman?' Judith asked. 'Marianne Kepler?'

Smiling, Merzig shook his head. He sat on the couch, squatting on his special knowledge, and let her wait for it. The impulse to pull out the gun and point it at Merzig was almost unbearable. Suddenly Kaiserley put his hand on her knee.

He immediately pulled it away, but Judith understood the gesture: stay calm, is what he wanted to tell her. Please stay very, very calm.

'I only know the alias she used back then,' Merzig said.

'And that would be what?'

'Rose,' Merzig answered. 'Like the flower.'

28

Colonel Hubert Stanz, in his early forties, a tall, slender man with pale skin and many freckles, stood in the terminal of the train station and watched the international Berlin–Malmö express, which was being searched by sniffer dogs in the light of glaring floodlights for the third time in the past half-hour. Stanz was nervous. The last time he'd had that feeling was during his final exam at law school, and that was at least a couple of years ago. Up until now, his focus had been on managing and carrying out interrogations, and this was his first 'open air' operation. It was dawning on him that the gap between theory and practice was substantial. For instance, while it was possible to plan an operation perfectly, it was far from guaranteed that the plan would be executed perfectly.

Theatre was being performed here, and the passport control officers had to follow orders. Everyone else was in position. He jumped when the telephone rang in the ghostly empty train terminal. Two steps and he'd reached the device and lifted the receiver.

'Thirty minutes,' it hissed. 'What's going wrong?'

'I don't know.' He looked at the train and knew that Lindner was sitting somewhere on the through coach. The rat. The turncoat. Together with a clutch of high-profile BND agents. And they couldn't get to him. Two coaches further on, in the Bergen locomotive, Sonnenberg sat with her daughter, carefully watched by the conductor. The rat's spawn. The vermin. They didn't move. And the longer they waited, the more likely it was that the whole operation would peter out. 'Maybe they have a signal arranged.'

'Yellow ribbons?' Rose's voice sounded contemptuous. 'We can't keep the train here forever. Tell your people to storm it.'

Stanz shook his head, even though she couldn't see him, because the train was between them. 'Out of the question. Too many witnesses.'

He didn't even want to think about the diplomatic complications that would ensue. Arrested in transit. Mother and child. Unbelievable. The tabloid press would eat it up. The interest-free trade credit had just been increased to 850 million West German marks, the West German government guarantee was at 950 million. Erich Honecker wanted to visit Bonn in September. Back in the day, they would have just pulled the woman and her child out of the train by the hair. Now they needed evidence. Ironclad.

'She knows just as much as Lindner. She can identify the BND agents,' she said.

And why can't you do that? Stanz was tempted to ask. *Didn't you do your homework, or what?* He was so tired of being treated like a yokel by these stuck-up Western women. He managed to swallow his words in time. From the very beginning she had made clear that she could only betray the BND plan, not tell them who would carry it out; she didn't know who would be doing the smuggling. Sometimes even the pushy women from the West reached their limits. Stanz looked nervously at the clock. Way past midnight. They were running out of time.

'Then pull them out,' was all she said.

She hung up. Stanz pulled another cigarette from his pack and lit it. That gave him a few more minutes to think. Why wasn't anything happening out there? The conductor had changed sides for a thousand West German marks. The Swedish! He didn't know what he despised more: the corruption in and of itself or the speed with which people let themselves be bribed. He was supposed to get them as soon as the woman gave the sign. But she hadn't done that. Did she have the feeling that her escape plan was in danger? Did she have a sixth sense? Had the dogs or the floodlights or ultimately her own crazy plan scared her? Stanz inhaled deeply. On that train sat two people who were committing high treason and a Western agent. And a child. The child was the weakest link.

He dropped the cigarette and stepped on it. Then he went to the platform and boarded the coaches that were to be uncoupled from the through train.

Stanz had committed the photo to heart long ago. The woman sat next to the window in a six-person compartment, her arm wrapped around her daughter, and stared at the border patrol with their German shepherds inspecting the underside of the coach again and again. Stanz pulled the door open with a jolt.

'Mrs Sonnenberg?'

She started and stared at him. Her face was pale, and she was more beautiful than the photos from the dossier had suggested. The girl clung to her a stuffed animal. She was tired and rubbed her eyes. The other passengers stared at him in fright.

'I'd like you to come with me. Come along.'

'Why?' she asked.

'Your husband would like to speak with you.'

In the bluish glow of the neon lights she appeared to lose her last bit of colour. She jumped up and grabbed the girl by the hand.

'My . . . husband? Has something happened?'

The fellow passengers received Irene Sonnenberg's confusion as a welcome change of pace from the tedium of waiting. Stanz knew that he didn't have much time.

'Yes. Please follow me.'

In that moment she had to know that her plan had failed. Stanz wasn't the conductor who should have brought her into the through coach. The cabin door rolled shut behind her.

'What's wrong?' She was breathless from fear.

'Mrs Sonnenberg, we want to avoid a fuss.'

'I'm here to go on holiday. The train will be uncoupled and continue to Bergen any minute now. We have a room in the FDGB-Heim Prora. Here.'

She nervously searched through her handbag until she had found a scrap of paper.

'Mummy? What's wrong with papa?'

She bent over to her child. A delicate girl with angelic curls; the similarity between them was impossible to overlook.

'Nothing, darling.'

'He's waiting for you,' Stanz said to the child. 'Over there, look. The coach next to the locomotive shed. Can you see it?'

The girl pressed her nose flat against the windowpane.

'Yes.'

'Your papa's over there.'

Irene Sonnenberg staggered but was able to catch herself. All life appeared to have been leached from her face. Stanz was familiar with those moments. Those were the seconds before a confession; the moments before the final collapse.

'That's Lenin's lounge car,' Stanz said. 'And that's where we're all going now.'

'Please,' Irene Sonnenberg whispered. 'Please don't.'

Stanz led the way, opening the door that led to the dark side of the tracks.

'Come on, little girl. Your papa is waiting.'

Two cops with machine guns accompanied them. On this side of the train there were only hallways, no cabins. The conductor made certain that no unwanted witnesses were milling around. No one would see how Irene Sonnenberg and her daughter were led away. It was less than thirty metres, but Stanz knew that for the woman it would seem like the last steps to the gallows. It had taken quite some time for him to suppress his empathy. He had led many interrogations. He had been the best in his class. He knew how to break people. They had been trained not to pay attention to the tears, not the stammered explanations, not the pleas and begging. They were even experienced at ignoring the inner voice that occasionally whispered that enough was enough.

Sonnenberg deserved the death penalty. Even if she looked like an angel, she still harboured corruption and betrayal inside her, and had put thousands of agents in immediate danger. He was remarkably moved by the child. The little girl had firmly grabbed her mother's hand and stumbled over the tracks and the rocks. Once the stuffed animal fell from her hand. Stanz picked it up, but Sonnenberg ripped it out of his hand and gave it back to her daughter herself.

The lounge car had been Rose's idea. And once again, Stanz couldn't help but admire the way that she had planned the operation and left nothing to chance. Stanz didn't work with a centralised command, and such an approach was new for him. As he pushed down the heavy door opener and let the two go ahead, he was glad they wouldn't have to bring all this to an end at the train station.

The child looked around in amazement. In her eyes, the thread-bare velvet and the spotted brass transformed into a palace.

'Where is Lenin?' she asked.

The heavy, red curtain moved. A hand pushed it aside. The child turned around and let a scream loose.

'No!'

Sonnenberg wanted to grab hold of the girl, but Stanz pulled her back.

'Stay calm,' he said. But the whole situation was spiralling completely out of control. 'Completely calm.'

'Lenin is on his way,' Rose said and aimed at the child.

The welder drank half of a bottle of mineral water in a single gulp, set it down, and burped loudly.

'Can I have my phone back now?'

TT cursed to himself. Why wasn't Kaiserley answering his telephone?

'Right away.'

He reached into his trouser pocket and pulled out another fifty. Shit. No idea when he'd get to another cash machine.

'I'll buy it from you. It's ancient anyway.'

'Hey!'

TT tossed the note on a pile of cobblestones and sprinted off. Dressed in his heavy work clothes, the welder was too slow to follow him. But he could still hear him yelling from two blocks away.

His landline, his laptop, his smartphone – all bugged. Someone had been following him each step of the way, the entire time, read every email he'd sent to Kellermann. And if what TT had just pieced together was true, then even Kellermann was in trouble up to his neck.

He dialled Kellermann's number from memory and fervently hoped that he had remembered it correctly.

Kellermann didn't answer. TT felt his throat tighten. Kaiserley had been right about everything, and TT despised himself for not having believed him. Pick up, he prayed. Pick up!

A hand grabbed him from behind and wheeled him around. He stared at the furious face of a strong man, flushed with anger.

'Phone,' was all he grunted, and grabbed TT by the lapels. It was the welder, and behind him his buddy appeared, ominously rolling up the sleeves of his checked shirt.

'It's an emergency,' TT squawked. 'Please! I need it!'

The welder pushed him against the wall. It knocked the wind out of him, and the device slipped out of his hand, falling to the ground.

'You want trouble? You can have it.'

He rammed a fist into TT's stomach. TT folded up like a pocket knife. A metallic taste flooded his mouth. He had bitten his tongue. Slowly he slid down the wall to the ground. He crouched on all fours. His hand reached out for the phone, but the welder was quicker. He stepped on TT's fingers. Not hard enough to break them, but hard enough for TT to howl in pain.

The other one picked up the phone and wiped it off.

'I have to . . . call someone,' TT groaned. 'It's urgent.'

The welder pulled back his foot, but only to boot TT in the ribs again.

'Remember that.'

They turned away. TT's head raced. There was no more room for cover stories and lies. The two of them walked off, and there was only a few seconds left for what was essential: the truth.

'Just one call!'

TT pulled himself together and ran after them. He was limping, and his hand was hurting badly.

'Let me try one last time. Please! Please!'

Passers-by on the other side of the street turned toward them. The whole situation was becoming embarrassing for the two workers. They walked faster.

'It's a matter of life and death!' TT bellowed.

One of them stopped, but the other one roughly dragged him further. TT ran past them and positioned himself in their way. The first welder wanted to push him aside.

'I have to try again. One more time. Give me your phone. I'm sorry, I didn't want to steal it. Let me use it for a call!'

'Shut up,' the welder said, but it no longer sounded so self-assured. 'Use your own.'

'I can't. It's bugged. Please. I have to warn someone.'

The two of them marched on.

'It's my father!' TT yelled. 'A woman is on her way to him. She wants to kill him!'

The welder stopped and turned around.

'Then call the cops.'

'Yeah, but with what?' TT yelled in desperation.

Judith stared past Merzig, looking at the fish, but not seeing anything else. It was as if someone had pulled back a velvet curtain in her mind, and suddenly everything was back. The barking dogs, the spotlights, and the 'clickety-clack, clickety-clack, clickety-clack', moving closer and closer.

'Judith?' Kaiserley's voice, from very close. 'What's wrong?'

'She . . . she told me something,' she whispered. 'She said she was leaving because she wanted to show the man something. She climbed out of the lounge car and the man followed her, and then . . . there was a locomotive. There was a bang, completely muffled. And then someone screamed. High and shrill. Someone screamed and couldn't stop.'

For the second time that evening something flashed in the eyes of the Stasi Lieutenant General. Empathy?

'That was you, Ms Kepler. You were severely traumatised. Your mother was shot before your eyes.'

Judith felt her mind powering down, section by section, as if she were standing at her own circuit box and flipping one switch after another. She resented, hated, despised this small, old man on his corduroy couch, who had still not reached the end of his, her, all of their story.

'She said she wanted to show Stanz the hiding place for the microfilm. No one could hold her back; she knew exactly what she was doing. And then the switch engine for the train to Bergen. She ran off. Behind the locomotive. Over the tracks. Into the floodlights. The snipers had no choice.'

Judith pulled the weapon from her bag, jumped up, and pointed it at Merzig.

'You pigs. You miserable, godless pigs! You shot her down like a rat!'

'Judith! No!'

She flipped down the safety, like Dombrowski had once shown her.

'Who was Rose?'

Merzig raised his hands. 'Child, put the gun away.'

'Look in there.' She pointed the barrel in Merzig's face. 'And think very carefully about what you say. Who was she?'

Kaiserley stood up, slowly and calmly, but Judith danced to the side, out of his reach.

'Tell me her name! Now! And fuck you, with Rose and Stanz, and Lindner, and . . .' She pointed at Kaiserley, who raised his hands. 'Weingärtner and all that shit! Who was she?'

Just then the window exploded with a loud bang. Cracks spread through the glass like a huge spider web. Another bang. Judith couldn't duck down fast enough. The walls of the aquarium broke into a thousand shards, tearing clothes and skin, and before Kaiserley flung her to the floor, she saw the water standing for a moment like a pillar in middle of the room, before crashing over in a single wave, a metre high. Under Kaiserley's weight, she slammed onto the coffee table, then the floor. The force of the impact flung the pistol out of her hand, landing out of her reach underneath the couch. A silver grey fish landed directly next to her face, twitching and flopping about. Kaiserley pressed his hand to her mouth. He was soaking wet, water dripping from his hair and onto her. Judith's heart hammered against her ribs. She was gasping for air as desperately as the fish next to her.

Then it was still. A quiet rattling, there was water dripping, forming puddles on the floor. Merzig lay across from them behind the coffee table, no more than a metre away. Blood streamed over his face. He twitched. And the flash in his eyes was no long the reflection of his strange soul, but rather came from razor-sharp shards of glass. His head fell to the side. There was a small, black hole in his temple. She felt Kaiserley's breath on her face. He slowly pulled his hand away and placed an index finger on his lips. She lay there and didn't move. And then the shards of glass crunched behind her as someone stepped on them.

29

Kellermann breathed a sigh of relief as soon as he had passed through the grey steel gate and let his car roll to a halt in the car park. Winkler's BMW was still there. A couple of days ago Winkler had not been much more than a kind of chauffeur for him. But the tide had turned. Now, he was the only one who might still be able to save something.

The office of the intelligence services coordinator was located behind the tennis courts. Two women were playing, and he hurried past, giving them a brief distracted look. He tried to order the sentences in his head, but never got past the one and only starting point: Eva. Where was she? What was she doing? What did she do? What will she do?

Winkler looked up in surprise when Kellermann opened the door without knocking and quickly shut it behind him. He was reading a dossier that looked like it weighed a ton, and carefully laid a ruler between the pages before closing it. Kellermann aimed the spinning chair towards Winkler's desk without wasting any time with pleasantries.

'Malmö,' he said.

Winkler furrowed his brow. 'I'm not following.'

'My wife is supposed to have been there. Can you explain why?'

Winkler attempted a polite smile. 'I really don't know Eva that well. Are you having problems?'

There was a portrait of the Federal President hanging behind Winkler. He was several years younger than Kellermann. Everyone was getting younger. Except him. He was becoming old and tired. Perhaps it really was time to step down.

'I had Kaiserley secretly followed. Him and Kepler. After the murder of Christina Borg it appeared to be the only way to find out more about the location of the Rosenholz files.'

'Rosenholz . . .' Winkler leaned back and looked at Kellermann thoughtfully. 'Only a couple of weeks ago we rejected establishing contact with that person from Sweden. You remember?'

'We'd been offered the microfilm on a silver platter!'

'For two hundred and fifty thousand euros. No, my dear. It's not possible to persuade the taxpayers that would be a good use of their money.'

Kellermann cursed this kind of bean-counting. He would only have had to delete one name. Only a single name.

'Since when do the taxpayers find out what their money is used for?'

Winkler motioned to the dossier. 'Five hundred pages. Annual budget of 430 million. And tomorrow I have to be able to explain every single item on it in front of the parliamentary oversight committee. New buildings. Personnel. Heating costs. And then the items that are never allowed to appear officially. Reconnaissance for the army outside of Germany. Fax machines and computers for the basement of the French embassy in Baghdad. Establishing connections with the ICO in Kosovo. Recruiting stooges for the international intelligence stations. Bribes for information about WMDs, terrorism, and money laundering. A quarter million for Rosenholz? Rosenholz is in the past. This here is the future.'

'We let our only chance slip through our fingers.'

'We?' Winkler studied Kellermann sharply. 'Don't you mean you did?'

Kellermann felt an icy chill run down his spine. 'What are you implying?'

'That you should either speak up now or go home and forever hold your peace. I can only help you if you're honest with me.'

Kellermann thought about all those years he had spent telling Winkler what was what. The leader of the pack. The grey one. The man in charge The commander who wasn't above wading through the muck of the front lines himself. Perhaps that was all over and the technicians, strategists, and analysts would now assume command. People like Winkler, who wore pristine white shirts and wingtip shoes, even in this heat. Kellermann had a sudden moment of complete clarity: his era had passed. Strange that he had failed to see it for so long.

'Kaiserley is meeting with a former Stasi Lieutenant General right now. And my wife is on the way there.'

'Then she has a more exciting private life than we do.'

Winkler pulled the tome closer. Kellermann took a deep breath.

'I think she's making a stupid mistake.'

'If this is about marital problems, you're talking to the wrong person.'

'This is about . . .' Kellermann ran his hand through his hair. Winkler waited.

'Eva got caught up in something she can't understand the implications of. I have reason to believe that she found things on my phone that she never should have been allowed to find. I believe she is in Berlin to prevent something from the past from surfacing.'

'What would that be?'

Merzig would tell Kaiserley everything. The whole story, in which a young girl played a role, a girl whom Kellermann had been head-over-heels in love with for ages. A girl he wanted to have, at any price. But that young girl didn't want a cynical, drunken lout twice her age. She fell for a dashing man who promised her the stars in the sky and treated her like an angel. Until the day he began to demand something in return . . .

'She only did it once. Twenty-five years ago she passed a briefing on to East Berlin. It's long past the statute of limitations. There's no way they could touch her now!'

'Your wife?'

'She wasn't my wife at the time. My first marriage was going down the tubes. She was young, inexperienced. When the catastrophe happened in Sassnitz, she turned to me. I swept it under the rug. Then I married her.'

So Kellermann protected the girl and didn't turn her in. They were married, and Eva Lange became Eva Kellermann. They had had good years, Eva and he. At some point he had repressed what had brought them together. They had worked so well together. If only the ghosts of the past had not returned.

'If Kaiserley finds out who had sent him to his doom back then . . . and Eva shows up there . . .'

'Eva betrayed Sassnitz?'

Kellermann nodded.

'Eva? *Your* Eva? Are you sure?'

'Yes.'

Winkler's hand shot forward and pressed a button on his phone. He lifted the receiver and waited until someone at the other end picked up.

'Geolocation, code red. Phone number?'

Kellermann gave it to him. Winkler waited, and opened a search window in the meantime.

'What's the name of this Stasi man?'

'Merzig. Lieutenant General Horst Merzig. Berlin.'

Winkler typed. At the same time he listed to what was coming through the receiver.

'Thanks,' he said curtly, and hung up. 'We're too late. Eva has already reached Merzig.'

Kellermann groaned. He noticed how Winkler studied him with a mixture of empathy and regret.

'I'll alert our colleagues in Berlin. The whole thing will probably end harmlessly. They'll exchange words, and then the issue will be off the table. But you should be aware this will have consequences for you.'

Kellermann nodded and stood up. 'Thanks. Let me know immediately if you hear anything.'

He was almost at the door.

'You could have come sooner,' Winkler said.

Kellermann drove back to Munich and was amazed. He should have been incensed. Angry about the situation he had got himself into. But all he felt was unending relief. They would find Eva. He would be disciplined and would be sent off to retirement. The statute of limitations had passed on her mistakes. The Rosenholz files could be closed, once and for all.

He reached the city centre and turned onto Maximilianstrasse.

I'm meeting up with a girlfriend at Bayerischer Hof. Kellermann drove past the hotel. Suddenly he slammed on the brakes. Eva didn't have a girlfriend at Bayerischer Hof. *He* had one.

Kellermann had Angelina's room number memorised, and went past reception with a slight nod. One of the many business travellers who just wanted to get to their room after a long day, get a shower and climb into bed. He took the elevator to the fifth floor. In his hand he held a master key card from IntSec, a company that made the security systems for the BND headquarters in Berlin and was also market leader in the area of mechatronics. This card gave him power over all HSPD-locks that used radio frequency identification. There weren't many cards of this kind. Up until now he had only viewed it as a status symbol. But now, as the heavy carpet swallowed his steps and he carefully looked around in the hallway, now, in his hands it was a weapon.

Angelina Espinoza. He swiped the card through the slot and took a deep breath. He had been here just last week, when they had exchanged text messages arranging that short, breathless encounter that now seemed as unreal as his breaking in. If she was there, then surprise was on his side. If not, then he would wait. He would take a seat in that midnight blue Italian armchair and stare at the print from Modigliani that he had seen from the bed, a female nude whose voluptuous curves and shyly lowered head had reminded him of Eva.

He opened the door to the living area. Silence. A glance confirmed that no one was in the room. Room service had arranged the books on the coffee table, fluffed the couch cushions, and pulled back the curtains. Apparently no one had entered the suite since this morning. But there was a hint of jasmine in the air. Kellermann knew the fragrance.

'Angelina?' he asked. No answer. 'Angelina? Are you there?'

He closed the door. Eva and Angelina had met. Had the mistress told the wife everything? Or had the wife confronted the mistress? What had happened? It must have pushed Eva toward Berlin, to prevent a second betrayal following the first.

His heart choked on concern and shame. He went to the window and looked down at the street. He had never done it before, and he wanted to know if it was possible to jump from there. Purely hypothetically, of course. He tried to open the window but failed. Air conditioning. Security risk. Both significant reasons.

He took a seat and looked back and forth between the voluptuous nude and the door. Damn smartphone. He had been too careless with it. Had too frequently left it lying around, with the fundamental trust exhibited when two people live together for twenty years. At some point he had stopped being careful. She must have been devastated.

Kellermann stared at the picture on the silk-lined wall. He was familiar with the original. He had once seen it at an exhibition, together with Eva. They had both stood in front of it, and he had told her she had the same way of holding a towel when she came out of the bath . . . the bath.

The sound was so quiet that he thought he had misheard it at first. A very soft, metallic ringing, a fraction of a tone, but in the quietness of the soundproof windows it was loud enough to make him jump. Kellermann held his breath and listened. Then he drew his service revolver and stood up. Finger on the trigger, he crept toward the door of the bathroom. He was angry with himself for not having searched the suite. Whoever was on the other side of the door had heard him and knew they were not alone.

Kellermann knocked the door open with an elbow. White marble, deep red blood. A lake of blood, fed by a continually flowing, red body of water. A woman lay in it. Her arm fell over the edge of the tub and the wound on her wrist was dripping into the red sea. There was an empty bottle of pills on the floor. It must have slipped out of her hand. Kellerman lowered his weapon. He knew that this was one of the moments that would change his life forever. There were only two things that had the power to do that: love and death. And he had never possessed love.

Judith squinted. Kaiserley was still lying on top of her. She couldn't move. The barrel of Dombrowski's gun was barely peeking out from under the edge of the sofa. But as long as Kaiserley believed he had to protect her with heart and soul, she was unable to reach it.

'How nice,' a woman's voice said. 'Although a drop too much water for decent tea, though.'

Kaiserley went to stand up.

'Keep calm. No sudden movements. Hands over your head, face to the wall, one after another.'

He rolled off Judith and stood up. She looked once more at the pistol, but the woman was so close that any wrong movement could be Judith's last. As she struggled upright, the silver-blue fish moved its tail one last time. Then it lay there, motionless. Except for its mouth, which opened, again and again.

The woman was perhaps in her late forties, and remarkably beautiful. A Mediterranean type with a narrow, delicate bone structure, but thoroughly fit, to the last fibres of her perfect body. She wore a dark, athletic suit and black leather gloves. Her brown eyes took in everything with surprising placidity, considering she was holding a bulky weapon with a silencer and pointing it alternatively at Judith and Kaiserley.

'Quirin,' she said.

Judith took a sharp breath. Of course. Wherever it got rough and dirty in this world, people knew each other. 'And you are . . .?'

'Warrant Officer Angelina Espinoza, Central Intelligence Agency.' When she saw Judith's confused face, she added: 'CIA. In real life, if there was ever something like it, my name is Gretchen. Gretchen Lindbergh.'

Her pronunciation was American, grating to Judith's ears.

'You haven't just worked for the CIA,' Kaiserley said.

'Hands up!' She pointed at Kaiserley, who instantly followed her orders. 'KGB, FSB, Stasi . . . I work for whoever pays me. And at the moment I'm here on my own account.'

She walked around the couch and stepped so close to Judith that she nearly touched her.

'Where are the microfilms?'

Judith spat in her face. Espinoza pulled back and Judith didn't duck in time. The blow caught the back of her head. She fell to her knees and out of the corner of her eye she saw how Kaiserley went to throw himself at the woman. The shot sounded like the pop of a champagne cork. Kaiserley screamed and collapsed. His hand pressed on his left upper thigh. Incredulous, he stared at the dark red spot that was expanding with rapid speed.

'Don't worry, I haven't forgotten how to shoot.' Espinoza pointed at Kaiserley's head. 'Today I'm just working in the style of a secretary. They usually don't hit the first time.'

'Who is it?' Kaiserley groaned. 'Who's taking all the blame for this?'

Espinoza pulled a phone out of her bag, flashed it triumphantly and put it back. Judith curled into a ball because she thought her head would explode. This woman was practised in knocking people out. Now it was directed at Judith. She swung her foot and kicked Judith in the side.

'That's the most important question. Right?'

Judith went down and stayed down. Once again, she saw the barrel of Dombrowski's gun. Merzig was no longer moving. His blood-shot eyes stared at the ceiling. The agent bent over her.

'Water under the bridge, that's what my German grandfather would have said.'

'Why are you doing this?' Judith groaned.

'The United States of America has a different legal system than you do. Over there things aren't swept under the rug so quickly. I'd be expecting three times twenty-five years. And I didn't even betray my own country.'

'You killed both of them. Lindner and Sonnenberg,' Kaiserley said. His voice was distorted with pain.

Espinoza jumped up. 'The woman got away from Stanz and ran directly into the border guards' line of fire. It was pure suicide. I had nothing to do with it.'

'But with Lindner.'

'Lindner would have betrayed me as soon as he was on trial. I would have been damaged goods for everyone, forever. I'd never have seen the light of day again. The microfilm, but no prisoners. Those were the directions from the Russians. Stanz wanted to take the soft approach, with tricks and bells and whistles and psychology. No drama. Nothing the valuable transit passengers from the West could have seen and reported. I didn't know that you were the person leading the operation.'

'Would that have changed anything?'

'Yes.' Her voice became a shade darker. 'Yes, it would have.'

She looked at Judith, who was trying to push her hand under the couch. The tips of her fingers touched the pistol but she couldn't grab it.

'He wouldn't be on your side today. You wouldn't have come this far.'

'Without him I would have been finished long ago,' Judith wheezed. 'More than anything, with you.'

'I doubt that.' Espinoza laughed thinly. 'You almost jumped off the cliff in Malmö. Was it at least a nice trip? I thought the dose would have pushed anyone into the hereafter, even a junkie like you.'

'It was cut. The dealer short-changed you.'

'I'm sorry. You were supposed to go out on a high. Not like the bitch who blackmailed us. Irene Borg alias Marianne Kepler. It went well for a long time. I set up an account under an alias and was able to deliver the money to Malmö. Everyone who had worked for the Stasi on West German soil was allowed to contribute. But at some point people didn't want to anymore. They were no longer afraid. They retired, they had nothing more to fear. What was a capital crime during the Cold War only gets a slap on the wrist today.'

She snorted with disdain. 'And then the bright little daughter had the idea of offering the files to the highest bidder. I'm somewhat particular when it comes to things like that. My name is my business.'

'What did you do to my father?'

'Stanz fetched a hooker from the Rügen Hotel who was also blonde. Or at least acted like she was. And a kid from the home. The he turned off the floodlights. It was dark. She was placed at the window of the station terminal. They were the perfect dummies. We only had to wait until Lindner went crazy in the train. But when we got him, he wouldn't say another word. So the hooker got the passports. She boarded the through coach with her kid. The agents should have recognised her and approached her. She would have identified them. Then we would have had them.'

'Would have,' Judith repeated. Her hand was still an inch from Dombrowski's gun. 'Would have isn't had.'

Espinoza's eyes narrowed. 'Yes,' she answered, stretching the vowel. 'We didn't know that she had fucked the Swedish conductor the night before. Coincidences like that happen. The Swedes went a little overboard with their neutrality. They were on the side of anyone who could sweet-talk them. He let the prostitute onto the train to Bergen. From there she took a taxi, immediately got on the ferry and sailed to Sweden, unrecognised and unobstructed, where Vonnegut made her disappear into the registry of his church. And we stood on the platform. When we finally sent passport control officers onto the through coach a half-hour later, they were long gone.'

'And my father?'

'I shot him when Stanz finally had the idea to look for your double on the train. No witness, no risk. He knew what he was getting into. You can only be a winner or a loser.' She raised her gun and took a step towards Judith. 'Where are the microfilms?'

'I don't know!' Judith yelled. 'And they're gone forever if you kill both of us!'

'Borg had them with her! The police didn't find them. The BND didn't either. But you, the cleaning lady, you have something. You know something.'

'No!'

'Those films are valuable. You carry them around. You keep an eye on them. You try to make them disappear at the last second. Where did you find them? In the rubbish chute? In the cellar? On the roof?'

She pulled the trigger. Judith threw herself to the side, and the shot just barely missed her. Espinoza was playing cat and mouse with her. She'd make her mark the next time. Not lethal. Not yet. Judith still remembered how Borg had been chased around the apartment by her murderer. How the killer had let her bleed out, just like Kaiserley was doing, who had been tossed half-conscious onto the couch, ashen-faced. She thought about the stains and the broken glass and the water and the cichlids and then thought that she must be in shock if her last worry in life was cleaning up.

She grabbed one of the slippery, twitching bodies of a dying fish and flung it in Espinoza's face. The woman yelled and stumbled back a step. Her face was distorted by disgust for a second, and distracted for the briefest moment, which was all that Judith needed.

She rammed her hand under the sofa, grabbed the pistol and jumped through the doorway. Two champagne corks popped, some sheetrock dust trickled down the wall. She looked around frantically. The front door was too far away. She went into Merzig's bedroom and positioned herself behind the open door. She tried to remember how tall Espinoza was. Then she placed the barrel of the gun against the door at the level where she guessed Espinoza's head would be and waited.

Her eyes must have adjusted to the darkness. She heard the crash of glass and quiet steps approaching in the hallway. She saw Merzig's narrow bed and the matte linoleum floor. There were a couple of certificates and old sports trophies, a small stack of books on a shelf over the bed. A photograph on the nightstand with a cheap, flimsy frame. The numbers 9:04 were glowing on the digital clock. The time that would be on her certificate of death. The steps came closer.

'Run!' Kaiserley yelled. 'Judith! Run!'

She held her breath. In the diffuse twilight she sensed more than she saw a shadow slipping through the door slightly ajar. She pulled the trigger. A deafening bang almost tore her eardrum, and the kick-back flung her against the wall. There was a hole in the door. She heard a body fall to the floor, but didn't dare move. Then she watched as the door opened slowly, very slowly.

Kellermann placed his gun on the washbasin. He turned off the water and pulled out the plug. He didn't know if he should move her, but even if he did, it would be impossible to lift her out of the tub.

'Eva! Eva! My God!'

He pulled her up and embraced her, shook her, pressed her face to his chest. He felt the warmth of the water, but her body was cold. An unnatural paleness covered her face. Blue veins shimmered through the thin skin on her temples. He placed his hand on her carotid but felt nothing. He blinked because there was suddenly water in his eyes and he was baffled. Helpless. There was a telephone next to the washbasin. Half-blind, he groped for it, and the receiver nearly slipped through his wet hands and into the water. He was connected with reception and registered an emergency. Only then did he see the note.

It was leaning against the mirror.

I can't live like this any longer. I killed because I love you. Forgive me. Because I also forgave you, what you did to me.

He didn't understand. He read the note several times but he didn't understand the meaning of the words. He folded it carefully and put it in his pocket. Then he held Eva tight and waited for the doctor.

Kaiserley reached for the crystal ashtray that had landed on the floor next to Merzig. He didn't have any other weapon available. His leg hurt, and when he saw the large, dark stain on the sofa he realised the extent of his blood loss. He stood up and tried to put as little weight as possible on his left leg.

The living room was literally a heap of broken glass. He was surprised the neighbours hadn't yet called the police. Then it hit him that no more than three minutes had passed since Angelina had showed up here. It had seemed like an eternity to him. Concern for Judith had almost made him crazy. There hadn't been any more sounds from the floor since the gunshot. He lifted the ashtray and stumbled to the door. Then he let it drop.

Angelina Espinoza's body lay in Merzig's bedroom. She wasn't moving. Whatever weapon had killed her, all that remained of her beautiful face were bloody scraps.

'Judith?'

He slowly climbed over Angelina's body and stepped into the room. Judith was sitting on Merzig's bed. The pistol was resting in her lap. She held a small picture frame in her hands and didn't look up when he came to her and sat down next to her.

There were four people in the photo: Lindner, a pretty young woman, a child beaming like an angel, and behind them Merzig, looking proudly at the camera. The similarity between him and Irene Sonnenberg was unmistakable. Tears ran down Judith's face, but she didn't blink and she didn't wipe them away.

'He signed the arrest warrant for his own daughter,' she said.

Kaiserley looked at the photo again. He wanted to lift his arm and pull her close but he was too tired even for that.

'He had . . . he was my grandfather.'

Kaiserley was silent. He felt her lean against him and let her head sink against his shoulder. She had done that once before. He tried not to move. Maybe she'd stay that way for a while.

'I'm sorry,' he whispered. 'Judith, I am so terribly sorry.'

Tears dripped onto the picture in her hand. 'I would have killed him. I would have, by God. And he knew it.'

'I wouldn't have let you.'

She removed her head. The warmth was instantly gone.

'You always presume,' she said. But it didn't sound as hard as usual. It sounded as if she had known it.

30

Judith wiped away the tears, pocketed the photograph, and stood up. She tucked Dombrowski's gun under her belt.

'How much time do we have?' she asked.

'None.'

'Are you badly hurt?'

'It was a flesh wound – went straight through. I'll live.'

She walked into the kitchen and found the kitchen knives exactly where they were stored in ninety-eight per cent of all households. She chose a small, sharp specimen with a pointed blade. Under the sink she found a bucket, detergent, and rags. No gloves. She didn't even look for them. She ignored the bucket and soaked the rag with undiluted detergent.

When she returned Kaiserley looked at her mockingly.

'You don't want to do an emergency operation here, do you?'

She shook her head and walked over to the opposite bedroom wall. She found the bullet hole and pulled the slug from the wall. Then she wiped away her fingerprints with the rag. She did the same thing with the door. She knelt next to Espinoza and searched through her jacket pockets until she had found the phone.

'Are you coming?' she asked and stood up quickly.

Kaiserley got up with a suppressed groan and hobbled behind her into the living room. She examined the destruction critically.

'Did you touch anything here?'

'The ashtray I think. It's still over there.'

Judith raced back into the bedroom. She found it and put it in her work bag, which Kaiserley was already holding out for her. She threw the phone in right after.

'Anything else? Think about it for a second!'

Kaiserley looked around.

'The couch.'

'No fingerprints on fabric. Maybe microfibres.' She studied Kaiserley's light trousers.

'The glass? The table?' he asked.

She looked at the floor. Then she went down on her knees and examined the glass of the coffee table against the light.

'Nothing,' she said and turned back around. 'They'll find your DNA. But they won't be able to connect it to you. Let's go.'

She tossed the rag in the sink, but not before hastily wiping down the handles on the cabinets and doors first. There was nothing more she could do. Maybe that would save them for a couple of hours. Then they left the house through the back door. The screaming of a police siren approached. The dim glow of the street lights blinded them like the floodlights of a sports arena.

'This way.' Kaiserley pointed to the paved garden path. It ended at a compost heap next to the back edge of the property. Judith looked around quickly. Somewhere in the neighbourhood someone was pulling up the shades.

'I'll carry you. Maybe the crime scene investigators will think it was an overweight giant. Come on!'

He pulled her close and lifted her. Judith held on tight. She heard him breathing hard through clenched teeth. He must be in severe pain. But he still fought his way through the bushes and reached the back of the neighbouring property. Judith prayed that there were no dogs running free. She tried to make herself as light as possible. She felt his arms and the strength with which he carried her, on and on. She couldn't remember ever having been carried.

He stumbled and she opened her eyes. They stood in front of a low wooden fence. Judith climbed over and helped Kaiserley follow. His car was parked on the corner. He leant on her and once again, for a moment, it felt like they were a couple taking a late evening stroll.

The flashing blue lights ghosted up the façades of the buildings. Two officers were ringing Merzig's front door. One decided to go round the house. He pulled his gun and was swallowed by the shadows. The other went back to the street and looked around.

'Keys,' Judith whispered.

Kaiserley gave them to her. She unlocked the car door and slid behind the wheel. Kaiserley sat on the passenger side. She started the car and slowly drove away. Two more squad cars drove past them before they hit the B1 motorway.

'Judith . . .'

'I don't want to hear it! Understand?'

'You have to talk about it. You killed a human being.'

'It was self-defence.'

'You found out things about your family . . .'

'I don't have a family! Not one like that! I don't want them, is that clear? I don't want them!'

'They loved you. They did it so you would have a better life!'

'Really?' she slammed into second gear and hit the next main road at fifty miles per hour. 'Great life then. A beautiful life! Thanks a lot! Ten years in a home! Out on the street at sixteen. On the needle at twenty! That's supposed to be better?'

'Judith!'

She turned on the hazard lights and let the car roll to a stop at the edge of the road. She held the wheel tightly with both hands. An ambulance raced down the street and turned off towards Biesdorf. It was followed by two police cars.

'I fucked it up,' she said finally. 'Just me.'

'No. You just defended yourself. There's something inside you that no one could erase. Your courage. Your empathy. Your strength. The first years of life are crucial for that. Everything that followed hurt you but didn't break you. You were alone, you are alone, and if you keep it up, you'll stay alone. But you'll have to decide for yourself.'

'Oh shit,' she murmured. 'Knock it off.'

'OK.'

She looked up; he smiled.

The traffic was flowing steadily, and they disappeared into the anonymity of the big city. They didn't say another word until Landsberger Allee. She turned left towards Kreuzberg.

'Where are you going?'

'To Dombrowski.' She cast a quick glance at her watch. Just before ten. 'The last office cleaning crew is just arriving. After that it's calm there. I have to bring the gun back before he notices anything.'

Kaiserley nodded and looked satisfied with her answer.

'The phone,' he said. 'Angelina wanted to incriminate someone. I'm just asking myself who.'

Judith shrugged her shoulders. 'In my bag. Just press redial.'

Kellermann sat at Eva's bedside and held her hand. Or at least her fingertips, because that was the only thing untouched by the bandages on her forearms and hands. The nurses checked the equipment in intensive care one last time – monitors with angular curves, the hydraulic hissing of the respirator, the IV solution that was dripping into Eva's body from a bottle – and gave him an encouraging smile.

Kellermann thought about her suicide note for the thousandth time. He understood her desperation. He could even appreciate why someone would take sleeping pills and slash her wrists. He attributed the suicide attempt to his failure, and his betrayal. But who did she mean when she wrote 'I've killed?'

Eva's eyelids fluttered. Her hands ran restlessly over the covers. She opened her eyes and looked at him as if he was a stranger.

'Eva?' The happiness spread his chest, almost seemed to make it burst. 'Can you hear me?' Can you understand me? Everything will be OK. Believe me. Everything will be OK.'

She touched the oxygen tube in her nose. 'What happened?'

'I'll explain it to you, Eva. One day. But first you have to get better.'

She looked at him, and the memories returned. His eyes were burning, as he let her gaze inside himself and waited for her accusation to be spoken.

'She said you wanted to leave me.'

'I won't leave you. Ever.'

'That you love her.'

'I don't love her.'

She took a deep breath. Her fingertips twitched. Kellermann rubbed her hand. *I don't love her*, he thought. *I don't know what love is. But this here, the two of us, comes close.*

'And then . . . it was black. I don't know anything else. What's going on?' She raised her arms and powerlessly let them sink again. 'What happened?'

'The pills?' he asked. 'You slashed open your wrists, Eva. You were almost dead.' His voice faltered. He was embarrassed. He had never experienced himself this way. 'You were almost dead.'

'I didn't do that,' she whispered. 'I would never abandon you. Only if you no longer wanted me.'

Kellermann produced the note. 'Did you write this letter?'

'A letter? No. What kind of letter?'

Kellermann crumbled up the paper and put it back. 'It's not important.'

She closed her eyes, her hand searching for his. She began to breathe calmly and evenly.

'Stay with me,' he said. 'Don't leave me. I still want you.'

The nurse crept back up quietly.

'Go back home. You need to change your clothes and sleep for a couple of hours.'

'I can't.'

She pointed to his blood-splotched trouser legs, which were protruding out from under the green protective apron. 'Do it for her. When she wakes up again.'

He looked down at himself and agreed with her.

Judith parked next to two moving vans, took her bag, and sprinted into the garage. Even if Kaiserley had wanted to follow her, he wouldn't have been able to in his state.

The door to Dombrowski's office wasn't locked. Surprised, she stared at the burning desk lamp and the figure who hastily jolted awake from a light slumber.

'Hi,' she said, and stood there, out of breath.

Dombrowski took the lampshade and pointed it at Judith. She turned on her heels.

'Stay here!'

Dombrowski stood up, had reached the door in three strides, and slammed it shut with such force that the stucco crumbled.

'Gun.'

She pulled the pistol out of her waistband and gave it to him. He checked the gun with practised motions. Then he sniffed at the barrel.

'What happened?'

'Nothing.'

'Don't lie to me!'

He ripped open the desk drawer and threw the pistol inside. Judith jumped. She'd never seen Dombrowski like this.

'Did you swim here?'

'No.'

'Listen up, girl. I'm able to smell it five hundred metres away if someone's in deep shit. And you stink! I covered your ass. I lied to the cops for you. Kai gave you an alibi with your time card. You stole my gun. You come back at night, you've fired shots, you look like death. Now tell me finally what happened!'

'I can't.'

'Then I'll call the cops. I haven't done it before, I swear. But now it's my only protection.'

He dropped into his Schalck-Golodkowski chair and reached for his telephone. Judith pounced on him and ripped the receiver out of his hand.

'No!'

'Then talk!'

Judith put the handset back. Her hands were shaking. She saw Dombrowski's furrowed face and the concern that was written all over it. And something else: affection. She thought about the photograph in her pocket, and Merzig's bloodshot eyes, and a family that had betrayed each other and knew that it was still better to know it all now. Because you could only despise what you knew. It seemed to be similar with affection.

She lifted her hand and placed it on Dombrowski's powerful arm.

'Come here,' he said hoarsely.

He pulled her onto his lap, embraced her and held her tight. At the same time, he clapped her on the back like a furniture mover. Judith let it happen because any rejection would have hurt him terribly. And because she could vaguely remember how she had pictured her father. Dombrowski's eyes were damp when she softly disentangled herself.

'I never had a daughter,' he said.

'Three, if I may remind you. From three different women.'

He nodded and attempted a pitiful grin. 'But they never came to me when they were in trouble. I thought I'd get to do it right at some point.'

'You did, Dombrowski, that you did.'

'Is everything OK?'

'It is now.'

She gave the drawer a shove. It slid shut and the pistol disappeared.

'Another incident like that and you'll get the public toilets!'

'Sure,' Judith said and grinned. She was about to open the door when Dombrowski called after her.

'Catch!'

She turned around too late. Something slapped against the wall, fell to the floor, and broke open. A penetrating odour of dog shit, urine and mould spread.

'Don't leave that lying around again. It almost knocked Josef out.'

Judith stared at the broken bin bag and the black, indefinable bundle of rags at her feet. A memory flashed brightly but couldn't be ordered. *Those films are valuable. You carry them around. You keep them in sight. You try to make them disappear at the last second.*

In your fear of death and your despair you throw it over the balcony railing. It lands in the hedges and is found by the dogs, buried and hidden. It stays outside, lying out in the rain, in the sun, by day and by night. Until it becomes rubbish that no one wants to touch.

She bent over and picked the thing up with splayed fingers.

'That's disgusting.'

'You said it. Get it out of here. Toss it. What is it?'

In front of Judith's eyes the rags transformed into something that had once vaguely resembled a stuffed toy. Arms, two legs, an empty space where a head must have been: a furry head with big ears and a black bobble for a nose. Arms and legs were now just chewed remnants. But she still recognised it. She gasped for air.

'It is . . .'

She ran her fingers over the belly of the creature. Her fingers suddenly froze. She looked up at Dombrowski.

'Carpet knife?'

He pulled open another drawer, found what she was looking for in a single motion, and went over to her. Judith placed the thing on the floor. The stench was breathtaking. She took the knife, extended the blade, and opened the creature's belly with a single incision. Metal scraped on metal. She tossed the knife aside and stuck her hand in the wet, ancient tatters.

'What is that?' Dombrowski asked.

One after another, Judith pulled out four tins of Florena cream.

'It was my teddy. My favourite toy.'

'And those?'

She tried to open the first one but it was either cross-threaded or rusted.

'Let me,' Dombrowski said. 'What's inside? Coke? Heroin? Uncut diamonds? Was this why everyone was after you?'

He groaned, and then he had the lid in one hand and the tin in the other. He looked at the contents in surprise.

'Film?'

Judith nodded. 'Film,' she answered. 'Holiday memories from Plattensee.'

Suspicious, Dombrowski handed her the tin. She stuffed it back with the others and the animal in the sack and made everything disappear in her bag.

'Just film?' Dombrowski still didn't appear to believe her.

Judith opened her mouth to say something and then closed it again. It was impossible. You couldn't explain it in a single sentence. All she could do was take the tins to Kaiserley and throw them at his feet. Words weren't necessary for that. He was the only one who would understand all of it. Everything. From beginning to end.

On the way to the bedroom Kellermann saw that someone had called. He paid no notice to the blinking light. Half-blind, he searched for something to pull on, climbed under the shower, dried off, and slipped into clean, dry clothes. On the way to the door he turned around and went out into the garden. He took the rose shears and cut flowers until he had a massive bouquet. Red and white. Then he remembered that he wasn't allowed to take flowers into intensive care. He let them fall. Nothing he did meant anything.

He checked the answering machine, praying it wasn't the clinic. Instead, Eva's name was glowing on the display. Kellermann furrowed his brow. Her phone was in Berlin. She herself was in

Munich. The two didn't fit together, and he had not devoted any attention to these confusing circumstances. He pushed the play button, but two seconds long he only heard a roaring sound, as if someone had been sitting in a car and had cut the connection too late.

Judith sat on the back seat of Kaiserley's car. The doors were open, her feet touched the asphalt. She was smoking. Kaiserley had turned on the interior light over the rear-view mirror and held the beginning of the roll of film up to the light.

'Well?' she growled impatiently.

Dombrowski was ruffling through the boot.

'I can't find your first-aid kit!'

'Under the spare tyre!' Kaiserley replied. Hushed, he continued: 'The only things I recognise are the index cards. It would have to be viewed on a reading device. But I'm guessing the film is genuine.'

Dombrowski began to clean out the boot. He cursed terribly while doing so. Kaiserley gave Judith a look of amusement.

'Nice boss,' he said.

She cast a fleeting glace back at him. 'He is. What are we actually going to do with this stuff?'

Kaiserley looked at her long and hard. He understood that 'we' was a gift. One he could accept or reject.

'There's a lot of people who will ask us that.'

Judith received the 'us' with a nod.

'Where's the rest?' Kaiserley deposited the film in the tin. 'We have to hand it over to the Stasi Records Agency.'

'*We* don't have to do anything.' Judith reclaimed the plural form. 'Those are my rolls of film. And I decide what I'm going to do with them.'

'You don't even know where to go with them. The VS will be at your door in a couple of hours. The BND will also want to take a look at them. These need to be put in the right hands.'

Judith stood up, stepped on her cigarette, and bent over the open passenger side to Kaiserley.

'These are the right hands.' She grabbed the tin and put it with the others. 'I had to pay for them. My whole fucking family paid for them.'

A phone rang. Irritated, she looked at Kaiserley, then at Dombrowski, who was busy uncovering a month's pay in deposit bottles. Finally, she realised that it was coming from her bag.

She pulled it out and took a couple of steps to one side.

'Yes?'

'Who am I speaking with?' An authoritarian voice, used to giving orders. Judith recognised it immediately. The last time she'd heard it was in the Underground. She immediately pictured the powerful figure of the man who had dared to put her under pressure.

'Mr Weckerle. I know I shouldn't name names. But in this case, and because it's certainly not your real name, I'll gladly make an exception.'

Silence. Then disbelief: 'You?'

Judith went a couple of steps further. 'Can you tell me who it is you wanted to call right now?'

'First I want to know how you got that phone.'

'The days when you were the one asking questions are past.'

'Where . . .'

'Didn't you understand me?' Kaiserley started listening. He looked over at her as if he would have liked to get up and hobble over to her. 'Who do you think should have been picking up in my place?'

'I don't know.'

'I can hear you lying, Weckerle. And you know why?' Because I come from an inferno. From hell. Because I . . .' She stopped because she was aware it wasn't a secure connection. 'Because I know who last had this phone in their hands. And I'm only talking with you because someone wanted to railroad you. And that, Mr Weckerle, is the only thing we have in common.'

The man on the other end was silent. He probably needed a moment to process what she had just told him. When he spoke again it sounded like the weight of the world had just fallen from his shoulders.

'We can speak openly. The smartphones were already swapped weeks ago.'

'Aha.' Judith didn't know what that meant. But apparently that meant a green light for this connection.

'The phone belongs to my wife,' he continued. 'She's in hospital now. She supposedly attempted suicide. In her suicide note it says she killed someone.'

'How's she doing?'

'They say if she survives the night . . .'

Weckerle, or whoever the man at the other end was, stopped.

'Listen. I'm very sorry about your wife. I don't know what else she did. Or if she was one of your killers, but she has nothing to do with this here.'

'She's not a killer. She's my wife.'

'Well perhaps she'll still become one,' Judith replied. 'Are you authorised to negotiate?'

'About what?'

'You know exactly what I mean. I have demands.'

'What?'

'Does the name Gretchen Lindbergh ring a bell?'

'No.'

'Mr Kaiserley knew her by the name of Angelina Espinoza. She's dead. She shot a former Stasi Lieutenant General. And if you're able to make it look like she subsequently killed herself, then I might throw this phone into the River Spree. Someday. When I can be sure that grass has grown over this business.'

'You're overestimating my scope of influence.'

'No,' Judith said. 'I'm sure I'm not. I have the film.'

Weckerle was silent. Presumably he was calculating what he could offer Judith.

'I don't want money. I don't want a passport. I don't want a cover story. What I want is for you all to leave me alone. Now and forever. Effective immediately, you're my attorney, Weckerle. I'll protect you and your wife if you represent my interests.'

'I don't know how a higher pay grade might rule on this issue . . .'

'I don't care how you get the higher-ups to get in line. People wanted to kill me because you guys fucked up. I defended myself. If that gets out, my family's name will be dragged through the mud. And I don't want that.'

'I'm afraid . . .'

'Weckerle? You should be afraid a little bit longer. Either you do for me what you would do for every one of your fucking agents or I'll rip you a new one. I'll have the entire Sassnitz case opened up again. I'll take everyone who covered it up and line them up against a wall. I'll have the graves dug up to reveal the ashes of two people inside instead of one. I'll have the money transfers to Malmö from the BND slush fund reported to the parliamentary oversight committee, and have posters printed with the names of everyone whose Stasi past hasn't been outed yet. I'll destroy you, understand?'

Silence.

'Understand?' Judith bellowed.

'You really found the films?'

'Fuck you. I sure fucking did.'

She ended the conversation and turned off the phone. Kaiserley stood behind her. He had heard everything. He wanted to say something but at that moment Dombrowski triumphantly returned from the boot with the first-aid box in his hand.

'The doctor would like to do an examination,' he called over to them.

'I'll be leaving then,' Judith said.

And she did. The whole way to the bus stop she still hoped someone would call her name. When the bus arrived, she got on and didn't look back.

The only thing he'd thought to say to her was a song about cemeteries.

Kellermann called Kresnick before he drove back to the hospital. He reached the State Director of the VS on a tennis court in Schwerin and spoke with him for exactly two minutes.

'Out of the question,' Kresnick said when Kellermann had finished.

Kellermann added thirty seconds' worth of a summary of the alternatives. Even if he made an effort to use politer expressions than Judith had done, Kresnick appeared unimpressed.

'It's still out of the question,' Kresnick said.

'Kepler will inflict immense damage on the intelligence services of this country . . .'

'Let me finish. Your request is absurd and unworthy of discussion. But I didn't say it was impossible.'

31

Two weeks later Judith stood in Merzig's hallway. There was already an empty waste skip that had been delivered the day before waiting on the street. She cut through the crime scene seal and opened the door with the key she had picked up from the neighbours beforehand. Kai followed her, lugging the bag of equipment over his shoulder, and looked around, his eyes large.

'Crazy,' he said as they walked pasted Merzig's bedroom.

The outline of the dead woman was still marked on the lino-leum with white chalk. The dried blood looked like a black cloud. Judith went into the living room. Forensics had tempo-rarily taped the window with plastic sheeting. The glass man would come that afternoon, and by then they needed to have the worst of it cleaned up.

'Fuck me.' Kai put the bag down next to the sofa and looked around. 'Was that an aquarium?'

'No idea.'

Judith looked at an ashen slimy blob that was protruding from a swarm of flies. Judging by the outlines and the smell, it could have been a cichlid. 'Don't step on that, otherwise you'll spread it over the entire apartment.'

'Oh man. Was there another one lying here?' He pointed to the line next to the sofa. 'Did he get shot too?'

Unlike her, Kai had not been informed about the event itself before his first crime scene. He was supposed to assist, no more. If Judith were to discover signs that he wasn't up to all of this here, she would send him home immediately.

However, he strolled through the living room as if it was an absurd movie set. Like everyone else, he had followed the heated speculations of the tabloid press. Gretchen Lindbergh, an ex-CIA agent, from whom the agency had immediately distanced itself, had broken into Merzig's house with an accomplice and had shot the former in cold blood. She was subsequently shot by her mysterious companion. The theories of the neighbours and press ranged from a large black man to Russian intelligence, frequently and enthusiastically called the KGB. Blackmail, Russians, the Cold War – Lindbergh/Espinoza became 'The Beauty Who Came in from the Cold.' It was assumed that Merzig had miscalculated the threat she posed and knew about some dark stain in her past. Because she remained equally colourful and mysterious, the murders in Berlin-Biesdorf would probably go down in the annals of unsolved crime cases. Many years later, an over-eager television producer with a lively imagination might reanimate the case.

Judith was surprised the house had already been cleared after two weeks. Apparently the investigation had been closed. A distant relative had been uncovered, who of course wanted nothing to do with either the house or with the mysterious incident. Because Dombrowski had his informants everywhere – even at the telephone desk of the local police station in question – of course the assignment landed in his lap. And just as naturally, he sent Judith to that house, to free it from evil spirits.

Judith pulled on some work gloves. First she had to remove the shards of glass, then provisionally clean the sofa, and then take care of the flooring. Merzig's relative wanted to come around noon. Dombrowski had told her something about an elderly woman from West Germany.

'Take out the broken glass,' she told Kai without responding to his question. Using the hand brush, she began to free the sofa from the shards of glass. Now and again, she paused and studied the bloodstain Kaiserley had left on the beige corduroy.

He hadn't got in touch with her. She wanted to ignore it, like you register a rebuff or a return call never made. But she couldn't. He had solved his puzzle, she hers. Their paths had parted. Should she have held him back?

The films were in her work locker. They would stay there until she could be sure that Weckerle would keep his word. Up until now it looked as if his networks would hold. But recently Judith had done a lot of thinking about promises and the breaking thereof.

By noon they had taken the remains of the aquarium and the window pane to the skip. Kai wondered about the crumbs that were spread all across the linoleum in the bedroom. In her own interest, Judith neglected to inform him what dried brain matter looked like. She handed him the dust pan and broom and instructed to simply remove everything that looked the slightest bit like dirt, crumbs, blood or chalk markings.

Then she climbed up to the second floor. There were only two converted rooms and due to the low-hanging rafters they seemed even more oppressive. Book shelves, an old rocking

THE CLEANER | 450

chair, dressers with bedding and covers. She sat down on the chair and began to rock carefully back and forth. She listened to the quiet creaking produced by the woven reeds rubbing together. The sun fell through the attic window onto her face, dust danced in the light. She closed her eyes.

The scent . . . so satiated by summer, harvest and hay. By wood and resin. The low room expanded, the walls shot up. It was dark, and she could see the stars through the window. They sparkled like diamonds on deep-blue velvet. Someone was embracing her. She felt the warmth of another body and cuddled closer. Over her Cassiopeia shone. She followed the tip of the 'W' and found the North Star. She would never lose her way again.

'I won't be paying you for that!'

Judith started. She saw the head of an elderly lady, who had stopped halfway up the stairs, out of breath.

'I'm sorry. Excuse me please.'

The woman climbed the rest of the stairs and looked around. She was a head shorter than Judith, with a delicate frame, and white hair arranged in neat finger waves. She wore a comfortable outfit made of cotton jersey and shoes that looked orthopaedic.

'My God,' she said and shook her head in dismay. 'All this junk. The young man downstairs belongs to you?'

'Yes. That's Kai. Judith Kepler, Dombrowski Facility Management.'

She shook hands with the woman. She expected to feel something. Blood ties? Recognition? The sudden flash of acknowledgement in the eyes of the other? Nothing of the sort occurred.

Judith felt a passing disappointment touch her heart and then immediately leave her.

'Are you cleaning up here? I'm Andrea Günzle. The deceased was my cousin.'

'My sincere condolences.'

Ms Günzle cast a look in the other room. Judith followed her. Two wardrobes were standing there. Merzig's cousin opened them and wrinkled her nose.

'Dear me,' she murmured to herself. 'Get rid of it, all of it. Do you declutter as well?'

'Yes, sure. We make houses broom-clean.'

Ms Günzle closed the wardrobe door. 'Horst, I mean – the deceased and I weren't very close. Terrible how his past caught up with him. He was, well, you probably know from the papers. So he hadn't made many friends.'

'Is there any more news?'

'They're looking for another guy. The third man. Apparently the American woman shot my first cousin and then tried to go for the other one. The hole in the door and everything, I'm not an expert, but the police tell me that it was probably self-defence.'

'Terrible,' Judith murmured. Ms Günzle nodded.

'Did he have any relatives beside you?'

Ms Günzle's face darkened. Judith was upset at herself that the question had slipped out of her. She didn't want to burden the nice old woman. The past was dead. Who did it help if she talked about it? She studied the old woman once more furtively, who had turned away and let her gaze sweep over the low walls one last time. Judith tried to find a similarity, but found none.

At most it was in the way she moved: pointedly, quickly, keeping everything in view. And she was apparently fairly restrained in saying farewell.

'No,' Ms Günzle finally said. 'He had a daughter and a grand-daughter. But they died in an accident.'

'An accident.'

'Yes. In Romania. Drifted off the road at night. The end. The whole family. He was a complicated man. But after that he didn't have any contact with anyone, actually. He just . . .'

Ms Günzle left the room and headed for the stairs. Suddenly she stopped.

'. . . locked himself in,' she finished her sentence. 'Yes. That's how you could put it. He was like those fish in his aquarium. We were standing around and looking at him, but he was in another world.'

Ms Günzle shook her head and felt for the rail to climb down.

'May I have the rocking chair?'

The old woman turned around to her once more. 'If you want that old dust catcher . . . broom-clean, yes. I believe he'd agree to it.'

Merzig's house in Biesdorf was the last assignment Judith completed. After a week it was empty, clean, and ready for the estate agent, to whom she handed the key. Afterwards she climbed into the moving van that was transporting all of Merzig's movable possessions to the Berlin dump, and didn't look back once. Kai, Josef, and two work placement volunteers lent a hand. Judith stood next to the open hatch and waited until everything had disappeared into the various containers.

She said farewell to Dombrowski, who called out several unpleasant curses, which she interpreted as indicating he would miss her. For at least the next three months that she would be taking off. She went to the locker room, took a shower, changed, and began to clean out her locker. She could understand Dombrowski. He wasn't sure she'd come back. She didn't know it herself. She had to work out a couple of things. This included the question of whether after all that had happened she could now turn her back on her job, or whether it actually meant something to her.

She closed her locker and watched the office cleaning crew returning from work and Josef parking a semi in the yard. Kai was already on his way home. Dombrowski had offered him an apprenticeship. Facility management, not crime scene cleaning. The boy was a little disappointed but his mood had brightened a bit when Dombrowski had signed him up for the Merzig house with Judith and promised to organise additional training if they came to an agreement.

She slung her bag over her shoulder and walked across the yard to the large rolling gate. Suddenly she heard a shrill whistle from behind her. She turned around and saw Dombrowski standing at an open window.

'Hey!' he called out and tossed something in her direction. She let the bag drop and caught it. It was the key to the old van. 'Make sure you bring it back!'

He rammed the window down again and disappeared. Judith lifted her bag and went to the car. The idea of taking a real holiday and just driving off was really beginning to take shape. She threw the bag onto the passenger seat, rounded the bonnet, and ran into a man.

'Where are you headed, Ms Kepler?'

Judith furrowed her brow and examined the man, from his carefully drawn parting to his hand-sewn wingtips.

'I'm sorry. I don't remember your name. So many of those recently, you understand?'

'Peter Winkler. Telecommunications and Communication Systems South. But you remember Malmö, right?'

'I don't know what you're talking about.' She reached past him and opened the door. 'What do you want from me?'

'Can we speak openly for a minute?'

'Are you wearing a wire?'

'Not at all, technically speaking. Beyond that, I know I would be in good hands with you.'

A charming smile flitted over his lips. Did they teach that at the BND? Smiling trustworthily at women? She looked around. There was no one to be seen in the car park. And the van was the only place where she could be sure no one was listening in.

'Get in.'

Once Winkler was seated, she started the car and drove off. She didn't know where to go, so she drove towards the city autobahn.

'What's up?'

'We kept our part of the agreement. Now it's time for you to do your part.'

'Who's going to tell me that the police won't suddenly have completely new information? The American killed at least four people, and would have killed me too, if I hadn't defended myself.'

'I know. And that's why we're making you an offer that is just as binding for us as for you.'

'And that would be?'

'We had the supposed grave of Marianne Kepler examined in Sassnitz. Mr Kaiserley asked us to do it. He was right to do so. There were ashes from two deceased in the urn. After all that he's told us we now believe that they are the remains of Richard and Irene Sonnenberg.'

Judith hit her indicator and watched the stop-and-start traffic at the Gradestrasse exit, trying to find a space to merge into. Kaiserley's name had hit her unexpectedly. The fact that he had talked to Winkler about her behind her back hurt her.

'You got that from Kaiserley?'

'We suggest a transfer of remains and the establishment of a new grave. You would have somewhere to go where you could pay your respects.'

'Who says that I want to? My father and grandfather were not heroes you shout from the rooftops about.'

'And your mother?'

Judith bit her lip. She didn't want to show any weakness in front of this man. Her feelings belonged to her alone. Still, she had to blink, and that upset her. Winkler reached into his suit and removed a passport.

'We've provided you with new documents. Perhaps you might want to carry your birth name again. Christina Sonnenberg. Here.'

He held out the passport. Judith eyed it briefly before returning her concentration to the traffic. Christina Sonnenberg.

She listened to the sound of the name and knew that it would always be strange for her.

'Keep it. I'm not so into names. I might end up forgetting it and would be standing there like Karsten Michael Oliver Asshole.'

Winkler let out a dry laugh. 'He'll be all right. Operative execution isn't his strong suite. His father was better than him by leaps and bounds.'

Judith shot a quick glance at Winkler. 'His father?'

'Kaiserley. I thought you knew that. If not, then forget it fast. Kaiserley was in Munich for a couple of days. I think the two gentlemen had a great deal to discuss.'

On the tip of Judith's tongue lay the question of whether he was back in Berlin. And if so, since when. And why he hadn't got in touch with her. But Winkler was the wrong person to ask that.

Winkler packed the passport away.

'Are you the registry office?' she asked.

'I do what I can.'

So Winkler was the man who had helped Kaiserley all these years. Maybe he had been the only person who had believed him. For a short, crazy moment she considered what it would be like to trust him as well.

'What would you do with the films if I gave them to you?'

'Up until this point we only had manipulated material available, which had gone through many hands before it reached us. We could compare them.'

'And make the names disappear.'

'In cases in which, after weighing all the possible consequences, it would appear advisable – yes.'

'No way.'

'That's what I expected. You can let me out over there.'

He motioned to a blue sign with the label 'Hohenzollerndamm.' Judith braked and turned off onto the exit. She reached a large intersection that had to handle traffic from all four directions, the feeder roads, and the S-Bahn. Winkler pointed to the train station.

'Over there, please.'

'No car either, right?' She stopped.

Winkler laughed. 'I have one more thing for you. I was supposed to give it to you from Mr Kaiserley.'

He handed her a small package. Judith kept it in her hand, but didn't open it.

'Are you concerned with the man who calls himself Weckerle?'

Winkler looked out of the window and didn't answer. Judith turned over the package. It was wrapped in an ordinary piece of paper.

'I don't know how forgiveness works. But I had the feeling he cares about his wife. Maybe you can keep out of it. He's an asshole. But one of those who admits it. It makes me almost sympathetic.'

Winkler nodded.

'I do want the grave.'

He turned to her and looked at her. 'You'll get it. I promise you that.'

Judith reached into her bag, pulled out the Florena cream tins, and gave them to him. Winkler opened one and immediately closed it again.

'There's a great copy shop on Silbersteinstrasse,' she said. 'They scan, digitalise, duplicate . . . I was there yesterday. If I find out that you left the little guys hanging again and the big ones get away . . .'

'Don't worry,' Winkler said quickly. He was still keeping an eye on the tins, as if he still couldn't believe what he was holding in his hands. 'Thanks.'

He got out, crossed the bridge, and disappeared into the station. Judith unwrapped the package. It was an MP3 player. Nothing else. She turned the car around and merged into the Kurfürstendamm traffic towards the ring road.

The first song she heard was Edith Piaf – 'Parlez-moi d'amour.'

She left the ring road at the next exit, turned and drove down the city highway towards Prenzlauer Berg.

About the Author

Elisabeth Herrmann is an exciting new voice in crime fiction. Her novels have captivated German readers since the publication of *The Sitter* in 2005 and have reached a broader audience with the subsequent adaptation into TV movies of *The Sitter* and *The Cleaner*. Elisabeth lives in Berlin with her daughter.